Caramel Flava

Zane Presents

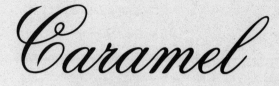

Caramel

Flava

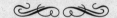

THE EROTICANOIR.COM
ANTHOLOGY

ATRIA BOOKS

New York   London   Toronto   Sydney

ATRIA BOOKS
1230 Avenue of the Americas
New York, NY 10020

Copyright © 2006 by Zane

ISBN-13: 978-0-7432-9727-1
ISBN-10:   0-7432-9727-X

First Atria Books trade paperback edition August 2006

1   3   5   7   9   10   8   6   4   2

ATRIA BOOKS is a trademark of Simon & Schuster, Inc.

Manufactured in the United States of America

For information about special discounts for bulk purchases,
please contact Simon & Schuster Special Sales at
1-800-456-6798 or business@simonandschuster.com.

COPYRIGHT NOTICES

A todos los amantes del mundo. No importa el color de supiel, la pasión es universal.

∽

To all the lovers in the world. No matter what your skin color, passion is universal.

CONTENTS

INTRODUCTION

Caramel Flava was a special undertaking giving me an opportunity to offer a great book to an underserved market. I have worked hard in my work as an editor and publisher to give a voice to black authors. I felt a similar push to do so far my Latino sisters and brothers who embrace sensuality. Love is the universal language, but erotic stories that specifically speak to the Latino market have been difficult to find. I know that *Caramel Flava* will appeal to readers of all ethnicities, as do the stories in *Chocolate Flava,* but they are tailored especially for the Latino heart. I was overwhelmed by the response to my call for submissions to the anthology. I got so many awesome stories that there are enough to do three or four collections. So, if you enjoy these—and I am confident that you will—there is more Caramel Flava to come.

Thank you to everyone who made this possible, and to all the authors who lent their talents to crafting these steamy, unforgettable tales.

So light the candles, get comfortable, and enjoy these other wonderful authors. Reach out to them, become avid readers of their work. They all deserve it. And then remember to pass on the love you gather in your heart from this special reading experience.

Blessings,
Zane

Caramel Flava

The Masquerade Party
LA FIESTA DE DISFRACES

❦

Tracee A. Hanna

*T*iara, a single, lovely, caramel-complexioned Venezuelan American, accepted an invitation to a masquerade party. She dressed in an all-white nurse costume: hat, corset, miniskirt, thigh highs, garter, and high-heeled shoes, with a stethoscope around her neck and a medical bag as her purse. Upon arriving at the party she was greeted by a handsome man, dressed in black slacks and a black mask. His muscular chest, magnificent arms, and his feet, were bare.

"Hello, may I see your invitation, please?" the usher asked. Tiara handed him her invitation. "This is a masquerade party. Everyone must be masked at all times," the usher said as he helped her put on a satiny white eye mask. He whispered in her ear, "Remember the rules tonight: no names, no business talk. Have fun and try the punch; it's delicious." He opened the double doors to the ballroom. The massive room was filled with masked people wearing beautiful costumes. "You are at table three. Follow me." He escorted Tiara to her seat.

"Thank you," she responded, smiling as she followed the sexy usher.

As Tiara walked through the ballroom she noticed, in the corner to her left, a table holding flutes filled with champagne; wineglasses filled with white, red, and blush wines; and goblets filled with an exotic punch (spiked with herbal aphrodisiacs). There was also a full-service wet bar for everyone's convenience. The dance floor was, to her right, filled with people moving their bodies to the beat. In the middle were several tables covered with white linen. Just beyond the tables was a host of people standing in small groups talking.

"Enjoy your evening," the usher said before taking his leave.

Just as she was taking her seat a waiter walked up to her with a tray full of drinks.

"Would you like a drink, ma'am?"

"Yes, thank you."

"I have champagne, wine, and punch or, if you'd like, I can bring you something from the bar."

"I'll try the punch, please." He placed the glass of punch on the table. "Thank you."

Tiara sat, people watching, as she sipped her punch.

"May I have this dance?" asked a portly man dressed as a sultan.

"Yes." As they danced, she asked, "What should I call you tonight?"

"You may call me Sultan. I believe that I am the only one here." He kissed the back of Tiara's hand. "You are a beautiful, sweet, toffee Latina. What should I call you, dear lady?"

"You may call me Nurse Taboo." Tiara giggled.

Tiara moved on to dance with and talk to several different men and women as the night passed. She had taken on the persona of Nurse Taboo, accepting touches and kisses from other partiers. She became one of the most popular people at the party. As the night progressed, the music changed to a dark African Cuban beat. Tiara found everything about the ambiance arousing, from the half-dressed ushers and servers to the genitalia-shaped ice sculptures; from the dim lighting to the life art hanging on the walls depicting several erotic and seemingly impossible sexual positions; from the exotic-tasting punch to the never-ending flow of champagne. But, what she found most stimulating was the people of all different sizes, shapes, and colors; drinking, dancing, and touching freely.

Tiara was standing in front of the drink table trying to catch her breath after an intense dance session with a sexy deep dark chocolate man wearing nothing but a leopard-print loincloth and matching eye mask. Her back was to the room as she took a moment to pat her face, neck, and breasts dry before getting another glass of the decadent punch.

"I know you and you know me," a man whispered in Tiara's ear. The man pressed his groin against her butt as he wrapped his arms around her waist.

"How do I know you?" Tiara asked, playing along.

"We were lovers," the man responded as he kissed her neck. "I would know those legs and that ass anywhere."

"Lovers, you say?" Tiara asked as she turned to face the man. He was dressed as the Phantom of the Opera, with his mask covering most of his face. "Why are we no longer lovers? Did it end badly?"

"Yes," the man sensually whispered in her ear. Just as he spoke the lights went out. Everyone in the room gasped, but they were back on within ten seconds. In that time the man had freed Tiara's breasts from her corset. "I know those breasts too."

"What are you doing?" Tiara asked as she pulled her corset up.

"Tonight I am reclaiming what is mine," the man responded in a deep, sexually charged voice.

"You are taking this a little bit too far."

"Am I?" asked the Phantom. The lights went off again but this time for longer than before. "You are mine, my Venezuelan Vixen." In the dark Tiara felt fingers being slipped into her pussy. "I am going to fuck you tonight right here at this party and you are going to let me."

"We can't, not here . . ." She moaned as the pleasure overtook her senses.

"Look around, I don't think that anyone would mind." The lights came back on. Tiara looked around the room. She saw that most of the women's breasts were exposed and everyone was touching or being touched, all the while dancing to the beat of the mystical music. There were couples, threesomes, and groups all doing what felt good to them. "Tiara," he whispered her name in her ear.

"You know my name!"

"I know more than that," he responded, still working his fingers within her pussy, gently massaging her G-spot.

"Who are you?" she asked.

"Let's see if you remember," the Phantom said as he unfastened his pants.

The lights went off again, but this time they were out for minutes instead of seconds. The Phantom spun Tiara around, spread her legs, and thrust his rigid dick into her hot, sopping-wet pussy. The enthralling force of his actions took her breath away. She held on to the table as if it were a life preserver. She was mesmerized by his adoration of her body. She heard moans and sighs of pleasure, from men and women both, rise above the music and mingle with her own. Familiar sensations fluttered then raced through her body. She was quickly approaching her zenith. However, just as the lights were coming on again, the Phantom stepped away and tucked his penis back into his pants.

"Tyree!" Tiara exclaimed, exasperated, as she spun around and slapped his face. No one even took notice; they were all lost in their own concupiscence. "I am not yours," she hissed. "And I never was!"

This was the man who broke her heart and left her not wanting to love. It had taken almost a year to get him out of her system. She had longed to be touched and caressed by him, at the same time vowing to resist being a doormat for him ever again. Tiara was tormented until she met Kibryia, who helped her erase Tyree from her system. He made sure that Tyree was a distant memory.

"We'll just see about that," Tyree stated as the lights flickered off again. He grabbed ahold of Tiara, lifted her up, and spread her legs as he slammed her against the wall, rendering her powerless to stop him. He freed his rigid dick once more and plunged it deep inside of Tiara; pushing hard and fast, burying himself as far into her body as he could go. "This pussy is mine and I can have it whenever I want it!"

Tiara didn't say a word in protest; she just took her punishment, crying out helplessly as the orgasmic pleasure swept her away. She held on to him tightly as she stared out into the darkness, completely lost in the intensity of his lovemaking. She was amazed by every familiar sensation as he moved inside of her. She could not think beyond that very moment in time; beyond her desire-enveloped state.

"Oh, Tyree . . ." She sighed.

"Yes, baby . . ." Tyree kissed and licked her neck. "Yes!"

The lights flickered on again, but they were too lost in their abyss of decadence to care. Tiara saw images of bodies entwined on the floor, tables, and up against the walls; the sight of others partaking in the same sweet taboos as she heightened her pleasure. The lights were off again almost as quickly as they flickered on. She felt naughty, uninhibited, and wickedly shameless as she gave herself over to Tyree completely. The lights were turned on and off slowly as if showing a slide show of life art. Tiara wanted more; every nerve ending in her body cried out for more touches, more kisses, and more caresses. She was drowning in a sea of carnal need. She freed her breasts from her corset.

"Touch me!" Tiara demanded as her body twisted and writhed beneath Tyree's. "Suck my breasts! Oh please!"

The aphrodisiac was taking over—Tiara and Tyree were quickly getting overrun by desire, drowning in a chemically induced lust. His ache to possess Tiara was all that Tyree could focus on as he licked and suckled her breasts. He wanted to touch more of her, taste all of her. He tucked his arms under her legs as he slowly slid her body up the wall. He twirled his tongue over her stomach, licking and kissing his way down her body until he got to her freshly waxed pubic area, where he took a playful bite. Tiara was captivated, so much so, she did not notice the small group of people walking toward her.

As the lights came on, the room came into focus again; Tiara saw the man in leopard print looking into her eyes intently. The lights clicked off and on once more and he was closer. The lights continued to slowly blink; she saw that there were two men and two women standing behind him, approaching with him. Tiara was delighted by the oral pleasures of Tyree licking her pussy and the intense stare of the dark stranger, which stirred a deeper passion. The group stopped about a yard away from Tyree. The leader waved his hand, directing the ladies to proceed. During every flash of light Tiara watched as both women dropped down to their knees and crawled over to Tyree. One lady, dressed as a belly dancer, positioned herself directly below Tiara, while the other, dressed as a sorceress, settled in behind Tyree. Simultaneously the women snaked up his body, slowly massaging and kissing his muscular legs as they went. The Belly Dancer took ahold of Tyree's dick with both of her hands and slipped the head into her mouth, while The Sorceress expertly massaged his balls as she licked his anus.

Tyree paused for a moment, looking up into Tiara's eyes as the lights continued to flash. He was in a conundrum of having to choose between reclaiming his lady love or giving in to wanton pleasure. In the blink of the lights his body made the choice for him and all was lost in a moment of reckless abandon. Tyree buried his head between Tiara's legs, licking, lapping, and sucking all of her juices away, forcing her to cum for him yet again. As the lights continued to blink off and on, he marveled in the ladies' skillful stimulation and the multiple sensations of pleasure. The ladies worked diligently while the men—The Jungle Man, The Caveman, and The Roman—patiently watched. When they saw that Tyree was growing too weak to stand up, much less hold, Tiara, they intervened. In a moment of darkness Tiara was taken out of Tyree's hands by two of the men and placed on the table next to him with her legs dangling off of the sides. Between the slow blink of the lights Tyree saw two men kneeling down on either side of Tiara. He watched as their hands caressed her breasts. In the next flicker of the lights The Jungle Man loomed over her. In the next flash he'd dropped to his knees, submerging his head between her legs while The Caveman and

The Roman started to devour her breasts with their mouths: licking, sucking, and nibbling until her nipples were hard.

Tiara and Tyree looked into each other's eyes, each a witness to the other's sexual decadence and gratification, presented like pictures in a slide show. She could not take her eyes away from him and he couldn't tear his eyes away from her. Tiara was spellbound by it all; the things that she was seeing as well as everything that she was feeling. She welcomed the new forbidden pleasures, all the while keeping her eyes on Tyree.

The Caveman and The Roman both reached for Tiara's buttocks, each grabbing a cheek, kneading and massaging their way to her anus, as they continued performing their lubricious manipulations on her breasts. Each man inserted a finger in her anus, which was already lubricated by the juices from her cum. The Jungle Man slipped two fingers into Tiara's pulsating pussy and sucked on her clit, making her cry out as her eyes rolled to the back of her head. She groaned in delight. She sighed and panted in pleasure. She welcomed the eroticism and embraced each taboo as she allowed her body to match the men's rhythmic caresses. Tiara's eyes fluttered open just long enough for the lights go on and off again, which allowed her to take a mental picture of what was happening to her.

Then, it all came to a sudden halt. Tiara's eyes drifted open once more and there was Tyree standing before her; no one else was there. He gripped her hips, pulling her close to him, and entered her body with a mind-blowing force.

"Mine, Tiara, mine," Tyree stated. "I don't want anyone else but you and I won't allow anyone else to have you. Come home with me?"

"All right." Tiara wrapped her arms and legs around him. "I'll come home with you tonight."

The lights twinkled on and then off again and again as they slowly made love, deliberately, passionately looking into each other's eyes.

At the end of the party Tiara couldn't find her purse. So she instructed Tyree to leave without her. She promised that she would meet him at his house, after she went home to pack a bag for the weekend. Once she kissed Tyree good-bye and saw him off she asked an usher to help her. He led her to a room down the corridor stating that any miscellaneous things—shoes, ties, etc.—that were lying about after the lights came back on were moved to that room. Tiara opened the door; her purse was sitting on the bed. As she stepped into the room to retrieve it, she looked around and noticed that there were no other miscellaneous items lying about, only her purse. Suddenly, the door closed behind her.

"You went to a lot of trouble to get me all alone tonight," Tiara stated as she turned toward the door, purse in hand. "Who are you?" she asked The Jungle Man, who was leaning with his back against the door. "Let me see your face," she demanded.

"You know who I am, Tiara—after all, I am your host tonight. Listen to my voice, look at my body, remember my touch, and tell me my name."

Tiara did as she was told. She listened to his voice. She looked over his magnificent body. She closed her eyes and reminisced about his touch. She opened her eyes and looked directly into his. She smiled an impish smile.

"I don't know your name," she lied.

"Yes, you do," The Jungle Man said ever so calmly as he locked the door. "I know that you're lying. I always know when you're lying. You have a choice, Tiara; we can do this the easy way or the hard way."

"The hard way!" Tiara said as she ripped off her mask and glared at The Jungle Man. She was thrilled, wildly excited, carnally electrified. She wanted to be taken. Adrenaline pumped through her body as she readied herself for his attack.

"You asked for it! Now I'm going to have to take you by force, just the way you like it, and ruin you."

"You have to catch me first!"

The Jungle Man lunged at Tiara; however, she sidestepped him. Just as she was about to flip over the bed he caught her by her ankle.

"This was too easy, Tiara," The Jungle Man stated as he pulled her to him.

"Well, hell . . . I had a busy night," Tiara responded, laughing.

"Come on, dear lady, let's share a shower."

"Gladly," she agreed. They continued talking while they undressed and got into the shower. "It's been a while, Kibryia."

"Yes, it has," Kibryia responded as he took off his mask. "When was the last time we saw each other, February of last year?"

"Yes, it's been about a year and a half. But I have a question for you."

"Shoot."

"What are you doing at the same party as Tyree? This party was by invitation only, no guests, which means that you invited him."

"I wanted to fuck you right in front of him."

"You almost did." Tiara laughed. "What stopped you? He was busy."

"I took my time with you when I shouldn't have. I wanted you to have a few thrills, to remember the things that we did and talked about the last time we were together."

"Oh, I remember—and I also remember how many days it took for me to recover. I really don't think that I can do this tonight."

"Bullshit! You can and you will. Now get on your knees and suck my dick while I wash your hair, baby."

"With pleasure, rinse the soap off." Tiara stroked Kibryia's dick, helping him wash the suds away. She slipped the head of his penis into her mouth while the water continued to trickle over the shaft. She stopped for a moment and looked up at him. "You know what, I just noticed something . . . your dick is just as thick as my wrist." She opened her mouth as wide as she could, being able to take in only about a fourth of his manhood before letting it slide out again. She gingerly licked, sucked, and kissed his cock. She slurped the water off of his dick as if she were drinking from a water fountain; all the while he lathered and rinsed her hair, twice. He applied the conditioner and massaged her scalp while she pleasured him, twirling her tongue over his testicles, sucking them gently one at a time. She licked her way over his shaft back to the head, tickling the tip with her tongue before taking it into her mouth once more.

"Stand up and turn around so that I can wash your back," Kibryia instructed. She did as she was told. "Brace yourself."

"*Por favor,* Kibryia, take it easy."

"No!" He gripped her hips and worked his monolithic dick into her already swollen pussy. "You should have chosen the easy way." His authoritarian voice roared. "Don't pretend that you don't know me—choose the hard way, and then beg for mercy later, damn it."

"Oooooooh! Daaamn . . . oh shit, Kibryia! Oh my God, man!"

"Damn, your pussy is tight. What are you doing fucking with that little-dick man? You know that you need to be filled to the point of overflowing. You know that you need a man that can stand up in it." Tiara could barely breathe; she gasped for air as she pushed at Kibryia. "Relax, Tiara, because you are taking this entire dick, tonight. I am going to fuck you like Tyree can't and then send you home to him ruined. Once you adjust to me I am going to lay you down and remind you why you will always make time to see me. I am going to make love to your entire body all night."

"I love the way you love me, Kibryia."

"And I do love loving you."

"Kibryia . . . you are just much too much for me tonight."

"I've got something that will help with that. Come with me. Here, stand in the doorway and hold on tight."

Tiara did as she was instructed. She closed her eyes and waited for Kibryia to work his massive dick into her sore pussy again.

Kibryia slathered his penis with a warming lubricant, stood behind Tiara, and whispered into her ear, "Are you ready for me?"

The question was completely rhetorical because before he even finished asking, he was pressing his penis head past her pussy lips. She was able to take the full length of him in just two strokes. She gasped in delight, arched her back, and bounced back against him. Stroke by stroke her body adjusted to his girth. After about a half an hour her pussy got accustomed to his dick. Once the feeling changed from a tight grip to a snug fit Kibryia carried Tiara to the bed. The different positions of lovemaking that they shared can be described only as manic Kama Sutra. Tiara came over and over again, her orgasms stronger, more powerful, and more sensational with Kibryia than with any other lover that she had ever had. They switched back and forth from oral to vaginal sex, prolonging their inevitable conclusion.

"I love you, Kibryia, I love you so much," Tiara hollered out helplessly as her cum exploded from her body yet again.

"I love you, too, Tiara," Kibryia responded breathlessly, "my naughty little minx."

They basked in all of the delights of their sexual enchantment; lavishing in the thrills that they gave each other. It was more than just a hair-pulling, ass-slapping, back-scratching romp. They truly made love to each other, taking their time to fully experience all that the other had to offer: every touch, every kiss, every lick, and every stroke was unhurried. They looked into each other's eyes to make sure that what was needed was given. Only with each other did they surrender emotional control. They gave in to more than just the moment, they shared devotion, desire, and ecstasy. They were wrapped in a vortex of passion ending in sensual rapture. They lay in each other's arms spent, breathless, lethargic, but more than that, euphoric.

"He can't have you," Kybryia stated as he pulled Tiara closer, tightening his grip on her. "I am not letting you go."

"Stop playing, you know that you can't keep me."

"I am here to stay, Tiara, and I don't like sharing . . . I *won't* share!"

"You have got to be kidding!"

"No, not at all . . . stay, Tiara. Stay with me tonight."

"I can't, love."

"You can't, or you won't?"

"I know that you are not serious, KB . . ."

"What if I am?"

"You're putting me in a precarious position."

"You are not leaving tonight, Tiara. It's not a request."

"Let me make a phone call."

"No." Kybryia kissed the top of Tiara's head. "No calls,

sweetheart. I'm not going to let you go anywhere. The house is locked, your cell phone has been confiscated, and the house phone won't be connected until Thursday."

"Damn."

"Remember that you said the hard way, Boo."

"So you decided to take me hostage?"

"Yes."

"What if I would have said the easy way?"

"I knew that you wouldn't." Kibryia shifted his weight so that Tiara was lying on top of him. "Sit up and slide yourself on this here dick."

Tiara spread her legs just enough for him to reenter her body.

"Mmm, oh Kibryia." She slowly descended on his pleasingly colossal cock. "This is so unfair." Using her PC muscles she pushed him out of her vaginal canal and closed her legs. "You know that I have to go."

"Nice trick but, um, by the time I unlock the doors you won't want to leave."

"I can't believe that you have taken me hostage."

"I have taken you more than hostage, Boo, you are going to be my sex slave. I am going to fuck you until your pussy is molded into the shape of my dick and you are going to love every minute of it."

"I'm going to have to fight you every step of the way, Kibryia."

"I know—that's why the house is locked. This is a war that I have every intention of winning, battle by battle. Now, get on this here dick like I told you."

"No!"

"Now see, you are going to learn how to obey as well."

"Obey?"

"Obey!"

"You?"

"Me!" Kibryia gripped Tiara by her hips and settled her on the head of his dick. He thrust his hips as he pulled her down on top of him, working his way deep into her body. "And no one else but me."

"Oh my God, Kibryia," Tiara moaned, "not again, no, baby no."

"Yes, sweetheart." He ground his hips, making her cry out and dig her nails into his shoulders. "Ride, baby, come on now, take a ride with me." Tiara moved up and down gingerly, riding slowly, softly. "No, my sweet, I will make love to you softly tomorrow, but tonight we are making love hard . . . hell, we're fucking. Your body is hot, wet, and ready for me to take."

"Then take control of me until I readjust to you, love."

"No repeats, Tiara, I did that a year and a half ago when we first got together. It's your turn today. This is your dick and I want you to ride it as such. You take control, baby, show me how much you want me; how much you've missed me; love me enough to be completely free with me always."

"I'll do my best." Tiara sat up as far she could. She looked into Kibryia's eyes. "Close your eyes, love." She moved her hips in a circular motion while he bucked. She took his hands away from her hips and pushed them up above his head. "Be still, just arch your hips up a little bit and hold yourself there," she instructed. She took over riding his massive cock as hard as she could stand. But before long, as her pleasure heightened to its pinnacle, she rode him with a mindless salaciousness. Her throaty, passion-filled cries escaped her body as if they were being forced out of her with every pummel onto his dick. "I'm going to cum, love! Help me!" Kibryia joined in, moving his hips, meeting Tiara in the middle stroke for stroke. Her body froze, caught up in ecstasy like a deer caught in headlights. She was held there suspended in an agonizing need, on the edge of the highest cliff wanting to dive into a sea of lubricious gratification. But her body would not relent. Her breath caught in her throat. Tears welled up in her eyes and spilled over onto her cheeks. Kibryia reached out and gave her clitoris a swift hard pinch, which instantly sent her over the edge. Her pleasure washed over her as she collapsed on top of him. She was worn-out, depleted, and somnolent . . . barely able to keep her eyes open.

"Oh no, lovely, it's not over yet." He continued to move inside her with deep, purposeful strokes. "I want your pussy to milk every ounce of cum out of my dick. Come on now, baby, do that little thing that you do. Work them muscles for me, baby, let me feel your grip. Go ahead and give my dick a little squeeze."

Tiara was frustrated; her attempt to even try to move her vaginal muscles proved fruitless.

"You can't do this to me, Kibryia, you can't push me this hard."

"I can and I will." He rolled her over onto her back, rolling over with her, on top of her. He held her legs open as he rammed deep into her, harder and faster still. Tiara's body responded, in complete contrast to her level of exhaustion. She thrashed about, her mind spinning, her very being on autopilot. Her desire outweighed her fatigue as she overexerted herself to the point of sure weariness. Her body trembled uncontrollably. Sexual yearning and pure lust raged through her body, boiled up inside of her, and pressurized to the point of combustion.

"KIBRYIA!!!" she exclaimed before falling completely still,

fainting, yet her juices still seeped out of her body. Satisfied with his effect on her, Kibryia sought his own release, after which he gathered her into his arms so that she lay on his chest, and settled in for the night.

All else was forgotten.

Cracked Butterfly

MARIPOSA DESHECHA

❧❧❧

Teresa Lamai

I can't stand human beings after a day in criminal court. So I'm glad the industrial district is deserted after six. As I make my way home, the desolate November wind smells like burning garbage. I stumble every time it the frigid current gusts out from between the buildings. Halfway home the misery is increased by a sideways, freezing rain cutting into me.

By the time I reached home, my breathing echoed in the dark hallways of my apartment building. I wanted to enter the door and fall on my carpet in the dark and turn up music so loud it would vibrate through my rib cage.

Instead I see a streak of warm light under my door.

A moment later I am in Tal's arms. My apartment is filled with the smell of tortillas, music, and Tal's voice. He squeezes my waist through the dank coat and I hold his temples between my palms. I refresh my eyelids in his glossy curls. I press my cheek against his and inhale. He has just shaved.

"I thought you were still on tour. Oh my God, don't move."

My voice squeaks. He laughs and kisses my forehead. His skin smells like cinnamon bread.

"I still have your key and I wanted to surprise you. You were going to sit here and read and eat caramel ice cream for dinner, weren't you, Rosa? And you're soaked." His warm mouth finds mine and we stand motionless, softly kissing and drinking in each other's breath. One by one, my cells came back to life.

I am still holding his face when he breaks the kiss and looks down at me. Tal's eyes are almond-shaped, tilting toward his temples in gorgeous arabesques. Their darkness is almost inhumanly beautiful, absorbing rather than reflecting light. I do everything I can to make them glitter like jewels. His lashes flutter uncertainly and I know he has a question for me.

His hands, long and slender as a pianist's, move over my hips. I squirm.

He starts unbuttoning my coat and slides it off, letting it slump wetly on the floor. My suit jacket lands on the couch.

He lets me kiss his wide cheekbones and smiling lips as he busies himself with my blouse. I rip out the last three buttons and sigh when he pulls it off. The air is cool, but my bones feel warm for the first time in weeks.

"No bra? I thought you were in court today. Good Lord, woman." I'm tugging at his curls, trying to pull him into the darkening nipples.

He runs his tongue along my belly, leaving a damp line just under my navel. Kneeling in front of me, he smoothes his hands up under my wool skirt. I kick my shoes behind me. My knees almost buckle when he hooks his fingers into the waistband of the panty hose and pulls. The skirt follows quickly. He pauses and I look down.

"When did you get a red thong?"

"It's laundry day."

"Damn. Let's see. Goddamn."

I close my eyes when he moves behind me. He fits one hand over my pubic bone and pushes my ass into his face, sinking his teeth into the cool mounds and lapping hungrily. His other hand is spread flat against my belly. When my pussy swells I move from side to side so that the lips can kiss each other. His hair tickles the small of my back. I shift my hips, tilting my silk-covered cunt toward his snaking tongue, panting "ah, ah" to the dark ceiling.

He stands and I turn, winding my arms around him, lifting one leg to circle his waist. I run my tongue from his collar to just behind his ear, warming his neck. His hands reach to my ass and he pulls the cheeks apart slowly, listening to the wet labia separate.

"There's plenty of time, Rosa." He covers my mouth again in a long, clinging kiss. "Mmm, that's just how your cunt kisses me back."

I don't see his hand moving up and I squeal when he pinches my nipples. He moves to grab my shoulder blades before I can step back. I laugh but his eyes are distracted. He takes several short breaths before he speaks.

"Rosa, I want you to let me use you like I did before. I couldn't think of anything else while I was away."

My breath catches. So that's the question.

Neither of us meant to go quite that far the night before he left, but the need exploded in us the instant his hand closed over my wrist. I've melted each time I've remembered being bound, bent over his desk, his right hand forcing my neck into the polished wood while his left hand held my vibrator. I came the way I'd always needed to, filling the house with long, braying screams like a woman giving birth.

"Okay, yes, yes." I look down. This compulsion is absurdly strong.

"Take off your panties and come into the bathroom," he begins, standing abruptly and walking in first.

I follow more slowly as he turns on the light. He already has a pair of handcuffs dangling over the shower curtain rod. I let out a snort. He turns to me and tells me a safe word. I toss my panties at his chest.

"Face the tub and put your wrists into those handcuffs." He leans back against the opposite wall. I pause when I see his expressionless eyes.

"In the bathroom?" I shove a nervous, simian smile toward him and he lets it go unacknowledged. I turn away quickly, reaching for the cold metal. It clicks benignly around my wrists. I don't quite believe the cuffs will hold until I start to pull on them. Tal is silent behind me.

"Um, okay—" I say after a few moments. I start to twist my head, looking for him.

The first slap, more on my hip than my ass, knocks me to the side. The cuffs cut into my wrists as I hang, feet splayed beneath me. The second slap burns, the third stings.

"Don't speak. Don't turn around." Tal's mouth is at my right ear, but his voice seems to come from every corner of the room. My nipples are tight, straining into the empty air.

I have struggled to my feet. "Ow," I say pointedly.

He fits his left arm around the front of my pelvis and lifts me backward, off my feet, spreading his legs to take the weight. He hits my ass with his right hand, swinging the weight of his back into five blows. Shock keeps me from yelling at first. Setting me down, he massages the shaking flesh gently, using both hands. It's unbearably hot and I feel bruises forming.

He has never spoken so gently to me. "I have a few large, uncomfortable gags I could use on you, Rosa. They'll stretch your mouth, they'll press on your whole tongue, most likely make you salivate over your chin. The ties will get tangled in your hair. I'd rather see you control yourself. Can you do that?"

I lick my lips when I can catch my breath. I watch the goose bumps rise along my arms.

"Good." He kisses the back of my neck.

I hear the scarf before I feel it. It's one of mine, wide red silk, filtering the light as it slides down my face. Tal fits it snug over my eyes.

I hear him move in front of me. A scraping in the tub, then his breath coming from down below. He's moved my stool into the tub. For the first time panic rises sharply, stopping just at the top of my throat.

"I have the gag ready, sweetheart, and several other things to hurt you with," Tal whispers. Something cold and hard probes rudely at my anus, then leaves. He grips my pelvis in both hands, tilting it forward.

The water is running. A warm cloth is on my belly.

I moan as softly as I can when his delicate hands are on my cunt. He lathers briefly and I feel one of my small razors working the hair off the mound. He shaves toward the center, then tells me to put my right foot up on the side of the tub.

He spreads the outer labia and lets one of his fingers stray just close enough to be sucked in. I gasp and rock toward him, my body ready to break into a rhythm. My cunt coats his finger and he stops once the scent begins to fill the space between us.

"Don't move, Rosa, I'm serious."

I feel a cold length of metal, flat against me. I freeze and bear down hard on my terrified stomach.

"The old-fashioned razor is the only way to get a close shave up in here." He tickles me and I clench my teeth.

"You know the safe word. But then we'd only be half-finished."

Just moments later he tells me to switch legs. My thighs are trembling now. I press my left foot hard into the cold porcelain. He finishes with a few efficient swipes, then sponges away the soap.

A long silence follows. The air tickles strangely.

I feel him whisper something just over my clit. His mouth closes slowly over the naked, slick labia. His kiss is thorough. I move in circles, trying to press my impatient clit against him. My inner lips swell toward him, as if begging for his tongue. He stops. I hear him swallow.

"Tal, fuck me." He must be ready to finish this game.

In answer, he stands slowly. He slides one hand under my hair, soft and firm, holding me still as his other hand lands on my cheek. My eyes sting. I hear him leave.

When he returns, he takes the blindfold off, sliding the knot tenderly from my hair. He is holding a key, and he unfastens the right cuff just long enough to turn me around. My wrist clicks back into place. His face is satiny with sweat. He is still dressed. His eyes are dazed and grateful.

He kisses my cheek. "I want to take you out, Rosa."

My blue silk dress is hanging on the back of the bathroom door. His rucksack is on the floor, some of the contents spilling out. I see the gags and he laughs softly.

"Oh, she's mad. You thought I was kidding?" He kisses my mouth and runs his tongue over my neck. He whispers into my hair, "I love you. Are you all right, really?"

"Tal, it's time to fuck me. We are not really going out."

He kneels and pulls something from the bottom of the ruck-sack. A tiny, plastic, powder blue butterfly, maybe one inch in di-ameter. Black straps hang from it.

"Hold on." He lifts my feet out from under me and slips the straps round them. I hiss when the cuffs cut into me. When I can stand again, I realize he is fitting the straps over my hips like a harness. I twist to look past his head.

The butterfly rests lightly over my mad, raging clit. The fat labia seem ready to swallow it. It looks ludicrously innocent. I can feel that I'm blushing hard.

"You know what the best part is?" Tal's narrow eyes are on mine.

"It matches my dress?"

His hand moves in his pocket and the butterfly jumps to life. It hovers, buzzing greedily as if I were a deep, thick-petaled flower. The vibrations spread through my labia to my ass. My cunt is furious and I pull at the shower rod. Plaster shakes loose at the bolts and settles to the floor. Tal looks ready to eat me.

"Tal, Tal." My voice sounds small and tight. "It's not enough. Tal."

"Pace yourself."

"Motherfucker." I am moving my legs together, then apart, grinding my hips in changing circles, until I see him crouch down to watch more closely.

"That sounds like a hurt word. I'm afraid it's quiet time again. But if you really want a gag, keep talking. I have this red one. It basically holds your jaws apart."

He opens my cabinet and finds some makeup. He grabs a fistful of hair at the base of my skull while he wipes the sweat off my forehead.

"You look fine as you are. You don't need any blush. I want to add some lipstick, though." He leans into my swinging breasts, still gripping my hair.

He murmurs like someone drunk with love as he licks the top of each breast. He can manage only two or three words between kisses. "You can either have them rouged or I'll make you wear bells on them, in public, until midnight at least." He takes the lipstick and smoothes my black nipples into long, sticky, crimson peaks. I want to cry but even that release won't come.

When he turns the butterfly to low, I can breathe again, but it still takes all my concentration to keep my hips still. I watch the long, smooth curve of his cheekbones as he reaches over my head. His throat is a little swollen.

"We've been meaning to go dancing for so long," Tal purrs, unlocking my wrists and massaging my arms briskly. He slips the dress over my head and helps me into my shoes.

He holds my head gently now, questions fluttering over his lashes again. I lean forward and bite his pink lower lip. When I pull back, his eyes are pure limpid bliss.

✍

Señor Frog's is always crowded on Friday nights. The club is a tiny neon box, tucked under the freeway overpass. Salsa rhythms beat through its thin walls. Crowds huddle against the wind, hurrying over the black ice that gleams multicolored throughout the parking lot.

Inside, the chairs and tables have all been pushed to the corners. The dance floor, the lobby, the dark hallway to the kitchen, every inch is thick with dancers. The crowds clear reverently for the best couples. A haze of smoke and perfumed steam hangs just under the low ceiling.

I'm brought straight back to my cunt when the butterfly

jumps again. My cry isn't heard over the music, but I turn to Tal's eyes, hard as ebony. I try to move away but we are pushed hip to hip. We've eased into a slow merengue, his hand resting on the small of my back. Our bellies touch, his shirt buttons flick over my nipples. In my mind, I undress him quickly, suck him into hardness, and impale myself on him several times, here on the uneven floor. I doubt many would notice.

Before I can speak, he tugs at my hair and kisses my ear. "Dance with everyone who asks you."

He's gone. The butterfly is on low and I clasp my hands together tight, looking down.

Soon I'm asked to dance. A tall, quiet man tries to lead me in country dances I never learned. I do my best to follow, watching his feet, almost forgetting the relentless little sting of pleasure. I look up to find his eyes transfixed on my vivid nipples. I can't keep them from pushing out farther. Just before the music finishes, the butterfly is turned to high and I have to stop moving, clutching my hands over my mouth. Two desperate moans escape. My partner stops, alarmed, asking if he's stepped on me, most likely thinking I'm about to throw up. I do what I can to assure him and thank him, panting, moving away into the crowd. I can't find Tal.

But he must see me because the torment ebbs as soon as another man asks me to dance.

A portly, quiet-eyed professor touches my back tensely as if I were a silk-covered bomb. He ignores the music and moves me in a slow, thorough orbit across the floor. He cries out at the end of the song when my fingernails sink into his wrist. I leave without looking at him.

A Haitian man, dreadlocks flying, twirls me on every fourth beat. The room spins in front of my eyes, changing direction as his dark hands nudge my shoulder or pull my wrist. Our stomachs meet as a new phrase starts, his teeth flash at me as he laughs. He is irrepressible, radiant as a bride. I press my forehead into his at the end of the song, watching his full lips as he begins to speak. They look soft. Tal turns me up and I pull away.

A young student asks me to dance. I wait for him to look up at my face before I say yes. His drenched silk shirt is nearly sliding off his smooth chest. He carefully strokes my neck as we settle into our rhythm and I smile, imagining it's step five in some article he's memorized: Ten Moves Chicks Dig.

He turns me and I see Tal, watching. Girls surround him like fireflies.

I reach Tal before he can move his hand to his pocket. He grabs my wrist but it's I who lead him to the women's bathroom.

Two elegant grandmas are sashaying out just as we arrive. One winks at me. I slam Tal against the far wall, harder than I meant to, then turn back to the door.

The ladies are still there.

"We're not well." I lock the door.

I turn back to a pile of clothes. Tal has undressed and is sitting on the counter, gleaming under the vanity lights. His skin is flushed and velvety like rose petals. His cock swings up, vein-covered. Stretched to its capacity, hard as an ingot of pure gold, shimmering like fresh honey. His knuckles are white as he braces himself on the counter.

I reach him in three steps.

My hair falls over his belly and clings to the wet skin. The sweet head of his cock nearly chokes me. I stretch my lips over him, tickling his balls, running my tongue over the crinkled, pulsing flesh. My jaws ache but I would do anything to coax that choked falsetto cry from him.

He's begging me now and I jump to stand on the counter, one foot on either side of his waist. I lower myself into a squat, letting him nuzzle into the slick folds.

There's a knock at the door. I slap Tal's face when he looks over.

"Focus. It looks like you'll need to work a little."

I start to come as soon as his fingers sink into my shoulders. I am bent over so quickly that the breath is knocked out of me. His fits his hand over my skull and presses my cheek into the countertop. He throws my dress over my back.

I try to reach back toward him, hands curling.

"Rosa, tell me it's okay . . ."

"Jesus, Tal, you have to do it."

He slides in as soon as I begin to speak, and the last word stretches into an unhinged wail. He has time for only one slow rotation of his hips, caressing the wet, aching inner walls. The little butterfly cracks when I grind it into the Formica. As he starts to thrust, I push my hands into the mirror so that I can writhe against him, the pleasure flashing from the base of my spine and spreading throughout my body. For a long moment I'm half-dead, stretched tight and still except for my cunt opening and closing on him like a sea anemone.

He releases my head and rests heavily on me when he comes, sobbing "fuck, fuck" with his last thrusts. Stars are circling brilliant in front of my eyes, white and gold and violet.

Five minutes later, the icy midnight sucks the air out of our lungs. We steal through the back parking lot, clinging to each other under our coats. The music fades into the wind behind us.

Closet Freak
SECRETOS DENTRO EL ARMARIO

❧⟡❧

Pat Tucker

The sensation of my flesh being stretched so wide it tears was overwhelming. My breathing quickened and I gasped for air, but I still gyrated my pelvic area and rocked my hips. I spread my legs wider; my muscles tightened and gripped him, pulling him in deeper. Humid warmth blanketed the room. Although it was nearly stifling, a sense of electricity hung in the air. Smacking sounds and heavy breathing filled the musky room.

"Oh, yes, *Papi*! Yes! Right there!"

"You like? You like?"

"SSssss, ooooooh yesss!"

I dug my nails into his muscular back, then I felt it. A little ripple that flowed from the very tips of my toes, shot through my veins and up my legs. Ripples turned to warm and flowing waves tingling up my thighs. I exhaled, shut my eyes tightly and clung to the feeling. Sweet pleasure danced back and forth with each stroke, almost teasingly as he slowly pulled out, then mounted tremendously as he pumped in.

I dug my nails deeper into his back, at first guiding, then all but shoving him into my wet bottomless hole.

"OHMIGOD! You hittin' my spot!" I screamed.

"Where?" He pumped. "Right there?"

"Oh shit yes! Yeesss! Fuck me—please fuck me! Yes! I'm uh, I'm cumming, *Papi* . . . Oh shit . . ."

My insides tingled, my heartbeat increased and my breath was caught in my throat. The waves crashed, sending electricity from muscle to muscle, vessel to vessel through my veins and shooting up to my brain. I felt my scalp searing and my eyes began to water. My nipples stiffened as spasms rushed through my entire body. Shock waves flooded my clit; my walls tightened, released, then throbbed. I felt him jerk, and I tightened my walls, determined to drain him.

"Ugh," he moaned.

I held on.

"Ugh." He grabbed my hair.

When he exploded, even though he was deep inside me, I felt an intense burning sensation. It had me teetering on the edge of pleasure and pain; satisfaction was within reach.

"Oh God! That was good," he mumbled.

"You dirty bitch!"

My head snapped toward the voice. My heart nearly came through my chest. Juan tumbled off me. His body made a thudding sound as he hit the floor. My eyes widened in horror as I scrambled to cover myself.

"Don't try to cover up now, you nasty bitch!"

"B-B-Bruce?" I blinked. "W-w-what are you doing in here?" I couldn't steady my voice as I swallowed back tears.

"Who the fuck is this?" Juan asked.

That's when the barrel of the gun moved from me to Juan. His hands flew up in surrender.

"Tell him who the fuck I am!" Bruce screamed, and pointed the gun back at me. My teeth clicked. When I opened my mouth to speak, nothing! The words had formed in my brain, but I couldn't find sound.

"What, bitch . . . can't talk now? Your nasty ass was moaning and screaming, got this Chicano all up in your pussy. You deserve to die!"

"*¡Eh, amigo, 'migo,* I didn't know she was married! We just hooked up, you know, on the Net," Juan offered.

"Oh, she's married, but I ain't her fucking husband. That mutherfucka got no idea what kind of slut he's married to."

Juan looked at me, then to Bruce. I could see confusion all over his face, but I was more preoccupied with images of the Reaper's cold finger on that trigger. I wasn't ready to die.

"If he ain't your husband, who is he?" Juan asked.

I shook my head. I clutched the sheets at my chin and tried in vain not to start bawling.

"I'm the man she claimed to love! Said she was thinking about leaving him for me! Now look at her, up in here fucking you like I never meant shit!"

He waved the gun as he spoke, using it to emphasize his traitorous words. I stared into his eyes, I had to try something—if this was how I was to die, I had to go out giving it my all.

"Bruce, we went out once," I reasoned. "Um, I never said I loved you." I swallowed, and blinked back more tears.

"We—" Bruce pointed at his chest with the barrel of the gun. "We connected!" he snapped. Suddenly, his arm jerked.

BANG!

BANG!

I screamed and thought I was going to wet myself. Beads of sweat laced my forehead and my heart threatened to explode. When I opened my eyes, the gun was back on me again.

Bruce waved the gun as if he was going to scratch the side of his head, like he was confused. Juan and I cringed.

I eased to the side a bit, trying not to become such a direct target.

Bruce shook his head, and frowned. "I've been following you for weeks, trying my best to figure out how to fix what went wrong with us." He shook his head again. "And you up in here giving up the ass; he ain't even black!" he snarled toward Juan.

"I don't even know her, amigo. Like I said, we just hooked up. I didn't know this was your girl!" he pleaded.

Juan's dick was good, but at that very moment he was acting like a scared little bitch. I can't say I blame him, we had met on the Internet only less than twenty-four hours earlier. Now here we were both on the wrong side of a gun with a crazy man threatening to pull the trigger.

"Bruce, what do you want me to do?"

"I don't want you to do a damn thing. You deserve to die!" he screamed.

Still trembling, I closed my eyes and willed myself to be anywhere but there, anywhere but in this situation, caught between two strangers. When Juan buried his head in his palms I felt so alone. I looked at my platinum and diamond wedding band and silently cursed my husband, Charles, for starting this madness in the first damn place!

I was seething when he unveiled his fabulous plan to put the spark back into our seven-year marriage. That had been a mere four months ago. Even with the barrel of a Magnum .45 pointed at my head now, I remember the day like it was hours ago.

"So are you gonna have an open mind?" Charles had asked excitedly.

I looked at my husband, all six feet five inches of his mocha-colored skin. His jet-black hair, eyebrows, thick lashes, and pencil-thin mustache always made his features stand out. Back in the day, just thinking about his striking features was enough to soak my panties. But time passed, work, responsibilities and life got in the way of our sizzling and passionate love affair. We sank into a comfortable and predictable life of boredom.

I didn't answer him right away. I thought he'd mention an exotic vacation—hell, maybe he wanted a threesome or some role-playing. We had tried the soft porn, regular porn and just about every sex toy under the sun—still, things in our bedroom always went back to humdrum. And humdrum was no longer getting the job done. I sighed and shrugged.

"I guess I'd be willing to at least give it a try, um, I mean, whatever it is. I guess it won't hurt to at least try."

A devilish grin crept across his face before he nearly pounced on me. "I'm so glad you agreed, baby." He hugged me and squeezed my body with such zeal, I was almost as excited about this magic plan that would salvage our union and take us back to marital bliss. When he released me, Charles dashed into the bedroom and returned with a black tote bag. He rushed to the sofa and patted a spot next to him.

"Come on, let's look through this stuff together. That way we can answer all of your questions and read at the same time."

I felt my heart take a nosedive when I saw the pamphlets and brochures he held with such care.

"I just have such a good feeling about this," he said, all giddy. "I've even talked to some other couples who say it's done wonders for them. I know it's gonna work for us too," he smiled.

"Swingers," I mumbled, my hands trembling as I read a brochure's title aloud.

Charles quickly put his hand over mine. He looked me in the eyes, smiled, then said, "I know, it's scary at first, but you promised you'd have an open mind."

I jumped from the sofa and dropped the brochure as if my fingers had been set ablaze. I shook my head, trying to deny what was so evident by all of the materials my husband had collected on what he suspected would save our marriage.

"You, um . . ." I shook my head and swallowed back fresh tears. "You want us to have sex with other people, Charles?" I tried to shake the images from my head again. "W-w-what would people say? Our family? Our friends?. I can't believe you want us to actually fuck other people! What about AIDS, what kind of shit . . ." I had to put a hand on my chest to keep my heart from failing me.

Charles stared up at me with hopeful eyes. The excitement that had invaded his face and voice had vanished. He glanced around at the pamphlets and brochures and shook his head. It was as if he found it hard to believe that I didn't see this idea for what it was: our last hope at reclaiming happiness.

"I thought you said you'd have an open mind. I'm just trying to save our marriage," he said.

"By bringing other people into our bedroom? What kind of sick shit is that? You want other men to fuck your wife? You think I want other women sucking your dick?" My voice was shaky despite my efforts to control it. I closed my eyes and shook my head. Silently, I prayed that when I opened them the nightmare would be over. I tried to convince myself that I was enough for my husband, that the solution to our problems lay with us, not with other sex partners, but I could tell his mind was made up. We sat for minutes until his next words pulled me reluctantly into a sordid and sinful world.

"I thought you'd welcome me including you in this, I wanted to do anything to avoid cheating on you."

His lips were still moving, but the only words that rang in my ear were "avoid cheating on you."

Against my better judgment I told myself we could try it, if only once, just to show him this was not going to be the "fix-it" he was looking for; then we could return to our normal life and go to counseling like other miserable married folks.

Boy, was I wrong. Dead wrong.

Two weeks after that dreadful day our time had come. From the day of inception to the day of action, Charles had consumed our lives with his magic bullet of a plan. The rules were simple. We'd go to a mixer and mingle. We'd find a couple we were interested in and go into a more private room to talk at first. If we decided we liked each other, we'd take it to the next level, whatever that was.

Every step of the way, something told me Charles would change his mind, or so I hoped. When we arrived at the private club and the valet took our keys, I thought okay, he'll say forget it. Then inside, where the lights were dimmed, couples danced, sat at bars and tables like regular clubs, again I fantasized. He'll see this isn't the answer, I assured myself.

But Charles seemed to soak up the atmosphere almost instantly; he reveled in the surroundings. He grooved to the music, drank and looked around, gazing almost longingly at other men's wives. And the other men, they smiled like they welcomed his stares. I found all of this repulsive, and had to excuse myself more than a few times to go gaze at my reflection in the mirror.

The last time I returned from the ladies' room, we had company at our table. I walked up to find a younger Hispanic woman and an older black man socializing with Charles.

"This must be the missus," the man said, and stood. Charles was too busy cheesing all up in his wife's face to even acknowledge my return. I burned with envy. She was pretty, full lips, olive skin, oval-shaped eyes, with high cheekbones and large breasts. I couldn't help but stare and compare her assets to mine. I shook my head.

"You must be Trish." She smiled. "I'm Mercedes. This is my husband, Philip." I looked at her, then Charles.

"It's okay, sit." He grinned.

Philip looked good for his age. I had no idea how old he was, but I could tell he was older. The gray hair at his temples added to his allure. But I was so jealous of Mercedes that I couldn't really appreciate Philip's attributes.

Until he touched me later, oh, when he touched me, my skin tingled beneath his fingers. His hands were firm, his muscular body was stiff and hard all over. I used my tongue to glaze over his six-pack and suckle his nipples and it drove him mad. I no longer cared what Charles was doing with Mercedes because I had found heaven right there in room 2354 at the Hilton.

Philip was a slow and meticulous lover. He was larger, thicker than Charles, and for the first time I realized just how much size really mattered. Philip used just the right amount of force. He filled me so much it felt as though he was tickling my ribs. He was sensuous, giving attention to each nook and cranny of my body.

The man had the nerve to kiss my elbows and made that feel sensuous. It was the first time I had ever experienced multiple orgasms. I never realized I could flow like that, heavy and freely. Philip gave me a tongue bath I won't soon forget; his lips traveled from the bottom of my feet and all over. There was this "no oral" rule, which we had no problem breaking.

I wanted to suck the color off his massive dick. When he exploded in my mouth, I slurped and sucked, trying not to waste his juices. Fucking Philip was a high I had never experienced and after one hit, I knew I was hooked.

When it was all over and we were on our way back home, I became sick to my stomach when Charles informed me that we can never repeat couples. I remember feeling like someone who thought they had won the lottery only to have the commission say oops, it seems there was some kind of mistake. That night I was overwhelmed with raw emotions. This stranger had peeled back layers and layers of sexual inhibitions for me. In the days, weeks and months that followed I began to yearn for him. But we never saw Philip and Mercedes again.

About three weeks later, we did Kim and Kevin, then Daniel and Sam, followed by Roger and Sonia. But they were just stand-ins for the real thing. I soon realized that I would never find another Philip, not at the parties we frequented. And after a while, Charles had lost interest in the swinging clubs all together. I was devastated. Here he had turned me on to a world of secret possibilities and he was no longer interested.

That's when I turned to the Internet. Images of Philip forcefully taking me from behind haunted me. With every stroke of the key, every dip into chat rooms, I longed to find him or his twin.

I lucked out and found a group that fit me just right: Closet freaksdotcom. It's where I met John, Steve, Eric, Nate and Bruce. I also met Melvin, Calvin, Brian and Juan.

It was cool, easy and most important, discreet. Once you became a member of the club, you type in your zip code and you're instantly hooked up with people who live within a 300-mile radius. You meet in the chat room. Then, if you start feeling someone's vibe, you request to go private. After that, you and your new friend go into a private chat room alone and negotiate hooking up. Most of the action happened within days. This thing didn't drag out for weeks, we were fuckers who were looking to get fucked. You hook up, fuck, then move on. No strings whatsoever.

Bruce's profile was alluring. He boasted his skills in the bedroom like it was a badge of honor. He was tall, like Philip. I started to get happy. They were the same complexion, similar build and both wore size 13½ shoes.

I just knew I had hit the jackpot once again. Bruce and I agreed to hook up in these abandoned row houses near downtown. The only people who frequented the area were druggies and other undesirables. This was not typically my style, but once in heat, I didn't mind. I had been creaming all day thinking about my rendezvous.

Bruce asked me to forget the bra and wear crotchless thongs, the kind where the string ran up my ass. So by the time I arrived, it was slippery wet between my thighs and my nipples were hard.

We didn't waste any time. He looked me up and down then said, "Damn, you're fine too."

I followed him to a house near the middle of the row. We glanced around in both directions before he forced his way through the rickety door. The house was small, smelled rank and there were several rotted areas on the floor. Bruce pulled out a flashlight and walked into a back room. I was right on his tail. A rodent scampered across the floor, I jumped. Our heads snapped toward a nearby window with a view of a couple arguing.

"Okay, this looks good," he said.

I just shrugged. Truth be told, I just needed room to lie on my back and spread my legs. We could've fucked in the car, for all I cared.

"This is the shit! My dick is so hard right now," Bruce teased. He stroked his crotch for good measure.

I was so looking forward to getting the shit fucked out of me. I tugged at my spring trench coat, and he stopped me.

"No, not yet, lemme find us a spot."

I watched as he walked over to a corner, kicked some debris out of the way, then spread a blanket he had brought.

When that was done, he sat back on the blanket; he used two flashlights to illuminate the room. I shed my coat and stood in front of him wearing stacked-heel boots, my crotchless thong and tassels taped to my nipples.

"Fuck, you are fine, and that body is banging." He rubbed his crotch again. "Here, turn around, lemme see that ass!"

I turned, but wondered when I'd see some action. I wanted dick in me and I wanted it bad. I didn't come for a damn fashion show. I had told Charles I'd only be gone two hours.

"Yes, see, that's what I like, when the string is buried so deep between your cheeks. That shit is a real turn-on. Just stand there for a minute."

I frowned when I heard what sounded like him beating his meat. When he moaned, I tried to turn around.

"Oh, no! Not yet, wait, just a sec," he cried. "Shake it for me," he begged, his deep baritone suddenly replaced by a shrieking sound.

Something didn't feel right, but still, I jiggled my ass and rubbed my cheeks for good measure.

"Aaaaaah, shit!"

I turned around to see that Bruce had cum all over himself. I was livid. I looked at him, frowning, then stepped closer.

"What's going on?" I asked. I thought maybe that's how he got down, you know, needed to release first, then his shit would be rock hard so I could get mine, properly.

"Here, come sit next to me, lemme hold you. That was good," he said, actually breathing hard.

Twenty minutes later, Bruce's dick was still limp. I took it into my mouth, what there was of it, and nothing.

"Um, I didn't think you were actually gonna suck it," he said. "That's not gonna work. I just needed to *believe* you were gonna do it, and now that you have, I'm afraid it won't do a thing."

I raised an eyebrow. I didn't know if he was for real.

"Okay, well, maybe if you sucked my pussy, that might help," I suggested.

"Help who?"

I tilted my head toward him, and started fuming. "What do you mean, help who?" I asked with much attitude.

"Look, this is a bust. I say we just chill, then we can hook up some other time and try again." Bruce looked down at his limp dick. "I'm down for the count." He shrugged.

I snatched up my coat and bolted toward the door.

"Wait, Trish, come on, let's cuddle. I swear it'll be worth your while!" he screamed as I stormed out.

That night I laughed at myself as I drove back home. I never thought I'd see Bruce again. I chalked it up as a loss and decided I'd find myself a sure thing the next night.

The following day I got flowers at work from Bruce begging me to give him another chance. It was a pleasant surprise, but not enough for me to consider his proposal. My mind should've been wondering how the fool knew where I worked, but I was hotly anticipating my romp with Melvin.

And he did not disappoint. Neither did Calvin or Brian. I took a break for about two weeks, then met this pepper named Juan. He was the first Hispanic man I ever wanted to fuck.

". . . So you see, that's why I've gotta kill your nasty ass." Bruce's voice jarred me back to my sad situation. The gun was still pointed at me, and Juan sat crying on the floor. He had started praying in Spanish and every so often would do the symbol of a cross, touching his forehead and each shoulder.

I knew I was on my own. "Bruce, I think this is all just a huge misunderstanding."

"You skank bitches are all the same. Just 'cause a nigga can't get it up every once in a while you think you better than somebody. All you had to do was give us another shot. I sent you flowers, I called you at work, I followed you around with your other niggas, I sat outside your house, waited for a chance to talk to you alone, but no, you just ignored me," he said.

My heart sank at his revelations because all this time I was hopping from dick to dick, I never even noticed I was being watched or followed. Yeah, Bruce had called, even got ahold of my cell number, but I just ignored him. I had no idea what he was capable of. In my quest to get more dick, I had developed tunnel vision. My biggest goal each week was coming up with believable stories for my husband.

"I bet I got your attention now, huh?"

"W-w-what do you want me to do? You wanna fuck me?"

Juan stopped praying and looked at Bruce.

"Yeah, amigo, that's a good idea. She got some real good pussy, man, just fuck her, she likes it."

I shook my head toward him. I was disgusted. Well, as disgusted as one could be with a gun pointed at them by a deranged stranger while they're caught cheating on their spouse.

When Bruce didn't respond right away, I allowed the sheet to drop, revealing my breasts. I fondled my nipples and palmed my breasts.

"Your tits are beautiful," Bruce admitted. The gun was still on me, but not aimed at my head. I began to relax a bit.

"Bruce, I don't want you to shoot me, but if you'll let me ease back a bit, I'd like to masturbate for you. You think you'd like that?"

He shook his head vigorously.

"Ssssssss." I licked my lips and noticed Bruce staring at my fingers. I pulled my lips apart and used my index finger to rub my clit.

With my legs spread wide, I kept trying to send a mental message to Juan that he should try to tackle Bruce. But that fool was watching the show too. When I heard Bruce release a heavy sigh, I started working faster. He licked his lips and used the gun to rub the side of his forehead.

"You like this, Daddy?" I purred.

"Shit, I love it when you call me Daddy, that shit makes my dick hard."

"I know, amigo," Juan said as he palmed his own erection. I couldn't believe him.

"Spread 'em wider, spread your legs wider for me," Bruce demanded.

I did. "Ooooh, ssssss," I squealed.

"Now, squeeze your nipples for me."

Juan looked back and forth between Bruce and me. I didn't understand how this shit could turn him on, but then again I realized he, like me, was just a big ole freak. I gyrated my hips, moving into my fingers. I could hear what I thought were sirens in the distance. But I didn't want to falsely hope help was on the way, so instead I focused on working my fingers.

Bruce tucked the gun in his waistband.

Everything was happening so fast.

Juan lunged for him, and I pounced. I wasn't about to leave this up to chance. If I had to die, I'd go down fighting.

We all tussled on the floor. There was pounding on the wall, and another shot was fired. Juan fell to the floor. Then there was more banging, this time on the door.

"Police! Open up now!"

Another shot rang out, I dropped back and felt a burning sensation at the side of my head. I reached up and touched my temple. I remember thinking, fighting naked really works up a sweat.

More time must've passed, but it felt like minutes to me when officers finally burst into the room. Shortly thereafter, everything became blurry. I started feeling light-headed.

One of the last things I remember is Bruce dragging my naked body by the neck as he held the gun to my head. "If y'all come any closer I'll kill her, I swear I will! You see he's already dead."

Warped sounds quickly replaced voices. My fingers started tearing at Bruce's arm that was squeezing my throat closed. The feel of steel against my temple should've been scary, but weariness washed over me so fast I had no time to feel fear. Bruce's heartbeat was pounding loudly in my ear.

"Okay, okay, let's calm down," someone said.

I knew I was losing my mind for certain when I looked up and thought I saw of all things a TV camera pointed into the room. I smiled, knowing for sure dementia was settling in. For a split second I wondered if Juan was really dead. Then without any warning, blackness swallowed me.

When I woke up, I looked around. Everything was white and sterile-looking. I tried to ease up but the pounding in my head forced me back down. That's when Charles appeared.

"You finally woke, I see," he said.

The look on his face wasn't sorrow, it was more like disappointment. I knew that he had found out about what I'd been doing.

"Where am I? How long have I been here? What happened? Is he dead? Oh God, what have I done?" I closed my eyes for a second, trying to regroup. "How did I get here? How'd you even find me?"

"Well." Charles sighed. "Honestly, I saw it unfolding on the news. I was in Target with about a hundred other people in the electronics department. The evening news came on, and I saw a flash of you being carried out on a stretcher."

I shook my head, trying to deny what I couldn't remember.

"I couldn't believe it either," he continued. "By the time I got over there, witnesses told me some dude was holding his wife and her lover hostage. It didn't take long for me to realize that it was actually my wife they were talking about."

Charles touched my arm. "Nobody's dead, that fool is in jail. The other dude is gonna be okay. A bullet grazed you. You'll have to wear that headwrap for a few more days."

I looked at Charles and closed my eyes. Tears that had been threatening to flow made good on their promise.

"Look, you need to rest, don't think about that madness. Just get better so you can come home," he said.

I instantly felt shame wash over me. "Can you ever forgive me?" I asked.

I watched Charles' Adam's apple move as he swallowed.

"Done," he said, and kissed my forehead.

I wondered how I could've been so foolish to think I needed more than what I already had.

Den of Pleasure
EL REFUGIO DEL PLACER

❦❦

Niobia Simone

The Den of Pleasure is the ultimate spot to have your mind—and your dick—blown. I walked into the brownstone, seemingly innocent from all outside appearances, ready to give in to the side of me that I keep suppressed. Hidden. Secret. Forbidden.

I put on my full face mask—a requirement of The Den— as soon as the front door closed behind me. Next I removed all of my clothes and slid them into one of the plastic bags sitting by fifty cubicles in the foyer.

I already felt excited just being here. My thick dick was stirring between my thighs.

"Welcome back, Adonis."

That wasn't my real name, but I turned around because it was the name by which they knew me. The woman standing before me was nude save for the Mardi Gras–style mask she wore. My eyes stroked her body familiarly.

The large pendulous breasts with the thickest nipples ever, which were deep chocolate in color. A tattoo of a blooming rose on the fat mound of her shaven pussy. Thick-ass thighs made to squeeze a man's sides as he stroked his dick deep inside of her, enjoying her inner pink lips—the petals to her rose—suctioning that dick. The thought of that made me so hard that my balls ached between my thighs.

I've fucked her before, but she wasn't on my menu tonight. And I was hungry for some ass, but for some new ass. Something I've never had before. Something to be surprised by. Would the pussy be slick and wet or tight with ridges? A quiet fuck or one of those screamers? A squirter while cumming? Yeah, I was here to tap some new ass. To hell with the same-o-same-o.

"What's your pleasure?" she asked in a soft and sultry voice meant to make a shiver race across your body.

"The main room," I answered.

"As you wish."

She turned and my eyes dropped to watch that lopsided up-and-down action of her pear-shaped, dimple-free ass as I followed her down the hall. We passed a spiral wrought-iron staircase that led to the six private room upstairs.

Anything goes behind those closed doors.

Just last week I fucked Raquel until she damn near passed out while her husband, Mac, sat in a chair and masturbated. Making her yell out my dick was better than his while I beat those walls like she stole something made me cum like crazy. Oh, Raquel and Mac were some real freaks. And the pussy was wasn't half bad either.

I wasn't ready for that tonight . . . not yet anyway.

We came to massive wooden double doors and she bent down a bit to open them both before stepping out of my way. I could almost hear the harps like I was being admitted to heaven.

Thirty people naked as the day they were born with varying

full-face masks to shield their identity were in various stages of sex play. The only furniture in the room were satin-covered beds and chaise lounges—fucking furniture. Some lounged and talked in low tones. Others massaged each other. And more still were fucking—footloose and fancy-free. Fast and furious. Slow and sensual.

I felt excited just being around people who were just as free and uninhibited with sex as me. Freaks like me. I took it all in with eager eyes, reaching down to massage down the length of my dick.

In the corner three women I didn't recognize were eating each other out like they were starving, uncaring of the onlookers. Pussy lips in varying shades of mocha with clitorises that all were plump and pink.

Reemy and Martin—a married couple from middle suburbia—were taking turns spanking a very willing woman. *Whap*. She wiggled her ass for more. *Whap*. More. There were lots of married couple here. Some just watched, others participated.

I couldn't even imagine asking my wife Marisol to come here with me. She knew nothing about this part of my life. She would judge. She would be hurt. She would leave me.

So once a week I fucked her missionary style, busted a nut, and rolled over wishing and wanting for more. Our sex was routine. Mundane. We didn't even leave the lights on when we had sex. I never ate my wife's pussy. She was a good girl, true enough, but it wasn't enough. I needed more. This place . . . this was my more. Three times a week I became Adonis.

I decided to enjoy the show the triplets mere putting on. It was a pussy-fest. I could cum just from watching them as they lay in a triangle formation eating one another like they were famished. Their moans mingled and the scent of their pussy juices clung to the air. The sistah with the skin as dark as semisweet chocolate—I called her Mocha—shifted to lie between the fair-skinned sister's open legs. In my head that one was Freckles—aptly named from the many dots on her fair body. Mocha moaned deep in her throat as she split Freckles' pussy open with her fingers, exposing the throbbing pink bud. With her snake-like tongue she circled that bud and then flicked it, causing Freckles to squirm as she in turn smacked away at Spanish Fly, the voluptuous olive-skinned Latin woman. Spanish Fly squat-ted her size-ten ass over Freckles' face with ease. And even though the other women on the bed were sexy and beautiful, they couldn't do shit with Spanish Fly. Everything about her ex-uded sex appeal. The squirm of her body. The quiver of her full buttocks. The way she flung her head back. The smoky lure of her eyes through the mask. Each and every curve on her glorious body. A simple moan in the back of her throat had the power to make me beg her for her pussy. My eyes stayed on her.

I didn't care about the kissing couple standing next to me or the men who also watched. Or the woman who leaned and finger-fucked herself with a vengeance. Fuck them. Fuck every-body. I found what I was looking for tonight. I spit on my hand and then jacked my dick, my fingers squeezing the throbbing tip as I felt that familiar excitement course through my body like a drug.

Spanish Fly turned and faced me, lowering her pussy back to Freckles, who waited with her tongue extended. Spanish Fly got on her knees, flinging her head of ebony hair over her shoulders as she began to circle her thick hips on Freckles' face and squeeze her own nipples like she was trying to twist them off.

Spanish Fly turned me the fuck on. She reminded me of Marisol. She was the freak I was too afraid to ask Marisol to be. I had to fuck her. I wanted to pull Freckles out the damn way and bury my tongue deep in her pussy, stroking that fat-ass clit until I made her scream in English and Spanish. I wanted to make her cum on my tongue and then bury every bit of my 10x3 dick—that's ten inches long and three inches wide—in her pussy.

She opened her eyes and looked me up and down, smiling slow and big as she watched me jack my dick so hard that my lips formed an "O" and a fine sheet of sweat covered my muscled frame.

My stomach was hot and my thighs locked as I circled my dick with my trembling fingers and stroked every inch until my wrist felt weak, but I kept going. I switched hands. She lifted her breasts until she could tease her nipples with her tongue. A long, agile tongue that I wanted to circle my dick like it was an ice cream pop on a steaming summer day.

"I wanna fuck you," I mouthed to her, meaning it.

She rose from the bed and Freckles moaned in disappointment, but that didn't stop her from walking away from her freaky ménage.

She had a banging Beyoncé body: wide hips, thick thighs, and titties small enough to suck whole. The dim lights glistened on her body as she walked past me, making my dick even harder just by licking her lips.

Every eye in the room seemed to be on Spanish Fly and she knew it. She reveled in it. She was bad as hell. It had been a long time since I wanted to fuck somebody so badly. And I reveled in the fact that she kept her eyes on me.

Still, I had to hurry. I'd told my wife I was going to a basketball game with the boys—that gave me just another hour.

She moved to the door and beckoned me with one bend of her finger. And I followed Spanish Fly with my throbbing dick in hand. We left the room and climbed the stairs. I could smell the good clean aroused scent of her pussy. I reached up and slapped her ass, loving the way it jiggled in a thousand different directions.

There were signs on the door to let you know whether the room was occupied and private, or occupied and public—meaning the people inside wanted to be watched. I didn't give a damn what sign Spanish Fly used as long as I got to slip this hard dick deep into her juicy pussy. My wife was at church and I wanted to fuck off this freaky nut that was hounding me and make it home before her.

My hands reached for her as soon as the door closed, but Spanish Fly took charge and pushed me down onto the bed. My dick was still hard and stood up from my body straight as an arrow and aching to dig her out. She climbed onto the bed between my open legs and headed straight for my hard-on.

"Te chuparé tu dick con mi boca."

I didn't know what the fuck she whispered. All I know was it sounded sexy as shit and that I heard the word dick, so I was good to go.

She licked every inch of it before she took it all in her mouth, until the tip tickled her tonsils. My ass arched off the bed and I clutched the sheets trying not to holler like a little bitch as she sucked me so hard that her cheeks caved in.

She knew what she was doing. First slow and deep, ending with a tickle of her tongue against the tip, and then fast and wet, causing her spit to drizzle down my dick and quivering thighs.

I sat up on my elbows to watch her; the sight of her lips suctioned to my dick was hot. She sucked that motherfucker like it had never been sucked before. I drew in air and my lips formed a circle as I squirted a little cum in her mouth.

Spanish Fly hummed with pleasure and sucked harder, her fingers squeezing my nuts. She shifted backward off the bed and slid her hands up my legs to jerk them roughly up high in the air until my ass was lifted off the bed. She ran her tongue up the crease of my ass and then circled the hole before she sucked it whole.

"Aaah," I cried out hoarsely, sweat dripping from my body, 'cause she had me sweating like a fiend.

Back and forth she went, from my ass to my balls to suck my dick deep and nasty and back down again. Ass. Balls. Dick. Ass. Balls. Dick.

Spanish Fly slapped my ass and roughly pushed me until I turned over on my stomach and then got on all fours. I felt the warmth of her body leave me. Before I could wonder where she went, she stood on the side of the bed and pressed her lush titties onto my back. Her hand tightly gripped my dick and jacked it downward until I started to pump my hips against her hand.

Suddenly I felt the first sting of a paddle to my ass—*whap*— followed by her sucking and licking the same area she just hit as she continued to stroke my dick, squeezing the thick tip.

She turned me the fuck out. An erotic mix of pleasure and pain that pushed me over the edge until I felt crazy from wanting to feel her pussy on my dick. The more I wanted her the longer she made me wait. She tortured me. Pleased me.

She spanked me till my ass felt raw and still I wanted her.

Feathers stroked across my body as she talked to me in Spanish, making me nearly nuts myself.

She tied me to the bed and then massaged oil over my body before she stroked me with her titties and her thighs, calling me *Papi*.

She pushed me, pulled me, stroked me, and sucked me.

She fucked me up. I lost awareness of time. I forgot everything and everyone but this Spanish Fly who was turning me out like a pro.

She slid her wet pussy down onto my dick and my muscles strained as I fought to break the bonds holding me. She was tight and wet, gripping my dick more like a fist than a pussy. Her thick thighs, wet from her own juices, pressed into my sides as she raised her hands to squeeze, pluck, and suck her own rock-hard nipples as she fucked me. I felt hypnotized by the way she circled her hips clockwise and then counterclockwise causing her walls to tightly grip and then release my dick. She was so wet that each move made a smacking noise.

She bent down and offered me her breasts. Eagerly I latched my mouth onto one, sucking her nipples like I was thirsty as she cried out in pleasure. I felt her ass bounce against my thighs as she fucked me harder. Spanish Fly rode me like she was trying to win the Triple Crown, her juices dripping down my balls. I felt spasms in her pussy as I licked her nipples wildly, sucking one whole breast into my eager mouth.

My heart pounded loudly in my ears. The smell of her pussy made my dick stone-hard. My stomach muscles tightened and I felt energy shimmy over our sweat-soaked bodies.

My wife. I loved her. I really did, but I needed this release. I needed this woman whose face I couldn't see.

Spanish Fly pressed her sweaty titties against my chest as she grabbed my head with her hands and licked my exposed lips with her tongue. When her tongue darted out of her sweet mouth again I suckled it deeply.

It was the first time I'd kissed a woman other than my wife.

Her tongue did tricks in my mouth as she made it flicker against mine. I thought of the way she ate Mocha's pussy and my heart swelled.

The familiar tension shimmied over my body. The feeling of expectation made me weak. I lifted my hips off the bed and rammed my dick up into her so hard that her soft body bounced up and down atop me. I knew she was cumming too because her pussy got wetter, more slippery, and the walls released and gripped like a vise, squeezing all the cum from my dick. With each spasm my dick jerked like a fired gun. I nearly died from wanting my hands free to hold that vibrating ass while we came like crazy.

She lifted off me and crawled back down between my legs to take my semi-hard dick in her mouth and suck the last of the juices from me. Her tongue circling the tip as she cleaned my thick white cum with a smile.

Fuck it. I cried out like a bitch and hit a high note.

"Shit," I swore, still trembling as she moved to untie my limbs.

My eyes drifted closed and I felt myself slipping into that good sex sleep zone.

I opened my eyes and saw that I was alone. Spanish Fly was gone.

I jumped from the bed. I had to see her again. I had to have her again.

When I left the room the door across the hall was open. A woman with a body like a video vixen was tied to the wall, spread-eagle. I didn't even pause to enjoy the sight as I flew down the stairs.

I had just stumbled around the curve, almost frantic, when I saw a glimpse of Spanish Fly's buttocks jiggling as she walked down the stairs. I caught up to her just as she neared the foot of the stairs.

I could still smell our sex and I wanted to fuck her again. Right there on the stairs.

I grabbed her arm. "Wait. Don't go."

She froze. I mean her entire body went deathly still. I felt a shiver race across her naked body as she turned to me. Behind her mask her eyes were filled with surprise and disbelief. She snatched her arm away. "Marcus?"

Gone was the sexy barely audible whisper-like voice from our sex play. This voice was clear and I recognized it well. I felt like my nuts had crawled up into my stomach. I grabbed her to me with one strong arm and wrestled her full-face mask off with my free hand to reveal her face.

I thought I knew it all.

I was wrong.

"Marisol," I said in disbelief.

Spanish Fly was my wife.

My Destiny

MI DESTINO

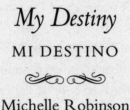

Michelle Robinson

*B*eautiful investment counselor Destiny Shannon didn't know it, but she was being watched! For several months now, she had been under constant surveillance. Her stalker was waiting for the moment when he would finally make her pay!

Destiny glanced at her reflection in Saks' window. Her dark red shoulder-length layered cut was a nice complement to her cocoa brown complexion. She would have to thank her stylist for convincing her to ditch her dull brown hair color. Although she was wearing a conservative gray pinstriped suit, nothing could conceal her beautiful, athletic body; her reward for years of high school track and field. She knew she shouldn't have come here on a weekday but she had lost her favorite shade of lipstick and, despite tearing the apartment apart, she hadn't found it. Saks was packed and she would have to race to get downtown. In the split second it took for her to glance at her watch and realize she was going to be late meeting her client, she ran into a gentleman entering Saks, spilling her latte all over his Armani suit. When she recovered from the collision, she realized how attractive he was.

Destiny retrieved a handkerchief from her suit pocket and nervously wiped at the coffee stain.

"Don't worry about that," he said.

Destiny grinned like a teenage girl with a crush on the teacher. This exquisite creature could be described only as an Adonis. The caramel-colored skin, the dark wavy hair and equally dark, seductively mysterious eyes; his features were so powerful, she could barely maintain direct eye contact.

"I apologize," Destiny offered. "I was in such a rush and wasn't paying attention. I've ruined your suit. I would be happy to pay to have it dry-cleaned."

"That's not necessary. I'm a buyer here at Saks. I have a closet full of sample suits at my disposal—it's one of the perks of the job. In fact, thank you," he added. "If we hadn't crashed into one another, I wouldn't have an opportunity to ask you to dinner tonight."

Destiny could feel the heat rising in her cheeks. She wanted to be cool, but she kept thinking how much she would like to be lying on a beach with this beautiful specimen of a man, fucking like minks. He oozed sensuality and it *had* been almost two years since she'd had sex with anything other than her shower massager.

He extended his right hand. "Hi, I'm Antonio Fernández."

"I'm Destiny Shannon."

"Wow, I can't wait to hear the story behind that incredible name. So, Destiny, how about it; dinner tonight at Haru's?" Antonio asked. "If you don't like Japanese, we can go somewhere else."

"No, Japanese sounds great; I've heard the food there is fabulous."

"Does eight o'clock work for you?" he asked.

"Eight o'clock would be fine," she replied.

"Where shall I pick you up?"

"I have a few errands I need to run. I'll meet you at the restaurant. Here's my business card. If anything should change, just give me a call. If I'm not there you can leave me a voice mail," Destiny said.

"Wild horses couldn't keep me away," he said.

They waved good-bye and Destiny hailed a taxi.

&

Destiny's day dragged on endlessly and she could barely concentrate. She raced home, showered, changed and got to the restaurant around 8:15 P.M. She was wearing a knee-length, clingy purple silk dress, gold hoop earrings and a gold lariat necklace. The jewelry brought out the beauty of her green eyes. On her feet she wore a pair of gold four-inch heels which gave her legs an ultra-sexy lilt when she walked. All eyes were on her. She wasn't accustomed to dressing this sexy, but she liked the way it made her feel. Antonio stood up when she got to the table. He leaned in toward her, put his arm around her waist and whispered in her ear, "Absolutely stunning." He smelled good enough to eat and his voice made her feel positively giddy. That black turtleneck and black leather pants he was wearing didn't hurt either.

They both ordered plum wine, Destiny had salmon teriyaki and Antonio had the sushi and sashimi. He was attentive, charming, intelligent—and only twenty-seven years old. Destiny was eleven years older than him; a difference she decided would have to be overlooked.

Although it was nearly the end of fall, it was a beautiful night and Antonio walked Destiny home to her apartment on Seventy-fifth and First.

"So," Destiny began. "Where are you from?"

"I was born in Puerto Rico, but my family and I moved to New York when I was four years old. What about you?" Antonio asked. "Where are you from?"

"I grew up in Harlem."

Antonio's eyes were piercing. It made Destiny acutely uncomfortable, so she prattled on and on about being named after her mom's midwife, going away to college and her job until Antonio suddenly asked, "Do I make you nervous?"

"No," Destiny responded quietly. "It's just—when you look at me, I feel like you're boring a hole through me."

Before she could elaborate, Antonio kissed her full on the lips, his tongue probing deeply, exploring her entire mouth. His kiss left her feeling dizzy.

"Does that help?" he asked, as he released her.

"Yeah, a little," she responded with a smile.

When they got back to her place, Destiny invited Antonio upstairs for a cup of coffee. She was still jumpy and Antonio knew just what would ease her tension.

"Destiny, I'd like to show you something." She was sitting on the stairs of her duplex and Antonio got up from her white leather couch and stood in front of her. He unfastened the belt to his pants. Her head kept telling her this was too soon, but unadulterated lust left her mesmerized and wanting more. Antonio allowed his pants to drop to the floor. The sight of him standing before her complete with bulging black bikini briefs and well-cut physique made her mouth water. Destiny barely had enough time to absorb the appeal of his masculine form when he removed all of his remaining clothing, including his briefs, revealing the largest dick she had ever seen in her life. He had to be fifteen inches long. Destiny had seen her fair share of dick, but this was not like anything she had ever seen before. This was like going to a museum and being compelled to touch the fascinating exhibit, but afraid of what would happen if you did. Destiny suddenly wondered if she could handle it.

"Touch it," Antonio said.

He didn't have to say it again. Destiny wrapped her hand around his cock and if it were even possible he got even harder. She got so hot and wet she could feel the lips of her pussy swelling. She would soon find out whether or not her pussy could accommodate his massive cock. She slowly began licking the tip. He was enormous and tasted like heaven. She licked and sucked the head of his cock; her sucking and his shallow breathing occupying the silence. Destiny relaxed her throat and bent her head further back, grabbed his muscular, toned ass and guided him 'til he was standing directly over her. And, as Antonio gripped both banisters for leverage, she took more of him inside of her mouth and began to stroke his dick with her mouth.

Despite his size, she managed to deep-throat his cock. She got as much of him inside as she could and fucked his cock with her mouth, gagging just a little each time the head of his cock hit the back of her throat, causing Antonio to moan uncontrollably. She released his lengthy steed and began flicking her tongue from his balls to the underside of his cock until he couldn't stand it any longer. She made sure there wasn't an inch of him that went unattended. She nibbled on his balls as his body trembled. When she grabbed his butt cheeks, he squirmed. She removed her right hand from his beautiful tanned ass and brought her fingers down to where she was still massaging his balls with her mouth. She used the nail of her purple, manicured index finger to trace a line between his balls and his ass, all while taking his entire sac into her mouth and sucking lightly. She released the hold her mouth had on his balls and began licking his sac. With her other hand she began jerking him off.

As she sucked and jerked him into a frenzy, she took the finger that was busy stimulating that place between his balls and his ass and put it into her mouth to get it good and lubricated before she slipped a finger inside his asshole so she could massage his prostate. She went back to licking and sucking the tip of his cock and just when she thought he was about to explode inside of her mouth, he withdraw and spoke. His voice was husky and filled with desire when he spoke to her in his native Spanish tongue: *"No mas, amor, yo no he terminado contigo."* Not yet, baby, I'm not finished with you.

Destiny had no idea what he had just said, but she was sure he would show her. He helped her up from the stairs, gently laid her on the floor and undressed her. Destiny lay there clad in a black silk thong, so aroused she could smell the scent of her own juices filling the air.

"Baby, I want to taste you," Antonio remarked. He stroked her face and kissed her so deeply he took her breath away. She needed him inside of her.

Antonio took turns kissing, sucking and licking the curve of her neck. His tongue traveled down to her breasts, sucking her nipples until they were so hard she could barely feel them. His artful tongue licked the droplets of sweat gathered near her belly button. While he licked her flat taut belly he took his fingers and entered her pussy. He fingered Destiny with first two, then three fingers until he was able to get his entire hand inside of her, fist-fucking her pussy 'til Destiny thought she might pass out from its intensity. She squirmed, but Antonio held fast to her all the while taking turns feasting on each of her nipples, now so hard, they seemed ready to erupt. Antonio removed his fist, soaked with

Destiny's cum juices and put his fingers in her mouth, whispering in her ear, *"Mira que rico pruebas."* (See how good you taste.)

Destiny attempted to speak and rise from the floor, but Antonio put one finger to her lips and said, "Shh." His lips traveled down to Destiny's clit and in no time it was as hard as Antonio's cock. He licked and sucked her pussy until she ejaculated all over his face. She lay there as each wave of ecstasy caused her body to shiver and tremble. Before her last quake was barely completed, Antonio had entered Destiny with all fifteen inches of his manhood. After being fist-fucked by Antonio, Destiny was more than ready for him. She gasped and cried out in a voice that was almost unrecognizable. Antonio held on to her body with her legs wrapped around him and stroked her nice and easy, finding her G-spot with great ease.

"This is so fucking good," was all Destiny kept saying.

Antonio looked Destiny directly in her eyes while he was inside of her and said, *"Estoy contento que te gusta, amor. Quiero que te guste. Quiero que me desees. ¿Me deseas, Destino?"* (I'm glad you like it, baby. I want you to like it. I want you to want me. Do you want me, Destiny?) Then he said in English, "Do you want me? Tell me you want me, Destiny."

This was more than Destiny could stand; his voice, the feel of him inside her. She was rocked by another earth-shattering orgasm. She cried out, "Yes, yes, I want you!" Antonio pulled out, removed the condom he was wearing, straddled Destiny's face, and eased his cock into her mouth. Destiny sucked him even more intensely than she had earlier. Within moments Antonio shot gobs of sweet, hot nectar inside of her mouth and Destiny gladly swallowed every drop. They dozed off on the floor and in the middle of the night Antonio carried her upstairs to her bedroom.

Destiny awoke to the aroma of bacon frying in the kitchen. For a moment she thought she had dreamed it all, until she looked under the sheets at her still naked body. She put on her red bathrobe and went downstairs to the kitchen to find Antonio standing over the stove preparing breakfast, buck naked.

"Good morning, love," Antonio said. "Sleep well?"

"Like a rock, thanks to you. I haven't slept this late in ages." It was 9:00 A.M. Usually Destiny was working on her third cup of coffee in the office at 7:00 A.M. The stale office coffee would have to wait today. She had a gorgeous hunk of a man in her kitchen fixing her breakfast.

"I assume you eat meat?" Antonio said, as he flipped the bacon in the pan.

Destiny chuckled. "Well, if I didn't, after last night, I guess I do now."

"Get back in bed; you're spoiling my plans."

Destiny raced upstairs and got right back in bed.

Antonio entered the room with a breakfast tray with coffee, bacon, scrambled eggs, toast, strawberries and freshly squeezed orange juice.

Destiny sampled some eggs, drank a sip of orange juice and sighed.

"I see your talents stretch above and beyond the bedroom," she said.

"I wasn't aware I had demonstrated any bedroom talents to you," replied Antonio.

"You haven't?" Destiny questioned.

"No, I haven't," Antonio said as he sat on the bed and inched closer to Destiny. "I didn't get an opportunity to demonstrate my

bedroom talents. You took advantage of me on the staircase before I had a chance."

"*I* took advantage of *you?*" Destiny laughed. "I remember it
differently."

"Well, love, that's my story and I'm sticking to it."

He grabbed a piece of bacon off of the plate and took a bite.
He fed the rest of it to Destiny with some scrambled eggs and
strawberries.

Destiny kept thinking how she could get used to this kind of
treatment.

Antonio gave Destiny a soft peck on the lips and jumped off
the bed. "I have to get to work. I'm gonna take a shower."

"Okay," Destiny answered.

While Antonio was taking his shower, Destiny realized how
much she liked this guy and hoped this wasn't one of those slam-
bam-thank-you-ma'ams. She wanted very much to see Antonio
again and again . . . and again. . . .

As if reading her mind, Antonio shouted, "Do you have any
plans tonight? I suddenly got this yen for hush puppies."

Destiny joined Antonio in the shower and gave him her answer. She walked into the bathroom and dropped her robe to the
floor, slid open the glass shower door and stepped in. She stood
directly behind Antonio and wrapped herself around him. She
picked up the bar of soap and lathered his chest. Before she could
give some attention to his lower region, Antonio had already
come to life. He turned to face her and put his arms around her.
He stroked her back and caressed her face. He kissed her so
sweetly, it was paradise. Antonio picked up the condom he had
placed on the bathtub ledge, opened it and put it on, picked her
up and slid her onto his pulsating cock. He gripped her buttocks

and slid her up and down his long, thick cock. She wrapped her arms around his neck and enjoyed the ride. The water from the showerhead splashed and splattered against their bodies.

Antonio's breathing was becoming increasingly labored. "Oh baby, I . . . I can't hold it. Here it comes . . . here it comes! Your pussy is so fucking tight." he roared. Antonio let out such a growl it was nothing short of primal.

Destiny's body convulsed as she came with him. Antonio set her down and held her to him. After they had both recovered, they soaped each other's bodies, stood together under the showerhead and allowed the warm water to revive them.

Antonio dressed and went downstairs. Destiny joined him and they locked together in a good-bye kiss.

"By the way," Antonio mentioned when their bodies separated, "you never told me whether you're free tonight."

"What did you have in mind?" Destiny asked.

"I was thinking maybe we start with dinner at Virgil's. It's a barbecue restaurant in Times Square with the best hush puppies in New York. You like hush puppies?"

"Yeah, I do," Destiny replied.

"Oh—she likes hush puppies! I think I'm in love," Antonio said.

Destiny believed she could actually hear her own heart skip a beat and tried to remain as cool and unresponsive to his words as was humanly possible. Somehow, though, she knew she failed. He'd have to be deaf, dumb and blind not to notice how his words affected her.

He glanced at his watch. "Tonight then," he said. "Eight o'clock. I'd like to be chivalrous tonight and pick you up at your door if you don't mind?"

"I don't mind at all. I'll see you at eight."

He kissed her again then turned to leave. "It's going to be difficult concentrating today," he said as he left.

"Ditto," Destiny added.

It was 10:30 A.M. and Destiny didn't feel like going to work. She was going to do something she hadn't done in a long time: lie in bed, watch the news, drink a cup of coffee and savor the moment. She called her assistant and told her she would be working from home, hung up the phone and ran upstairs to her bedroom. Destiny slept late into the afternoon dreaming of many more days like this one.

∽

Antonio and Destiny had been dating for six months now and things were almost too good to be true. They both enjoyed the same things and seldom had any conflict, yet Destiny often thought Antonio was hiding something. He seldom spoke of his family and she had never met any of his friends.

One afternoon Destiny was on her way out of the office to a meeting when the telephone rang.

"Tammy, could you grab that for me?" she asked her assistant.

"Good afternoon, Ms. Shannon's office," Tammy said. "Destiny, it's Antonio."

Destiny ran back into her office. "Hi, baby," she said.

"Hi, love," Antonio responded. "Did you know today is six months to the day that we met?"

"Really," Destiny responded. She couldn't believe how romantic he was. She knew, but was surprised he had remembered. Most men didn't remember six-month anniversaries.

"So, my dear, to commemorate this momentous occasion, I am cooking dinner for you tonight at my place."

Destiny was elated; dinner at his place. She seldom spent time there. The most she had ever done was meet him in the lobby of his building. They spent all their time at her place. She hadn't pressured Antonio and figured it was because his studio in Chelsea was less comfortable than her large two-bedroom apartment. "So, what are we having?" she asked.

"Lobster tails, rice pilaf and steamed mixed vegetables. Does that meet with *mi Destino's* approval?" Antonio asked.

Destiny's heart began to race. It had been fifteen years since she had heard those words— *"mi Destino"*—Spanish for my destiny. Only one man had ever called her that. He had been the love of her life and he was dead!

Destiny left her office and caught a cab to Antonio's apartment. She was happy to get a quiet driver. She didn't feel up to idle chitchat. She needed to calm herself and to stop rehashing old memories.

Destiny got to Antonio's around 6:00 P.M. His place was decorated with lots of leather and glass and was larger than she expected. On the round glass dining table was a chilled bottle of champagne and a dish full of strawberries. As soon as Destiny walked in Antonio grabbed her and kissed her full on the lips. He engulfed her; tugging at her lower lip with his teeth and sticking his tongue so far down her throat she thought she might choke. His kisses were different than usual; or was it her uneasiness at being reminded of her past?

"*Mi Destino.* come, have a seat." Antonio removed Destiny's coat and flung it across the recliner.

Destiny was agitated. "Why do you keep calling me that?" she asked.

"What?" Antonio responded; "*Mi Destino?* Because you are—you are my destiny."

Destiny couldn't put her finger on it, but there was something strange about Antonio tonight. He popped the cork on the bottle of Dom Pérignon, poured each of them a glass and proposed a toast—"To momentous occasions," he announced. After they each took a sip of the champagne, Antonio grabbed Destiny with such force she almost lost her footing. He kissed her, sucking the breath from her body with each kiss. He grabbed at her breasts, pushing her down on the couch. Usually Antonio was slow and gentle with her. This time, however, he ripped her silk blouse from her body along with her red lace bra as he proceeded to pinch both her nipples, sucking her breasts, feeding on them like a starving man, taking turns biting at each nipple as they began to grow more and more erect. Destiny was frightened by this sudden change in his personality. She was wearing a red thong, which he also ripped from her body, causing a searing pain to course through her as the cloth ripped into her pussy. Antonio wasted no time in bombarding her body with bites—to her breasts and to her belly before seeking out her clean-shaven mound. His tongue licked and sucked her pussy while his teeth nibbled at her clit. Destiny was frightened, yet there was an element that excited her.

He finally spoke. *"Esto es lo que usted quieres?"* she heard him say. It sounded to Destiny like a question—or was it some sort of challenge? She couldn't begin to know what he had said. Just when Destiny thought she would explode from a mixture of anticipation coated with fear, Antonio picked up the bottle of champagne. He took a long swig straight from the bottle, grabbed the back of Destiny's head, pulling her hair, and pulled her lips close to his, releasing the champagne he had in his mouth into hers. Champagne dribbled out of the corners of her mouth. Before she could recover, Antonio had doused her body with half of the champagne in the bottle. He licked and sucked hungrily at the liquid that now soaked her. Antonio raised himself from atop Destiny just long enough to remove his clothing. His dick was rock hard and he was still holding the bottle of champagne in his hand.

He kept asking, "Is this what you want, *mi Destino?* Is this what you want?" Before she could answer, Antonio plunged the champagne bottle deep into her pussy, causing her to gasp, and began fucking her with the bottle. Trickles of champagne streamed down her thighs, when he pulled the bottle out, it poured from her pussy onto the floor. He ended by jerking off and ejaculating a massive quantity of cum onto Destiny's face before collapsing on her and falling asleep.

Destiny was dumbfounded. His lovemaking was usually so tender. She thought maybe he had been drinking before she got there. But he didn't seem to be drunk. She couldn't sleep, so she just watched Antonio for a moment. She couldn't shake the feeling that he reminded her of someone. She decided to get out of bed and make herself a cup of herbal tea. She was looking for the tea in Antonio's kitchen cabinets, and in the corner of one of the cabinets was an envelope. She didn't usually snoop, but there was so much she didn't know about Antonio, and the evening had been so strange. She opened the envelope. And was stunned. There was a picture of what appeared to be a very happy couple and their son. The boy looked to be about eleven or twelve years old, the woman she did not recognize, but the man in the picture she knew all too well! It was Julio, the only man she had ever loved—that is, until now. As she tried to make sense of this situation, she heard footsteps behind her. It was Antonio.

"I guess we can add invasion of privacy to your list of crimes," Antonio said.

"Antonio, I don't understand," Destiny muttered.

"Don't you? You're a smart girl, *mi Destino.* Why don't you put two and two together: Julio Vargas, the man in the picture, he was my father. You took him away from me and my mother when he needed us the most. You stole from us; robbed us of what was ours."

"But . . . but your name is Fernandez," Destiny stammered. She was so overwhelmed, she couldn't think of anything else to say.

"I changed my name. Otherwise the plan wouldn't have worked. I've been planning this for close to seven months now— ever since you killed my mother. The woman in the picture—my mother—she died of cirrhosis of the liver; drank herself to death after you stole her husband. I was going to ruin your career, your home, all the things that matter to you, and leave you sad and alone, so you could feel what my mother felt fifteen years ago."

"Antonio, what are you talking about? I didn't even know your mother!" Destiny yelled.

"That's what makes it all the more sinful. Do you know my mother was never the same after my father left us? She couldn't understand what she had done. Hell, I couldn't understand what *I* had done. What would cause a man dying of cancer to leave the family who loved him and spend his last moments on earth with a twenty-three-year-old whore! I have to admit, though, after blowing out that pussy I can understand why Papa couldn't resist. You really are the fuck of the century!"

Destiny could feel his rage and pain. It was as if he was twelve years old all over again. She knew she had to make Antonio understand. She'd loved Julio and now she loved his son, and that made her protective of Julio's memory, even under these circumstances. Antonio might not listen to her, but he *would* listen to his father.

"Antonio, I have something for you. I've carried it close to me all these years thinking it was what I needed. I now know I was just holding on to it until the inevitable happened."

Destiny picked up her pocketbook. From her wallet she retrieved a folded piece of paper and handed it to Antonio. Antonio snatched the piece of paper out of Destiny's hand.

"What the fuck is this!" he yelled, yet he began reading.

Mi Destino,

By the time you read this I will be gone. Do not grieve for me, my angel. You have given me immeasurable joy in my final days. If I had not known I hadn't long to live would I ever have grabbed for the spontaneity I so craved in life? Would I have reached for you? Your love breathed new life into me, while the love of my beautiful wife and son has sustained me, and I pray that my final selfish act will not hurt them too deeply, for I have greatly loved them both. My wish is that all those I have loved most of all will inhale of life and not get lost in their grief. I hope my son will one day know the passion and love I have known. Although I am only thirty-eight years old, I feel as though I have lived a lifetime . . .

Love, Julio

Antonio dropped to the floor and sobbed, deep racking sobs that rocked his soul. Destiny embraced him, kissing his hands, his face all the while saying over and over again, "I'm so very, very sorry. Antonio, can you ever forgive me?"

Antonio looked into her eyes and in that instant Destiny

knew—she knew that she had been forgiven. All she wanted to do now was to make it up to Antonio.

"I really do love you, you know. No matter how hard I tried to hate you, I couldn't help but fall in love with you in spite of myself," Antonio said.

"I love you, too, baby." Destiny answered. They didn't talk anymore that night. Everything that needed to be said had already been said. Destiny kissed Antonio from head to toe, wiping away years of pain. She thought of father and son; both were with her tonight. Destiny lay on top of Antonio and wrapped around him great walls of passion, protection, and—yes—love. As each stroke brought Antonio closer to releasing torrents of pain, he whispered the words Destiny knew all too well—*mi Destino.*

"*Y tu eres mío,*" she replied. And you are mine.

Shameless

DESCARADA

Nikki Sinclair

I don't care where we go," Melissa said, hooking her bra before a mirror. "As long as I can show off my pussy."

This might have disturbed him a month ago. But a month ago she stood on the bed in their Baltimore hotel room and asked, bending over, "Have you ever seen an asshole like that?"

No, he hadn't.

But then he hadn't actually seen anyone's asshole or thought much about it until he met this short young woman with smooth round arms and pretty breasts and a good-size but not too large behind and . . . Well, there wasn't a part he hadn't seen. She was a nudist is what she was. She was also an epicurean and music lover and wine lover and sex lover, and she was wild with excitement this morning as they packed suitcases because she had never been to Mexico and she was, of course, a travel lover.

"Will you teach me Spanish?" she asked, pulling on thong underwear. She put her arms around his neck. "I mean, real Spanish. I already know the bad words."

That was true.

Right away she wanted all the bedroom words. "How do you say it in Spanish?" she asked, sticking her pussy in his face. He had been lying on his back. She was on top, facing his feet, stroking his cock. They had known each other a week.

"It's—" His voice caught as she stuck it in her mouth. "*Sesenta y nueve.* I think."

She sucked loudly. Then paused. "Don't you know? I thought you were Mexican."

"I am."

"*Sesenta y nueve,*" she said. "Sixty-nine. I'll remember."

He knew she would.

This morning, wearing only her thong, with their suitcases half-packed, she stared into Oscar's eyes. "Teach me," she whispered. A tall, brown, handsome man, Oscar pulled her hands away. She wanted it most when it was most impractical.

"We'll be late," he said. "I'll teach you all the Spanish you want in Mazatlán. If there's time for anything besides . . ." He looked at her a bit sadly. In their short time together they already had a history of going places and not seeing too much of anything. Well, that wasn't entirely true. Among other things he had seen her asshole.

Oscar worried about taking Melissa to meet his father and brother but reminded himself she always behaved very well outside bedrooms. Attractive and intelligent, happy, enthusiastic and a little childish, this little blonde would impress his father. She would impress him for no other reason than she was an American. For a father who sent his boy to American schools, who encouraged Oscar to learn English from the earliest age, and delighted in Oscar's American business and American connections, it would be all too good to be true.

"But, Papá," Oscar reminded him on the phone. "We have

only dated two months." This to the old man's enthusiastic inquiries about marriage.

"You're too cautious," Papá warned. "It's like business. Make a decision."

"Let's see if you like her first."

"I love her. Get married here."

"That won't happen," Oscar said.

"You'll make more money."

"Yes, I know."

"It's the same with your brother. He won't marry either. Or make money."

"I make money."

"Not enough. Get married." That was Papá.

At the airport the lobbies were crowded with people in shorts and loud shirts. "Tell me about Carnaval again," Melissa asked. As they sat she snuggled next to him. Looking down he saw her pretty cleavage. He'd made her wear a bra.

"It's like Mardi Gras," Oscar said. "Pretty much everyone in Mazatlán throws a big party, just before Lent. Sin before repentence, that sort of thing. Crazy costumes, Mexican food, seafood, shrimp and music. It's mostly Latin, you aren't going to see a lot of Americans. Or many rules."

"I'm liking Carnaval already."

"You would. I thought we'd go down to the Avenida del Mar, where the real action takes place. Just stay close to me."

"Why?"

"This is a local festival. That blond hair might get you in a little trouble."

"Sounds like fun."

"Just stay close."

They slept on the plane. Sere mountains and naked valleys

rolled beneath as the jet crossed into Mexico. The day was bright, blue, hot, Mexican. Oscar was dozing and woke when Melissa excused herself. After she wiggled her ass past him he closed his eyes once more.

"Excuse me, sir," the flight attendant said a moment later. She touched Oscar's shoulder. "Excuse me, but your wife needs your help."

"Wife?" he mumbled groggily.

"Yes. She's asking for you. She's in the bathroom and she wants you to bring her purse."

"My wife needs . . . Oh, yes." Oscar grasped the situation. "So she asked for me, did she?" he said to the flight attendant. His legs were stiff. "I ought to send you."

"What?" the flight attendant asked.

"Nothing."

At the bathroom door he knocked, lightly. He heard Melissa's muffled reply. Oscar called her and she opened the door an inch. "Get in here," she said. Her pants were off. Oscar glanced as the flight attendants, who were in plain sight preparing serving carts. In an instant he pushed his way in.

"What the hell is this?" Oscar asked. Was she nuts? She stood on the seat.

"Lock the door," she commanded. There was no room, Oscar could barely move.

"I won't. Melissa, put your pants on."

"C'mon," she said, breathing fast. "Let's join the mile-high club." Her pussy was in his face.

"You're going too far. We're in Mexico now!"

"Come on. It'll be over in a second."

"You're crazy," he said. But he wasn't going to leave, not with a bottomless girl for all to see, and he couldn't turn around, not

in that cramped space, not with her pussy in his face. With difficulty he reached behind and locked the door.

She was hot. Her intoxicating odor filled his nostrils. She
rubbed it in his face, her hands were in his hair and she rubbed
her pussy up and down in his face, the gray-blond patch soft and
coarse as she rubbed and rubbed. His cheeks, his nose were wet.
"Do me!" she gasped. "Do me!" Oscar's head bumped the door.
She had him trapped, she was rubbing her pussy in his face in a
tiny bathroom at 30,000 feet with three flight attendants two
feet away and there was nothing he could do. Well, he thought,
he could do something. He could finish her. And fast.

He put his tongue between her legs. Melissa gasped. Too
loud, he thought. Too loud! He licked and licked, carefully, skillfully. She fought, rubbing. "C'mon," she said. "C'mon." His hand
ran down her legs to the top of the toilet. There it was. Okay,
then. Sticking his tongue deep into her he heard her moan, and
bringing it up, bringing his tongue up, he licked and licked re-
lentlessly, grinding away on her swollen clit. Melissa grunted,
gasped, and as she came, ass shaking, the ear-splitting flush of the
jetliner's toilet drowned out her loudest cries.

They washed as best they could. "That was a pretty good
trick," she said to Oscar. "Flushing the toilet like that."

"I think fast," he said, combing his hair, his moustache. He
smelled like her. They both smelled like her.

"You act fast, too." She kissed him. "Sure you don't want me
to do you?"

He said no. God no.

"'Cause I'm fast, too," she added.

He knew. And wondered if the trip down the aisle to their
seats wouldn't make them as obvious as he imagined it would.

As the jet approached Mazatlán, Melissa slept on Oscar's arm.

The picture of innocence. He knew he was taking a chance with her. He might have snuck her into Mexico and not told anyone. Then there would be no mess, no questions and no inquiries. Melissa could be as shameless as she pleased. Instead he told his father and brother she was coming, bragged, even. "My girl-friend," he called her, proudly, even though she wouldn't let him say it to her or their friends. Or to anyone.

"I don't want that," she had said.

"Then what are we?"

"Friends," she told him, rubbing her forehead. "Just friends."

She woke in her seat beside him. Kissing him, she looked out the window with sleepy, lovely eyes. She looked every bit the professional, handsome American woman he had fallen for. Good manners, intelligent, poised. She would impress his brother, Jorge, whom she would meet first. He would try her out on him. Then Papá. Papá would love her. There was nothing to fear.

"Seat belt time," he said. The plane tilted low over the city. As he buckled his seat belt he leaned close. "Excited?" he asked.

She held her compact and lipstick close to her face. "Oscar," she asked, "have you ever seen a tanned pussy?"

They rented a car. It was the clear blue day and the brown mountains of Sinaloa Province and the chaos and color and dirt of Mazatlán gleaming by the sea that brought him the real feel-ing of being home. Despite Papá he was Mexican. To the old man America was the Land of Oz, where all wishes were granted. He wouldn't mess with the old man's fantasy. He turned onto the Avenida del Mar, as Melissa insisted. Preparations for Carnaval were everywhere, including flowers and wreaths; beer signs; handmade, makeshift stages; and Mexican flags and bunting—green, red and white—on balconies and power poles and trucks and clotheslines. Men drank beer in the sun, at tables and in bodegas, in Mexican saloons, on benches and in the streets, workingmen getting a jump on the holiday. They stared brazenly at Melissa as she and Oscar bumped along in traffic.

"My God, what's that?" she asked. A great stone building stood before them.

"That's the Cathedral of Nuestra Señora," Oscar said. The cathedral rose above them, all ledges and arches, a massive structure, embellished with a hundred saints, villains, devils engaged in a frozen battle for the hearts of man. Heavy stone steps held a score of women, resting peasants and children. Great doors opened to a cavernous interior. "Want to see it?" he asked.

"Is it open?" Melissa blinked, staring.

"It's always open."

They parked and walked up the steps. She stood beside him while Oscar crossed himself and walked carefully up the wide center aisle. Here and there a woman, an occasional man, hunched, kneeling in prayer.

"Is there a priest?" Melissa asked.

"We can't talk," he whispered. He pointed along the dark walls. A candle glowed here and there. "We'll visit the stations," he whispered. "You can see the artwork."

In the gloom Melissa began to make out people, small women, some in rags, shuffling along the walls. Arched grottos held painted figures in bas-relief, and before these flowers were placed coins, bits of food, votive candles. It was an eerie sight. Oscar held her hand and released it at each station, each depiction of Christ's journey to Calvary. His lips moved silently. They walked the perimeter and then returned to the great doors. Outside the noise and brilliance of the midday city assailed them. They found their car.

"Who are the people on the steps?" Melissa asked.

"Poor people. Sick people. Children." They drove past the cathedral and continued down Avenida del Mar. "It's a safe place for them."

"Does anyone give them money?"

"They don't get money," Oscar said. "They get hope."

"I see."

A few blocks down they parked and had lunch at a little bistro Oscar knew. The food was good, and the waiters knew Oscar and greeted him like old friends. They spoke volubly in Spanish, and Melissa swore she would not return without knowing at least a little. At their hotel in the Golden Zone they made love. Afterward, Melissa spoke of the cathedral. Oscar, feeling very close to her, thought she had been impressed by its beauty and mystery. He was wrong.

"Want to hear a story?" she started. He didn't. And he did. "When I was working in a church bookstore I went home with two boys. We were in college. They lived in a trailer on the other side of the river. We got drunk and fell asleep and in the morning there was two feet of snow. The city was paralyzed. Well, you know how I am, and around these two guys, and we're alone and stuck and I'm hungover and we're playing cards and I'm really really horny.

"We played strip poker and pretty soon we're in our underwear and I'm teasing about having sex with one of them and how I'd love to suck the winner off. I knew neither one could get up to get another Bloody Mary. Their cocks were sticking out pretty bad so I said the heck with the winner, I suppose I can do ya both. We cleared out the living room and I got on my hands and knees. The one guy has a big ol' hard-on and he sits down in front of me and I go to work on him. I sucked him up and down and the other guy puts a condom on and slides it right in from behind me. He pushes in and out while I suck up and down. It was every girl's fantasy and soon we got a really good rhythm going: Push, suck, push, suck, and it gets faster and better and I feel something happening deep in my stomach. I came and when I do I really suck and as his cock spurts I gulp and gulp and deep down I feel it all the way in one big rolling orgasm from my cunt to my mouth and back down again.

"Afterward, drinking, we figured we all came together. End of story."

"Impressive," Oscar said. What did she want him to say? They slept.

An hour later Oscar kissed her ear. "Señorita," he said. It was early evening, and time to visit Jorge for drinks and dinner. She came dreamily awake. Smiled. His angel. Sleep seemed to wash them both clean.

After dinner with Jorge, they went to see his new condo. Jorge gestured grandly. "My abode," he said to Melissa, sweeping his arm as they entered. He spoke English as well as Oscar. They had dined at an expensive restaurant and a nightcap was in order, Jorge insisted. Oscar knew he would take any chance to show off his big condominium, the ocean view, the beautiful carved bar, the ten-thousand-dollar couch. Jorge made plenty of money with his four pizza parlors. "In the pizza business you have to be a drunk not to make money," he liked to say, usually as a toast. He claimed his own girlfriend was unavailable for dinner, but would love for Melissa to meet her some other night. Oscar knew this was a pose. Jorge spoke of girls, of beautiful girls, of one-night girls, of girls in the coffee shops and girls in the offices. There weren't any girls. Jorge was the type of shrewd businessman who learned to live without girls. He learned to distrust them, to place a value on them, and ultimately, to refuse to meet their price. Oscar knew him too well to be fooled.

When Melissa excused herself to use the powder room his brother poked Oscar in the ribs. "A real tigress, that one."

"Yes, Jorge."

"You having fun with her?"

Oscar rubbed his temples. It had been a busy day. "She meets Papá tomorrow. And then Carnaval."

"Yes. Watch her."

"I hope Papá—"

"I was speaking of Carnaval," Jorge interrupted. "Papá will love this girl. He will love her no matter what. She could fart in front of him, tell dirty jokes, take off her clothes."

Oscar gulped. Was it that obvious? "He wants me to marry her."

"He wants the whole world to get married." His brother laughed. "He wants me to marry all my girlfriends. Just tell Papá the same thing you tell this gringa. 'Maybe tomorrow.' Right?"

"I don't tell her anything like that. And don't call her names."

"You can't be serious about this woman, Oscar. Not the way she swings her ass."

"That's enough, Jorge."

"C'mon," Jorge said, raising his glass, eyes alight. He didn't have to wink. "A little fun with the American girls."

"Careful," Oscar said, his face darkening.

"C'mon," Jorge said. "Don't make it more than it is."

"I said be careful."

The playful light vanished from Jorge's eyes. "You be careful," he said to Oscar. Hadn't he the right to speak openly? Would he watch his brother be made a fool of? A man who hurt easily, Jorge refilled their glasses. "You be careful," he repeated.

⌇

The next morning Oscar hugged his father. It was good to see him. Better than he expected.

"But where's your girl?" Papá asked, oiled and ready.

"She's sleeping," he lied to his father. "I didn't bring her because she's sleeping and I thought it was best, you know."

The old man frowned. He had a big comical moustache, the ends curling and shining with Brilliantine. Short and round, he looked all the world like little Mario in Donkey Kong. He still thought himself good-looking. He had the unassailable vanity of the once-handsome. Today he wore an expensive sport coat, brown. It set off his flashing hazel eyes.

"I'll bring her tomorrow," Oscar said.

"I want to meet her now," Papá grumbled. "Let's take my car."

"Papá, you'll meet her."

"When? What is this?" He had been a cattle-buyer. He knew rough dealing when he saw it.

They talked. The old man complained about Mexican business, his many enemies. He said he hoped Oscar stayed in America. "It's better there. If you're going to get cheated get cheated honestly." Oscar didn't quite follow that one. Papá was retired, a bull who had chased the matador from the ring. Snorting, furious, but there was no one left to fight.

A maid brought coffee. Oscar watched her closely. Broad-faced, matronly, he couldn't help thinking it would have been his mother, should have been his mother, had she not died ten years before. The thought made him wince.

The old man moved from business to his second-favorite topic, marriage. "Tell this boy to get married, María!" he shouted at the maid.

"Oh, you," she teased him. "How come you don't call my sister?"

"I intend to. I am preparing the proper introduction."

"Yes, I know." She smiled at Oscar. She knew. She knew as well as he knew. And it dawned on Oscar as the old man prattled away about girls and money what a great lie it all was. It was a lie because there would never be another woman for Papá, who could not speak of his mother, who was so heartbroken he clammed up and never spoke to the boys of his grief or consoled them in theirs. He put her pictures away and busied himself with his enemies and after that the comical pursuit of nonexistent women. Right then and there Oscar knew that he, Jorge and Papá lied to one another and all the world every day. His father lied when he said he was cheated by Mexico. His brother lied when he said he would marry. He would never marry but instead form a much more permanent union and make money his mistress. Jorge would love money and never cheat on her and in twenty years tell his nieces and nephews a sad story of being left at the altar by the most beautiful girl in Mexico. He would tell them how all the angels cried for him but all along he and they and everyone knew he had married the richest girl: money.

"Papá," Oscar said. "I want a picture of Mamá. I want the big picture we kept in the hall when she was alive." He saw these words were like a whip upon his father.

"There's no pictures," he said. "I've thrown them away."

"I don't believe you. I want a picture of her. I want to start remembering her again. I want to remember her every day."

"There's no pictures. And don't talk about it."

"Please, Papá."

On the patio beyond their chairs birds flitted among the banana trees. "A man," his father said, looking away, his voice subdued. "A man lives his whole life with a plan. That plan can't be changed."

"Sometimes our plans change," Oscar replied.

"No. Not my plan."

"You need to adapt."

"To what? Failure?" The old man rose. "I have to rest now. You've worn me out with your foolishness."

While his father lay in his room Oscar spent time in the neglected garden, meditating. It was his mother's garden. In her absence it had grown and changed. He hardly recognized the banana trees, the bushes and banyans. The garden grew all by itself. Soon it was time to go back to the hotel and pick up Melissa. At the door María stopped him. "It's from your father," she said. "He told me to give it to you."

She handed it to him with solemn eyes. It was the picture of Mamá.

∽

It seemed to her the whole of Mazatlán had quit working, put on a straw hat, and gotten drunk. In front of the hotel Melissa hailed a Pulmonia, a sort of golf cart–cab, and rattled off in the direction of the Avenida del Mar and Carnaval. She was dressed for fun, in a sleeveless blouse, white shorts, light sandals.

She tried to call Oscar. "What's wrong with the phone?" she asked the cabbie, pointing at her cell phone.

"What?" the cabbie shouted back.

"The cell phone. It doesn't work."

"Soon it work." He smiled pleasantly.

Progress was slow. Buses clogged the Avenida, and the side streets were just as busy. They passed under a great decorated arch, where the cabbie stopped and she paid him. He turned the little Pulmonia and bouncing over the curb putt-putted away. The throng was so great Melissa could barely move. Pushed along, she found herself finally outside the bistro she and Oscar enjoyed the day before. It was much changed. The chairs and tables were missing. Men stood slopping beer on the wooden floor, shouting back and forth to each other. Melissa looked for the friendly waiters, Oscar's waiters, but they were nowhere to be found. She pushed her way back onto the sidewalk. She didn't like the way the men in there looked at her.

A sudden explosion sent screams and laughter rolling up the street. Some men were knocked down. Cries were heard as it continued up the street. A hand took her arm just as horses pulling a wagon tore past. "You shouldn't be here," a voice said. It was the man who'd pulled her to safety. He wore thick, round glasses. An old-fashioned camera hung from his neck.

"What?" Melissa asked.

"You need to leave. That way." He pointed up the street. It was even more crowded than the one they were on. She asked him why and he simply shook his head. A parade and passing throng swept him away.

The crush was incredible. Melissa felt a hand on her neck. When she turned the hand was gone, and so was her necklace. She was pushed along, past drinking men, past stages of blaring musicians, past costumed dancers, past donkeys and horses. Some men in soiled T-shirts and police hats stood laughing and drinking beer. She tried to cross to them but a booming and tinkling mariachi band rolled past, followed by buses and more buses and she was swept along in their exhaust. More explosions, and screams, real screams this time. Waves of people ran back against the crowds. Firecrackers or machine guns rattled. A rocket burst overhead, spraying them with cinders. Melissa tripped on something. Looking down she saw a man, passed out or dead, lying at her feet. Someone threw beer. She was wet, men were laughing. In a panic she pushed ahead. Dirty hands reached from everywhere. Stained, filthy fingers touched her bare shoulders, pulled at her blouse. They grabbed her breasts, grabbed her ass as wild-eyed men leered with laughing, drunken faces.

∽

It was Oscar who found her.

"Melissa," he whispered in the cathedral.

"Oh, Oscar!" she cried, jumping up from a pew and throwing her arms around him. "Thank God!"

"Are you okay?" he asked.

"I'm fine," she said. "I mean, I'm scared, that's all. But how did you know I was here?"

"You weren't in the bars." He smiled. She was in no mood for jokes. They walked toward the great doors, part open, with sunlight slanting in. "Why did you come here?" Oscar asked her.

"You said it was safe," she said. "Why did you look here?"

"I'm not sure."

"Oscar, listen." Melissa took his arm once they were outside. "I've been lying to you. All the stories about other men? It isn't true."

"How could it not be true?" he asked.

"Because it's not."

"So all those stories . . ."

"Made up."

"The orgy?"

"Made up."

"Two men?"

"Made up."

"The girl at school?"

"Well . . . That one's kind of true. I'll tell you later."

"Then tell me: why did you say those things?" Oscar asked.

"I wanted you to think I was bad. So you wouldn't . . ."

"Wouldn't what?"

She burst into tears. "So you wouldn't love me!"

Some of the force, the violence of Carnaval had ebbed, moved on. Oscar looked at this girl, this most unusual girl. Tears stained her miserable face. Mazatlán rushed by, the streets, the clutter, the noise. Sunny Mazatlán. "What," he asked her, "is wrong with love?"

"Only someone who's never been hurt would ask that." She wiped her eyes. "Why are you looking at me like that?"

Oscar laughed. "I'm getting used to being with a good girl."

"I suppose I could be a little bad. For you."

"Bad is good," he said. "Sometimes." They kissed, and he held her close.

Open House
CASA PARA LA VENTA

❦❧

James W. Lewis

Man, this will be fun, I thought. I can't wait!

"Welcome to Rancho Hills," the pretty redheaded sales rep said, interrupting my private conversation. "Have you two been here before?"

"No," I replied, staring at dozens of toy house models under a large glass table. Red "Sold Out" magnets covered at least ninety percent of the mini-homes, which was typical for a new housing development in Northern California.

"What's the square footage of your largest house?" my wife, Sonya, asked.

"Plan three is a 3,680-square-foot, four bedroom, our largest model." The rep pointed to a corner table. An older woman stood next to the table with a wide customer service smile. "We have brochures with the info you need."

The older woman handed us two brochures. "Thank you," I said. I tapped Sonya's elbow, turned, and then pushed the glass door that led to the three models.

The older woman held the door for us. "Just a reminder, we'll be closing in fifteen minutes."

"Okay," Sonya said, slipping her hand into mine. "We'll be back soon."

My wife pulled me away. Outside, we double-timed past the first two models. The hem of Sonya's white summer dress bounced against her ample backside, her dark-brown legs as smooth as buttermilk.

"Slow down, babe," I said, laughing. "What about the other models?"

She didn't turn. "Don't have much time. Gotta hurry. *Anda más rapido.*"

I smiled. "I'm walking fast, babe!"

My wife . . . boy . . . damn! I loved when Sonya would flip between English and Spanish. Her tossed Spanglish vocabulary always boiled my horny blood cells, even after years of an up-and-down marriage. Because of her, I *"hablo español"* with the best of 'em.

Of course, being Dominican burned something within me, too. Ever since I saw Rita Moreno on *The Electric Company* back in the day, I always had a lit flame for Latinas. No wonder I married one.

While run-walking, I stared at the Spanish Colonial–style mansion with multicolored concrete tiles for a roof. It definitely had a trendy, *MTV Cribs* look. Very nice.

We stepped up the curvy entryway. I peeped at the sectional garage doors and thought how perfect it would be to have separate spots for our rides.

"Nice, huh?" Sonya said, now standing near the entrance. The raised panel door stood at least ten feet high.

"Yup. Can't wait to see the inside."

She pushed at the door. To my surprise, classic jazz welcomed us. We stepped inside and admired the marble tile. Central air-conditioning cooled us from ninety-degree summer heat.

My wife's eyes grew wide as plates. *"Que bellezal!"* She grabbed my hand. "Come on, babe, upstairs. *Vámonos!"*

I didn't say a word; I just did what she told me.

She skipped up the hardwood steps, giggling like a kid on her way to Magic Mountain, with me close behind her. I gazed at the crystal chandelier hanging from the mile-high ceiling, bobbed my head to the jazzy percussion and drum bass that reverberated through the house.

We reached the top of the stairs. With my wrist still locked under her tight grip, Sonya guided me toward the loft. She didn't peep into the bedrooms, bathrooms or family room; she already knew her destination.

In the loft area stood a large pine bookcase, a La-Z-Boy recliner and two ottomans—the perfect chill spot. Sonya placed the brochures on the La-Z-Boy, stepped between the ottomans and placed her hands on the steel rail that overlooked the living room.

"All right," she said, looking at her watch. *"Solamente tenemos trece minutos."*

Thirteen minutes, huh? I thought. I didn't waste time. Once I flipped up my wife's dress, slid my hands under her panties and rubbed her cocoa-skinned *culo,* we commenced the real reason why we came to the house.

I pulled her panties down her legs and onto the floor. Her flesh warmed my hand—as if anticipation singed her flesh. I unzipped my shorts. Down to my ankles they went.

"Damn," I said, tingles tickling my face. "We didn't check for anybody in here."

"No time," Sonya replied. No fear, no hesitation in her voice. I loved her on-the-edge-of-danger nerve. "We'll take our chances."

The loft became the perfect lookout spot. I could see most of the living room and outside through a large window next to the front door. I surveyed our vicinity one last time before I lowered my hips and positioned myself for rear entry. Heart thumps jabbed me from within.

"Hurry up, baby," Sonya whispered, pushing her butt against my steel-hard *pinga*.

I grinned. "Here I come."

The surround sound of jazz added a seductive melody to our risky business, setting the stage for a perfect "slow dance." Nine inches slapped Sonya's firm butt cheeks; then I maneuvered, and slid my cock inside her. The walls of her pussy . . . shit . . . so wet! Ain't nothin' like it in the world.

With me swallowed up, her warmth dented my watchdog composure. It made my body relax, eyelids slump and mouth drop into a crooked grin. I wasn't inside a $400,000 house anymore; I was inside my wife—the only place I wanted to be.

We grooved against each other, releasing sweet purrs like the sounds of the jazz player's trumpet. I buried my forehead in the nape of her neck, her thick wavy hair rubbing against my nose and lips. Moving strands of hair, I lapped my tongue along the lines between her shoulders, tasting trickles of sweat.

"Maldito!" she cried. "You feel so good! I can't believe we're doing this again."

My eyelids shot open. Sonya forced me to remember our illegal sexcapade.

I twitched when I saw the chandelier, but maintained my slow, steady strokes against dark-brown cheeks reminiscent of

Jennifer Lopez's onion. I could tell Sonya's eyes were still closed, obviously relying on me as lookout.

I checked the window next to the front door. Didn't see anyone outside and couldn't hear anything but my wife and jazz music. I knew that could change any second.

My heart kicked into fourth gear. I started pumping faster. Sonya's moans grew louder, my grunts deeper. She spread her legs into a wide upside-down V and nudged her butt further against my steady grind. She felt so damn good! Fuck! My panicky thrill had collided with the explosive sensation of my cock skinny-dipping inside her—spreading my haywire hormones into an internal wildfire.

The smooth groove of trumpets resonated around us. Nice melody. I think the jazz player was Norman Brown, but who cared, anyway? Shit, I didn't. Sonya and I made our own music.

Sweat rained down my forehead into my eyes. I gritted my teeth, then dug my nails into Sonya's wet ass cheeks. She snapped her head back against my shoulder, expelling a sharp cry. I snaked my hand under her shirt, cupped her *tetas,* and then caressed her nipples. While circling deep inside her, I slowed my pace—then pounded her pussy with hard strokes. Her cries pierced the soft whine of a sax solo.

Tingles raked through my back, my legs—even my toes. I yanked my arm from under her dress, then wrapped my fingers around the rail next to her hands, my hard flesh so deep inside.

Fuck!

Again, I forgot where I was. Or, maybe I didn't care where I was. I began reaching my peak. A primal urge mushroomed in me, but I restrained myself from yanking Sonya's hair and piledriving into her. Our cries could've cracked windows.

Then I heard voices outside.

I thought my heart would implode.

We froze—then gasped.

I looked toward the window. Before I said a word, my wife whispered, "*Coño!* It's the sales reps!"

I swear the thunder rumbling inside me could've severed my rib cage. Both reps were walking toward the house but had stopped in front of the window to review a stack of papers the older woman held. All they had to do was turn to the glass, look up—and catch the last stages of our public porno.

Heat rushed across my face. I swallowed—but commenced the backstroke. We could see them—but they hadn't seen us . . . yet.

Sonya pushed back into me. "We'd better hurr . . . *ay, mierda*"—her body jerked, then their knees banged each other—"I'm 'bout to . . . to come!"

She pounded her ass against me . . . gasping . . . cursing . . . moaning. I turned to the window. Shit! The reps started walking toward the door! Lost sight of them—but didn't stop. Sonya's mini-explosions had seized control of her body. I cupped a hand over her mouth to muffle her cries as spasms ripped through her. Her teeth nicked my finger. I endured the pain.

Uh-oh. *"Ay, mierda"* for me, too.

My stomach tightened, arms twitched, eyes shut. My head dropped between her shoulder blades, teeth clamping strands of Sonya's hair. Heart booming . . . hips slipping and sliding . . . our faces pouring sweat. So fuckin' intense.

My legs went limp. I lost balance momentarily, pushing my knees against the back of Sonya's legs. The voices outside grew louder; I thought I heard footsteps. Couldn't stop, though.

Almost there. I gripped Sonya's waist—then came with the force of a volcano.

A long-winded percussion of horns serenaded our coital finale. Voices were just outside; I could almost understand their words. For a second, I didn't give a shit. Sonya and I were riding earthquake tremors—but a tap on the door shook us. I opened my eyes, swiping away strands of Sonya's hair that had stuck to my wet forehead.

The front door opened, but still shielded them from us. Frantic, Sonya shoved me backward, slamming me against the bookcase. She stumbled, regained balance, and then bent to pick up her panties. My cock dripped semen on the bottom of Sonya's dress and thigh as I struggled to pull my shorts up.

I saw the redheaded sales rep emerge from behind the door, so I ducked, smacking my face against Sonya's left ass cheek. She slapped my arm, giggling.

"Hello?" one of the women said. I think she heard the ruckus. "It's five minutes to six. We're about to close."

We bent down low and back far enough where the reps couldn't see us—but I heard footsteps at the bottom of the stairs. Sonya crawled onto her back while yanking up her panties. So much exhilaration in her pretty brown eyes. I stood, finally yanked up my underwear and shorts, and then pulled Sonya to her feet . . . just in time.

I heard the rep at the top of the stairs. "Excuse me," she said. "We have to close up."

"Oh . . . uh . . . okay," I said, zipping up my shorts, my back turned to her. Breathe, breathe! "Give us a se-second. My wife . . . uh . . . tripped on the ottoman."

I didn't turn around. Sonya stood in front of me, trying to

tidy up as much as she could. She finger-combed strands of out-of-whack hair that had covered her eyes, stuck to her forehead, and the sides of her face. Damn, we couldn't stop giggling. Just like teenagers.

I hadn't realized how much I missed Sonya's hearty chuckles. Hadn't seen so many smiles in a while. Her face exuded such a glow.

The redhead walked up to us. "Is everything okay?"

I grabbed Sonya's hand and scrambled past the redhead. "Yeah. We're fine."

Sonya banged her knee against an ottoman, then stumbled into the La-Z-Boy. I caught her before her face collided with the cushion. She exploded in laughter.

When we reached the stairs, I turned, saw the sales rep lift her head, and noticed the puzzled look. I guess she was trying to figure out those sticky wet spots on the carpet. Before she could say a word, we jetted down the stairs.

The other rep was walking out of the living room when she saw us. "Hello," she said, "how did you like this model?"

I pulled the door. "Love it! We marked our territory here. Can't wait to come back!"

A gazillion wrinkles furrowed the woman's head, but she still maintained that customer service smile. Sonya covered her mouth to keep from exploding.

"That's . . . um . . . nice," the woman said. "Hope to see you again soon."

"Okay," Sonya replied. She grabbed my arm and gave me the evil eye. "C'mon, you knucklehead."

We darted to freedom, the hot sun almost sitting on us. Summer heat outside couldn't compare to the inferno we'd created inside, though.

Sonya hotfooted a few feet in front of me. I looked down and noted a wet spot glistening on her calf. I didn't say anything about it, just smiled. A little memento for my eyes only.

We got in the car—then got the hell out.

I leaned the car seat back, my fingers tapping the steering wheel. We sat quietly, paging through our thoughts, small grins strapped to our faces. Shoot, the only thing missing were cigarettes.

Never thought we'd be in this position. Married seven and a half years and almost succumbed to the so-called Seven-Year Itch. Kisses had pretty much died out; hugs were every so often. The passion in our marriage had slipped away somehow.

Man, how our secret getaways changed all that. A renewed sense of adventure had resuscitated our dying attraction; made two thirty-six-year-olds act half their ages.

Our new magnetism had driven us to Rancho Hills—and dozens of other outdoor spots. That's one more check mark on our long list of "pubic" places to conquer.

It's a wonderful thing to rekindle a flame and keep it blazing.

Sonya grabbed a newspaper from the backseat. She flipped through several pages before she said, "Hey, that movie is still in theaters. The one with the really bad reviews."

I grinned. "Yeah? What times?"

"The last showing is ten-fifteen tonight."

A minute or two passed. I turned to Sonya, saw the corners of her red-glazed lips creep up.

"So," I said, "I hear that movie is really, really bad."

She chuckled. "Yup. Only made a couple mil its first weekend."

Sonya stroked my knee. She had a naughty glint in her eyes; the same look she'd given me minutes before ending up at Rancho Hills.

"So that means the movie's so bad there won't be anyone in the theater, right?"

She nodded. "That's right." Her hand crept up my thigh. Yup, that look got more evil by the second. "So," she said. *"Quieres ir al cine esta noche?"* Movie tonight, huh? I smiled. We damn sure won't be watching a thing.

Just Damn Good Sex!
SÓLO SEXO CRUDO

Naleighna Kai

*W*ell, if you won't talk to me or let me make love to you . . . then just stick your honey pot out the front door so I can taste you. At least feed me something, damn it!"

Niyah's jaw dropped. Her fingers went limp, sending the fine bone china plate tumbling toward the marble floor, where it shattered and flew in a thousand directions. Dinner landed everywhere. She closed her eyes, trying to block out the fact that her neighbors had just heard Mario's outburst.

Instead of being embarrassed, she said, "Awww, no he didn't say that!"

She'd never heard him get angry or raise his voice, but now Mario had just told the world he knew her more intimately than some men knew their women—and he wasn't ashamed!

For a woman who was used to giving up pussy out of both panty legs, his words were more than a challenge—they were a return to the natural order of things.

Her body started melting at the thought of what that man could do with his tongue, then it trembled at the memory of their steamy nights together. Since she had picked religion over sex, she was surprised by the loneliness of her empty bed. Now, after three months of holding it together, keeping her legs closed, and staying knee-deep in church, Niyah wanted to give in—she wanted to fill that emptiness and her bed again.

Contrary to popular belief, Satan didn't have a pitchfork, tail, horns, and a red suit. He came under the guise of a surprisingly tall, lean, muscled, well-groomed, curly-haired Puerto Rican with enough fire and passion to start a five-alarm fire.

Mario's expert tongue belonged in the Porno Hall of Fame. His matching dick techniques would put Doc Johnson products to shame. And since the good "doctor" had been memorialized in some of the world's most well used dildos and vibrators on the planet—that was truly saying something. Mario's massive hands could drape across her skin with whisper-soft touches or grip her in the waves of a thundering orgasm and keep her in place until he was done giving as good as he got. He navigated the soft recesses of her dark brown skin and the even softer folds of flesh with unmatched expertise. Cherished the full-curve measurements that pushed her into plus-size status, separating her from the slender sisters. And he enjoyed every inch, exploring her each time as though it were the first.

And she had given him up! What planet did she live on? If giving in right now meant going to hell, Niyah was ready to take a ringside seat by the fire. Mario was that good!

Her wavering resolve, coupled with the fear that Mario might say something else that would put it all out there for her neighbors, should have stirred her to action. Instead, she stood motionless in the center of the living room floor, her bare feet covered with the macaroni and cheese, glazed turkey ham, and string beans she'd reheated for a late-night dinner.

Struggling between desire, common sense, and logic, Niyah broke down. She wanted to be with him so badly it tore her apart. But she had changed from the woman with a For Sale sign on one thigh and an Open for Business sign on the other, to a Bible-wielding, four-days-a-week churchgoing sister. She wanted to stay on the righteous path. Why is this so hard? Why do I miss him so much? Why do I feel so lonely even though I'm doing the right thing?

The phone rang, interrupting her thoughts and giving her a slight reprieve from the confusion and pain. When she grabbed the receiver, her next-door neighbor's voice came through loud and clear.

"Girl, you're passing up a lickin'? I know you're losing your damn mind!" Shari snapped in her famous Southern drawl. "Church or no church, girl, if it'll soothe your damn conscience, don't look at it as oral sex, just consider it baptism—by tongue. Give that boy some ass, so we can all get some sleep around here!"

Niyah could imagine Shari's golden skin flushed with color with every uttered word. She wasn't the only one losing shut-eye.

Niyah had been sleeping with Mario, the mailroom manager, for nearly two years—with an occasional movie and dinner thrown in for good measure. Then misery began three months ago with six simple words: "Mario, I can't see you anymore."

His expression crumbled, causing her heart to restrict, then pound wildly. A sudden stab of pain flashed through the muscle in the center of her chest that signaled the ultimate sign of life. Deep in her heart she knew she didn't mean a single word.

Everything else in Niyah's life was going haywire. Her finances had taken a serious nosedive. Family members were driving her crazy, pulling her into the middle of one dispute or another to mediate madness and bullshit. When her downtown

Chicago law office started laying off people left and right, she almost went into a panic. Her life was a stalemate at best, inching
slowly backward. Time for a change. She distanced herself from
her family's bickering and greed and decided she needed religion to get her life in order. The first step was going back to
church, the second was cutting out the greatest temptation in
her life—Mario Barajas.

∞

She had decided, after a string of bad relationships, that being
alone was safe, that masturbation was safe. These days, a man and
his dick had to be worth dying for. And she hadn't found many
she trusted—until the gorgeous, curly-haired man had set a
brother straight one day after an argument in the office cafeteria.

The argument was about an age-old subject—the preference
of men, skinny women versus plus-size. Mario, in a strong, certain tone, made heads turn in his direction when he defended his
love of fleshy, voluptuous women: "Say what you want about
what I like, but I can tell you this: they don't smell, they don't
swell, they don't tell, they're grateful as hell, and they make love
real well."

Sisters, Latinas, and white women alike stood and applauded.
Niyah was among them. She noticed Mario a lot more after that.
And he found it a lot easier to pursue her. She didn't resist.
Curiosity wouldn't allow her to take a backseat to her needs—
which by that time were plentiful. Masturbation could fill the
void, but the real thing could put a vibrator or dildo on the un-
employment line in a Chicago second.

She felt warmed when his dark brown eyes drank her in the
moment she walked past the mailroom. Her mocha skin, fleshy
and generous hips, and full breasts, which lifted teasingly from

her bra in such a way that the average man screamed "Milk!" when she walked past, combined in such a way that even a few of the slimmer sisters eyed her with envy. The proud chin, full, sensual lips, arched eyebrows, and high cheekbones were classic.

But what stirred the attention of men was her walk—especially if she ventured out wearing three-and-a-half-inch heels—allowing her hips to sway sexily and her smooth gait to range somewhere between businesswoman and high-class hooker. Sometimes she could almost "hear" the question as she walked past: does she or doesn't she make love as well as her hips promise with each sway? Yes, she damn well did.

Fortunately, Mario was not one to boast of his conquests—so speculation still ran high. And she'd like to keep it that way.

Their law firm was extremely conservative. She wouldn't lose her job over an office romance, but she could gain the disapproval of people who signed her paycheck—and that would be most unfortunate.

Younger than her thirty-four years, Mario could make love like no one she'd ever known. But for Niyah, his talents stopped there, even if he truly loved her. She was hell-bent on a man with a six-figure salary. A mailroom manager just wouldn't do.

As he stood in the center of her bedroom that day when she told him it was over, she watched him fight for control. Finally, his handsomely chiseled face, reflecting only calm, looked up at her as he asked in his lightly accented English, "*Mi vida,* why end this?"

He had called her his life. God, how could she end this?

"I'm not going to have sex again until I get married."

Mario didn't blink. "Then marry me. What's the big deal?"

Shocked that he would be so easy about things, Niyah searched his face for signs of humor.

"I didn't say that to get you to propose to me. I want to find a man in church, turn my life around." She blamed her currently bleak situation on being with the wrong man—in the wrong way—and not setting foot in church for years. But how could she explain that to him?

He had been her first venture into interracial relations—a sister's way of saying she's crossing from "brothers" to "others." She had weathered the brothers' storm as they glowered at her if she happened to be hanging on Mario's arm. Inside, she felt a little self-conscious, but that went away when she realized that the brothers who were angry weren't the ones stepping up to move Mario out and take his place. A dick in the hand was worth the promise of dick to come—so she could tough it out. And Mario had been worth it—then.

After she broke it off, Mario refused to stop seeing her even though she returned his letters and wouldn't take his calls. For ten minutes every night for more than three months he stood just below her bedroom window calling to her in his accented English that she had come to love.

"I just want to be with you. I want to marry you. Just let me in. Talk to me, Niyah. We can work through this."

Some nights he said he missed her, needed her, and loved her. Mario sounded so sincere, but Niyah knew getting back on the righteous path required some sacrifices. Sex with him was one—but oh, what a sacrifice!

The neighbors started commenting on Mario's nightly chants. They were the talk of the block, with men hoping Mario would take the hint to move on because he was giving them a bad name, and with the women cheering for him, praying he'd get positive results because it was romantic.

Much to Niyah's chagrin, people actually began placing bets.

The stakes got higher every night when Mario walked away with no results.

One night, Shari finally banged on the door.

"All right, spill it, girl. What the hell has he done that you're leaving that fine specimen of Latino out in the cold like that?"

"He hasn't done anything," Niyah said, stepping aside to allow the petite woman into her fashionably furnished townhouse.

"He didn't hit you?"

"No."

"Try and steal the pussy?"

Niyah laughed. "He was really good to me, but church is the main part of my life now."

Shari paused in the middle of taking a seat and stared at Niyah. "And what's that got to do with getting some dick?"

"Fornication is out of the question."

"Honey, what part of the Bible are you reading?" Shari snapped. "Half the sex in that book is good, old-fashioned fornication, with a man 'knowing' a woman to seal the deal. You better recognize it and quit holding that pussy so tight that fresh air can't get in, and a good orgasm can't get out." Then she punched a single finger into Niyah's chest. "Quit playing around, woman. Let him tap that ass. God didn't make pussy and dick to just look at them—we're supposed to use the damn thangs!"

Point taken. "But I want a man that's making at least a six-figure salary."

Shari leaned back on the sofa. "Do you travel in six-figure circles?"

"Well . . ."

"Just what I thought," Shari said with a grimace. "You'd do better making your own money."

"And he's . . . he's not a brother."

Shari's hazel eyes narrowed. "Don't make me slap you. The kitty cat doesn't check for passports as the dick goes in. It might check for diseases, condoms, length, thickness, and curves, but not color and native country," she said without cracking a smile. "And I still don't understand what that's got to do with you getting some nookie."

Niyah thought about that for a moment. "My family would trip if they knew I was sleeping with a Latino."

"But your family's not the one with an empty bed."

Damn, the woman did have a point.

Shari leaned forward, resting her elbows on her knees. "Get laid, go to church, repent, come on home, and start all over. That's how it works for everybody else."

Niyah held in a laugh as she plopped down on the sofa across from her friend. "But that's not right."

"Girl, you'd better check around. Read that book Mario gave you. You might learn somethin'."

Memory kicked in as Niyah gasped. "*A Dictionary of Sex in the Bible*? Can you believe he'd leave something like that on the doorstep? Suppose my mother had come over and found that?"

"Then she could've learned something, too. I read it, and personally, David was a man after my own heart. Screwed everything with a striped robe and a smile and still managed to be the apple of God's eye. Whattaman!"

"Yeah, but it cost him the life of one of his children."

"That was because he killed a husband to get to the pussy," she shot back. "It had nothin' to do with sleeping with that woman. Read the story, girl. Ease your mind and go get that man before he wises up and moves on, leaving your pussy to grow dust bunnies and a layer of cobwebs."

Niyah burst out laughing.

"Then somebody'll need a road map and a toolkit to find it." Shari glared at her. "He loves you, and you're making things harder than they should be. All for the sake of a book that has changed hands and interpretations too many times to count. Before all those others came into the picture, the first commandment was actually Be fruitful and multiply." Her friend patted her breasts proudly. "I'm doing my part."

Others, with even less of an argument, tried to convince her to give in, but Niyah held fast. The men on the block thought a woman couldn't go without sex for more than two months. The women knew better. New arguments and a different betting pool began. Niyah stopped going to block club meetings, especially since the meetings began to be about her and Mario.

All the while, Mario kept trying to whittle down her defenses. When his words didn't work, he serenaded her. That would have been beautiful—if the boy could sing. Everything from "I Want You Back" to "Who's Loving You," sounded pitiful, just pitiful. His singing made her smile, but also a little sad.

Niyah was surprised at how much she missed him. It was just sex, right? Mind-numbing, toe-curling, speaking-in-tongues, out-of-this-world sex. Just damn good sex. Only that.

At first Niyah had been afraid to go to work, thinking there would be problems. But Mario looked at her only if she happened to be nearby, and never made a scene. She looked at him, wanting him, longing for him. Mario respected her space. He knew personal confrontation had no spot in the workplace. He brought it to her doorstep. Or more precisely, outside her bedroom window.

Mario's voice was the last thing she heard before falling into restless sleep, and the first thing she remembered when waking in the morning. Not to mention the single white rose, which he laid on her doorstep each night and which greeted her every day as she left for work. Romantic, nonthreatening, and persistent. Then he had dropped off a book that really brought things home—*And Adam Knew Eve: A Dictionary of Sex in the Bible,* which only reinforced Shari's point about sex and fulfillment. Mario made things so hard for her. Why couldn't he just leave her alone and accept her decision? But, then, did she really want that?

She kept going to church, and kept her legs closed and her mind on the Lord. The memories of the smooth, sensual, but comforting way Mario treated her made him a temptation and pure torture at the same time. He was the reason she did so much praying.

Then came the depressing realization: with the number of men that actually came to church, her attempt to find a mate within those walls would be slim to none, with even slimmer chances for that six-figured mate. Niyah accepted the fact that she would be alone for a while. Not a pleasant thought, but she had made a choice and planned to stick with it.

Until tonight.

Out of pure anger and frustration, Mario had yelled out, "Well, if you won't talk to me or let me make love to you . . . then just stick your honey pot out the front door so I can taste you. At least feed me something, damn it!"

Then Shari's words kicked in on her phone line: "If it'll soothe your damn conscience, don't look at it as oral sex, just consider it baptism—by tongue."

Niyah started to protest, but Shari didn't give her a chance. "Quit playing, girl, and give that man some lovin'! From what you've told me, he's been good to you. He's also been out there trying to win your ass back and you've been playing hard to get—and looking like damn-it-to-hell the entire time. Now get on with it. Give him some pussy and give us all a break! 'Cause if you don't, I'm gonna toss him some of mine so he doesn't go to waste."

Niyah didn't need any more encouragement. Hell, she'd been thinking some of the very same things! She didn't bother to clear the mess off the floor. Instead she hurried to freshen up and slipped into one of the nightgowns Mario loved. The black lace always made his eyes light up.

She scrambled down the stairs two at a time like a kid at Christmas, hoping she wasn't too late. He never stayed a minute longer than ten. She believed he timed his nightly visits to be there just before her normal bedtime. Anticipation welled up inside her unlike anything she could remember as she took a long, slow breath before opening the door.

Mario stood in his usual place next to the front porch looking up at her bedroom window. All six feet of his rugged, golden self looked so damn good. His sexy lips, keen features, small goatee, and dark curly hair made him look even more handsome. She felt the moisture pool between her thighs. I'll be damned, I'm actually gonna do the damn thing! Her heart did a flip as she found she could actually breathe again.

His dark brown eyes, always his most dangerous feature, looked tired and sad. He'd apparently experienced a few restless nights, too. Mario's jaw went slack, then snapped shut. His moist lips parted slightly, and his eyes widened as he turned and gazed at her standing in the entrance.

Scanning her face first, those intense dark brown eyes traveled over her body as though committing every inch to memory. He slowly licked his lips, then sprang into action, embracing her warmly before lifting her up, then placing her gently on the cool floor.

Smoothing the silky folds of her nightgown out of his way, his tongue trailed the soft length of her thighs to the dark nestle of curls that signaled the center of her universe. Every curve, every stretch of skin, every fold of flesh, tingled at the touch of his hands, first with a loss of sensation, then an awakening that filtered through her body like a slow trickling stream.

A sudden movement, and seconds later he buried his head into the quivering flesh—providing the much-anticipated return to normal pleasures, a return to sanity. Cupping her buttocks in his warm, massive hands, he snaked his tongue out, flicking across her pearl in quick, short bursts, then a slower steady rhythm.

An almost feral growl escaped her lips. Three months without sex of any kind—borrowed, bought, or stolen—was hell for any woman who was used to getting a side order of good nookie on a nightly basis.

Gripping his head, she thrust upward, moving herself across his tongue as he encircled the lips, shaking his head from side to side and leaving a trail of fire with every movement. She arched, lifting the rest of her body from the ground. His hand reached out, steadying her, holding her. The orgasm hit hard, building from the base of her womb, shooting down to her legs and numbing them, preparing them for the next burst of pleasure. The moisture trickled at first, then rushed out to greet his tongue with a hearty, Where the hell have you been?

Mario stayed down there so long she had to beg him to stop. Her pearl was singing and the kitty cat was hoarse!

After making her reach orgasm a couple of times, he lifted his head. "I want you." Warm hands stroked her buttocks, then a single finger branched out to touch her pearl. "I want this."

She opened to him, allowing his body to fill the space that rightfully belonged to him. A sudden shadow that appeared on her driveway reminded her that they were on the front porch. Thank God it was enclosed or the world would have received an education that night! Niyah was certain the neighbors would take bets on that.

"Let's take this inside."

Picking her up, he carried her toward the door. They didn't make it past the spot just inside the doorway, barely allowing the door to close.

The sound of material ripping echoed through the foyer. Seconds later, the hard length of him pressed at the center of her thighs, demanding entrance.

She opened to him, trembling with anticipation, as he thrust into her moist heat, her flesh gripping him like a long-lost friend. His hands splayed across her hips, guiding every move as he kept them joined, working in a slow, steady rhythm. The hands trailed along her flesh, holding her as though he had found pure gold, thrusting into her heat with long, measured strokes. Their lips joined in a frantic rush of pleasure as his tongue, laced with her nectar, explored the soft confines of her moist mouth. His lips were softer than she remembered. He tore them away, teased them down her neck to her chest, and lingered lovingly on her breasts, tasting them, teasing them as though her moans were his only source of life and nourishment.

His fingers gripped and held on to her for dear life as he took her to the edge of reason, then tipped her into a pleasure-filled oblivion.

Niyah thanked God, Yahweh, Jesus, Yashua, Allah, Buddha, Confucius—covering all the bases—for any and every number of reasons, and maybe even ventured as far as speaking in tongues for a few minutes. She damn near blacked out, but her body and mind held on—unwilling to miss a second of his touch, a second of his feel, a second of release only this particular dance could provide.

Her fingers laced in his dark, curly hair, then trailed down his back, resting on the base of his spine. A slow descent down the smooth curve of his tight ass only incited her more.

She moaned as her thighs lifted, wrapping around him tightly, shaking with every thrust, following as his rhythm increased. The tempo became driving, almost animalistic—branding—pure ownership. "This is mine, this is mine, mine—all mine," he whispered into her ear.

She couldn't agree more.

Several hours later as they lay wrapped in each other's arms, her back began protesting against the hardwood floor. As she stood to take the party to a softer place, every part of her body ached and felt good at the same time.

He stood and watched her walk up the stairs. She turned just in time to see him pick up his work clothes, holding them steadily in his hands, as he held her gaze for what seemed like forever. Neither spoke. She thought of what happened and for a split second she believed she'd used him, and felt a twinge of regret—but only for a second.

Finally, Mario realized she would remain silent, and he slowly lowered his jeans, with his briefs still tucked inside, and stuck one leg in.

He was never one to press her for more than she wanted to

give, and she realized that this time wouldn't be any different. She always admired that about him.

Telling herself that she had already messed up a three-month sexual fast, she might as well do it all the way. As she watched him get dressed to leave, she extended her hand.

"Mario, come upstairs with me."

She could repent tomorrow.

He halted, searching her eyes, wondering if she meant it.

She nodded.

He dropped the rest of his clothes and took the steps two at a time. As he embraced her again, she wrapped her arms around him, holding him as close as possible, savoring the scent of sex surrounding him. It felt so right. Absence didn't make the heart grow fonder, it made the dick get stronger and the sex last longer. No lie!

Mario kissed her passionately as he carried her to the bed. This time his lovemaking was so intense that letting herself flow with him took away her sense of reasoning. They made love until the orgasms caused a three-second blackout—pleasure overload. That had never happened before. Mario wasn't bullshitting this time, not one single bit.

After they burned every last ounce of energy, they slept. And for the first time in months the sleep was hard and dreamless, comforting and safe.

She couldn't walk the next morning, and to tell the truth, neither could he. They missed work that day. The next day they established a comforting routine of making love, then falling into more comalike sleep.

Niyah wanted enough memories that would last until . . . when?

On the second day of missing work, they finally came up for air. They showered together before she fixed a hearty breakfast. Mario always had a healthy appetite. That morning, since she was equally famished, she almost made a career out of cooking. Meanwhile, the man could barely keep his hands off her, wanting to hold her or kiss her every chance he got, and making her giggle like a little girl, showing her at every possible turn how much he had missed her.

Feeling lighter and refreshed, Niyah had to admit it—she had missed him, too. She didn't feel so—lost? Unsettled? Alone? He felt good to her. Just him holding her was right. And it wasn't just the sex—it was Mario being . . . there.

After their two-day makeup marathon, they ate, then talked and talked. Well, mostly he talked, having so much to say that all she could do was listen. And that, too, was unlike him. She had known him for his quiet strength and reliability. He told her everything that happened during the three months they were apart, but it was his last words that got her attention: "Baby, don't send me away again. Let's talk about making this work. Let's talk about what bothers you so much about me." He reached out, gently stroking her face, his finger trailing a fiery path. "I love you."

Mario never said anything he didn't mean. And she knew for certain that he meant those three words.

No words came to her mind to say she felt the same. He opened his mouth to speak, but she tried to interrupt, preparing to halt any further words of love. "Mario, I just don't think—"

"No, Niyah," he said sharply. "Listen to me for a change. I've had enough of how you've sidestepped the real issues here. We need to find some common ground. I need to get some things out in the open. This time you will not brush me off. You will listen."

Holding her hands, his tenor voice was strong, sure, and his manner kept her a willing prisoner. This was a first for her. She was normally the one to say what would and would not happen. Evidently things were about to change. She didn't know how she felt about that.

As he gazed into her eyes, he almost dared her to disagree. She felt a little flustered, and opened her mouth to say something, testing his strength. She didn't get a sound past her lips as he leaned forward, circling his tongue in the opening and silencing anything she had to say.

When he pulled away, Niyah was a little miffed, but she also secretly admired what he was doing. She'd always taken pride in her stubbornness, so she prepared to say something anyway. This time he leaned forward, kissing her even more passionately until she couldn't think straight, then he pulled away once more.

He watched her. Dared her.

She sighed, but remained silent, brewing a little, but respecting him and his wishes. He didn't rant and rave the way some people did when they wanted to get their message across. Mario used a calmer method to get her attention and make his point. The corners of his mouth drew up into a slight smile as he watched her frustration.

Taking several deep breaths, she remained silent, waiting.

His smile widened as he pulled her even closer. His deep, resonating voice penetrated her heart.

"Respect, Niyah. That's all I ask." He took a long, slow breath. "I didn't want to pressure you and I almost made a mistake. I'm not going to let it happen again."

Pulling away, he placed his finger under her chin, gently lifting it until her eyes met his. "I will not make that mistake again." His voice sent shivers up and down her spine.

She wanted to say something, but thought better of it. His kisses were dangerous and effective.

After a few moments, he pulled away, sprinting to his clothes. He searched through them until he found a small velvet box. He opened it, turned it around, and handed it to her.

A ring! Beautiful. God, it was beautiful!

"It's real," he said as she stared at it, mesmerized by it.

When she didn't reply, something in his expression crumbled. He dropped his shoulders and looked away.

"I'll get you something better if you don't . . . like this one."

All she could do was shake her head and stare at the size of that diamond. She knew it had taken a few of his paychecks to buy. She knew exactly how much he made. A few times, in between layoffs, his entire paycheck came her way. She never had to ask. He would just say, "Take what you need. It's a gift, not a loan."

She didn't love him, didn't want to play with him or his emotions. She'd done enough of that already. Every time she got on her feet again, she returned every penny, but he always found a way to get the money back into the house one way or another— paying her bills ahead of time, buying things for the house, or for her.

Mario was a good person, but the only thing they had in common was great sex. He wasn't as educated as she thought her man should be—he had only a high school diploma. She had never considered him permanent mate material. She had been comfortable with the way things were, and saw no reason to change—until her need for religion took over.

Glancing at him, she thought about his proposal. She thought about him: handsome, so very handsome, sweet, kind, loving, and passionate. She felt a sharp pain pierce her heart. She couldn't take his ring. He deserved her honesty.

"Mario, I care for you, but I can't say that it's more than that."

He crooked his mouth into something that wasn't quite a smile.

"I know that, baby," he said, stroking her face gently. "I know you try to keep it that way. You've never talked to me about your true feelings, or even tried to explore what we have. I still want to be with you. It'll be all right. You'll love me in your way. It's only a matter of time."

Amazed at his determination, she silently studied this gorgeous, generous man.

"Niyah, you're the only woman I've ever been with who treated me like I was worth something. I might not be the man you think you need, but for the last two years, I've been more than enough. You've shared some of your feelings, your good times and bad. You've shared yourself." He smiled warmly, stroking his hands across hers. "I might not have a lot, but I would have the world if I had you." Mario looked different as he poured his soul out to her, stating his case with confidence and strength.

Why didn't she see that before in him? How had she missed it?

"Even though you've held back sometimes, you've always thought about what I wanted, too." Mario kissed her gently on the lips. "I've been with other women. I know when a person tries to use me. You never did—even when I gave you everything I had. I know you even stopped mentioning when you needed help because you knew I wouldn't take back the money." He shrugged sadly. "It hurt me when you wouldn't come to me. You know I would give you anything. I've always considered you my woman, not just someone I sleep with."

She winced. Because she'd been trying so hard to keep her

heart safe, that's all she saw him as—a sex partner. The guilt washed over her. She wondered how often the man had looked at her, read her, understood her.

Mario glanced at her, taking in her grim expression, and lowered his gaze.

"Maybe you saw things differently, Niyah, but all I know is that you've shown me in many ways that you really care. And you give yourself to me in a way that's pure . . . *cielo.*" Heaven! She looked away, but he softly turned her face toward him until she was looking deep into his dark brown eyes. "Helping you is the least I want to do for you. That's what a man does for the woman he loves."

Shocked and moved by his admission, she found it hard to breathe.

Mario placed his warm hand over the delicate curve of her fingers. "I want to show you something." Pulling a slip of paper out of his pants pocket, he presented her with the receipt for the ring. Scanning the description, she noticed he had used Wite-Out on the price. She smiled. Mario wasn't trying to impress her. That's how he was. Simple, giving, and honest. He wanted her to see the date of the purchase—two years ago. He had been holding on to the ring for a long time—long before she decided to stop seeing him!

Speechless, overwhelmed with emotion, tears welled up in her eyes and overflowed down her cheeks in spite of her best efforts to keep them at bay. She wanted to pull away, but his embrace kept her in place. He brushed his lips gently across her cheeks, licking away the tears one by one, and reaching deep into her soul.

Slowly lowering to one knee, he kept her hands in his.

"Niyah, will you marry me? I understand how you feel. For

a while I'll just have to have enough love for the both of us. Anything you want is yours. I need you and I would be wrong if I didn't fight for this, because I know deep down you need me, too."

Her heart raced and hurt all at the same time. Her emotions wouldn't allow her to speak or even whisper a single word.

Mario's eyes were intent in their constant contact. "I never asked you before. I was afraid of what your answer would be." His gaze lowered slowly. "If you said you wouldn't marry me, it would prove you weren't looking at me as a man—you only saw me for how good the sex was." He shrugged. "I wasn't ready to hear that. I wanted you to see that I could be so much more to you. At times I thought you did."

He stood slowly, linking their hands. "Sometimes when I'm at work and I'm around all those other men—men who are supposed to be smarter, or who are older—I see and hear their unhappiness. They talk about how their wives and girlfriends don't seem to love and respect them. But you've never been like that. You treat me with love and respect in the way you do things and how you talk to me. That's all I ask."

His piercing, dark brown eyes reached into her soul. "Before you stopped seeing me, you'd treat me like a husband: loving me, listening to me, caring for me, cooking dinner for me every night, making sure I had everything I needed for work."

His beautiful smile tugged at her heart.

"You didn't have to do that. But I needed it. I needed you." He kissed the back of her hand, sending shivers of pleasure through her body. "It's so hard to find a woman with the right combination of everything. I had to do this, Niyah. I had to make things right for us. You have always been . . . *mi vida*—my life."

He wrapped his arms around her as she laid her head against the beat of his heart. His deep, resonating voice penetrated her soul.

"Baby, my apartment has been the loneliest place since you've sent me away. That's why I'm here every night, standing outside, not trying to hurt you, not trying to stalk you. I'm only trying to make my way in. This is where my heart is. You're holding it hostage. You always have, but you've been too stubborn to see it." He began stroking her back.

"If you had another man, I could understand and I'd let this go. But just being in church isn't a reason to push me away. Marry me and do whatever it takes to make you feel good in church. But don't let this go—even God wants us to be happy." He entwined his warm, strong fingers with hers. "Doesn't it say somewhere in the Bible that we're supposed to make a joyful noise and serve God with gladness and thanksgiving?"

She simply nodded.

"Well, you've been in church for the past three months and at night it doesn't sound like you're making a joyful noise. It sounds like you're crying because you're lonely and have an empty space right here," he said, placing his hand gently over her heart. "Marry me and make me happy and I'll make you happy. You can have two men in your life—God and me." He smiled slyly. "I'm sure He won't mind sharing just a part of you with me. That's what He intended."

She smiled as she thought about what Mario said. And how the simple things she did meant so much to him. She did them naturally because of his kindness and because he appreciated everything. When she placed a meal in front of him, he savored every bite, even the new dishes she tried strictly to please him. He enjoyed them mostly because she took the time to do it for him. The thought made her tremble as reality struck. She'd had to jump through hoops for other men—flaming hoops at that—and the relationships still never seemed to make her happy.

She realized that maybe the fact that she felt settled and more peaceful when Mario was with her said it might be something more. The everyday relationship was far from the fireworks she had experienced with other men, but those fireworks had made her do some foolish things, and she'd ended up unhappy anyway.

Sometimes a woman had to go for sparkle instead of fireworks; sparkle could stay consistent, fireworks died out. As Mario held her, she felt warm, loved, and complete. That sparkle was fast turning into pure dynamite!

She reached up to touch his face, fingers trembling as she tried to hide her emotions. "I'm scared, Mario. Really, really scared. This is so different than what I want. So different than what I . . . expected. I'm afraid and I don't know how to stop being afraid."

"You think that I'm not afraid, too? I see the looks that couples like us get on the street—brothers ready to tear me a new asshole because I'm with you. My people believe this is all about sex and that I couldn't want more from you than that."

He kissed her then.

She pulled away. "My family won't agree with this and they—"

A single finger silenced her. "Your family's not here right now. They don't get a vote. Mine don't get a vote. You do. We do. We say what's right for us. 'Cause at the end of the day, when the door is closed and the outside world isn't looking in—there's only us."

She took a minute to absorb that, then said, "But what if I

want a man that's already successful, not a man that's just making it? My father and mother struggled all their lives."

"Why does it have to be one person making that money? Why can't it be something we build together? A business maybe?" He sighed, letting out a long, slow breath. "Six figures isn't hard to make with a good plan. Keeping it is another story. It takes strength. It takes determination. It takes teamwork. I think we'd be a good team. Don't you?"

She searched his eyes for a moment, as the real reason she had held back for so long came to the forefront. "Mario, I don't know how to say this . . ."

"Just say it, baby. We're laying it all on the line now."

Niyah swallowed hard. "I probably won't ever love you as much as you love me."

He winced just a little, enough to know that she had hurt him again, then his sexy lips lifted in a small, bitter smile. "Has that ever really been the problem?" He kissed her fingertips. "Open your heart, Niyah, stop trying to find excuses. If it wasn't me, it would be some other man you'd push away for the very same reason— or one like it." Mario pulled her into him. "I won't hurt you, *mi vida.* Hurting you would only be hurting myself."

At those words, she began to cry. Tears that she never knew she'd held inside. Tears for him. Tears for all she'd missed out on. He leaned in, kissing away the salty wetness flowing down her cheeks, then held her until her sobs had passed.

"I'm not unreasonable about things, you know," he said after a moment. "We can always talk and work things out. Communication. My parents talk all the time." Then he laughed. "More like argue and fuss at a hellified volume. Mama's no joke with a rolling pin."

Niyah laughed with him.

"But they've been together for fifty years." He took a moment to let that sink in. "Mom wasn't in love with Dad at first—but it happened. And no one could tell the difference—not then and not now."

With that, he curled her into his arms, carried her to bed and made love to her so tenderly the only thing she could do was cling to him, hold on to him—and admit one thing: It was better to have a man who loved her more than she loved him, than to be as lonely and miserable as she had been for the past three months. She opened to him slowly, allowing him to penetrate deeply, then he froze, pulling her to him, holding them connected—sensually, completely—as he whispered over and over, "*Mi vida,* my love, *te amo, te amo . . .*"

Within a few weeks they were married, with her neighbors looking on. The neighbors actually used the money collected from the women's "Mario should make it back in" and the men's "Niyah won't last another day without sex" funds to buy the newlyweds wonderful wedding gifts.

Mario was right. She fell in love with him a little more each day. She appreciated him and his unwavering love for her. He was a good friend, a good provider, and a damn good lover. What more could she ask for?

Mario was also a lot more intelligent than he gave himself credit for—than she gave him credit for. She was ashamed she didn't see that in the beginning. She'd been too busy trying to stay "safe." Now her heart was safe with him!

At the beginning of the year, he proposed an idea for a document services business that encompassed his managerial skills and what he had learned at the law firm. She helped him put the plan into action. That six-figure salary might be within reach after all.

Content with what they had, he loved her like no other, always treating her like a queen. She accepted him as her true soul mate and watched him become stronger and more confident in their relationship—the way she wanted him to be in the beginning. The way he always was, but was afraid to be with her. She became happier, softer, and more loving.

She also started going to another church, one that Mario had begun attending during her months of celibacy. His church wasn't about religion. It was more about positive affirmations, and being joyful, prayerful, and true to one's self.

Lord knows they still needed to be in church. As much as they made love, it had to be a sin.

Found in Translation
ENCUENTRO EN LA TRADUCCIÓN

Susan DiPlacido

I meet him on the beach outside the Melia Habana. It's magic hour, that luscious time of day between sunset and dusk. That twilight time that lingers, where a divine light glows with soft edges and misty rapture. Hazy clouds frame the background as he strides out of the forbidden azure ocean, water skimming off his muscled skin, dripping from the ringlets of his shaggy dark hair.

I know he's trouble right away.

He drops to his knees in front of me. With a perfect accent, he says, *"Señorita bonita, mi nombre es Javier Santiago y seré infeliz por siempre si usted no cena conmigo."*

This guy, Javier, that's what he says to me.

I sigh.

In English, that roughly translates to: "Pretty lady, my name is Javier Santiago, and I'll be unhappy forever unless you have dinner with me."

And in my American, thirty-year-old, single-girl jaded dialect, it translates to: "Nice tits. Wanna fuck?"

I didn't come to Cuba to get laid. I don't need to travel to a foreign country when I've got a perfectly good Hitachi Magic Wand in my bedroom at home that does the job more efficiently (and reliably) than any man can. I don't know why I came here. I guess maybe it was to experience something so ancient, once so idyllic. After all, it's in vogue these days to consider Cuba to be the final fragment of Atlantis, the once-majestic city built by the god of the sea to protect his mortal beloved.

Havana is a place that makes you realize that humans don't fuck up everything. The landscape alone is breathtaking, with the city rising beyond the deep sea, an enchanting marriage of civilization and natural beauty. Silky sand leading to the luxury of resort life. It was more than I expected.

And then, just as I thought I'd seen heaven on earth, out of the ocean comes this godlike-looking creature. This, this— Javier. He could be an angel.

But as he looks up at me, he reaches out, wet fingers circling my wrist, skimming and tickling the underside of my palm, sending an unmistakable spark up my spine. And the glint in his eyes tells me he's closer to a devil.

What the hell, I'll go to dinner with him. I'll do more than that with him.

It startles me when he meets me in the lobby and immediately puts his hand on the small of my back. Such a bold and familiar move for someone I've just met. I step away and put space between us. But he takes my hand as we walk and though it stiffens me, again that sinful spark keeps me from pulling back.

At the restaurant, instead of sitting across from me, he takes a seat next to mine, presumably so he can enjoy the view of the placid sea at night. Leaning back, he rests his arm on the back of my chair and twists his fingers through the locks of hair that hang down my back, across my shoulder. It's appalling at first, but as I sip on a mojito that warms my belly while the evening *brisa* kicks up, cooling the air, I reluctantly relax into it.

It's presumptuous of him, almost cocky, as though he's taking it as a given that I'm his for the evening. But I like the confidence, and besides, even though I didn't come here to get laid, his good looks and sultry demeanor are making me look forward to it.

Later, sitting on the terrace framed by palm trees, I stick a forkful of escabeche in my mouth, my toes curling with the tartness. Javier says, "Your face, it bewitches me." He's been pouring this impromptu poetry to me since we've been here, lacing it with compliments, presumably to weaken my defenses.

This guy, Javier, is he serious with all this?

Of course not. I decide to cut to the chase.

"Javier," I mumble with my full mouth. Chewing, swallowing down a gulp of wine, I say, "*Por favor.* Stop it already."

"You are angelic," he says.

"Okay." I wipe my mouth with the napkin and lean back from the plate of food. "Listen," I tell him. "You're very nice. But this isn't necessary, you don't have to sweet-talk me. With a few shots of rum, I'll sleep with you anyhow. I'd prefer it if we kept it honest like that."

He frowns and says, "*Americana.* I say these things not to have sex with you. I say them for they are true." But he motions with his hand and calls over the waiter. He orders rum for us.

"I knew it," I say, smirking.

He leans forward and looks me in the eyes, saying, "*Por supuesto que te deseo.*" Of course I want you.

"Then stop trying to make it more," I tell him. "It's not nice."

He looks shocked. Stricken. "*Mami chula,*" he says. "This was not my intent, to anger you by telling you how beautiful you are."

"I'm not angry," I say, feeling guilty for offending him. "It's just, it's leading when it's not true."

"Ahh." He nods. "*Entiendo.* It is not that I'm making more, *ángel mío.* It is you trying to make less. I should have expected. Come now." He flops his napkin on the table and stands. Looking down at me, he says, "We go now, and have the sex, then?"

"But," I stall, slinking in my seat, glancing around to see if anyone heard him. "The grappa hasn't come yet."

"So we can finish the meal?" he asks.

"Yes, we can finish our dinner, Javier."

"You are sure?"

The waiter arrives with our brandy but hesitates as Javier still hasn't taken his seat.

"Yes, I'm sure," I say and motion for him to sit.

This guy, Javier, I guess he is serious.

He pulls his chair closer so that his knee brushes against mine as he sits. He raises his glass and says a traditional toast and we both take a deep swig of the brandy. I close my eyes, letting the sweetness fill my mouth as the pungent scent hovers. Upon swallowing, a liquid heat courses down to my belly. He nudges my shoulder, leans close and whispers in my ear, "You are not without hope, yet, *Americana.*"

Tingles ripple across my skin as my face flushes, but my head doesn't swim from the effects just yet. Whether it's the effects of the booze or his sultry breath, I'm not sure. "Without hope for what?" I ask him.

"If you can enjoy your food the way you do, if you can enjoy the drink, then all is not lost. You are not in that much of a hurry."

"What the hell are you talking about?" is all I say.

He laughs and places his arm on the back of my chair, directs me to look out on the night waters of the dark ocean. "Why did you come here, Americana?"

"I, I . . ." I stutter like a fool. "I just wanted to see it, it's so exotic."

He puts his arm around my shoulders, his thumb lightly stroking my naked arm. It's still disconcerting, all this physical closeness. But I figure it's a difference in our cultures. Nearly everyone around here is snuggled close, though I assume they're longtime lovers.

He says, "You come here, looking for the exotic. And yet you'd deny me looking at what I find beautiful and exotic. *Americana,* you're all in such a hurry. You make it about the satisfaction, no the joy in the act itself. Even your women. Even you. Fast food, fast cars, fast phones. Everybody in a rush to finish everything."

"Yeah, well, we get a lot of stuff accomplished that way," I tell him.

"Ahh." He raises his brows. "But it is not all about the finish. We enjoy ourselves."

His stilted English in tandem with the stroking on my arm starts a subtle vibration in my lower tummy. Maybe it's not all about the finish to him, but suddenly I wish we'd at least get started. He purrs in my ear, now in Spanish, calling me *bonita* again.

I don't mind if he wants to call me beautiful, but I know he has other motives. I know that because I'm not beautiful. I know I'm not beautiful because other men never bother to tell me that I am. They just get down to business once it's been established that's where things are headed.

I put my hand on Javier's knee to let him know that I'm with him. He nods but refills our rum glasses, deliberately clinks his against mine, and drinks his slowly. In the soft glow of candle-light, his Adam's apple bobs as he swallows; the soft scruff of stub-ble can't conceal the that single, strong vein that runs down the side of his neck.

I lean into him, pressing my body against his side. He's firm and warm and he dips his head and meets my mouth with his lips. Soft, tinged with the liquor. He moves his hand off my shoulder, places it on my exposed thigh. As he kisses me gently, his fingertips trace patterns upward on my leg. Thrumming in-side, I kiss him more deeply as his hand snakes up. I uncross my legs to give him easier access.

Javier moves. Instead of kissing my mouth, he drops feather kisses on my cheek, his fingers rubbing the inside of my upper thigh. The *brisa* kicks up again, and I bite my lip to control a shudder as his breath tingles in my ear. Instinctively, I slide my hand up his leg, his muscles tensing beneath my touch. Not lin-gering, I take hold of him and he sighs in my ear again, a heavy breath, hot and moist.

The waiter comes to check on us. I freeze, but Javier doesn't. He nuzzles my ear again before turning to the waiter and an-swering in Spanish, "Bring us the dessert list," while his fingers dance dangerously higher, now brushing against the smooth fab-ric of my panties.

I blush and tuck my head down. It's dim, but I'm not sure the waiter is oblivious. He bows, but loiters to refill our glasses. As he does, Javier slides his fingers directly across the crotch of my un-derwear, firmly.

I reel. I don't know if it's from the sensation so much as shame. Shame that it does feel good, shame that I don't cross my legs or push him away. But he picks up my brandy glass and feeds me a sip, a rather large gulp. As I'm swallowing, he kisses my neck and works his hand smoothly up my stomach, then back down, this time beneath my panties.

I squirm and take hold of him again as the waiter retreats. He sets down the glass and moves my hand off of him. Saying, *"Suave, señorita. Suave."* Slow. Slow down? That's what this guy with his hand down my underwear in a public restaurant is telling me . . . slow down.

But before I can protest or take hold of him again, he slides his hand, his strong, sure fingers, back down. Inside my panties, parting my slit, two bold fingers slip down the length of me, then roughly, heavily back up, and again partway down, settling this time on my sweet spot, pressing against the nub of my rapidly sensitizing clit.

My breath catches, my shoulders tense, and my insides quicken. The rush from the grappa taking hold in my brain, warming my body as surely as he's tuning me up, turning me on.

I'm wet already, it's slick as he slides up and down, again coming to rest and pressing against my pleasure button. This time, shortening the length of his stroke, moving those two fingers only an inch. Sliding up, waiting, kissing my neck, and then gliding down, sucking on my earlobe. It's so nasty, so risky, I know I should pull away, or push him away, especially before the waiter comes back. But I'm pulsing and as I allow him to slide a few more times, I'm wired on it.

Shallow breath and rapid pulse, champagne blood rushes through my limbs, concentrating and knotting at the delicious tension he's creating between my legs, begging for satisfaction. The waiter comes back with the dessert tray. And oh sweet mercy help me, I still can't pull away. Even as the waiter looks me in the face. I meet his eyes, he's explaining the desserts, pointing to samples on the tray, and Javier keeps working his fingers rhythmically over my engorged clit. I tell myself the waiter can't possibly know what's going on as long as I keep it cool. Yes, Javier's nuzzling my neck, but the waiter can't see his hands under the table, beneath the tablecloth, especially in this flickering light. I can do this, I can hold it together.

But as the waiter starts reciting the menu, Javier picks up the pace, moving quick and firm, taking me higher, higher. God, this is awful, I'm close to getting off, I should stop this but I can't, it's within reach, it's just too good. I stay still, dropping my eyes to hide the telltale twitches. And when the waiter finishes his descriptions, just as I'm on the edge, Javier stops his movements. I can't stop myself, I just can't help it, my back arches and my pelvis pushes forward, seeking satisfaction, pressing myself, subtly grinding against his hand.

He moves his fingers away, pulling up slightly, rubbing small circles against the base of my stomach as he orders us a chocolate torte to share. It's horrible, even worse than the tantalizing indiscretion was, my nerves are screaming for release, my whole body in a knot and head swimming. The waiter takes his leave and instead of putting his hand back between my legs and finishing me off, Javier removes it completely. Languidly, he brings his fingers to his mouth and licks them with a satisfied smile, telling me I'm sweeter than any dessert.

Now I can't decide if I want to fuck him or claw his eyes out. I slowly come back down as he feeds me the cake, adding a sinfully delicious balance of sweetness to round out the spice and heat of the meal. And by the time we walk back to the hotel, I'm melting to him as he holds a strong arm around my waist, leading me up the marble staircase and through the dimly lit hallway.

Once inside, I nod to the bed, but he wanders out to the balcony and beckons me to join him. We have a panoramic view of the ocean, possibly concealing not-yet-forgotten treasures of a mythical civilization below. I slide into his arms and kiss him deeply, full tongue, arms around his neck. He responds, running his hands up and down my scantily clad back.

Releasing his neck, I reach down and unbuckle his belt, unzip his pants. I dive beneath his clothes and take hold of him, hot and hard already, caressing the silky hardness that I'm already burning for. Just moments after I start pumping him, he pulls my hands away and sets them around his neck again. His hands stroke my back, his kisses fall on my throat, my chest, he sucks deliberately on a nipple, sending silvery spikes of pleasure down my spine. I press against him, now shamelessly rubbing myself against his erection, the friction alone amping me up.

I can feel the tension building in him, palpable waves of lust coming from him. He brushes my hair aside; the breeze cools my neck as he warms it, massaging it with those strong, sure fingers. He runs a finger down my spine, his hands caressing the cheeks of my ass. I groan with desire, reach down and take hold of him and stroke demandingly on his erection. But he whispers in my ear, *"Por favor, Americana. Suare."*

And then he kisses me. Strong and deep, stopping to mumble, *"Señorita bonita,"* into my mouth, and then kissing me some more.

My knees go weak.

No one's been able to do that to me since I was a teenager. My Hitachi Magic Wand has never done it.

This guy, Javier, he's done it.

I bite my lip and finally understand.

We humans, we haven't fucked up everything just yet.

So I bend to his touch, letting the insistent buzz between my legs build while concentrating on his touches on my shoulder. His fingers curve, the slightest rake of nail teasing my skin, feeling electric everywhere Javier touches me, making everywhere else want the same attention. Twining my fingers in his hair, the soft ringlets tickle my palms; his eyelashes flutter against my cheeks when he kisses my ear. I kiss his sinewy throat and he moans, I trace the lines of muscle on his back with my fingertips, taste the brine of his lips on my tongue. His skin is warm and smooth, the musky smell intensifying as he heats up.

When he finally picks me up and carries me to the bed, I'm not just pulsing between my legs. My whole body is attuned, my slick skin smells like him, just as he's tinged with me. Finally, lying on top of him; he puts a hand behind my head and draws me in for an extended kiss. As his tongue thrusts into my mouth I straddle his hips. One hand on my neck, insisting on kissing me, tonguing me, with his other hand he lines himself up and finally, mercifully enters me with a forceful thrust.

Just like the rest, he takes his time. Pushing into me, rubbing against me, until I have to beg him not to stop. Finally, mercifully, he sets a pace that puts all my hypersensitive nerves on edge. The orgasm builds, and when I come the shock and shiver isn't just a release in my cunt, though that's the epicenter of sensation. Tiny shivers sweep across my body, reverberating through my limbs, shaking through my core and up my spine, radiating outward.

Even after he comes, I can see the devilish glint in his now exhausted eyes as he flips onto his back, one hand reached over, stroking my stomach.

He says to me, "Cuba. Some say it's the last romantic remnant of Atlantis. But all our treasures are forbidden to Americans."

"I know," I say. Admitting, "That's why I came here."

"It was worth it?" he asks. "You have found what you were seeking?"

Outside, the soft misty light of dawn illuminates the quiet blue of the sea, a diffuse glow that's never able to reveal what's supposedly sunk beneath. Built for love, then destroyed in vengeance when it became corrupted with power and greed, Atlantis was forever lost. I wander out to the balcony to watch the day begin, filled with a magical hope that I thought had been permanently eroded. Americans aren't supposed to travel here because of the politics. What could a Caribbean island offer that we don't already have anyhow? But I did find something here. Something perhaps not forbidden in our culture of haste, but something rapidly getting lost.

It's already humid outside, a penetrating, sultry heat. Before long, the sun will intensify and warm the day, but the mild *brisa* will keep it in harmony, much like the sweetness of rum complements its heat. Then, it will be beautiful. But right now, for a few lingering moments, it's perfection.

I go back inside, stretch myself next to Javier. I run my hand along his chest, slowly, carefully.

I sigh.

I Want You

TE DESEO

༄᠆᠆᠆᠆᠆᠆᠆᠆᠆᠆᠆᠆᠆

William Fredrick Cooper

Te deseo.

I have to tell her so. The sun-kissed beige complexion, close-cropped black hair and beautiful hazel eyes captured me first, but her magnificent movement on the dance floor has the veins in my dick rearranging themselves, aroused in anticipation.

Exuding sensuality in every step, she is, simultaneously, divinity and purgatory in motion. I wonder if her sexual inclinations would be as nasty as my fantasies tell me they would be. Longing to bring a bunch of powerful orgasms from her, the thought of us moving through marathon sessions of mutual pleasure has me squirming in my seat.

Te deseo.

I am dying for her to know. Igniting my flames with her racy repertoire, that she has me lusting after her is insane. I can't help it: she is tilting my world off its axis with her rapture of twists and turns. Los Bravos, the persuasive percussion blaring from the speakers, agrees with me. The ocean of motion under that spaghetti-strapped red dress waves fluently, back and forth, fucking with me even more. I wonder if the garden under that outfit is in serious need of watering.

Our eyes meet, and hold. Acknowledging the spell cast, she puckers those pouted red lips, then bats an erotic eyelash at me. Pirouetting back into the arms of her partner, the look of a seductress revisits me. Her smile is alluringly spicy. Seeing her cute dimples wink as well, the length of me crawls further down my trousers as I yearn to part her paradise with an active, artful, animated mouth. Mm, I wonder if the taste of her cunny is as sweet as caramel syrup.

Te deseo.

I pray she won't say no. My goodness, I love the wickedness of the seduction. The light coat of sweat on this temptress blends perfectly with the spinning colored lights overhead, and steady blue background. That it makes her skin glisten further accentuates her mystique.

Knowing every man in the place wants to fuck the sense out of her tonight, I notice her enjoyment of her power, working everyone watching her into a sexual frenzy. Cutting through a thick haze of cigarette smoke on deliciously defined stems, the firmness of her ass is seen by all. If she did a zipper check right about now, the congregation of hard-ons would be solid as steel, ready to pop.

Te deseo.

Would she like my strokes forceful, or slow? Watching her glide on those three-inch black stilettos has me delirious with desire. The thought of hearing her purr *"Ooh, Papi"* as I massage her bud with my mouth has the throb of my pecker out of control. Scurrying upward in her with my tongue, the exploration of every crevice of her pussy would make her scream praises, as well as the name of her god and son in foreign octaves.

Now, I'm supplanted in wonderland. Invading her insides with an urgent chocolate stick, the electricity at my waist unites with her well-saturated energy. Working myself deep, then deeper, the strength of my lust made her shudder from temple to toes, causing orgasmic overload. Then, as my release built up, she pays tribute to the passionate pounding with strange guttural sounds, vulnerable mutterings and ecstatic rambles. Through these groans of pleasure, she'll be admitting that no man had ever worn out the kitty like I had.

Te deseo. Te deseo, ahora.

Or shall I say, "Let's go"?

"Stop with the obsessive staring and go ask her to dance," Crazy Hec says, disrupting my vision. "Or are you scared to?"

"He's not scared, Hector. He's a *racista,*" B.K. adds, eliciting gales of laughter from our whole crew with his translation.

"Kill that noise, dawg," I respond. "I don't discriminate, you know that."

Crazy Hec's other half, Martha, begs to differ.

"Yeah right, Coop. How come you never go on our Pocono retreats?"

"Because I don't want to stand out like a sixth toe, that's why. Remember, I'm older than you guys, as well as the only unattached one."

Anthony, always the comedian, sniffs my black silk shirt.

"Is that bullshit I smell?"

Again, laughter.

"C'mon, Will. You know we love you," Jahira says. "I just think you're scared."

"Scared of what?"

"Scared that a Latina will put a hurtin' on you," B.K. notes.

"Debbie and I have been telling him that for years," Anthony adds.

Nodding, Debbie agrees.

"Coop, that woman out there will have you begging for mama."

Nothing liked being roasted by the crew on your first night out in eons. It's all good, for I love my second family like play cousins. After all, it's been some time since the crew—Anthony Lopez and his wife, Debbie, Crazy Hector and Martha Gonzalez, Jahira Santiago and B.K. Simpson, and yours truly—convened at Tavola's, our after-work hangout by the Manhattan Courts. Claudia, the world's sexiest bartender and model extraordinaire, always brings us steamed clams to go along with her over-the-top Long Island Ice Teas. Buzzing with merriment (as well as tipsiness), our posse is akin to the ensemble that meets at that place in Boston where everyone knows your name.

Now we're at Cafe Remy, a downtown nightclub near the South Ferry Terminal. In a few, Louis Arroyo and his lovely Torri, Jesus and Aida Hernandez, Mike, Gail Carr, and Icsom and Krista Jones, as well as more party troopers from the legal system, will arrive. Rolling about thirty deep, we usually take over the place, partying the night away.

Or shall I say they do such, as I am so self-conscious about dancing salsa. This is an irony to all who know me, for when it comes to hoofing, steps to me are effortless, like they were to Bojangles, Gregory Hines, Sammy Davis Jr., and the Nicholas Brothers. Full of confidence and expression while becoming a slave to the rhythms of a neat beat, "a fish in water" is what I've been called by many.

The moves of my midsection command the most attention.

If I had a dollar for every time a woman asked me if I moved in bed the way I do on a dance floor, I'd never have to work again. My hip action is innate; whenever a steady beat catches me, the swivel is immediate. Keeping time to almost any rhythm, some may think of me as an exhibitionist when I launch into my gyrations; however, nothing could be further from the truth. Instead of listening to melodious fusion of rhythm and song, I feel it.

The throbbing of its pulse is enticing.

The passion of its groove is exciting.

Like a mouse behind a pied piper, put on a thumping bass line, and my feet are sure to follow. From hip-hop to reggae, house to merengue, I close my eyes and enter a zone where nothing else matters except the music and my partner.

Maybe it's just me, but the connection between dancing and sex is fiercely intense. Intoxicatingly arousing, synchronicity in motion unleashes primitive, passionate impulses begging to escape the bondage of everyday routine. The inhibitive storm set free, when coupled with a woman that gets down, sparks really fly. Melding into one, the joining of like spirits on the dance floor is the perfect precursor to the primal carnality we both desire. Sometimes, all that stands in the way of such is confidence.

Something I lack when it comes to the most sensuous dance. Every superman has his kryptonite, and mine is salsa. While not green with envy while watching Anthony, Jesus, B.K., Hector and Louis lead their ladies with the right combination of machismo and grace, I long for the day where I can share chemistry to the sounds of Tito Puente, Eddie Palmeri, Johnny Pacheco, and Willie Colon, as opposed to R & B grooves I mastered.

Maybe my Spanish Fly leaving the dance floor will show me someday.

Not now, however.

The club just went old school.

It's Shabba and Maxi's "Housecall," a dancehall groove from back in the day.

Damn, it's been a minute since I heard this jam.

Head bouncing, my torso is turning.

It's time for a house call of my own.

Scanning the establishment, I see her.

The chocolate woman in the bar area, wearing that sexy black dress and matching fuck-me pumps, bobbin' her head, fits the bill.

She's been checking me out on the low all night.

The Cosmopolitan she's nursing needs a time-out.

With the boldness of a cobra, I strike. Using nary a word, my hand tickles her fingertips, then abducts them. Deaf to her feeble "Wait, can I finish my drink" plea, she's my prisoner now. The direction of our escape is to the left, where the hardwood floor will supply everything we need.

Okay, I see that she needs this liberation as badly as I do, for her sway intrigues me.

Let me reel it in by pressing her backside against the firestorm at my groin.

The purring sound leaving this lady is nice.

Decoding her movements, I can tell she's wavering between nice and nasty. The aggressive language of her body waves tells me that she doesn't want to leave the spot alone tonight, yet her hesitance to look at me indicates she wants to remain a lady.

In case I didn't understand her mixed message, her hands caress the nape of me.

She wants me to ride her ass through the whole song.

Okay, I'll play along.

My hands and arms form a waist wrap, and our bodies are one.

Rocking and rocking, anyone watching us can tell we're balanced on the tightrope: one that separates a one-night stand where bodies move in concert in bed from a night of fantasizing about what might have been, had the right words been said. The former thought consumes her; she rotates her hips in a slow circular motion, ticking her pelvis like the second hand of a watch. Glancing back, she looks amazed that I keep up with her. Doesn't she know that when she's too bad for everyone else, she's just right for me?

Her frame shudders.

I can tell I'm getting to her.

After the cut, she faces me.

"Damn, baby. You're too dangerous for me," she says, and leaves me stranded on the island of grooves.

Oh well. I guess freedom isn't for everyone.

The deejay feels my disappointment; he's got on soca now.

Continuing my naughty wind, I saunter back to my table, where B.K. approaches me as if he's on fire.

"You have an admirer, Coop."

Pointing left, I see her, and my eyes widen.

It's the lady in red, staring deeply at me while hypnotically moving in place.

Swerving seductively with an authentic sexiness, her body is a vision of polished perfection. I could see her legs pulse, enhancing the musculature of her chiseled calves. Her well-placed curves excite me with their generosity, but not as much as the rose tattoo above those perky breasts. Look at it sitting there, begging for me to pick its petals. Mm, I love her hazel eyes. Passionately penetrating my senses as they smolder with sexuality, they are stalking me with a look of want.

A man extends his hand, inviting her to the floor.

She politely says, "No, thank you," while never once looking at him.

She's already dancing with someone in her mind.

Me.

"Man, you better go get with that," B.K. says.

I peer back at my crew sitting at the table, and see twenty-plus different shades of skin, the looks on their faces screaming in unison, "Well, what are you waiting for, stupid?"

∞

Well, what are you waiting for, stupid?

Why am I standing here, four songs later? Hasn't the messenger from Oz returned with my nerve? And why is the essence of my fantasy still waiting, and smiling? For the past twenty minutes, men have begged to invade her majestic presence on the dance floor, and all have been turned away. That she does so while looking in my direction makes me sweat.

Does she know something that I don't?

Maybe she does. Maybe, just maybe, she came here to share her exotic femininity with me. Maybe she's chosen me to drink of the warm juices that lie in abundance between those smooth thighs, and quench her insatiable lust. Maybe it's me that'll have access to what everyone craves.

Wait, what's Hector whispering in her ear? He's always starting something. Why is he pointing in my direction, and why is she laughing?

And why are they headed this way?

My heart, threatening to come through my chest, is beating fast as she nears. Damn, her shoulders are round and ripe, and I love the muscular definition in her arms. I can tell she works out. Mm, those lips are so sexy. Smiling with anticipation, she's licking her bottom one as if famished. That heated gaze is making my dick stiff.

There's no time to sweat.

Be cool, Will, like the other side of a pillow.

"Estoy enamorada de la azúcar negra," she announces sexily while extending her hand.

She's in love with brown sugar, I see. Nervous, two seconds seem like two hours before I respond.

"Gracias, señorita." Feeling the soft texture of her touch, I kiss her hand.

I'm entangled in the web of a spider, a red widow.

"I'm Alicia. Alicia Morena," she says.

"My name is William."

"Ooh, Guillermo. That's such a strong name."

Guillermo, William, Ed the Baker from around the way . . . whatever. The tree trunk at my groin is encouraging me to be anybody she wants me to be.

"I hear you want to learn how to salsa," she says.

Startled by my blown cover, I look at Hector, who's grinning like a Cheshire cat. Don't you just hate tattletales?

Embarrassed, I nod yes.

The deejay must be smiling from his booth while sensing the attraction of our different worlds. The calypso cuts cease, and *"No Soy Para Ti,"* a salsa cut by Ismael Rivera, fills the air.

"Guillermo, *quieres tocarme?*"

Hell yeah, I want to touch her, all over. Damn, the way she

says my name in Spanish has my blood on fire. This woman is sexy. And she knows it.

I want to rip that red dress off her and suck on those thick, eraser-sized nipples, but the dance will suffice, for now. As I grab her hand, she feels my insecurity, but allows me to lead her to the hardwood floor. Hopefully, our flames won't burn the place down.

The combination of beats and brass create a mild rhythm to the song, one we both feel instantly. Capturing her size-six waist, I follow the fluidity of her hip roll and flawless footwork. Back and forth, side to side, I feature her to the nightclub through a series of seductive turns and sumptuous spins. Taking her on a sensuous trip by my table, I notice my posse with their mouths agape.

Anthony and Debbie start clapping, and the rest follow suit as I pull Alicia close.

"Papi, you never danced salsa before?" she asks.

"A little bit, Alicia. My crew shows me things."

"Well, let me tell you that you're a natural. Seeing a black man dance Latin well turns me on. It shows me he's aware of all cultures."

She has me blushing as the bongos, maracas, trumpets and cowbell of Hector Lavoe's *"Mi Gente"* quicken the tempo.

"Time to step it up," Alicia announces.

Peering at me, she launches into a torrid display that has Selena beaming from the heavens.

"C'mon, baby, control me," she commands.

I'll try. Reaching for her hand, my freefall into a passionate inferno is now complete. Not much spinning this time, I let her freestyle, occasionally matching her seamless steps with my own.

My God, it's working. Feeling my lead, she's working with me. Hmm, let me try some hustle turns. Damn, I'm rolling *siete* with my dancing. Our hips are close now. I release her, and watch her go. Seeing her cha-cha-cha while I clap has my crew going crazy.

"Do that shit, Coop!" Martha screams.

"He's got it," Debbie says.

"Coooooooop!" Hector, B.K. and Anthony shout.

Suddenly, I feel the eyes of the population on us as *"Siembra,"* a scintillating Ruben Blades song, cooks in the background of our heaven.

"Gracias, Alicia," I say, turning away to walk off the floor.

"You can't stop now, Guillermo."

The insistence of her tone tells me she's in the sinfully hot zone that blends the lines of dancing and sex. Her hazel eyes, now glassy with euphoria, are on the precipice of combustion. What I can't decipher is if it's the music or my masculinity that is the key to her ignition.

"Come finish what you started," she orders.

The pace is even quicker. Watching her twist and turn has the temperature in *mi corazón, cuerpo y pobrecillo* rising. After a twirl, I pull her close once more, and our lips touch slightly.

Damn, what's coming over me?

Whatever it is, I think she likes it, for her face resembles an erotic explosion.

"Ay, Papi," she coos. Then, as a gesture of further appreciation, she pinches my ass.

Finishing the song, Alicia and I share another dance; this time it's a slow waltz to *No puedo dejar de amar te,* Michael Jackson's Spanish version of "I Just Can't Stop Loving You."

Moving her hands from my triceps, up and down my slender

frame, Alicia holds me tight through this song, as well the ballad playing now, *"Heroe,"* by Enrique Iglesias.

Feeling the heat of her core as we move together, her pointed nipples against my slim chest are driving me crazy. My lust for her now undisguised, my dick is granite-hard, and wants to take a dip in her pool of ecstasy.

She notices. Pressing those luscious petals to my neck, she licks my earlobe with her lovely, Latin lizard, thoroughly enjoying the taste of sweat and cologne.

"Estoy tan mojada," she purrs. *"Estoy tan mojada."*

Damn, is your kitty that wet? Can I taste it, right here, right now? I bet a river of your juices will escape you, and drench my chin. I bet you are sweet, like pears. Can I search for your G-spot with my fingers while humming on your clit with my mouth? Can I trace the length of me along your lustfully lubricated labia, then slip and slide in a succulent, sensational, sweetly saturated sex sauce?

Guillermo wants to be your love slave, Alicia; so fucking bad.

I never experienced a Latina before, and would love for you to be my first, and only. Is it any different, honey? I hear that you spoil your men in *el dormitorio.* Can you treat me like a king, if only for a moment in lust? Will you sing marvelous, melodious moans if I ease open those legs, lick, then love your clit right with the fluent flutter of my oral flute? Will my manhood feel like it's in heaven when it plays hide-and-seek inside your Spanish garden? *Te deseo;* if only for a night.

If my mouth admits this now, the animal stirring in both of us would be unleashed. Can you picture us being arrested for screwing in front of a midtown audience? As much as our bilingual libidos roared, a mutual dam was constructed, stunting the natural flow of our soulful connection.

Someday would not be tonight.

"Where do you live, Alicia?" I ask as we leave the floor.

"In Upper Manhattan, William . . . "

Damn, she even says William sexy.

"In the Inwood section. Right off of Two Hundred Seventh Street."

Hmm. That's within walking distance from me.

"When can I see you again for more salsa lessons?"

"You don't need any more, Guillermo."

Disappointed that our association seems momentary, my eyes search the carpet below for consolation.

"But if you insist, *Papi* . . . "

In a millisecond, I make the transformation. I'm no longer the luckless "agony of defeat" skier of ABC's *Wide World of Sports* fame. Once again, I am faster than a speeding bullet, more powerful than a locomotive, able to leap . . .

You get the picture.

She continues.

"Come to my place tomorrow, and bring a bottle of Licor 43. Be there by nine, and I promise I'll give you a lesson I'm sure you'll never forget."

Giggling, she kisses my cheek, then fades into the crowd of dancers on the floor.

Gee, I wonder what she meant by that?

∽

Here I am, still in a stupor, almost twenty hours later. Reliving the cosmic chemistry shared with Alicia had my groin tingling with anticipation all night. Shit, I even placed a pillow between my legs, so that I could hump on it. Masturbation was an option for release, but I wanted to save my scalding seed for tonight. Just in case.

One by one my boys have been blowing up my phone, giving me pointers on how to deal with an exotic princess like Alicia. Though none of them dared ask, I know they all wanted to know if I'll be inside of her wet, watery resting place. A true gentleman never tells.

A beautiful arrangement of red roses sits in the refrigerator, and I purchased the bottle she requested. This golden brown stuff, from what I recall, is sticky and syrupy.

I wonder what we'll be mixing that with.

The vision of me tasting her salty secretions with my hungry tongue has me feeling like an anxious puppy. Man, I would love to suck on her gravity-defying breasts. I bet her luscious nubbins are so ripe and sensitive. Wondering if her vagina can accommodate the full engorgement of my thick rod, I want to make those pretty hazel pupils roll to the top of her pretty head with hot, hectic, hellacious hip thrusts. Envisioning her astride my dick, I see her flexing those firm thighs while squatting, then kneeling.

Shit, I'm getting worked up again.

Will the muscles of her channel massage the length of me with short strokes or long, languid ones? Will it spasm once I turn her over and penetrate her to the hilt with my hunger? Will the measured motion of my midsection send her spiraling into a place where nothing matters except the womb-twitching waves of orgasmic bliss? Will she gasp for breath while trying to escape an insane ecstasy? Will I bathe the walls of her sex with my milky pudding?

In a few hours, all questions will be answered. For now, I'm at my computer, cruising through the Black Singles Connection website. I shared an excerpt of last night with the Relationship and Dating Message Board—a tame version, of course—and asked for suggestions as to enhancing the ambiance tonight. Many of my online friends were amazed that I sought assistance, for I constantly brag about my . . . ahem . . . romantic prowess. Together, they came up with ideas ranging from a G-string striptease to kissing her the minute she opened the door. All of them were awesome.

However, Isabel, a woman from Spain excited that my spirit was intoxicated by a new culture, suggested that I write her a sonnet in Spanish.

"Women from spain are very passionate. The suave approach works every time," she said.

I'm a little rusty, but I think I'll give it a try in this blank card:

Aunque sea sólo por una noche
(IF ONLY FOR A NIGHT)

Me duele el corazón por ti
Mi cuerpo te desea ardientemente
Mi alma te anhela tanto, mi amor,
Aunque sea sólo por una noche

Aunque sea sólo por una noche, tócame
Aunque sea sólo por una noche, saboreame
Aunque sea sólo por una noche, deja que nuestros cuerpos hagan
    música
Te deseo, mi amor
Aunque sea sólo por una noche

For effect purposes, the translation of my lust will hammer my point home:

My heart aches for you
My body longs for you
My soul wants you, so bad my love
If only for a night

If only for a night, touch me
If only for a night, taste me
If only for a night, let our bodies make music together
I want you, my love
If only for a night

Damn, I want Alicia so bad I can taste her skin. It's delectable, delightful and delicious. Her body will tremble from my warm embrace; my gentle touch will make her quiver. Undressing, then caressing her, teasing and pleasing her, hopefully I won't miss a spot with my tongue. Testing, teasing while tasting, by the time I'm done eating her, she'll shudder and shiver through an endless series of orgasms.

Then, as we feel ourselves climbing into uncharted heights of lust, the heat of my dick will be relentless once it breaks the skin of a new world. Once embedded and entrenched within her spicy walls, our bodies will stretch the imagination of contortionists everywhere. Pumping and pleasing her, I'll be determined to see the trembling tremors from a sexually sedated seductress. Swirling from peak to peak, we'll share the grunts, groans and pleasurable moans that our horizontal mamba brings, as well as the uncontrollable contractions of nerves exploding in ecstasy. I will make this woman cum until she joins me in the ultimate cluster of climaxes that pure, unadulterated passion brings.

Damn, I sure hope she craves chocolate tonight.

❧

So, here I am, on the fourth floor of her walk-up building, at the doorway of paradise. A smoldering bachata tune with a steady Dominican beat heats up the hallway, compliments of the apartment below hers. Maybe that's what we'll be dancing to tonight. Or better yet, maybe I could show her the steps I practiced this morning while listening to Marc Anthony. Maybe . . .

"Well, aren't you going to come in?"

There's nothing like a fantasy disrupted by an even better reality.

"Close the door," the voice of a siren orders.

Glancing out in the hallway, the other gray apartment doors smirk at me. I just hate being the last to know shit.

Obliging, I shut the door to the real world and enter a surreal yet serene place, an erotic world where you can neither run nor hide from inhibitions. I follow the cadence of her sashay; Alicia's natural movements are so precise, so deliberate and rhythmic.

I'm scanning my surroundings, wide-eyed and open-mouthed, curiosity etched all over my face as to what lies ahead. The only degree of normalcy is Gloria Estefan singing *"Tengo que decirte algo"* on her stereo. Someone left the bathwater of questions running, and it's overflowing my mind.

Why is she dressed in a black, formfitting catsuit? And why are there scented purple candles lit throughout the house? What's up with the red lights, and the chair in the middle of the living room floor? And why are there towels and long red scarves on her red velvet sofa? Wait a second: Did I walk into a scene from an Alfred Hitchcock movie and meet the seductive Spanish half-sister of Norman Bates? Or, in the alternative, did I walk onto an adult movie set and meet Vanessa del Rio?

"Thanks so much for the roses," Alicia says, removing both the arrangement and libations from my arms.

She reads my card.

Closing it, her eyes, piercing my soul, are warm and watery.

I struck a chord in her heart; the right chord.

"I see you . . . um . . . " I stutter, alluding to the scenery.

"That's for later."

Then she takes my hand, leading me away from one flytrap, steering me in the direction of what I'm thinking is another.

I'm wrong. It's the kitchen.

"Come, William. Sit and let Mamá feed you."

⌖

Damn, this sister can burn. The paella, complete with lobster tails, bits of octopus, chicken, calamari and shrimp, was so filling. Initially, Alicia looked disturbed that I couldn't eat two helpings, but I explained to her my disdain for walking around on a full stomach. That's one reason.

Reason number two? Who likes having sex on a full stomach? It's so uncomfortable. I have to leave room for dessert; that is, if there is any.

My goodness, Alicia sure set a stage. If the cream-flavored scents these candles give off are an aphrodisiac to awaken sexual impulses, then it's working. Before she went in the back to freshen up, she asked me to push the "2" button on the CD changer in the living room, then make myself comfortable on the sofa.

"It's a surprise," she added.

Fulfilling the request, the music I'm now listening to caught me by surprise. To my utter amazement, it's the scintillatingly sinister street radio mix of "Downtown," by SWV. The background vocals of this song tell me exactly what Alicia wants tonight.

She wants to get freaky.

"Going downtown is the way to Alicia's love, William," she yells.

I gulp.

Did I walk into a mine field, or what?

She reemerges, winding those sexy hips better than a Jamaican woman, with the Licor in hand. The brazen blaze in her eyes has a tremor racing down my spine.

"Stand up and strip for me."

Following her directive, I rise. Off go the blue jeans, then my blue sweater.

"Them too," she demands, tugging at my red-and-white Snoopy boxers. "I want to see what I'm working with tonight."

A nervous laugh escapes me, as I roll down my shorts.

The brown torpedo is at attention.

"Aaayyy, Papi, is that all for me?"

"Yes, Alicia," I mumble.

"Hmmm, I can't wait. But for now, you must close your eyes and dance with me."

As if on cue, *"No me dejes de querer,"* a sexy Estefan cut, fills the moonlit evening. I feel its pulse, and pull my Spanish kitty close. Fred Astaire and Ginger Rogers have nothing on us, except clothes.

"Keep those eyes closed," she reiterates.

Slowly, I nod. Shit, I'm on the brink of overheating. Wait, where is she going with my fingers? Ooh, shit . . . That feels so good.

"You like that, Guillermo? You like the way Mamá sucks on your fingers?"

"Yes . . . I do."

She does them one, two, three at a time, submerging them deep in her mouth, leaving a teasing trace of her sloppiness on each of them while sucking the sense out of them. Is this a subliminal message as to how she'll handle something bigger?

She pulls me close once more. Ooh, what's this oozing down the side of my face?

"Mm, Guillermo, you're my chocolate sundae."

These candles, this liqueur on my bald head, running down my body, her free hand massaging me as we share a forbidden dance . . . I feel the fear of fulfilling a fantasy melting . . . melting . . . mm, I love this shit.

"Pour some more on me, Alicia," I say.

That's it, baby, make a nasty mess out of me.

Now it's your turn.

Like Daredevil, I am blind, but my other senses are stronger. Let me get that bottle . . . got it.

"Didn't think I would find your soft hands with my eyes closed, now did you?" I brag.

"Make me sticky, Guillermo."

I'll do her one better.

Pulling her into my blaze, our lips peck once, twice, thrice, then part in exploration of the oral pinkness within our fire. Finding the sources of our arousal, first gently, then urgently, the tongue wrestle is ravenous. All the while, I am pouring the sticky solution upon us.

I'm feeling Alicia shudder from the electricity between us. Those hips grind against me, hard and steady, the momentum of her dance building by the beat. My dick is as hard as a black diamond, and the peaches surrounding them are drawing tight.

You do mix Licor 43 with milk, right?

Because I think I'm going to cum . . .

Not yet.

Who do you think I am, Minute Mouse?

I'm breathless, having collapsed in the metal chair in the center of the floor, dim-eyed and dizzy because my sex sword is still filled with excitement.

"Let me get out of this outfit, *Papi,*" my fantasy come true announces. Alicia must forgive the eager look in my eyes; I've been dying to see this Spanish goddess naked since our eyes met last night.

She looks amazing: anatomically astonishing, absolutely appetizing and incredibly intimidating all at once. Her beige complexion is flawless. Slimly muscled, yet curvaceous, that taut abdomen is taunting me, and those well-developed, track runner thighs that complement her sex-, I mean six-pack are titillating, tantalizing and terrifying. I swallow saliva while gawking, for the combination of her hard calves, firm thighs and great stomach muscles means one thing:

Mamá Morena can ride good dick all night.

Good, chocolate dick is what's she's going get tonight, provided I can break her erotic spell and leave this chair.

"You are the most beautiful woman I ever laid my eyes on, Alicia," I say.

"And I'm yours, Guillermo," she responds. "*Aunque sea sólo por una noche.*"

Bravely, I try to stand up and greet her with my fever, but she won't let me. Why is she pushing me back into the chair?

Reaching back, Alicia hands me a glass of her witches' brew, mildly disguised as ice water.

Though my body is defenseless, weak to her touch, the lion

at my waist, fully alert once more, wants to mute its roar in the moistness of the tigress straddling me.

That idea might have to wait. My goodness, I feel her strength as she climbs my sticky, slim frame.

"*Papi,* I was taught to always to treat my men like the kings they are," she says.

"I . . . I'm speech—"

A lusciously long index finger stills my thought.

"Please don't talk," Alicia whispers. "Just enjoy my dance."

Taking my face into her soft hands, she's alternating between kisses and lustful kitty licks. Mm, I like that shit. Her purr, oozing a new sexiness, reestablishes my trance as she slowly, gently nibbles on my ears. Eagerly embarking on an arousing journey, I can hear her panting as her lips touch my nose, then peck my mouth.

I can barely take this. Her tongue is so well trained, tasting my neck as if bloodthirsty. The tenderness of her touch is exciting places on me I never knew existed. I hear the hitches in her breath as she grinds her hips against me, a trickle of her lust juice is oozing down my thigh, and I can feel her clit throbbing, and swelling.

I'll take care of that later; that is, if I can regain control of my body.

A wet trace of Alicia's saliva has caught up with drops of syrup. Mixing while meandering to my navel, the trail meets up with its creator, who just parted my thighs and found the place where the dance will end.

Her red lips are introducing itself to my swollen purple knob, savoring it like it's an alien stranger as she wraps her hands around the stiffness of my thick shaft.

Our eyes meet yet again. Her look is altered, haunting and horny, unmistakably naughty.

"Ay, Papi. Estoy loca por esta caña negra."

Rocking forward, she sweeps her tongue along the tip of me, tasting the pre-cum that drips from me. I feel like all the blood in my body is going south of the border as she licks the underside of her black sugarcane.

"Nice hook, baby," she moans.

My breath is short once more, for her flooding mouth has latched onto me something fierce. Swirling and slicking, oiling and polishing my shaft in a slow, insatiable rhythm, she's a hungry python, eagerly engulfing its prey, the fluidity of her head bob instinctive. I love the way she relaxes her jaw and throat muscles while maintaining her slobber.

Damn, she's moving from dick to testicle sacs now, flicking her talented tongue along them. Her hedonistic taming of my tool has intensified my surge within. Recapturing my meat in her oral goblet, she makes it disappear, then reappear easily. Her oral strokes now manic, she's really enjoying her delicious chocolate bar.

And, I'm enjoying the greasing of my magic stick.

I'm tensing as her pace quickens even more, and the sloppy, slurping sounds get louder. The throbbing nerves in my dick must be exciting, for her wet, succulent moans are ones of intense pleasure.

My toes are curling. I feel my thighs tighten, then sag as she slows the tempo of her tribute. Then she speeds it up again as she feels me getting harder and harder.

Shit, she's greedy, and so, so good.

Feeling my explosion reaching the point of no return, like engineer Scotty says on *Star Trek:* I don't think I can hold it any longer.

I'm about to . . . Oh, shit . . .

A spurt of white lava leaves me . . . then another . . . three
times . . . four . . . All I hear is her gulping . . . my breaths . . . so
short . . . my tip . . . so sensitive . . . Please stop sucking it . . .
No, don't . . . Yes, do . . . oh, shit . . . I can't stop trembling . . .
regroup, mind . . . body, stop shaking . . .

"I know, *Papi,*" she says, finally draining my pipe completely.
"I know how bad you needed that."

She must have cum as well, for I hear her breathing heavily.

A boyish curiosity leaves me as I search the room for air.

"Alicia, I want . . . "

"I already know, baby. You want to know what my pussy
tastes like."

A dancer, seductress and psychic all rolled into one.

Damn, I feel lucky.

Finally, we're both on our feet, kissing passionately as we stick
together in the mixture of saliva, sweat, syrup, and semen. The
only thing missing are the spurts of satisfaction that leave a happy
vagina when eaten properly.

And I'm about to fix that problem.

Alicia senses my newfound aggression, stretches her beauty
out on the sofa and spreads her muscled stems.

"*Guillermo, quieres tocarme?*" she asks slyly.

"*Sí, Mamá,*" I respond while pecking the lips that took my
phallus to heaven and back. It's time for my voyage to the center
of Spain.

Like an obedient compass needle, I begin my journey. Licking her rose tattoo, I hear a slight moan. Hmm, those pointed
nipples are sensitive to touch? Okay, let me skim the surface of
them lightly with itsy-bitsy tongue flutters.

The involuntary wails leaving her are so nice.

You see, while I pleasure Alicia, I'm performing anatomical

reconnaissance. Charting out her peaks and valleys, by the time I'm done examining the gorgeous terrain, surveying and scanning this foreign land for sensitive spots and erogenous zones, she'll be quaking and quivering like a bowstring.

Oh, I see she likes the way I suck on her abundant orbs. Mm, Papá wishes she had milk, for it does a body good. The remains of the liqueur mix well with her natural taste. Mm, that cute navel of hers is indescribably delicious.

"Please get to my pussy, Guillermo," Alicia pants.

Peering up from between her thighs, my face wears the look of a burglar.

"Not yet," I respond. "I'm saving that for last."

I want her body to generate enough electricity to illuminate a city, her face to fight the feminine gestures of bliss that taste-testing her tangy triangle will bring. But I must try her toes first, one at a time.

First planting tender kisses, next I engulf them, causing the tides of her inner sea to simmer.

She's caught a small wave with that act. Her calves are so strong I must suck them. She barely conceals her pleasure. Next focusing on a different kind of hole, I lick around her anus, lube my finger with the slick ooze trickling from her saturated rainforest, and insert one slow, then slower. Multitasking, I lick the outer lips of her honey pot lightly with my oral lizard.

"Ay, Papi, ay, Guillermo" she moans. "Do that shit, baby."

I feel her body tense, then spasm slightly. Jerking, then sighing, Alicia succumbs to her mini-tremor.

That was minor. It's time for her to experience a major orgasm.

Moaning and murmuring as I neared her magnetically attractive garden once more, I share a reverential moment with its musky aroma before I begin to lick her inner thighs.

"Please eat my pussy," she begs.

Licking and lapping her thick, fleshy folds, her coos are that of a kitten as I slide a finger, then two, within her honey. However, I refuse to be content with a purr. I need the roar of a mountain lioness.

Resuming my exploration of her delicious depths, the inner walls of Spain clutched at my oral telescope. Piercing her pussy with my nose, then chin, I am on a deliberate course to bring a multitude of mini-explosions from my Latin lovely. Moving from cunt to clit to cunt again, the taste of her drenched garden is awesome; and addictive, I might add.

I feel the muscles in her legs tighten as my face latches onto her drenched pussy. The needle of my compass now flat, the need to decorate every pink pussy wall with my tongue art is overwhelming. Mixing my saliva with her moisture, I was on a scavenger hunt of pleasure, looking for that special place that brings Alicia off many times over.

"Aaay, Papi . . . get that . . . oh, William . . . just like that . . ."

Her moans are an indicator of the sensational bolts of pleasure taking possession of her awesome body; her circular motion against my face tells me I found her land of milky honey.

Licking slowly, in circles around her slick, swollen clit, I flatten my tongue against it and move like a paroled butterfly liberated from its cocoon.

Peering up at my princess, I see heavenly contortions. A chorus of moans leaves her as well.

Damn, her pussy tastes good. It's time to immerse myself once more. Munching on her precious interior, I taste the beginning of an intense orgasm. Her thick walls are absolutely scrumptious.

"Ay, Papi, you do that shit . . . eat that . . . so . . . fucking . . . good . . . Yes, baby, yes . . . "

Her purrs excite me further, so I become more determined to make her hips rise from the velvet.

She bucking against it now, trying to fight the same feeling I warred with.

Like me, she's sees her resistance to orgasm is an exercise in futility.

"That's it, baby . . . Make it cum hard . . . ay . . . ay . . . ay, yes . . . Make it cum."

She can't anymore. Alicia shoots a river of hot, salty juices from her hot spot, nearly drowning me with what I couldn't drink. Damn, I love women that squirt.

Rising, she steps over me, her breathing staggered as she wobbles into the back of her apartment.

For two minutes, I hear water running, then silence. She returns with a soapy washcloth and basin.

"Like I said, Guillermo, I take care of my men. Now, get up," she says.

Rising, I feel the gentle touch of hot liquid, terry cloth and tenderness wash then rinse me. Cleansed of the sticky scent of soiled foreplay, I return the bathing, and feel my flaccidity leave me once more.

"Ooh, William," Alicia says while gently stroking its puffy rim. Our hips meet again, this time without music, and begin a slow dance. Grinding slowly, low moans escape us.

Her hard nipples feel so good against my chest. They are making the blood vessels in my dick swell even larger. It's eager to explore something wet, warm and welcoming.

Peering deep into Alicia's hazel eyes, I touch her vagina and feel her nice, sloppy mess again.

"Sit down and let me ride that perfect dick."

After nearly two hours of pleasure, her voice is still like Spanish fly.

My desire to kiss her grows as long as the fire at my groin.

I sit myself on the towel that protects the velvet from our lust, and she immediately straddles my quivering column of manhood.

"Hands behind your back," she commands.

Obliging her request, I feel my hands fastened together by the scarves. That she does this while pumping up and down on my dick is amazing.

A slow rise, then fall, then hip wriggle by this wonderful lover takes me deeper into her Spanish garden. I flex my hips to meet her strokes, only to be humbled by vibrant vaginal muscles that massage my dick as they clench it, then retreat. Alicia moves in circles, causing my toes to curl and my breath to grow short.

I'm being handled like I was an amateur lover. My eyes blink open and shut in ecstasy as she presses her hands on my chest and flutters her backside like a moth. Bravely, I lunge forward and suck on those beautiful mounds.

"That's it, Papi, suck my nipples . . . Ay, Guillermo," Alicia purrs while not breaking the connection. Soon, I hear names and curses in a foreign tongue as her legs tense.

"Cum with your eyes open," I urge. "The orgasm will be more intense."

Alicia listens, then shudders and staggers like a punch-drunk boxer, then screams while soaking my staff with her waterfall.

"¡Dios mío! ¡Dios mío!"

That sounds so sexy.

"Untie me," I say.

She does, without realizing that she's lost control of my hunger.

I turn her over, place her legs on my shoulders, hold her calves hostage with my forearms and rub myself against her clitoris; very gently.

I could go inside right away, but I want her to beg for it.

"Please, William, please."

Inch by inch, I slowly sink my erection within her sex once more. Again, the key fits perfectly.

"*¡Dios mío, Papi! ¡Dios mío!*"

God, that sounds better than a sigh. Starting slowly, I give her tip, then root, then tip again. In circles, figure eights and, when her pussy becomes more accommodating, deep push-ups on my fists. Pumping while pulverizing it, I'm insistent with my need to take her to the summit of sexual sensation, so I increase the urgency of my thrusts.

"Fuck it harder, harder, fuck it, baby . . . "

From English to Spanish to English again, the melody of her moans intoxicates me, intensifies my dance. Seeing her grab but not hold the towel, then the sofa makes me try even harder than Avis does.

"*¡Dios mío, Papi! ¡Dios mío!*"

Alicia trembles as she gets the whole concert of movements: swivels and rhythmic gyrations; long and looping, then short, staccato strokes; slow, circular hip motion; semi-withdrawals; then, total immersion.

"Those hips . . . and that dick are fucking me so well," she announces through rapid pants.

Ay, Papi, ay, Guillermo, aaayyyy. Papi, *que rico.*

Shivering, her fists pound me in pleasure, then her nails invade my back. I know she feels the beat of my pulse. Holding her ass now, I go deeper, where no man, I think, has gone before.

"Stir that dick in my pussy good," she says. Obliging, the motion of my midsection moves from "O" to "V." Alicia's vagina involuntarily clamps onto me like it needs the companionship of my dick forever.

Shivering and shaking, I hit the right chord inside her tunnel repeatedly, and with relentless repetition; her eyes are tearing as she stares at me.

Thinking something's wrong, I pull out.

"Please, don't take it away, baby. Give me my dick, baby. Please, Guillermo."

She's so greedy, lost in the rapture of our shared gyrations. And I love it.

The wetness of her fused with the slick sounds of sopping sex and Kegel-enhanced contractions are causing my teeth to grit and thrash as an explosion rises. Already being the fix I crave, my dick gets harder within my Spanish garden.

"That's it, baby. Be a good boy and fill Mamá up," she urges.

The power of my pumping gets stronger as I glue my lips and tongue to hers, trembling violently. I'm close, so close to that dizzying, light-headed rush I want so bad.

"Come on, Guillermo . . . Shoot it all in me, baby . . . Cum for me, Papi."

I'm about to lose it again . . . Shit, she's fucking good . . . Oh shit . . . Damn . . . fuck, she took it out and is sucking it again . . . she's so nasty . . . and good . . . Fuck . . . she's coming too as she sucks . . .

I run my hands through her hair as she drinks from her well.

"Mm, that's a good boy, Guillermo."

My breath slowly returns to earth; as does hers.

"So, Guillermo," Alicia says, "I hear you want to learn to salsa."

Kissing passionately, our shared laugh is breathless.

"You know what I think, Alicia?"

"What?"

"I think we make beautiful music together."

"So do I, Guillermo. So do I."

Not Tonight
ESTA NOCHE NO

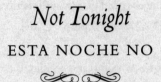

Curtis L. Alcutt

𝒦enji loved his job. He worked as a janitor at TechRealm Communications for a dozen years. Thursday nights were his favorite because, he had the pleasure of seeing Mrs. Colleen Bailey's curvolicious body, when she routinely came into monitor the network servers.

I know Mr. Bailey ain't puttin' it on her right, Kenji thought as he watched Colleen set her coffee cup down and press her security badge against the pad to gain entrance to the ground-floor lobby.

"How are you, Kenji?" Colleen asked as she put her access badge into her black leather Tavecchi laptop briefcase.

He put his feather duster in the back pocket of his dark gray uniform pants and grinned. "I'm doin' good now that you're here."

"You've fed me that line for over eight years now. When are you going to come up with a new one?"

"Just as soon as you stop lookin' so damned good."

"Watch it. That's borderline sexual harassment." Colleen self-consciously pulled closed her hip-length black Liz Claiborne suit jacket. She could feel Kenji's half Spanish, half African-American brown eyes travel over her forty-D redbone breasts.

"Borderline? I must be slippin'. Usually you threaten to at least call security."

"If you didn't keep this place so clean, I would've had you fired long ago."

He looked into her freckled face once more as she walked past him toward the elevators to the basement. He thought to say something else smart but decided against it. It took nearly two years before he was able to get more than a simple hello out of her. She wasn't the finest woman in the building, but she was one of the few he wanted and hadn't fucked yet. He'd cheated himself out of two wives since he started working there. He found that most of the stuck-up executive women he worked with were freaks on the down-low. His basement office had doubled as a mini motel many times.

Since TechRealm occupied a relatively small office building in downtown Berkeley, they needed only a three-person janitorial staff; one for each floor. Kenji, being the owner of Klean-Sweep Janitorial Services, always worked the ground floor and basement. He usually worked days, working nights only when he knew Colleen was scheduled to come by. At night the building was a ghost town. The only living soul there was the silver-haired security guard named Archie who worked the graveyard shift.

∞

Colleen used her access code and entered the server room. She placed her laptop bag on the main console and logged into the mainframe. On top of the console were two monitors. One gave a view of the hallway outside the server room and the other a view of the security guard desk. Six other monitors displayed detailed information on the status of the humming servers.

"Wake up, children, Momma's here," she said to herself. She removed her jacket and hung it up next to her smock on the black metal coatrack in the corner. She put on her white smock and checked the wall-mounted thermostat. The server room was the normal sixty-seven degrees. She slipped out of her Via Spiga "Alvita" pumps and into her well-worn Minnetonka moccasins, which sat beneath the coatrack.

Shit! I must have left my coffee cup in my car, Colleen thought as she sat her forty-six-inch rump in her ergonomic black leather chair. *I should ask Kenji to get it for me.* She smiled at the thought. Even though she dared not admit it, she wanted to give in and get some of his exotic cock. She'd heard the rumors about how freaky and well-equipped he was. Her being the sister of the cofounder of TechRealm, Reginald—don't call me Reggie—Helton, meant she could ill afford to be added to the rumor mill. After she got her master's in Computer Science from San Francisco State University ten years ago, Reginald gave her a job as the head network administrator. Tonight was her weekly system checkup. For the next four hours, she'd be locked in with her "babies."

Colleen heard the click of her automatic coffee machine as it began brewing. Archie always made sure to set it up for her on the nights she was scheduled to come in. "Mmmmm, that smells good. Maybe I can get Archie to get my cup for me," she said as she drew the hazelnut aroma into her nostrils. Colleen glanced at the console and saw the intercom button labeled with Archie's name. Just as she was about to push it, she looked at the monitor and saw him walking away, putting on his cap. He was going to make his scheduled rounds.

Oh hell. He's gonna be gone for at least an hour. Her caffeine demons demanded to be fed. She looked at the phone and saw the word JANITOR labeled as the fifth button on the speed dial list. If she pushed it, it would first ring Kenji's basement office. If she got no answer there, it would automatically forward to his cell phone. *What's the worst that could happen? He would come down here and give me his "meatsicle" along with my coffee cup?* A sudden throb of her clit told her what she'd been denying for years: She wanted Kenji's multicultural dick.

∽

How the hell did they get sunflower seed shells get on top of the refrigerator? Kenji wondered as he wiped down the white Kenmore fridge in the employee lounge. Next to the sink he picked up a used Styrofoam cup that had lipstick stains on the rim. The lipstick was a similar color to that Colleen wore.

Colleen.

Just the thought of her a floor beneath him began the running of blood to his sleeping penis. Her sexy thickness flipped his switch. He didn't care much for the model-type woman. Kenji liked his women with a little "girth." Colleen certainly fit the criteria. At about 5'5" and one hundred sixty pounds, she was right in his sexual wheelhouse. As stiff as she always appeared to be, he *knew* she wasn't gettin' the "whammy" on a regular basis. *I'd do her even if she was on the rag,* he thought as he tossed the cup in the trash. His concrete-hard dick agreed.

∽

To take her mind off of raping Kenji, Colleen plugged her laptop into the console and began her automatic antivirus update of the network. The mere act of pushing her plug into the console networking jack hole made her moist. She felt her reddish brown nipples grow. *Maybe I should've screwed Jasper before I left home,* she thought as she let her hand fall in her lap. *On second thought, I need a long stroker.* After thirteen years of marriage, Jasper had become a sexual minute-man. A sigh escaped her as she rubbed her throbbing clit through her thin polyester Liz Claiborne pants.

After leaving the employee lounge, Kenji went to empty the trash cans in the visitors' area. He passed Archie's empty desk and absently rubbed the countertop to check for dust. He found none. He made sure his access badge was clipped to his retractable key ring before opening the bulletproof double doors that led to the visitors' area. He pushed his rolling cleaning cart through the doors and emptied the two chrome wastebaskets and relined them with trash bags before straightening the magazines on the low-slung coffee table.

On the table to the right of the access pad, he noticed a stainless-steel coffee cup. It had the TechRealm logo emblazoned on it along with the initials "C.B."

"This must be Colleen's," he said as he held the cup. Only the head honchos had their initials on their cups. The smooth feel of the cool stainless steel made him think of how soft and smooth Colleen's ass would feel in the palm of his hand. How soft and smooth her large tits would feel to his lips. Stiffness, once again, invaded his sperm-shooter.

I think I'll take Colleen her cup. I need to go downstairs anyway and refill my glass cleaner bottle. Kenji put the cup on his cart and headed toward the elevator.

After prying her hand out of her lap, Colleen battled to regain hold of her senses. Between her caffeine and sex cravings, she had a fight on her hands. *If I can't get any dick, I have to at least have some java,* she thought. As she stood up to search for a cup of some kind, she glanced at the security guard monitor and spotted Kenji. He held something in his hand.

Her coffee cup.

What the hell? she wondered. *How did he get my cup?* Before her wonder turned to panic, she retraced her footsteps in her mind. *That's right, I put it on the table by the entrance door so I could get my access badge out of my bag,* she recalled. A beep from her laptop informed her that the antivirus update to the system was completed successfully. That gave her about forty minutes of free time as the system diagnostics ran.

She bit her lip as she thought, *If I call and have him bring me my cup, I'm gonna end up giving him some.*

Colleen watched Kenji push his cart to the elevator and push the down arrow. *Oh shit! He's on his way down here!* A mix of fear, desire, and excitement filled Colleen. Her years of loyalty to Jasper were on the verge of being ruined. She knew she would let Kenji have her tonight. She *knew* it.

∽

In the elevator, Kenji lusted for Colleen in his mind. He rubbed his stonelike rod as he imagined rolling against her soft, spacious ass. "Down, boy," he said to his stiff member. *Mrs. Colleen ain't just another office slut. She'll mess around and tell her brother if I overstep my boundaries, and bye-bye, contract.* He exhaled loudly as the elevator doors parted. Forty-two steps to the right and twenty-one to the left and he was at his office door.

When Colleen saw Kenji appear and disappear as he left the hall camera's viewing angle on the way to his office, her nipples became rigid. *Why am I trippin'? That man's probably not even thinking about me,* Colleen thought as she filled a tiny paper cup full of water from the Alhambra water cooler. She'd nearly fooled herself into being in control until her phone rang.

"Hello?"

"Hey, Colleen. I found somethin' of yours."

"What are you talking about, man?" His voice added another log to her freak-fire. She sat back in her chair and twisted one of her red dreadlocks.

"If you're missin' a cup with your initials on it, I'll return it for the reward."

"What reward?

"The one written on the bottom of the cup. It says, 'If found, return to owner for a generous reward.' " Kenji sat on the corner of his desk grinning into the phone.

"I don't have time to play with you right now, Kenji. Just bring me my cup, please? 'Bye." After hanging up, she realized she'd just invited the fox into the chicken coop. *Okay. All I have to do is make sure to keep some furniture between us,* she thought as she pulled her compact mirror out of her bag and applied a fresh coat of plum lipstick.

Kenji listened to the dial tone for almost a full minute before he hung up. *Damn, this'll be the first time I'm totally alone with her.* He went into his small bathroom, pissed, and made sure he was presentable. *Don't mess this up.* He lifted her coffee cup off his cart and left.

∽

Colleen's eyes never left the monitor as she watched Kenji approach her door. The way his uniform fit his slim frame and the confidence in his walk made her kitty purr. He was her height, but she outweighed him by about twenty pounds. She wanted to lick his walnut shell–colored skin from top to bottom. He wore his unruly African-American/Spanish hair in a bushy ponytail.

"It took you long enough," Colleen said into the intercom as she buzzed him in.

"I'll take that as a thank-you." He held the cup out to her.

"You're welcome." She gave him a smile. When she took the cup, her hand touched his. The heat from his skin made her swallow hard and take a step back.

"You okay? It looks like you just got stung by a bee."

"I'm fine."

"Yes, you are."

"Do you ever give it a rest?"

"It's against my religion to rest." Kenji's eyes surveyed her body as though he had X-ray vision. He wasn't aware that he was at a full salute behind his zipper.

Is that his dick? Colleen wondered as she glanced down at the front of his pants. It looked more like he had a billy club in his pocket.

The silence between them was awkward. The hum of the servers could have easily been mistaken for the energy which flowed between Colleen and Kenji.

"Don't you have work to do?" Colleen could feel her panties

getting soggy. *Thank God the computer console is between us,* she thought.

"As a matter of fact I do. It's about time I gave you a good cleanin'." He walked slowly to the end of the console.

"Excuse me?" Colleen's hand knocked her coffee cup to the floor.

"Calm down, woman. Just relax." He continued to close in on her. The horseshoe shape of the console offered Colleen only one exit: past Kenji. When she bent over to pick up her cup, she found her face about a foot away from Kenji's bulge.

"What do you think you're doing?" She spoke directly to his crotch while in her crouch.

Well, it's now or never, Kenji thought. He'd already crossed the line by walking up on her the way he did. *I can always find another building to clean.* As she slowly got to her feet, he took another step toward her, backing her booty against the console. She had nowhere to go.

"Kenji . . . " That was all she could say before she found his tongue attempting to part her lips. She was amazed at how quickly she accepted it. His tongue seemed to do somersaults in her mouth. Colleen had a vise-like grip on the edge of the console as she sucked his tongue. When he pressed against her and she felt the hardness of his stick rub against her leg, she broke the kiss.

"What's wrong, Colleen?" Kenji continued to kiss and lick the side of her neck.

"You know . . . what's . . . wrong. You . . . Me . . . Us . . . This." She found a tiny bit of strength and pushed him off her.

"Can you honestly tell me you don't want this?" Kenji took her hand and placed it on the throbbing beast in his trousers. He took a glance at the monitors and saw Archie walking down the hall to the computer room.

"I'm married." She closed her eyes and squeezed his hard joint as she spoke those words. Kenji gyrated his hips and nibbled her ear as she held his meat. Mental snapshots of Jasper, the women gossiping in the break room, sucking Kenji's dick, and her son played behind her closed eyelids.

Kenji broke away from Colleen and pointed at the monitor. "You got company," he sighed. Colleen reluctantly let go of his manhood and sat in her chair.

"Evenin', folks," Archie said after opening the door. "Just checkin' to make sure everything's okay."

"Everything's fine. Kenji just bought me my coffee cup and was on his way out," she said as she got up and walked past him to the coffeepot.

"Yeah, I just have to finish the bathrooms down here then I'm done for the night."

"Glad you reminded me. Can I get a box of tissue from ya? My allergies are kickin' up somethin' fierce!"

Thank you, Lord, Colleen thought.

"You ready?" Archie asked the disappointed Kenji.

"Yeah, let's go."

After going back to his closet and giving Archie his tissue, Kenji decided to give Colleen one more go. *What the hell do I have to lose? If she's not on the phone with her brother right now, I'm damned lucky.*

∽

Oh no! I just know he's not coming back, Colleen thought as she watched Kenji walk toward her in the monitor. *Good thing he doesn't have the access code to this room.* That thought gave her a little comfort.

"Let's finish what we were doin', Colleen," Kenji said into the intercom.

"It *is* finished, Kenji. I'm sorry but we can't . . . it's not right." Her vagina had other thoughts, though. She was still hot as fish grease.

"All right," he said with his head against the door. "But if you change your mind, you can have this." He stood back and looked up at the camera over the door.

"What the hell is he doing?" Colleen said as she looked at the monitor. It only took seconds for her to understand.

"This is for you, baby," Kenji said to the camera as he unzipped his pants.

Oh no he's not! Colleen intensified her stare at the screen. Kenji's hard, massive light-brown dick hung out of his zipper.

Although she couldn't hear him, she read lips good enough to see him say, "Come get this." Colleen watched as he stroked his thing slowly from the bulbous head to the hairy base. *Damn! Even with his hand around it, there's at least another six inches sticking out.* It was fat and long just how she liked. Colleen pushed back in her chair and put her hand inside her pants. She found her throbbing clit and rubbed it gently as she watched Kenji's show.

She imagined being bent over in front of him as he slid in and out of her wetness. Colleen added a second finger inside her slit. Kenji jacked off faster. His eyes closed as he pictured lying between Colleen's warm, thick legs, digging her out. His balls were heavy with semen. He felt it demanding release as he added more friction to his dick . . . head.

Colleen put a finger in her mouth and sucked it like she desired to suck the penis on her monitor screen. Three fingers massaged the inside of her wet pussy at the same time. She longed to have one of her "toys" hidden in the shoe box in the back of her closet.

Kenji leaned back against the wall for support as he got ready to let his load flow. In his mind's eye, his dick was inside Colleen's twat trying to knock the walls down. The first drops of pre-cum let him know it was time to let loose.

Colleen split her legs as wide as she could. She felt the warm wave moving inside her, signaling climax was approaching. "Ummmmmm . . . fuck me, Kenjiiii!" she uttered at the screen as a violent orgasm shook her body.

"Ohhhhhhhhhhhhhhhhh shitttt gonnnna cummmm!" Kenji's knob stiffened up and got cherry-red right before it began pumping baby juice out in a thick spray. He lay back against the wall panting as the final drops of cum dripped out. It looked like someone had spit vanilla milk shake on the floor. He looked into the camera, grinned, and said, "I'll be back to clean that up in a minute" as he turned and left.

Colleen eased her hand out of her pants and staggered to her feet. She hadn't cum like that in months. She decided right then she would have to give sex with Kenji serious consideration. *Yes, he might just get this pussy one day, but not tonight . . .*

Mandatory Overtime

HORAS EXTRAS OBLIGATORIAS

❧❧❧

Keeb Knight

*S*he stood at the front of her desk poring over contracts. Engulfed in her work she never heard him come in. All she heard was the door to her office slam shut behind her. Before she could turn around he reached in front of her, grabbed both her wrists and held them at her sides. She tried to wriggle free of his grip.

"Stay still," he commanded. He ran his large dark hands along the lines of her stomach and chest. He pressed her body against his chest, cupping and kneading her breasts through her blazer. "Are you ready for me?" he whispered in her ear.

She recognized his voice. "Yes, I've been waiting a long time for this," she replied. Her body tingled all over. "Take me."

He ripped open her suit. The buttons took flight across the room and her unharnessed breasts were now his to seize. He pressed his cock firmly between the cleft of her bodacious buttocks. The only thing separating them was his trousers and her skirt.

"Ro—"

He quickly put his hand over her mouth. "Sssh. Don't say a

word, baby," he said in a hypnotic whisper. He released her and slowly turned her around so she could face him.

He was beautiful. She got lost in his mild brown eyes, throwing her arms around his chocolate neck and rewarding him with a kiss. She slipped her tongue between his soft full lips so they could devour each other's sweetness.

Still in their amorous embrace, he backed her up to the desk, pinning her against it with his lean muscular frame. His hands caressed her hips, then trailed their way back to her buttocks. Her fully rounded ass fit nicely in his large hands. He felt through her soft skirt that she wasn't wearing any panties. He picked her up, sat her on top of the desk, and forced her legs apart, exposing her glistening toffee-toned pussy.

"Take it, Rome! Don't make me wait any longer." She could see the emergence in his pants as he stood there holding her by the ankles, spreading her apart even wider. It was if his cock could smell what was waiting outside the wall of fabric. Like a wild snake trapped in an opaque sack it was waiting to strike the first thing it saw. She reached across her open legs, unbuckled his belt, unzipped his pants, and with both hands took hold of his lengthy beast. She couldn't believe her eyes. She pulled his thick-headed cobra to her dripping wet pussy and slowly slipped him in as she tilted her head back, enjoying the warm reception. She slapped his bare ass, coercing him to give her all of it. "Fuck me, Rome! Don't hold back! Fuck me until I scream."

With each pounding stroke her triple Ds swayed back and forth, moving in an elliptical motion. Sliding in and out with methodic thrusts, he pushed her submissive body further back on the desk to a point where both her head and breasts hung over the other side. From an upside-down view she could see two voyeuristic window washers outside her office with their pants down, each giving her a thumbs-up and a couple tugs at their cocks for good measure. This moment was too special for her to care who the fuck was watching.

He rolled her legs back until her knees touched the surface of the desk and were in line with her chest. With one long deep stroke he teased her with the fullness of his massive cock, stretching her, throbbing against her vaginal walls.

"Oh . . . oh . . . oh, fuck yes," she gasped deeply.

He was finally ready to give her what she craved. His dangling walnut-size balls and long stiff cock dripped her juices on her breasts as he straddled her torso. His erection swung like a pendulum looking to be centered. He cupped the back of her head in his hands and he pulled her forward. And like a skilled African hunter who has found his prey, he was ready to immerse his tool. Then he beckoned her.

"Is this what you wanted?" he said.

Yes, Rome! Fill my mouth with that fuckin' Zulu dick!

"Regina. Regina," he called out.

"Yes! Yes! I said give it to me, dammit!" she shouted out loud.

∽

Regina was slumped in her high-back executive chair awakening from her intoxicating daydream, facing the window with her mouth wide open and her fingers tucked in her moist pussy. Two smiling window washers wearing white coveralls were waving hello. One of them tugged at his crotch a few times just for good measure.

"Regina, you okay?" said Rome.

"Ye . . . yeah, I'm fine." She shook her head, quickly straightened her skirt and swiveled her chair around to see Rome standing there in confusion with a manila folder in his hand. "Is that the updated Navan contract I asked for?" she said as she regained focus.

"Yes, it is. They want to finalize the agreement by Monday."

"Perfect. Just leave it here on the desk and I'll look at it. Thank you."

"You sure you're okay, Regina?"

Somewhat embarrassed, she kept her head down, focusing only on the sales reports she had before her. "Everything's fine, Rome. You may leave now. Thanks, dear."

Rome placed the file on her desk, shook his head, smiled, and walked back out.

She looked up briefly as he walked out the door to gaze at his juicy behind. *Damn you, Rome!*

∽

It was Friday, 4:01 P.M. Regina Pechos, vice president of business development for Incite Media Group headquarters in Philadelphia, leaned back in her chair as she stared at her monitor, her mind wandering. She could see and hear every one of her employees with the customized hidden security cameras she had installed a year ago. But today the thirty-two-year-old, five-foot-seven, raven-haired, gray-eyed, chestnut-skinned, buxom, onion-assed VP focused on one prize employee. She'd been having the same daydream for the last ten months—since she hired her new fine-looking, dark-skinned, six-foot-four marketing manager, Rome Black. She admired his talents in marketing and the assets he brought to the company, particularly that phenom cock she'd heard so much about. Rome transferred from the Memphis division of Incite Media to Philadelphia because he heard about an opening there. His prowess was highly praised by Regina's colleague and friend since childhood, Chelita Blanco, director of marketing down in Memphis. Though she'd never seen it for herself, Regina often created her own image of how that cock would feel submerged in the depths of her greedy pussy.

Today was no different. As she watched him from her monitor she continued to pleasure herself. Her skirt was pulled back exposing her open thighs and cherry red lace thong, which she tugged to one side with one hand and in rapid motion flicked her clit with the middle finger of her free hand. But a quick masturbation was not enough on this day. The self-torment had to stop. She grabbed more than a handful of tissues from her side drawer, quickly dabbed herself dry, fixed her thong, and gathered her skirt. With her dry hand she reached for the desk phone and auto-dialed his extension.

Rome answered in his velvety bass voice. "Incite Media Group. Rome Black speaking."

She nearly melted at the rhythm of every word. *Damn!* "Rome, you know it's me. Why are you giving me the company greeting?"

"I—"

"Oh, never mind. What time are you leaving today?

"Five o'clock."

"I need you to stay after five today."

"How long do you need me to stay?"

"As long as it takes to get this project done. I'm sorry for the short notice, but I really need you to stay."

"What . . . is it that Myers project you need help with?"

She thought quickly. "Yes. I need to you to help me get this damn thing off my desk so I can get to more pressing projects."

"Uh . . . yeah, I can stay for a little while. I'll just have go to the gym a little later than usual," Rome replied with a curious expression on his face.

"Oh! You work out?" As if she couldn't tell by his buff-ass chest, broad-ass shoulders and his beefy-ass thighs burstin' through his goddamn tight-ass trousers.

"I do work out, but I also have a personal training gig down at the Eighteenth Street Gym."

"Don't we pay you enough here at Incite?

"You pay me well, but living up here in Philly is just a little more expensive than back when I was living in Memphis. And I only hold training sessions three nights a week."

After tonight you won't have the goddamn strength to walk let alone make it to the gym to hold any type of personal training session, she thought. "Do you have a scheduled appointment with a client tonight?"

"Yes."

"I think you better postpone going to the gym tonight— we're gonna keep you real busy."

We? He knew in the back of his brain that she wanted his black ass to stroke her pussycat, but what the fuck did she mean by *we?*

"Well, I expect see you in my office in about an hour. Wait about five minutes or so before you come in. I don't want everyone knowing about you staying late. They may think I'm picking favorites and that won't be any good for morale. You've been doing good work over the last few months and I'm highly impressed with your productivity. Just thought I would utilize you a little more today on this project."

"You got it, boss." He hung up with a shrewd smile on his face.

After hanging up she stood at the window with a devious look in her eyes and thought, *¡Sí, Papi! Mamasita is about to get her torch lit.*

She turned to the full-length mirror that hung on the wall near the window, rotating her body from left to right with extreme confidence. She noticed that the impressions of her hardened nipples were showing through the blazer of her gray Marni suit. She never wore a bra to support her voluptuous 38DDDs. She didn't give two shits in a rat's ass if they swirled and jiggled under her suit. She could proudly say her mamms were all natural. She believed that if her breasts were happy, then she was happy. Fuck the rest of the world.

∽

He only overheard Rome's side of the conversation, but he knew what it meant. "Hey, Rome?"

"What's up," he replied to the voice.

"You know she wants to fuck you, right," whispered Jake Tyson, senior sales manager, from over the wall that separated their cubicles.

"Huh," Rome replied with a fake surprised look on his face. He peered up and saw Jake grinning like a Cheshire cat. All Rome could see was his light-skinned round face with both his paws on either side supporting him on the wall.

"Yeah, man. Haven't you seen the way she's been eyeballin' you?"

"Uh . . . No, I haven't," he lied with a straight face. Rome knew from past experience that he was about to get into a fuckfest with his boss, but he didn't want to let on that he was hip to her game. In his last meeting with Chelita she recommended that he do anything Regina requested him to do if he wanted to advance in the company. She said all this while his head was buried in her pussy under a table in a dark corner of Nouveau Restaurant in downtown Memphis, where they had their last dinner meeting together. He almost didn't hear anything she said because the inside of her thighs nearly covered his ears as she pulled his head in tight so that his snakelike tongue could slither into the abyss of her vagina. He knew she wanted to leave her taste in his mouth before he left. And she did. She wrapped her legs around his head and rammed her cunt hard against his mouth as she went into a buck wild wave of ecstasy, squirting her love juice down his accommodating throat. "Yessss! Get all of it, Dyson," she decreed. And he complied. Slurping her pussy clean inside and out. Because of his pussy-eating skills she'd nicknamed him after the vacuum cleaner known for powerful suction and cleaning performance. If that's what it took to keep his pockets lined and his dick flexed, he was down.

Jake walked around to Rome's desk so he could talk to him quietly. He stooped next to him and whispered, "Come on, man. You can't tell me you haven't sensed something. Think about it. You've been here for over ten months and up to now how often have you seen her stay after five?"

Rome thought for a second. "I can't recall."

"Right. We're salaried employees, Rome. We don't get overtime in the sense of earning extra pay. We do a mandatory overtime when required." Jake looked him dead in the face. "Hey, man, I've been working here at the headquarters for three years. I used to be a cock diesel pretty boy like you when I started here. I got the same request you just got, but the only difference was that she asked me for a dick-down within six months of my being hired. I was engaged at the time, but since I got married I put on some beer-gut weight just so I wouldn't appeal to her anymore. My wife thinks I put on the weight as my way of showing moral support during her pregnancy."

"So did you say no?"

"Did I say no to what?" Jake asked with a puzzled look.

"Did you say no to her?" Rome tilted his head in the direction of Regina's office.

Jake brought his tone back down to a whisper, grabbed his cock through his pants, and grinned. "Damn skippy I tapped dat ass, bro. Yo. Let me tell you somethin'. That is Grade A *punani* up in dat office. Tap it right and it's job security for you, my brotha. She's like that fine-ass schoolteacher you dreamed about fuckin' when you were in high school. I'm sure you had a lust for at least one of your teachers back then."

As Jake babbled on, Rome's mind flashed back to Ms. Sandra Buttlan, his homeroom history teacher, when he was a senior back at Central High. The only difference was that he actually fucked her. She was thirty-ish and fine as all hell. His classmates nicknamed her Ms. Butt Land. Her nickname matched her bootylicious ass, which was onion to the tenth degree. One day she was showing a film about Egyptian pyramids and as she stood behind the projector just alongside his desk he remembered how he slid his hand up her two-sizes-too-small dress, right between her thick silky thighs. Turning only her head to look down at him, she noticed he was looking straight ahead at the film as though nothing was happening, and he continued to move his hand high enough to caress her dense pubic hair. She conformed by moving her legs further apart so his long fingers could get full access. Ten minutes into the film his fingers were soaked from her dripping pussy. He remembered like it was yesterday, assaulting her clit to a point where her juices poured down and off the sides of his elbow before the film ended. She did everything she could to try and stand there as though she hadn't been finger-fucked for the last twenty-five minutes with her knees almost buckling. After class was over she pulled him aside and told him that he'd have to stay for detention for his naughty deed. He was just glad he didn't get expelled.

"Rome, if you make it through this detention on your best behavior, then you and I will get along just fine," she said.

That day she actually fucked him six ways to Sunday. He was okay with fucking the finest teacher in Central High. He spent numerous detentions at her apartment down the street right up until graduation. They even dated for a while after he graduated.

"Rome, you listenin' to me, bro," said Jake.

"Yeah, man, I'm listening. I was just having a flashback. Sorry, man."

"That must've been a hellified flashback. I don't think you heard half of what I just said. Anyway, handle yo business."

∽

Regina watched and listened in on the conversation Jake was having with Rome. Everything Jake was saying was true. Rome's job was secure, regardless of what she desired. She couldn't deny that Rome's marketing talent was off the charts and with the growth they were seeing in the Philadelphia area in promotional advertising for real estate, alcoholic beverages, high-end apparel, and the city's tourism projects, it was going to be a banner year for Incite. But she usually got what she desired. And on this day she desired to devour Rome. Every delectable inch of him.

Her desk phone rang. "Good afternoon Incite Media Group this is Regina."

"*¿No han chingado todavía?*" the voice on the other end inquired.

Knowing who was on the other end, Regina smiled blushingly. "No, Chelita, I didn't fuck him yet. I'm waiting on you." She knew ahead of time that Chelita would be in town for a business meeting with a client today, so she'd invited her to come down as a tag-team partner. "Where are you?"

"I'm on the corner of sixteenth and JFK Boulevard. I just came out of my meeting. Hey! Did I tell you Rome's dick taste like Godiva chocolate?"

"Chelita, puleeze! Godiva? No dick taste that damn good."

"I'm tellin' you, *chica*. It's not that usual salty-ass-tastin' dick. I don't know what the fuck he puts in his system, but that muthafucka got sweet meat. Look. My taxi is here. I should be there in a few. Okay?"

"Okay."

∽

It was 4:45 P.M. Chelita entered the reception area of the fifteenth-floor office of Incite Media Group. The five-foot-six Latina vixen had straight fawn-colored hair down to her shoulders, flawless fair skin, huge brown eyes, and fine features that were dominated by her full temptestuous mouth. She was wrapped in a full-length black mink coat.

"Good evening, Ms. Blanco," greeted the receptionist. "You look absolutely stunning."

"Thanks, Roslyn," she replied with a wink as she headed in the direction of Regina's office.

Rome looked up and nearly fell out of his chair when he saw Chelita coming around the corner heading in his direction. Her coat was open, revealing what was underneath. She looked super fine in her black fuck-me mink coat and her little red fuck-me dress and black knee-high *Miu Miu* fuck-me boots.

She walked up to him as he sat there still in shock and placed the ball of her foot on his crotch, exposing her pouty eat-me coochie pie.

Caramel Flava

"Hi, Dyson. Good to see you again. Sure hope you haven't had a big lunch."

"Good to see you too, Lita. I had a light lunch. Why?"

"Well, this could be a long night at the office. We're gonna have a lot for you to chew on tonight." She tossed her Hermès fuck-me scarf over his face and strutted to Regina's office. "Bring that with you when you come in. We might need it," she called back.

~

Regina was clearing off her desk and discussing some business with Chelita before they prepared for their sexploit with Rome.

"Were you able to get the Rapture, Inc. deal today?" asked Regina.

"Not only did I get it. I zipped it back up when I was done. And when was the last time I didn't close a deal?"

"Umm . . . Last year when there was a woman who was the decision maker. We almost lost that five-year, hundred-thousand-dollar contract."

"That's not fair. Rome subbed in for me. You know I don't *do* women. Present company excluded, of course."

"Uh-huh," Regina said under her breath.

"Now that you have my Dyson, if sales numbers begin to drop down in Memphis, then you'll know why," said Chelita.

"You don't always need sex to make a deal, Chelita."

"Fuck if you don't! I damn sure can't play any goddamn golf. Speaking of sex. Can we call his fine ass in here now? I haven't seen my Dyson in almost a year and you stallin' with all this bullshit. He does know why he's coming in here, right?

"Well, if he didn't know before, then he damn sure knows after you gave him a peek at that vanilla pussy of yours."

"Oh. You saw that, huh. You should've seen the look on Rome's face when he saw me walk in."

"You ready?"

"The question is, are *you* ready? Miss Closet Freak."

"Oh, shut up," Regina said, rolling her eyes. She dialed Rome's extension, but he was already walking through her door. "I was just calling you. Come on in and close the door."

"This must be an important meeting for Chelita to fly all the way up here to help us out."

"Yes it is. Like I told you I need you to help us get this Myers project off my desk so we can get to more pressing projects." On top of her desk were three things. Her computer, the Myers project file, and Chelita sitting on the edge of the desk with her legs crossed and showing a lot of thigh. "Do you think you can handle it, Rome?"

"I can handle anything you dish out." He stared Regina dead in her gray eyes.

"Oh! He likes a challenge," said Regina holding his stare as she sat behind her desk fingering her pussy.

"That's my Dyson," chirped Chelita.

Rome walked over and removed the file from the desk, leaned over toward Regina, and reached for the center drawer. As he opened it the back of his hand brushed against her left breast. "Excuse me." He slipped the file in the half-open drawer and then closed it. Still leaning across the desk, his face was just inches from hers. "Done."

She took his hand, directing it inside her suit and onto her braless breast. "No. We're not done yet. I think you need to check if I'm okay."

He squeezed her breast and tweaked her erect nipple between his thumb and forefinger.

She closed her eyes as a warm sensation trickled throughout her body.

"It feels okay to me," he replied.

She guided his hand out from under her suit. "Well then, I guess we're done, but since we're finished so early with the Myers project you can probably help us with our other project."

"What project is that?"

Chelita walked up to him, unbuttoned his shirt, and undid his belt buckle. She reached in his underwear to grab ahold of his lengthy semihard dick. "Oooh! Feels like Precious gained some weight. Nice! I'm surprised you found underwear to even hold this monster."

Regina, now standing in front of Rome, waited for the unveiling.

Chelita slowly rolled his underwear and pants down to his ankles.

Regina couldn't believe what sprang forth. It was the biggest, longest, weightiest-looking dick she'd ever seen. She couldn't wait. Her dream was coming true. "That's what's been hangin' in your pants for the last ten months? You've been holding out on me, Rome."

She got up close to his face and grabbed his dick, slowly slipping it under her skirt, rubbing its bulbous head against her wet, thong-covered pussy. "I think we're going to have to show you a thing or two about not holding back." She removed her blazer, slipped out of her skirt, and peeled off her thong, revealing a huge pair of big brown-eyed titties and a cleanly shaven slit.

He thought he was gonna bust a nut just from getting an eye full of her Brickhouse Betty Bangin' Body. *Whoa!*

"From this day forward we don't hold things back from each other. We share. Right, Rome?"

"Yes, ma'am," he replied as he took off his shoes and stepped out of his pants.

"Let me help you take your first stab at sharing." She dropped to her knees and with her adept hands began jerking his cock. She licked the tip of his black-brown erection in a slow seductive manner, then hungrily licked along the length of it. Stopping only to suck on one of his nuts. His cock responded by expanding and hardening until it became a thick, veined monster. Then she began sucking and slurping the massive surface of his appendage.

"Mmm . . . Mmm . . . Mmm!" *His dick does taste chocolaty.* She quickened the pace, he began to buck, and his thighs trembled before he slowly fell to his knees.

He closed his eyes and threw his head back at the pleasurable intensity of her warm, wet mouth still enveloping his manhood. He now lay flat on his back. When he opened his eyes he looked up to see a white pussy heading toward his face. It had *Puta de la Reina* tattooed just above the slit.

"Say ahhh," said Chelita, who'd long awaited having her pussy detailed.

Regina also had Rome where she wanted him and drew as much of his dick down her throat as she could. She needed his dick to be nice and slick before she rode him. She wanted him to feel the depths of her throat, making him disappear until her lips met the base and connected with his skin.

His warm tongue worked on Chelita's clit for a while. He moved his hands behind her ass cheeks so he could force her pussy further down into his mouth. He ate her pussy like it was a juicy peach. He worked his tongue like a cock, thrusting in and out of her wet pussy. He teased her by blowing cool air on her wet skin, then went back in with his tongue and sucked on her clit until it became swollen.

Chelita gained strength when she was on the verge of climaxing. She pulled his head in tighter against her swollen lips. She was suffocating him. "Ooooh! Find my spot. Work that tongue, baby. Yes, yessss," she hissed. "Don't you fucking stop!" Her eyes rolled up into her head. "Oh, Dyson, I wish I could just stuff your entire fucking head up inside my pussy!" She tried with no success.

While he was occupied with a mouthful of Chelita's coochie pie, Regina was preparing to straddle him. Supporting herself on his smooth, buff chest and rock-solid abs, she got into position above his slick erection. Her wet pussy lips spread as they touched the head of his cock and slid down easily to its base.

Rome grimaced as she began to do figure eights with her pelvis and then bounced her apple-bottom ass up and down like a buck wild cowgirl riding an untamed horse.

"Damn! You feel so good! Oh, Gawd." Regina moaned at the wonderful sensation of Rome's enormous cock hitting her spot on every stroke.

Chelita pulled her legs back and opened them wider for Rome's long slithering tongue. She fell back and nestled her head between Regina's thirty-eights and began nibbling and sucking on one of her nipples until it became a long, stiff delicacy. Her legs quivered violently. "Oooh shit, yeah," Chelita screamed. She could feel the contractions deep inside her. Everything seemed to just throb with pleasure. Rome always brought her where she wanted to be. "I'm cumming, baby!" Regina pushed Chelita forward. Chelita grabbed Rome's head again, pressing him tight against her throbbing pussy, and let out a guttural moan as the flood of her juices spurted into his mouth. "Oh . . . yeah. You love mommy's milk, don't you, Dyson?"

"Um . . . Mmm," he grunted as he slurped her clean.

Rome rolled Chelita off his neck so he could focus on Regina, who was still grinding on his dick. He arched his back, gave one hard thrust, pushing deeper into her. She gasped. He sat up, had her lock her legs around his hips and in one full motion he stood up, switching into a gangsta-style, gun-drawn position. He carried her over to the window, pressing her shoulders against the glass and giving her a few more deep thrusts.

"Oh, Rome! I love the feel of your cock inside me," she whispered as she clawed into his back. He thrust faster, harder, deeper, cradling her ass in his hands, opening her wider, stroking her dripping wet pussy up and down his shaft. He then turned her to lie on top of the desk, firmly kneading her breasts and stroking her, over and over.

She couldn't take it any longer. She went into a frenzy. "Ah . . . Ah . . . Ahhh! I'm . . . cumming! Cum with me, Rome!" she shouted. Her pussy contracted, squeezing tight around him, sending her into a cry of ecstasy and an explosive orgasm that showered his throbbing cock.

Rome joined her in a long satisfying climax, pumping her pussy with every drop of his Zulu semen. "Oooh, yeaaaah," he moaned. Still inside her, sweaty and almost out of breath he collapsed and laid his head between her snuggle puppies. "Regina."

"Yes?"

"I would be glad to assist you with any more upcoming precious projects."

She smiled. "Oh, Rome, you're such a dedicated employee."

It Is What It Is

SEA LO QUE SEA

❧⨾❧

Petula Caesar

I've always valued a great personality, intelligence, and inner beauty in women. But as a very handsome man and a partner at a very successful law firm, I had access to what my brother calls "top shelf girls." So I dated them, and really didn't pay much attention to other types of women. I've always tried to remain modest about my "Brad Pitt good looks" (as one of my exes described me once) and my accomplishments, but honestly, I knew in my heart I deserved the "top shelf girls." I went to the gym regularly and kept myself well groomed. I was well dressed and interesting. Most important, I made sure I treated the ladies well no matter how serious or casual the involvement. I wasn't a bad guy. I was just very busy with my career and preferred that a woman's beauty be . . . easily accessible. I could get past a not-so-great personality if the woman had a frame that still managed to balance generous breasts, a flat abdomen, and a thin waistline, combined with alluring eyes, a pouting mouth, and a pretty face. I could muddle along for a good while without stimulating conversation or common interests. Or, to quote my wife Evangeline's words (the very words that bought us together in fact) *"Sea lo que sea,"* which roughly translated means "it is what it is."

The first time Eva and I were naked in bed I stared at her rounded, cocoa-colored abdomen and her breasts topped with fudge-colored nipples that were beginning to slope softly downward. I would watch her breasts sway, bounce, and swing while she rode my dick. I would imagine the wind moving the trees on Isla Verde Beach near her home in San Juan, Puerto Rico. I was surprised that she allowed me to look at her fully undressed the first time, but she did. Her body was sexily imperfect. Her face was pleasingly plain to me at first glance. She possessed two slightly sad, coffee-colored eyes, an ordinary nose, two pale pink full lips, and a smooth, spacious forehead. Her body was a collection of voluptuous, slightly oversized curves that easily led one into the next. When she smiled it was a haunted-looking, closed-mouth curving of her lips that faded quickly. Her hair was long and hung straight down to her generous hips, like a thick sheet of midnight silk or a heavy dark waterfall. But she was completely honest about all these things in her personal ad.

I started reading *El Diario* when I was transferred to my firm's headquarters in New York City. I was looking forward to starting a life far from the comfort of the familiar. Once I got settled I started checking out the personal ads. I wasn't really sure why. I hated to think of myself as the stereotypical white guy looking to have a sexual experience with a Latina now that I was in the Big Apple. There had been minorities of all kinds around me in college and in law school; they were nothing new to me. I quickly realized how prejudiced that sounded, and stopped trying to prove to myself that I wasn't racist. I didn't like struggling with political correctness when I contemplated my dealings with women. Having a conscience was inconvenient as hell sometimes.

I scoured each ad with my most discerning eye, scrutinizing every word and phrase, looking for any hint of dishonesty, deceit, or mental illness. Anything that sounded too good to be true was immediately dismissed, as was anything sounding too desperate, too freaky, too underage, or illegal. Evangeline's ad was the only one left at the end of this process. The headline for her ad was *"sea lo que sea."* In it she said she wanted a man who would have a "sexship" with her. Not a relationship . . . a sexship. She said she was looking to "create a sexual rapport with a man, but not necessarily any other kind." When describing herself she said she was "no great beauty" but "one wouldn't throw her out of bed." I was intrigued. There was something about the way she presented herself that had the ring of truth to it. She seemed at ease with herself . . . which I admired and even envied slightly. I sent her an email, she responded, and we agreed to meet at the Starbucks near my office. On the appointed day she was sitting near the window, peering out anxiously, obviously looking for someone.

"Excuse me," I asked as I approached the table. "You're Evangeline?"

"And you're William," she replied, motioning toward the empty seat at the table.

"Please sit down. Would you like a cup of coffee?"

She had a beautiful voice. It was very carefully modulated, and precise. It was soft like a caress. It had a rhythm to it that my dick seemed to be able to hear because it began dancing to it as soon as she spoke my name. I had never reacted to a woman's voice like that.

I shook my head in response to her as I sat, and began taking mental notes about her physical appearance. In spite of the sexy voice she was just what her ad said she was . . . an ordinary-looking woman. I released my disappointment with a sigh. Only in that brief moment did I acknowledge that I had some precon-ceived ideas about what my new Puerto Rican lady-friend would look like. Even though my mind's eye recorded all the things I didn't much care for, my dick still seemed interested. She pushed her long hair back from her face and said, "Let's get down to business. Why did you answer my ad?"

I hesitated for a moment. She answered her own question, saying, "It's the no-strings sex, right?"

"Yeah." I chuckled. "The whole idea of sex without emo-tional attachments seems nice on the surface. Not sure how well it really works, though."

"So why are you here?"

"I liked your 'it is what it is/it is as it is' headline, once I looked up the translation."

"Thank you." And she smiled her closed-mouth smile.

"You were pretty up-front about everything you had to offer and everything you wanted. I liked that, so I had to see if it was real."

"And what do you think?"

"I think you have the most beautiful speaking voice I've ever heard."

"Again I thank you."

"As for whether or not I think you're being honest, I'll have to see." We locked eyes and I felt as if we were about to do battle. "Why are you looking for a no-strings-attached thing, and not a 'serious relationship'?" I made quotation marks in the air with my fingers as I said "serious relationship."

She drained her coffee from her cup and sighed, closing her eyes for a moment. The air around us suddenly filled with ten-sion and sadness. It was as if she were prying herself open with a crowbar. She paused, trying to decide if she wanted to tell me why I was in Starbucks with her today.

She finally plunged forward. "I'm originally from San Juan, Puerto Rico. I came to the States to attend Columbia University. Once I finished my undergrad, I got my first real job, my first little apartment on my own. I invited my parents here to visit me for Christmas. I was always the one flying there to see them, and I wanted them to come see me for a change. I wanted them to see New York during the holidays. The tree in Rockefeller Center, the Rockettes at Radio City, the decorations everywhere. A complete tourist's Christmas in New York City. They agreed. I saved up money for months, even took a part-time job so I could pay for everything and make it just perfect. The plane had difficulty landing, it was icy . . ." She halted there. Her eyes pleaded with me not to make her say the rest. So I didn't. I could see the shadows of pain and grief lying on her face, completing the sentence for her.

She continued. "My family, my friends wanted to help, but I didn't want help. I wanted to mourn quietly by myself. But they were all around me, trying so hard to say the right thing, to do the right thing. Everyone around me saying, '*Pobre bebé. Que triste es.* So much tragedy in her life.' "

I figured that the Spanish she'd spoken probably meant "poor thing" or "poor baby."

Clearly becoming uncomfortable, she finished her story. "They asked me to come back to San Juan. I didn't. I stayed here, went to grad school. It's been hard sometimes. But I built myself a life on my own terms. And my sex life is built that way too. Anyway, I feel more comfortable with strangers now. I can tell them what I want about myself, or not tell them anything."

I took her right hand into mine impulsively. It was cold, even though she had just been holding a hot cup of coffee. The skin was smooth. I rubbed it between both my hands to warm it. I managed to pull an "I see" from my throat. Once her hand got warmer I released it, and I took her left hand into mine to warm it as well.

"Where do I fit into all of this?" I asked.

"I do allow myself one form of comfort and release . . . sex. It is my pain reliever of choice. But I am not promiscuous or inclined to seek out random encounters, so I want one regular partner. A man with a killer tongue and a dick that understands a pussy like it used to be one."

She had a way with words. I remembered in her ad she said she was a writer. She looked down at my hands.

"William," she said, "your hands are very sexy. Strong. Even though you're only touching my hands, I can feel your hands all over my body."

The way she said my name was driving me crazy. It was the only time her speech was accented, and it was sexier than any naked woman I'd ever seen. And her directness was causing my dick to ache and moan softly. I wondered if she could hear it crying out for her.

She removed her left hand from mine. Then she took my right hand in hers. Reaching underneath the table, she placed my hand between her legs. Though her hands had been cold, her pussy was hot. Her hair brushed my arm and grazed my hand as she reached for me. It was as soft as her voice. Goose pimples formed on the places her hair had touched. The smell of it wafted over to me . . . wildflowers. I could taste the sweet scent in my mouth. I looked deeply into her eyes and got lost in their sorrowful cloudiness. My dick got harder, and my breathing became slightly ragged.

Was I turned on by her words? Was I moved by her story? Her hair, her voice, her eyes . . . when had I ever cared about any of these things? Tits, asses, hips, legs . . . that's what I was into. Accessible beauty. Surface sexiness. Was I experiencing a sympathy erection? I tried to focus on her plain face, too round and too open. But I kept returning to her eyes. The momentary sadness had passed and I found myself gazing at the desire in the pools of cherry blackness. I became more aroused.

"You mean to tell me it's that hard to find a man to fuck you," I asked forcefully, trying to snap myself out of it. I wanted to see if bluntness would unnerve her.

She met it head-on. "A lot of the men I've met assume casual sex means I'm a slut. A lot of men still have that serious Madonna-whore complex. Good girl or bad girl, pick a side and stay on it. My sexuality isn't that simple by a long shot. They think I'm promiscuous, so they treat me disrespectfully. They seem to feel the absence of a 'relationship' "—now *her* fingers were making quotation marks in the air—"means an absence of courtesy and consideration. That's not what I had in mind."

My hand was still between her legs, somehow caught there. I pulled my chair closer to her. I extended my index finger and began slowly rubbing against what I estimated to be her clit. The way her hips shifted in her chair told me my aim was perfect.

"What did you have in mind, Evangeline?"

She opened her legs a bit. She pulled her chair closer. I added another finger to the first and continued to rub her clit. I could hear and feel it throbbing and pulsing.

"What I want is a man who'll respect and befriend me enough to make the verbal exchanges that are the preamble to sex comfortable. Then I want the shit fucked out of me." She reached for my dick, squeezed it, and ran her fingertips across the head. "Very nice," she said. My dick lunged forward like a race-horse heading for the final stretch.

"I want casual sex with the same level of respect and deference that occurs in more evolved relationships. How do you feel about that, William?"

"Evangeline, your hand's on my dick right now. How do you think I feel?"

She squeezed me again. I swear I think my dick called her name.

"I think you feel . . . just right," she said. She licked her lips. "I want to suck your dick right this minute. You're a very handsome, sexy man. Clearly smart. Definitely appealing. I've hit the personal ad jackpot. If this interview is over and if I've answered all your questions, could we go to my place now? It's not far from here."

"Now?" I repeated. My dick grew frantic at the thought that it might lose this opportunity.

She said, "Well, if you must go, you must, but . . ." She trailed off, continuing to rub my dick. "It seems a shame to waste this." And she tossed her hair back again.

Twenty-six minutes later I ripped open a condom, fresh from a shower we took together where I sucked her breasts while she cried out my name. Once in bed, I hovered over her fleshiness as I rolled the prophylactic onto myself. She was a wide expanse of uncharted territory. A new sexual frontier. I grabbed her caramel legs and hoisted them over my shoulders, and she locked her knees there. I slid my hard dick in her to the hilt, and felt like a king when she drew her breath sharply inward and bit her bottom lip. She was so fucking soft, like a thousand down pillows, and tighter than I'd known a woman could be. With her legs locked over me, she pushed her pussy against my dick, bearing down on it and looking up at me. She grabbed her own breasts as her eyes stared into mine. She flicked her tongue across the nipples, and then sucked them as I watched from above. I fucked her harder, pounding into her with stronger, deeper strokes as I watched her partake of her own chocolate brownness. The look on her face and the wet, mounting, tightening pressure around my dick almost made me come immediately, but I managed to focus and to fuck the shit out of her as she fucked the shit out of me. I liked her cool, independent, and self-possessed nature. I loved her acceptance of everything life was, and everything it wasn't. I loved *sea lo que sea*. I wanted to be her friend. But she didn't want a friendship . . . she wanted a sexship. So be it.

Once a week I went to her home. I usually brought food with me, but occasionally she would cook. I loved her cooking and marveled at the seasonings in her cabinet that were foreign to me. She always made a huge pitcher of sangria. I turned on the television, and she'd bring our food and drinks into the living room. She always served my plate, and asked about my day at the office. I'd tell her few stories about my meetings with my partners, or my day in court. Sometimes we'd get into heated philosophical debates about this or that. Those conversations were foreplay for the brain. (I never realized before Eva that the best fucks start in the mind.) I would ask how the writing was going, and she'd tell me about her latest assignments, her insane editors, or her impossible deadlines. Occasionally she'd let me read something she was working on.

Once we'd eaten and cleared up, we'd watch TV. After a while she'd turn off the television and go up to the bedroom. I would follow her. She had a wrought-iron candleholder on her dresser, and I would light the candles before I got in bed. We would lie together, marinating in each other's personal space.

Some nights we would bask in sweet, silent complicity. Some nights we'd laugh and joke and tickle each other. It was the only time I could get her to laugh out loud and smile with her mouth open. Eventually I would reach around to rub her swollen nipples, or kiss her neck. Sometimes I would wind my fingers around her hair with one hand, or I'd snuggle close enough to her so she could feel my hard dick against her backside. She'd sigh, turning to face me. We would kiss once. It was always a long kiss, a wet and passionate kiss that would go on for minutes. My tongue would enter her mouth as she sighed and let her tongue find its way into my mouth. We would kiss and breathe each other, inhaling and exhaling and giving and taking each other's mouths and lips until we were satisfied.

I would spend a good deal of time bringing her to an initial climax with my hands and mouth. Gently finding her clit with my thumb and forefinger, I would touch it ever so slightly, enjoying the arch of her back that was her response. I would dampen my forefinger and thumb with her juices, then bring my hand up to our faces, placing my thumb in my mouth and my forefinger in hers. We would taste her in unison. She'd lick my finger and begin to suck it, and my dick would rise up, jealously wanting to take my finger's place. After we had both eaten her essence from my fingertips, my head would find its way between her legs. Her pubic hair smelled like summer rain and was just as humidly moist. I tongue-kissed her fleshy insides until my thirst was quenched and her orgasm had flooded her pussy. I would then kiss her nipples with the utmost reverence. They would be slick with sweat by now, and I'd lap at the saltiness, thinking of drinking margaritas by a clear blue sea. She would grab my dick like she did that first day, stroking it, begging it to come inside her with low Spanish murmurings and with sensuously gyrating hips. By then she was more than ready to fuck me, and I was more than ready to fuck her.

She was the best I ever had. It was never the same with her, but always perfect. She had split sexual personalities. And I loved them all . . . had no favorites. I was always glad when each one showed up and always sorry when they left. Some nights she was porn star good. She'd put on these ridiculous five-inch heels and would stand over me on the bed, lowering herself down on me, playing with her titties, doing me like an adult movie superstar. Some nights she was standing-on-her-head-doing-a-split-in-midair good (yes, she could actually do that). Some nights she was freaky-scary S&M good. She took handcuffs and long silk scarves and feathers and tongue vibrators and warming gel out of her nightstand, and our imaginations would have us climaxing all night long. She was reliably and consistently satisfying, as open and honest at her ad. She knew what I liked, and always gave it to me. Her consistency was as sexy as her honesty.

She gave me excellent head exactly how I liked it . . . shamelessly and skillfully. She'd clench her hand around my cock and run her hand up and down, squeezing it as her mouth bobbed up and down on it. Not a nick even in the throes of our most heated sessions. And she never forgot to give my balls attention too. She would fuck me excellently from any position, at any time. I could wake her up from a sound slumber and get the shit fucked out of me. Even if we skipped the foreplay, she would still be ready. Missionary—she fucked the shit out of me. Doggy style, both kneeling and lying down—she fucked the shit out of me. She could make her ass clap too, and I had only seen that kind of action in strip clubs. Cowgirl and reverse cowgirl—she fucked the shit out of me. In a buck with her legs over my shoulders—she fucked the shit out of me. Pinned against the wall after returning from the bathroom, early in the morning with the sun just starting to rise and the candles going out, with me standing on the floor as half her body hung off the bed and she hung on for dear life—she fucked the shit out of me. With Prince screaming from the CD player or Luther crooning love tunes—she fucked the shit out of me. In dead silence in the dead of night in the dead of winter—she fucked the shit out of me. With it pouring down rain outside, with thunder and lightning crackling the sky—she fucked the shit out of me always. I kept up my end of the deal and fucked the shit out of her.

Slowly pieces of her began to cling to me. I took over the task of making sangria and got to be good at it. I began to pick up the occasional Spanish phrases she would utter when my dick was in her. I recited them to myself on the nights I masturbated alone in my bed, my brain clogged with sticky sexy thoughts of her. I became obsessed with her long dark hair, and loved to look at it and feel it falling down over and around me when she was on top. I learned to enjoy grabbing her wide hips as she offered her mind-blowing, wonderful pussy from behind, watching her head bury itself in the pillow, trying to hide from the intensity of my rock hardness in her sweet softness. I found a supermarket not far from her house that carried Goya products and tried to score a few brownie points by picking up things like adobo seasoning for her.

After several months of seeing each other, she started to occasionally ask me if she was fulfilling my Latina fantasy. She would jokingly apologize for not being intimately familiar with *West Side Story,* or for not having Jennifer Lopez's ass, or for not liking the Latin house music I had come to enjoy since moving to New York, or for hating Taco Bell. I would laugh warily at these jokes, hoping she was not serious. Sometimes she would laughingly referring to herself as my "*El Diario* ho." I always got angry and told her it wasn't funny. I didn't like her calling herself a ho. Since I showed our "sexship" respect, I felt she should too, and her words were hypocritical to me. In spite of those occasional bumps in the road, we hung on together for fifteen months. The sex continued to be amazing, and so did she.

And then late one night in bed after giving me one of her mind-blowing forty-five-minute blowjobs that left me dry as the desert she said, "William, how would you feel about me seeing other people?"

My state of post-ejaculatory bliss evaporated.

"Excuse me?"

"Well," she began as she sat up to lie back on the pillows propped up in the bed, "I went on a date with a guy before I met you, but it went badly, so I didn't see him anymore. I ran into him a couple of months ago, and we talked about that horrible date we had, and we've talked a little more since then, and . . ." Her voice trailed off. For the first time in fifteen months her voice was ugly to me.

I sat completely up.

"What's his name, Eva?" I asked, swallowing hard.

She hesitated a moment. "His name is Harold."

I paused, trying to figure out if she was just being coy. "His whole name, Eva," I said, biting off the words.

She paused, finally catching my meaning. "His name is Harold Manuel Ortíz."

"Ah," I said.

She frowned. "Does it really matter, William?"

"Is it because I'm . . . I'm . . . not . . ." I tried another way. "Is it because I'm white?"

She seemed to grow angry.

"Is what because you're white? *Sea lo que sea,* William. We have never gone out on a real date. I have never met your family though you've gone to visit them twice and they've come here once. I have never been to any of the functions at your job, nor have I met any of the friends you've made here. And I'm not angry, William. *Sea lo que sea.*"

I was speechless.

"You've kept me in a tiny corner of your life," she continued. "And I haven't complained. But if you had really wanted me, you would have made a bigger place for me. You're a smart man, a successful man. Hell, a gorgeous man. Master of the universe. You know how to get what you want out of life. Half the time life hands it to you and all you have to do is reach out for it! So I know you would have tried to get more from us if you really wanted more."

"It wasn't that I didn't want to, Evangeline. But I've just been . . . trying to figure out how to . . . and you're always acting like nothing between us can ever be serious because of how we got together. So I—"

She cut me off dismissively, waving her hand at me as if to shoo away a fly. She raised her voice to me for the first time since we'd met. "William, you have dated many women before me. 'Top shelf women,' your brother calls them, right? You mean to tell me you have no idea how to let a woman know you're serious about her? You didn't know how to let me know you wanted more than what we have now? Face it, because I already have. *Sea lo que sea.* I just want to try something a little different now. I want to be more than—than—someone's personal J-Ho."

Now I was enraged. She didn't get it. I really didn't know

how to be serious with a woman, a woman I respected and admired who had a huge impenetrable wall built around herself. Why would she automatically assume I did know?

I raised my voice to her for the first time since we'd met. "I'm so sick of this shit! Why can't you try 'something different' with me? The way we are now . . . you set this up! These are the terms you set! *Your* terms! Was I supposed to assume you wanted me to sweep you off your feet? And by the way, Evangeline, you aren't the easiest person to get to know. Since your parents died you've pretty much shut everyone out, so forgive me if I couldn't figure out how to get in, or if I was waiting for you to let me in. I'm not a lover boy with all the answers. You think because I've dated a lot of women that I automatically know how to handle every woman I meet. I'm not Prince Charming or a mind reader. I'm not some Mighty Whitey *americano* that goes around sweeping women off their feet with flowers and candy and shit. I'm not some smooth operator who knows what women want and can just make whatever he wants to happen happen. Why would you expect me to know what to do when you're different from every woman I've ever known?"

There was silence.

"Mighty Whitey," we both repeated. Then we cracked up laughing because we had spoken simultaneously.

I caught my breath first. "That was a good one, huh?"

She continued to chuckle. "It was. I think my way with words is rubbing off on you."

"Maybe so," I agreed.

There was silence.

"What do we do now?" she asked.

"Well, you're the one always saying it is what it is," I replied. "Maybe we finally need to find out exactly what this is."

I saw her face grow cloudy for a moment. She was still afraid, not quite ready to trust me.

"We'll take as long as you need," I added. "I'm not going anywhere."

She smiled one of her rare, openmouth smiles, and planted her lips around my dick. "Don't want to attach bad memories to the blow job experience," she explained as she began to suck my dick back to life.

Muchas gracias, I thought to myself, and rolled my eyes to the back of my head as the sensations shut them tight.

Saints and Sinners

SANTOS Y PECADORES

❧

Geneva King

ello. You've reached Sister Adele at The Center. Please leave your name, number, and a brief message. God bless." *Beep.* A familiar voice rang out.

"Morning, Adele. I was hoping to catch you before you left your room. I need a favor. Call me back."

Adele groaned. Frank's favors usually involved her mentoring some juvenile delinquent. Normally she wouldn't mind, but she had too much on her plate already. Her eyes fell on the Jesus portrait in the corner. From His perch, He looked more disapproving of her than usual.

"Fine, I'll call him," she muttered. "Maybe I can help him find another place."

She plopped on her bed and dialed Frank's number.

His secretary answered on the second ring. "Frank Meyer's office. How may I help you?"

"Hi, Carrie. It's Adele. Is the boss in?"

"Sure thing, Sis—I mean, Adele. I'll transfer you over."

Adele grinned into the phone. It had taken the perky receptionist a while to figure out how to address her. Adele still wasn't sure whether nuns inspired a sense of reverence or discomfort in the woman.

"Adele! How are ya?"

"Fine, Frank. I trust all is well with you?"

Her friend sighed dramatically on the other end of the line. "It is now that you called. I need a big favor from you. You see, I have——"

She cut him off before he could get too far. "About that. You know I'm always willing to help, but I don't have the time. Why don't you call Jennifer across town? I'm sure she'd be happy to work with the child."

"It's not a kid."

Adele was momentarily nonplussed. "But I thought you only dealt with juveniles."

"We've had some staff cuts, so I get more to do. Which is why I need your help." He sounded so tired, she felt herself melting.

"What did he do?" When there was no answer, she spoke again more sharply. "Frank?"

"Assault." He scrambled to explain before she could refuse. "The guy he assaulted hurt his sister. Beat her bad enough to put her in the hospital. That's why he's not in jail right now. The judge went really easy on him. Probation and community service."

Adele squeezed her eyes shut. "Dear Lord. Okay, okay, you win. What's he like?"

"His name is Miguel, he's twenty-two, from the old neigh-borhood. No father, lives with the mother and sister." Frank hes-itated. "He's got a rough exterior. I really think he can be helped . . . if he'll let anyone in."

"That's always the catch." She pursed her lips. "All right, when can I expect him? And how long will he be here?"

"The judge gave him a hundred hours. I'll bring him over first thing this morning."

"Sounds good. Take care of yourself, Frank."

"I'll try. 'Bye."

After hanging up, Adele locked her apartment door and headed down to The Center. Sure enough, things were swinging into high gear. The staff bustled in, ready to get to work. Various women dropped their children off at the daycare center.

"Morning, Sister," several called as she descended the steps.

Adele waved back, smiling at the children. She made a mental note to stop in after lunch. By then, the attendants usually needed a break from the little angels.

Adele got settled into her tiny office. She flicked on her computer, a gift from the local electronics shop. A few people had responded to her request for donations. She found an e-mail from her sister; she'd deal with that later. Right now, she had more important things to arrange.

Adele had been engrossed in her work for about an hour when a knock interrupted her. She looked up to find Frank standing in the door. A strange man stood behind him. Adele assumed he was Miguel. For reasons she couldn't fathom, he was still wearing his sunglasses inside the building.

"Frank, come in." Adele stood up, extending her hand to the stranger. "You must be Miguel."

Miguel nodded curtly, shaking her hand quickly. "What's up?"

Adele studied his face, searching for signs of his character. He didn't give her much to go on. She supposed he would be handsome, if he relaxed his mouth into a smile. Or at least less of a scowl. His brown skin contrasted sharply with the white tee and the diamond studs in his ears.

"There's no sun in here."

He shot a quick look at Frank. "What's she talking about?"

Frank pointed to the glasses. "Take 'em off. Adele likes to look into your soul." He chuckled as Adele swatted him playfully.

Miguel sighed, and then pulled the shades from his face. Adele was struck by the intensity in his gaze. So many emotions swam around, vying for attention: anger, fear, distrust, could that be lust? He did have gorgeous brown eyes. Adele wasn't one to wax poetic, but they looked like deep brown pools, pulling her deeper into their abyss.

"Adele?"

She realized that Frank was talking to her. "I'm sorry, what were you saying?" She resisted the urge to look back at Miguel; those eyes were hypnotic.

"He's all yours. I'll be in touch." He walked out of the office and clasped Miguel by the shoulder. "She's a good woman. She'll take good care of you."

You bet I will, Adele thought before immediately flushing with shame. *Lucky for me, my skin's darker than his.* She turned to her charge. "It's good to have you. Let me show you around."

Adele led Miguel out down the hall, suddenly very aware of her body movements. She realized that her hips were sashaying and her breasts bouncing more than normal. She wondered briefly if Miguel was watching her walk, but she shoved the thought guiltily from her mind.

"These are the offices." They left the narrow hall and entered the main space. "This is where most of the activity happens. It's still a work in progress. We've partitioned off the daycare, kitchen, and storage closet so we can renovate the rest. Mornings are usually pretty calm. At least 'til school lets out." She smiled at him. "Any preferences?"

Miguel shrugged. "Wherever."

She thought for a moment. "How's your Spanish? We could use a tutor."

"Don't speak it."

Adele's cheeks were starting to hurt from holding the smile. "Can you cook?"

"Nah."

"No."

He looked at her. "Why you surprised? My mom and sister did all the cooking."

"No, the word is no, not nah. By the way, helping verbs are your friends."

He stared at her. To Adele's surprise, a small smile spread across his face. "You sound like my mom. She used to teach English before we were born."

"You have dimples," Adele blurted out before she could stop herself. "I mean"—she pulled herself together—"she didn't go back to teaching?"

The smile disappeared as quickly as it had come. "No."

Adele waited. When no explanation came, she decided to pry. "What does she do now?"

"Some clerical work. When she can get it. Are you gonna show me what I'm gonna be doing? I don't really care what it is."

Adele made a mental note to find out a little more about his background. "Well, I have a lot of little jobs that need doing." She pointed at a window. "See the lawn? Not through that window you can't. But if you could, you'd see it needs to be cut. The windows need washing. Badly. All the supplies are in the utilities closet and the shed out back. Most of what I'll have for you now will be cleaning or repairwork. Can you handle that?"

He nodded. "Where can I put my bag?"

"I'll keep it in my office, if you like."

He hesitated, then handed it to her. "Oh, wait." He pulled out a small MP3 player and headphones. "See you later."

"Let me know if you need anything," she called to his retreating back. Unlike most guys his age, his pants actually rested where they were supposed to and he definitely had a little junk in the trunk. *Get a grip, woman. You have better things to do than ogle this guy's ass . . . I mean butt! Lord forgive me!*

Despite Adele's best intentions to keep her mind focused and pure, she found herself making excuses to go past the window or take walks outside to watch Miguel cut the grass. On her second peek, she noticed he had shed his tee in favor of the tank underneath.

"That boy must be nearly dehydrated. It's only right I bring him something to drink," she told her assistant, Kim.

"Mmm-hmm. I'll go take it out."

Adele grabbed her arm before she could hurry off. "He doesn't need some hot-blooded woman panting after him. Besides, you have stuff to do. I'll take it." Mindlessly, she adjusted her hair in the window.

Kim burst out laughing at her friend. "Okay, Sister. But I don't think it's me he needs to look out for." With a wink, she strode off to her office.

Five minutes later, Adele went outside carrying a pitcher of ice-cold water and a glass. "Miguel!" She yelled to be heard over the lawn mower.

He turned and waved to her. She lifted the water and motioned him over. As he got closer, she could see that his shirt was soaked through with sweat. The thin material clung to his chest. Suddenly, she felt a heat spread through her body, one that she couldn't attribute to the warmth of the sun. It started somewhere so deep inside, Adele was hard-pressed to put her finger on it.

"I brought you some water," she heard someone giggle. To her horror, she realized that she had uttered the words like a silly schoolgirl.

"Thank you, Sister."

"Adele. No one calls me Sister." She pointed to the tattoo on his arm. "What's that about?"

He shrugged. "That's past."

"You have nice muscles. You work out?"

"Yeah, sometimes." He gulped the water, then poured another glass. "That hit the spot. Thanks."

"You're welcome. There's more when you need it. I don't want you getting dehydrated."

He nodded and walked back to the mower. Adele grabbed the pitcher and went back inside. This time, she didn't even fight the urge to sashay back to the building. She never turned around, but something told her that his eyes were on her the whole way.

The rest of the day passed uneventfully. Adele finally pushed Miguel and his sculpted biceps from her mind long enough to get her work done. He poked his head in at four to collect his things, but she was too absorbed in her duties to do more than wave.

Adele finally made it to her apartment after nine that night. Her eyes were heavy, but the heat had made her sticky with sweat. There was no way she could go without a shower.

She relaxed under the warm water, feeling the tension seep from her muscles. She reached for her special supply of aromatherapy bath gel. She used it only on days like today, when she felt particularly drained. The tightness was good. It meant that she was getting things accomplished, things that would affect her community positively.

She pulled on her bath gloves and lathered up. First her neck, then shoulders and breasts. She shivered as the coarse nylon slid across her nipples. She hesitated before drawing them back over them, playing with them until they hardened. The heat had returned full-force, but this time she could identify the source of the intensity.

Adele hadn't masturbated in years. Ever since she had taken vows, she relied on sheer will and prayer to get her through the temptation. This time, she found her fingers sliding cautiously down her belly to the swatch of hair between her legs. The gloves proved to be too rough for her sensitive nub, so she tossed them aside.

"I don't even think I remember how to do this," she muttered.

The initial touch silenced her doubts and gave her the courage to press on. Her fingers worked her clit, rediscovering the joys she had long ago buried. She traced her lips lightly and made her way further back until she felt her fingers slip inside her pussy. She pressed one in carefully, and added a second more urgently, thrusting wildly.

When she was younger, she used to imagine she was with Willie Mansfield, the boy who lived across the street. He had been the sexiest guy in their graduating class. After high school, he had joined the service, she couldn't remember which branch. Too shy to talk to him back then, she'd contented herself with imagining his penis buried deep inside her, while he whispered sweet nothings in her ear.

Years later, she knew a lot more about sex and her thoughts weren't nearly so innocent. This time, it was Miguel's cock thrusting inside of her and his teeth grazing her nipples. His fingernails dug into her butt cheeks, the pain vying with the pleasure.

"Yes! Oh God, yes!" Adele cried into the water. She could feel the orgasm coming; it was so close. She moved quicker, trying to hurry it up. To her dismay, the more she tried to force it, the more the sensation slipped away. With it went her image of Miguel and his large muscles.

"Agh!" she yelled in frustration. "God da—" She broke off mid-shout. She had already broken one rule tonight. She didn't think God would be particularly forgiving about her taking His name in vain.

The next morning, Adele went downstairs earlier than usual. After the failed attempt in the shower, she spent a tormented night tossing in bed. When her alarm had gone off, she'd already been up and dressed.

It was too early for the staff to arrive, so Adele went outside to check the previous day's mail. She tripped over something on the doorstep and fell, scraping her elbows.

A pair of strong hands hauled her upright. "I am so sorry. I must have been asleep longer than I thought."

Adele rubbed her arms. She wasn't sure if she was more bothered by the fact that Miguel was sleeping in The Center's doorway or that he had seen her sprawled over the walkway. "What are you doing here?"

"I work here, remember?" He offered a little smile. "You sure you're okay?"

"I'm fine. And I'm waiting for a real answer." Her voice got steely. "Now."

He sighed and looked away. "I can't live at home anymore. The project doesn't let you live there if you have a criminal record. I had to leave so my mom and my sister wouldn't get kicked out."

Adele nodded. She wanted to reach out and touch him, comfort him in some way, but she knew he would just pull away. "That's a very noble thing you did."

He turned to face her. "How so? Now I'm just a homeless bum with a record."

"I remember this kid when I was younger who got out of prison and went back home. When they told him to leave, he refused and his whole family was kicked out. His grandmother, parents, siblings all forced out because he refused to leave and his mother wouldn't make him go." She stroked his arm gently. "You were being selfless."

"Well, now I have to find someplace to live and money to pay for it." He buried his face in his hands. "This sucks."

She plucked him. "Stop griping. We just need to figure out how to fix it."

He glanced at her incredulously. "You'd really help me? What do you care?"

"Yes. And because I do. Now come follow me before I change my mind. It's been a long night." She didn't bother mentioning that he was the cause of it.

She walked back upstairs, past her apartment to another door. "I live there and this is an empty apartment. A friend of mine used to live here, but she retired last year." She opened the door. "It's small, it hasn't been cleaned in ages, and the dust is lethal. But if you like it, it's yours. Until you get on your feet. It's got a kitchen and a bathroom." She stood aside. "See for yourself."

Miguel moved past her, taking in the apartment. "I can't take this. I have no way of paying you."

"I'm sure I'll find something for you to do." She winked at

him. "Why don't you spend the morning getting settled in? You can get cleaning supplies from downstairs."

"Look, I want you to know." Miguel fidgeted in the doorway. "I really appreciate you doing this. Thank you."

Adele gazed back into his eyes. The raw emotion she saw melted something inside her. "You're welcome," she said simply, before walking downstairs.

Adele didn't get a chance to check on Miguel until after closing. She took her shower, then knocked on his door.

He answered the door in boxers and a black tank shirt. "What's up?"

Don't look at the thighs, don't look at the thighs. "Did you eat dinner?"

He nodded. "My mom gave me some food. She sent over some dessert for me to give you." He pulled the door further open. "You want?"

"Sure, thanks." Adele felt like a teenager, instead of the thirty-seven-year-old woman she was.

"Sit down. You want something to drink?"

She sat on the old couch. "Water, please. You did a good job in here. I need to hire you to clean my place."

"It's the least I can do." He handed her a plate and her water. "I hope you like flan."

"Love it."

They settled into a comfortable silence. Adele was enjoying the baked custard until she caught Miguel watching her. He looked amused. "What?"

"Nothing. I'm just glad you're enjoying it." His full lips curved up in a smile.

"This is so good!" Adele waved her fork in the air. "I'm serious; your mother is a genius."

"I didn't think you'd enjoy it very much."

Adele stopped mid-bite. "Why not?"

He shrugged. "I don't know. Aren't nuns all about denying themselves?"

Adele thought guiltily about her shower escapade. "That's not what it's about. It's about improving life for everyone through God."

He regarded her solemnly. "Is that why you became a nun?"

Adele nodded. "More or less."

"But what about everything you have to give up?"

"Such as?"

He thought. "Nice things. Marriage. Children. You don't want any of that? I'm not prying, am I?"

"I don't mind. Okay, I have nice things. Not expensive things, but I think they're nice. I am married. To God. And my children are the people I help."

"And that's enough for you?" His eyes bored into hers. She suddenly felt naked in front of him. And not the way she would have liked to be.

"Yes." She raised her chin a notch, as if to emphasize her point. "No muss, no fuss. Although, I might have liked to have a child of my own. But that's water under the bridge now."

"You still could."

She laughed. "Miguel, I'm thirty-seven. It's too late for me. I'm too old for that."

"Thirty-seven ain't old. Shoot, all you need is a man and you're in business."

"Right. And where am I supposed to find one that I want to share my life and my child with?" she challenged.

"You're a pretty lady. There are plenty of men who'd want to get to know you." He spoke softly, looking into her eyes.

Adele looked back at him, then wished she hadn't. It was like looking into a mirror. His eyes were cloudy with lust. Every nerve in her body screamed at her to give in to his unspoken invitation. Adele was floored; until now, she'd thought the attraction was all in her head.

"I should go!" she blurted, mentally kicking herself for her juvenile reaction. "It's late. Thanks for the dessert."

"You're welcome." He stood up and stretched. Adele watched wordlessly, her brain greedily storing the image for later.

"I'll see myself out. Good night." She hurried to the door, but he followed her and pulled the door open.

"Good night, Adele." He looked at her with those eyes again.

It took all of Adele's willpower to walk back to her apartment. She didn't breathe until she got inside and bolted the door.

Uncomfortable with her reactions to Miguel, Adele spent the rest of the week avoiding him. Any conversations were held with plenty of people around. In an effort to get her mind right, she went to confession. She was too embarrassed to visit Father Matthew, so she went to a church in the next county.

By the weekend, Adele felt ready to pop. Since fervent prayers hadn't worked their usual magic, she was at a loss. *One more time. Then I'll quit. No more masturbation.* She removed the scowling Savior from the wall and placed Him carefully in her desk drawer.

A few years before, at her sister's bachelorette party, each guest got a bag of goodies. Adele had stashed the bag under her bed without another thought. But if she remembered correctly, one of the favors had been—

"Got it!" Adele held the vibrator up to the light. "If this

doesn't work . . ." she shook her head, hoping for the best and trying to forget she was a nun. What was it about that boy that made her want to throw sixteen years of devotion to God out the window?

Two AA batteries later, Adele was stretched out on her bed, panting. One hand grasped the headboard while Miguel's tongue lapped at her pussy. Having learned her lesson, Adele kept the toy vibrating on a low level even though she craved the stronger sensations. She drew it around her clit, enjoying the attention Miguel was paying to her. She pictured his muscular thighs and his snug boxers and increased the intensity. *Oral sex deserves reciprocation. I'll have to return the favor.*

She peeled her hand from the headboard and slid a finger over her tongue. Her mouth accepted his dick eagerly. She loved the taste of him; it was so . . . earthy, so manly. Her tongue raced over the damp flesh, trying to memorize the bumpy ridges and smooth skin.

The combination proved to be too much for her. She felt the blessed shivers start in her core and radiate outward. She tried to cover her mouth, but some moans escaped into the air. Sated, Adele tossed the toy aside and curled up on top of her sheets.

A knock sounded at the door. Miguel. She shot up, pulling her pajama top down and buttoning it up. "Just a moment."

She pulled on her pants and robe before opening the door a crack. "Is something wrong?"

He leaned against the door frame. "I heard some noises. For a minute, I thought it was . . . but you're a nun, so that's out. So I figured something was wrong."

He gazed at her with such concern, Adele was sure she was going straight to hell. "I, um, just had a bad dream. I'm sorry to have woken you."

"I wasn't sleeping." His voice had taken on a deeper, more guttural tone. "I couldn't sleep." His hand reached out and hesitantly stroked her cheek.

Something inside Adele broke. She grabbed his shirt and hauled him inside. His arms circled her waist, pulling her toward him. It had been a while since Adele had kissed anyone other than family and friends, but she found her rhythm quickly. She drew back slightly, drawing her tongue along his bottom lip. It used to drive men wild when she was younger, and she was pleased to see it had the same effect on Miguel.

"I shouldn't be doing this. Especially not with you." She tilted her head to the side to give him better access to her neck. "This is so wrong."

Miguel paused briefly. "We can stop if you want."

She pulled him back. "No."

Miguel unbuttoned her top, peeling it off of her body. He cradled her breasts in his hands, drawing his thumb across her nipples. "You are so sexy. I thought so the first time I saw you walk." He took one in his mouth, biting it gently.

Adele groaned. In another minute, her knees would be too weak to support her. "Bed," she croaked.

She lay on the bed and he loomed over her, exploring her body with his mouth. He ran his fingers over her stomach, coming dangerously close to her cunt. "Be right back."

She waited anxiously while he tinkered around in the kitchen. He came back a moment later with a glass, which he placed on the table. "The day you brought me water, all I could think about was running ice all over you." He took a piece from the cup and put words into action.

Adele shivered. The ice was so cold it nearly burned her skin. Neck, breasts, belly, thighs, nothing was spared.

The ice found her clit and she jumped from the shock. His mouth replaced it a moment later. He alternated the ice and his warm tongue until she was shouting and shaking from the orgasm.

He kissed her mouth. She could feel his cock pressing against her pussy, begging for entrance. "You ever done this before?"

"A long time ago." She glared and poked his shoulder. "Be gentle!"

He chuckled. "Don't worry. You're in good hands."

Miguel kissed her again. Adele deepened the kiss, getting lost in his mouth until she felt a sharp pain. "Stop."

Miguel stilled immediately. "It's okay, baby. I'll get it in and then it'll be all over."

She nodded, burying her head in his shoulder. Either Miguel was enormous or her vagina had generated a new hymen. The pain mounted, but he took it slowly, taking the cue from her reactions.

She snuck a look at his face. "You okay?"

"You feel so good." He kissed her neck. "I want to make you feel good." He smiled at her. "There. It's all in."

Adele lay beneath him, getting accustomed to his penis inside her. "Move a little."

He withdrew, but stopped when she winced. "No, keep going."

He started moving inside her, slowly at first. Adele could tell he was straining to stay in control of himself. "Thank you for your patience," she murmured.

He started thrusting faster. Somewhere along the way, the pain dulled. Adele realized she actually felt good. No orgasm loomed on the horizon, but the sensations were bearable.

Miguel pulled her legs around his waist, dipping deeper into her. His breath got more rugged and shallow. She reached around and gripped his back as he shuddered and shot his cum inside her.

It wasn't until they were drifting off to sleep that she realized neither of them had remembered to use a condom.

Adele was worried that everyone would know what she had done. Fortunately, Miguel's work kept them separated the entire day. If people knew, no one made any comments. However, Kim did say that she was smiling more than usual.

"Just blessed to be alive," Adele replied.

Adele didn't even bother trying to convince herself and God that she'd never do it again. She knew exactly where she planned to spend the night. As planned, midnight found her draped across her lover's body, taking his penis into her mouth.

"This thing gets bigger every time I see it."

He grinned, running his fingers through her hair. "See if you can take it a little deeper. There, that's it." He closed his eyes and settled back. "I'll try to warn you before I come."

Adele's jaw was starting to hurt. His penis filled her mouth, leaving little room to maneuver her tongue. Still, she could taste him and it was just as she had imagined. Luckily for him, she was in a good frame of mind. He didn't warn her until it was too late.

Their days settled into a routine, although the sex was anything but. She and Miguel explored her office, the kitchen, and even the daycare. After hours, The Center seemed like one big bed.

And while Adele knew that it would all come to an end, she wasn't prepared for the cessation of her period. Initially, she told herself it was just late, but after two weeks, she had to face the facts. A home test confirmed her worst suspicion. She was pregnant with Miguel's child.

Her choice was clear. She had to give up either her baby or her work. She couldn't have both. Adele walked aimlessly around The Center. The whole building held special memories. Every weekend, they fed the homeless. The daycare was up and thriving. Could she possibly leave everything behind? There was so much work to do. But how could she stay, knowing she'd be living a lie?

She heard footsteps behind her, but she didn't turn around. She could sense Miguel's presence a mile away. Miguel! She hadn't even thought about him yet. For the millionth time that day, Adele started to mentally kick herself for her stupidity.

"You never showed me this." He waved her toy in front of her face. "We could have some fun with it. It'd be a good way to celebrate my new job."

He bent to kiss her, but she pulled away. Tears threatened to fall at any moment, but she didn't want him to see her cry.

"Hey, what's wrong?" He walked around until they were face-to-face. "Adele, baby, talk to me."

The concern in his gaze touched her. In that moment, she knew what she had to do. Miguel needed a helping hand, not an ex-nun wife and baby. She took his face in her hands and kissed him as tenderly as she dared. "Nothing. I'm fine." She put on her best smile. "Now, come tell me about this new job."

Overhaul

REVISIÓN

❧❧❧

Sydney Molare

I'd seen the signs—new haircut, faint bruises on her neck . . . bite marks on her inner thigh. We'd been married thirteen years and I knew this woman like I knew my own self. I was an authority on what she liked, disliked and how she liked it served up to her. Fun-loving, sporting a sexy damn body with "hello, there!" tits and a "ride me" ass, she was a wild woman . . . or rather, she used to be. Lately, she'd been standoffish, prone to headaches and excuses, and that just wasn't like her. Sex had been major in our marriage. Now it's "I'm not feeling so good. I'll make it up to you some other time." I tried to ignore it but if I were a betting man, I'd put everything I had on this: My wife was having an affair.

Moonlight flooded the room. I stared at her lying next to me, golden sun-blushed skin, long hair curling around her pillow. She looked angelic sleeping there, head atop her hands. I ran a finger over her soft, honey flesh. She flinched slightly; moved away. Oh how I wished she'd open her eyes, turn into my hot body, make me believe she was mine and only mine. But she didn't. She rolled onto her stomach, head facing away from me, awake now. I knew if I touched her again I would feel clenched muscles unresponsive to my touch.

I threw back the covers, headed into the kitchen for a glass of Coke, just to think. I left the lights off. I'd memorized the layout of our house too well to need it. Grabbing a soda, I stepped onto the terrace, wanting to look into the starry night as I sorted out my thoughts.

Just as I popped the top, I heard a muffled, "Ahhhhhhhhhh . . ." My hand stilled as I searched for the origin of the sound. I was surprised to see the drapes open in the rear room of my neighbor, a mousy woman who skittered away whenever I spoke to her. She wore her hair in a tight bun, wore schoolmarm clothes, but she was a librarian so I guess it went with her image or something.

I heard the moan again, then the librarian popped into view . . . except I'd never seen her looking like this. Her hair cascaded around her shoulders, bullet breasts I didn't know she possessed were encased in some sheer fabric and a G-string barely covered the essentials. Damn, she was hot! Who knew?

A dark man followed behind her, grabbed her hair, pushed her against the wall, ripped the scrap of bra off her body. I grew apprehensive, not sure if I should dial 9-1-1 or just watch. The devilish side of me said *Watch* so I waited. I had second thoughts as the man lifted a short riding crop and began lashing it across her heavy breasts. Just as I'd convinced myself to call the police, she leaned back, held the reddening orbs out as he continued to lash them. My cock surged to life as she grabbed his head and sucked his tongue into her mouth, head rolling as they tongue dueled to the death. Damn!

The man ripped the panties from her hips, dropped his pajama bottoms to reveal a curved average-size dick. I felt precum forming as I watched him lift a leg, position himself, surge into her pussy. Our librarian surprised me further as she pistoned back on him, groped his ass, propelling him forward, giving as good as she got.

Precum leaked when the man suddenly pulled out, turned her around and rammed back into her. The man rode his mare, hands twisted into her long hair. She bucked her cowboy high, *tetas* bouncing in the air. The cherry nipples were distended at least two inches. I licked my lips, imagined suckling those berries.

I stroked myself then, pulled at my tight, wet head, as our librarian thrashed and contorted on the unknown man. I couldn't close my eyes, couldn't imagine any other image than the one in front of me. I stroked and watched as they rolled and pitched, his pelvis melded to her ass. Finally, he pulled out, shot his cum over her back.

My hand was slick with my juice. I wanted some loving. I started to keep stroking, get myself off, but no, this hard-on I had was too good for a hand job—especially when I had a wife.

My brick rod bounced as I walked back to the bedroom. She hadn't moved an inch. I pulled the shirt over my head, dropped my bottoms and slid into bed. She was snoring a little so I knew this was no act.

I skimmed knuckles over her sumptuous JLO ass before palming it. Lifted her hair and rained kisses across her back and neck. I glided lightly up and down her satin skin; was rewarded with a sigh. I ran my hot hands between her knees, rubbed them as they parted for me. I took my time running fingers into her bush . . . *gawddamn, she was already wet* . . . flicking across her clit.

A sharp intake of air.

Good.

My cock pulsed as I slid down her back, between her legs, dipped my head. My tongue already knew the route as it sliced between her lips and headed for her clit.

She moaned then.

My head rotated as I wrote the alphabet and the numbers one to one hundred in her pussy. Her wet lips grasped, clenched . . . snapped around my tongue. *That's it, talk to Daddy.* Her hands could no longer be still. They rubbed over and over my head, nudging, pushing, guiding me.

I lifted, slid her down the bed to my throbbing cock. I seated those lush hips on my thighs before I pushed into her, swerved and pistoned into *my* hot snatch. She hiccupped, pulled a pillow to her mouth and bit the fabric . . . but worked her ass like she knew who owned the pussy.

I was in heaven as my slick dick hit all the right spots. Her belly quivered, legs shook as I showed her pussy how much I loved it. I *am* The Man! Then . . . she threw her legs over my shoulder and clenched. Her pussy muscles groped, caressed, fisted my cock. *Got*damn! She was tight! My balls swelled, head mushroomed as she brought the thunder, lightning, hail, cannons and . . . milked my ass dry.

∽

The following day, it was business as usual. No mention of the great sex the night before and believe me, we hadn't had mind-stunning sex like that in a minute. It had gotten routine, stale, no real passion behind it. Just convenient.

Clad in a short, but tasteful, skirt that hugged her bountiful ass and nipped in her waist, she rinsed out her coffee cup, gave me a peck to the lips before grabbing her jacket and purse. I watched through the window as she stabbed a number in her phone and smiled as she spoke into it as she backed out of the drive. I had to wonder who she was calling this early and, more important, what was said to make her smile like that.

I stood there, mind heavy, watching the rain tapping against the panes. As our undercover sexpot librarian darted through the drizzle to her car—a dead ringer for the woman from *That '70s Show* today—I was determined to get *us* back on track.

∾

I cooked dinner and had a dozen red roses waiting when she arrived home.

"What's this about, Tonio?" she asked, flicking her long hair off her shoulders, eyes apprehensive.

I wanted to blurt out, "Your affair," but instead I just smiled and served her dinner. Besides, I had no proof and didn't plan to hunt for any. Like my *abuela* always said, "If you go looking for a booger, you're bound to find a fat one." Things would come to a head one way or the other.

I played some Santana, slow-danced her around the room, tried to show her what she meant to me as I grooved her to my groove. But soon, the smile she'd had earlier faded and she excused herself, said she'd had a long day, was feigning sleep as I lay next to her a few hours later. *Shit!*

∾

The gunning of a motor woke me. I walked to the living room, stared out, smiled as I saw the man from last night hopping off a Harley. My gut clutched, cock lurched as the memory flooded back. I hoped and prayed for a rerun.

My prayers were answered.

Librarian Lady walked into her back room wearing a black shiny getup that had those tits front-and-center, nipples free, ass cheeks hanging out and high-heeled boots. The man crawled on his hands and knees behind her. She held a leash fastened to a choker around his neck in her hands.

This ought to be interesting.

She said something to the man who nodded, head facing the floor. She slapped him then. *Oho!* I threw my fist over my mouth, stopping the chuckle about to escape as his head snapped back like a boomerang. Chick packed a wallop!

Ms. Librarian then sat on a stool, legs crossed. I watched her red lips bark something to the man. He began licking the tips of her boots. Her lips moved again. The man licked up the boots and to her knees. She parted her legs; revealed those shorts had no center. Her pinkness seared my brain; made my half-mast cock wake to high alert.

The man nibbled inside those skinny thighs as he drifted higher and higher. Our local librarian's head was thrown back, chest heaving as he reached the mother lode. Her head and neck twisted with abandon as he tongued the hell out of her. Face contorted, body writhing, I lip-read the "Oh God! Oh God!" she spoke to the ceiling.

Shit!

The man switched places, took charge as he pulled the librarian from the stool, shoved her to her knees, pushed his cock between her red lips. She opened wide, swallowed him whole. Her cheeks sucked in, face bounced against his pelvis in relish.

I don't remember pulling my cock out, stroking myself, hips pumping in the air, but I was. The man grabbed those long nipples, pushed her tits around his cock as he mouth-fucked her. Librarian cupped his balls and he went ballistic. His hands tangled in her hair as he slammed into her mouth again and again. I watched in amazement as she grabbed his ass, added her muscle to his momentum. In seconds, he pulled back and spurted white viscous fluid over her chest, which she rubbed into her skin.

∽

I was past horny. I was about to explode!

On anxious legs, I strode back to our bedroom. I shed my clothes, slid beneath the covers again. My hands roamed across María's belly as I nipped her shoulder, licked her earlobe, rubbed my rock-hard dick against her ass. I ran my hand into her panties, was feeling for her clit when she stopped me.

"I'm sore," she protested.

"That's all right," I assured her. I turned away, felt for the tube of K-Y jelly in the nightstand. I lubed my pole, then squirted more on my fingers. I rolled back, began sliding the slippery lubricant between her ass cheeks as I sucked her neck.

"We haven't done this in a minute," she reminded me.

Way too long. "I know. I'll be gentle," I said, mouth reclaiming the patch of skin I'd been sucking. I blew into her ear and she seemed to *ignite.* Her body moved against me, her ass ground against my hardness, hands reached behind, rubbed my head. I directed my cock into the high hole and pushed. She moaned as I slipped past her sphincter. Relaxed as I slid in further.

"Damn," she said before reaching into her nightstand, pulling out her mini-bullet.

Her Milky Way was tight as heck! My breath was labored as I held back, tried not to let my body take over, piston into her in my need. I stroked slowly, stretching an inch at a time as I fed my dick into her ass.

She inserted her bullet . . . and took me over the edge. *Aw shit!* I couldn't stop as the vibrations made me pump, hump, grind into her. She pushed back, hand reaching around grasping my ass cheek. I rode her chocolate highway in eighth gear.

Then . . . she put the bullet on my balls. I double-pumped as the vibration radiated through my sac. She put an arch in her back, made me sweat, slobber, speak in tongues, bite my tongue. I don't remember cumming. I just remember bliss flooding my body before my eyes rolled into my head.

∽

The following morning the conversation was a little livelier.

"What's gotten into you, Tonio?" she questioned as she sipped her coffee.

I'd slipped into the shower, massaged her fully before I bathed her down. "You mean us, don't you?"

"Okay. What's gotten into us?" A smile played at the edges of her mouth.

"Ain't nothing wrong with a husband loving his wife, now, is there?" I replied, leaning over to kiss her. She opened her mouth, gave me some tongue action. I flicked, glided, sucked and bit her tongue. I wanted her to understand that whatever she was looking for was already here.

She pulled back first. "If we keep this up, I'm gonna be late." Her chest heaved.

Not a bad idea. But instead I fixed her mussed hair and ran a finger down her cheek, locking eyes with her the entire time.

She stood there, mouth agape, as I turned to the refrigerator. I flexed my butt as I reached in for the orange juice. She was in the same spot when I turned back.

"What?" I teased.

I saw the questions in her eyes; refused to answer them.

She smiled again and shook her head. "Nothing. Nothing at all."
She picked up her purse and glanced back at me. "See you
tonight."

I walked over, pulled her into a hug and gave her another
tongue lashing before releasing her. She wobbled, reached for
the cabinet to balance herself. Said nothing more as she walked
on unsteady legs up the hall, head shaking the entire time.

I watched her as she entered her car and backed out. No
phone today. Good.

∽

I kept up the sex pace. Thanks to Librarian Lady and her man,
my dick surged to life whenever I heard a car next door. It was
like we were on our honeymoon again. I was happy when I
woke in the morning, satisfied when I closed my eyes. But Paradise doesn't last forever. My wife finally had "The Chat." I'd
expected it sooner than this but in any event, I was ready.

"Honey, we've had sex five times this week. We've got to
slow down. It's wearing me out," she complained.

Trying to love two ain't easy to do. But one thing I'd decided:
If one of *us* was gonna be missing out on the pussy, it wasn't
gonna be me.

"Aw, baby, you know I never could get enough of your good
loving," I smoozed, pulling her into my arms.

She tensed, held me at arm's length. "I enjoy you too. It's just
that . . . " Her eyes looked everywhere but at me. "I'm getting
worn out from . . . " *Sexing two men.* " . . . From us staying up so
late and everything," she finished lamely.

There were fatigue lines around her eyes and her mouth was
tight. Most likely, her other lover was sweating her and she'd had
to put him off, couldn't work him over since I'd been laying

down the pipe like I had a plumber's degree. She wasn't tired, she was worried.

I smiled slyly as I answered, "I'll try, but I can't promise anything. As a matter of fact, why don't you take the day off and let me *refresh* you?"

She grabbed her purse and ran out the door.

∽

She came home, arms heavy with folders. "I'll be up half the night trying to finish these," she said for clarification.

I wondered briefly why she couldn't complete them at the office but held my tongue. Sometimes work did follow you home. She'd said nothing when I'd done it so I stayed silent.

I missed her as she worked in the office. I watched television, tried not to think about sex, but that's all that was playing in my head—good sex with my wife. I finally went to bed around eleven while she sat there pecking at the computer, files all around her.

∽

The revving of an engine woke me again. I felt across the bed, realized my wife wasn't there. I heard footsteps and my heart clutched. I wanted to get up, see if our local librarian was putting on another show, but how to explain my forays into voyeurism to my wife?

I lay there as footsteps advanced into the kitchen. Heard the refrigerator door open and close . . . gulps of soda and light coughs afterward . . . the terrace curtain being slid aside . . . the door opening. I sat up then, wanting to stop her; wondering what was happening. Instead, I sat there frozen as a sweat broke out on my forehead.

After fifteen minutes, I couldn't take it anymore. I crept to the patio door. My wife stood on the terrace staring at the same room I'd been a front-row voyeur to. My eyes glanced at the room window. Ms. Librarian was being reamed out, the man straddling her back, his tongue hanging out.

I walked behind my wife; wrapped my arms around her waist. She leaned into me, whispered, "Have you ever seen anything so fucking delicious?" Her body began rocking, pelvis thrusting slightly. My cock picked up her vibe and reared his big-ass head. I licked and nibbled as she stared.

When Ms. Librarian buckled on a strap-on cock and stood behind the man, my wife lifted her skirt, spread her legs. I slid those panties down her golden legs, pulled her skirt over her ass.

She watched. I kissed those beauteous globes.

She moaned. I alternately sank my tongue into both of her holes.

She rolled. I sucked her clit, feasted on her honey loving.

She raked her nails across my head. I lifted, slung her over the railing, pulled her titties free.

She spread wide. I surged in, pumped for all I was worth.

We made the terrace quake in our passion. A chair tap-danced across the floor as I put my back into it. A potted flower splattered to the floor as she pumped back.

I fucked with everything I had. I yielded no quarter. Give me everything or give me nothing. I wanted her to know what she had, what she was working with.

A light was switched on. Still we fucked.

A surprised "What the hell?" was uttered. Still we fucked.

Ms. Librarian and her man now watched us, clapped, goaded us on. Still we fucked.

The *slap! slap! slap!* of our bodies made the neighbor's dog bark like crazy. Still we fucked.

We fucked, *fucked,* Fucked, FUCKED, *FUCKED* until we both howled to the moon in ecstasy. Made car alarms go off in response. Collapsed onto the chaise lounge still fused. Dreamed in each other's arms in the morning dew.

∽

That night, my wife walked into the house, strutted to the bedroom and returned half-naked. She said nothing as she melded her mouth to mine, cupped my balls before stroking my cock through my pants. I held my breath as her fingers slid my zipper down. My dick saluted. She stuck her tongue out, lightly flicked the tip, her eyes trapping my own.

"Your turn," she whispered.

I do believe we are back on track.

Sugar and Butter Poured over Muscle

AZÚCAR Y MANTEQUILLA
DERRAMADOS SOBRE UN MÚSCULO

❧⸺❧

Anne Elizabeth

Skin like caramel, sugar warmed with butter and poured over muscle. He was the most gorgeous man she had seen in ages, and she ached for him.

It had been a long time since she indulged her sweet tooth. She hungered in a way that made a craving for chocolate pale in response.

Unconsciously, her tongue licked over her lips. She pursed the perfect pout of her mouth together and pantomimed a kiss.

Okay, maybe it wasn't an accident he was staring back now. But she wanted him. Needed him. She had to have him.

Taking a long breath, she let her chest fill. Her breasts swelled under the hold of the tight blouse and shook with the release. Yes, she was depending on him watching now.

Running her tongue over the upper lip to encompass first one tip of the cupid bow, then the other, until she reached the edge, then swooped down over the thickness of her lower pout. She watched his eyes track her. Bite Me Strawberry was the color of the bright red lipstick she wore, and she wanted him to—bite her, that is.

Eyebrows lifted. Thick, dark and temptingly soft-looking male eyebrows arched high into his forehead as if reading her mind.

"Gorgeous," she sighed. Leaning forward, she let the button on her blouse strain. The material gapped to show the sheer lace bra beneath. Never in all of her days had she been so grateful she was wearing her push-up. The things Wonderbra did for her breasts was beyond tempting, it was downright damnable. Of course, she would not have it any other way.

"Excuse me, miss."

It was the porter. She did not let her eye contact with the muscular hunk waver.

"Miss. You are being paged."

"Am I? By who?" She was curious enough to give the porter her full attention. She broke her eye contact.

"Didn't say, miss."

"How do you know I am a miss?"

"No ring."

She smiled at him. "That's not always accurate."

"Should I say Mrs.?"

"No. Not married. Where do I answer this page?"

"Over there, miss. In the Airline Club. Across the way, through the door and first room on the right."

"You wouldn't be accompanying me?"

"No, miss."

Opening her Prada, she fished inside for a tip. A five and a twenty came out. She stuffed the twenty back in and gave the porter a five.

"Thank you, miss."

Nodding her head, she gathered her possessions. After finding her Hermès scarf on the ground, she shook it to rid the silk
of airport dust and stood.

Her man was gone. She felt her facial features pull into an
unattractive expression and forced herself to release it. She
sighed. "Figures."

Setting off in the direction bid, she wondered what the issue
was. Did work track her down, because she refused to turn on
her cell or bring a BlackBerry? Was it her family? Did the airline
have an issue? Questions rattled in her brain.

As she pushed through the last door, she could not help
freezing in her tracks. Nothing could have prepared her for this.
It was him. "You?"

"Yes." His voice was deep, melodic and rich. The image of
sugar warmed with butter came unbidden again and she licked
her lips.

He walked toward her and his stride was long, graceful.
The play of muscles was extraordinary and her mouth opened
slightly.

Hands pulled her purse from her, the travel bag, and her coat.
Her arms were suddenly empty save for the silk scarf which he
drew around her waist to pull her closer.

"How? Who?"

Lips turned up at the corners. "They like the military in
airports."

She looked at him blankly.

"I told them I'm with the military."

"Are you?"

"Yes. Do you doubt me? Do you doubt what I am capable of?"

"I don't know. It's just that I—"

"Don't know what I want?"

"Yes." She couldn't keep the quiver out of her voice. Every fiber of her body screamed for him to touch her, but her mind, now that it was faced with the moment, was a little scared.

"It didn't stop you earlier."

Her body wouldn't let her betray this need. She leaned toward him, wanting this gorgeous man, and she was getting closer to him by the second.

The next words bathed his chin. "Your—"

"Name is—"

"Isa." She could hear the quake in her voice. Damn, she hated that she sounded scared.

"Rafael." His tongue tripped over the syllables like a licking caressing. "You have skin like milk."

"Oh." Her mouth opened wider, and his descended.

All thought disappeared as his tongue touched hers. It teased, tickling the tip and tantalizing the length. Slowly he stroked her tongue until she moved beneath him.

Her mouth stroked, wanting to drink from his mouth as he did hers. The fingers, so carefully manicured hours earlier, dug into his shirt and pulled.

He made a sound and drew back from her.

Her eyes flew open, though she couldn't have told you when she closed them. The arched line of her eyebrows drew together and she knew she was making that face, the unhappy, stressed one she so desperately sought to eradicate.

A smile played over his lips. He leaned in and kissed between her eyebrows and the wrinkles faded into relaxation. "Yes, my red-haired beauty. I shall make everything better."

Sugar and butter, her mind mulled. *Skin so hot, like savory, creamy caramel.*

"Will you allow me?"

"Yes." The words left her mouth before she could stop them. But as his hands started unbuttoning her blouse, she wasn't sure she could stop.

Clothes seemed to strip away in a blink of an eye until she was standing there naked. Hands ran over her. Instead of making her feel bare, the caresses made her feel beautiful, sexy and desired.

As his hands grazed the inside of her thighs, she parted her legs wider and his fingers found her. She sighed as he rubbed her clit.

Lust pushed away the lull of the steady stroke as she pushed herself toward him. "My greedy redhead. Did you know there is a vine which bears grapes called Isabella? Do you need to be picked, my Isa, my beauty?"

"Yes." Her voice was a whisper. She wanted him. Yet somehow, she still felt disconnected.

"Open your eyes."

She did. Responding immediately to the command in his voice.

Teeth stretched his face in a long smile, like he was baring them. His fingers played over her gently. "Is this what you want?"

She nodded slowly.

"Liar." He squeezed her labia.

Her body quaked.

"You want something else."

"Yes."

"Louder."

"I want something else."

Her eyes looked down. She couldn't bring herself to say it. Her needs were not allowed in her world. It was too straitlaced, too staid. It was the reason she could not help flirting with the gorgeous Latino man in the airport, the one who held her now so intimately.

"You want me to master you."

Her eyes snapped to his. She knew if she had a mirror they would be large and very, very green. "Yes."

"Light or heavy pain."

"Light."

"But you want some now?" A hand was in her hair, rubbing and massaging her scalp.

"Yes."

He twined the length of hair around his hand and used it as a handle to place her head where he wanted it. His mouth was back. Rougher this time.

He ate at her, taking her mouth and claiming her skin. A hand tweaked her clit and she felt herself come. It was small, but joyful. If this was it, she promised herself, she would be happy, could be happy with just—

Without prep, she was turned. The front of her body grazed the wall and the shock sent her pleasure/pain receptors into "receive" mode.

The sound of a zipper, the crinkle of foil, prepared her this time, but him entering her from behind, stretching her wide, took her breath.

"Big. So big." She panted.

"Hmmm, you are tight, my milkmaid. Very tight."

This part of him felt as thick and muscled as the rest of him. She couldn't help it, she tensed.

He stopped, half in and half out of her. "Ease."

She was drawn from the wall. Fingers played over her breasts, stroking, pinching, teasing until she relaxed. Her uterus eased.

"You know me."

"I know pleasure. Never doubt a Navy man knows his way around a woman."

He surged and sank himself to the hilt.

She cried out and her body convulsed around him. The gush of liquid was huge as it bathed his cock.

A growl came from his mouth. He set his teeth against her skin and bit, leaving a ring to mark her. At the same time, he squeezed her nipples hard and she came. He released them, tenderly mended the ache. Then pinched again and held tight, and pumped hard and fast.

Her fingers dug into his thighs and he groaned. There was wet beneath her fingertips and he lifted her up and away from anything to grab.

Turning her, he placed her on the conference table, so she squatted on the table. He was still in her and he drew her tight, all folded up, against him.

The position bunched the muscles of her legs together. It was uncomfortable having her knees tucked into her chest and she squirmed against him. He was too big for her in this position and her body started to force him out.

He acquiesced and drew all the way out of her and laid her body out on the table with her butt in the air and legs dangling over the side. Drawing back his hand, he smacked her skin.

The first swipe was shocking. The second brought a smile to her lips. She sighed after the third and pushed up to meet him for the next ones.

Ease flowed through her body, making her heart beat faster and her pulse thud. The part of her brain that longed to let go finally released and she felt the tender touch of floating. It came sometimes, when she was being attended in such a way, but it had been so long. So long.

His cock brushed against her leg and the beat faltered.

She shivered. *Hot, so hot.*

He pulled her against him. The heat was too much, and she fought to pull away, but he thrust his cock into her.

She was wet. It made a sound, like the smack of a kiss or the swat of a behind.

He sighed. The pace he set was fast and steady.

Fingers played over her, rubbing, kneading, pinching, prodding, until the pleasure/pain line was so blurred every part of her flowed into him and his next movement.

She felt her climb, and it wasn't a mini climax building, but one of those multi-orgasmic, triple-tiered episodes that shimmered with aftershocks. "Permission to—"

"No." The word ground out, the sound gravel-hard and deeper then before.

She concentrated on her breath, trying to pull it back in, but like her body it was out of control. She panted like she was running a race and her body was so hot, so wet.

"Please." The word hung plaintive between them. She wouldn't beg, she couldn't, though her body cried its own tears for release. She was so wet. So wet.

Hands squeezed her breasts and yanked her from the table.

The rhythm was broken. She shook and shuddered in his hands.

He pulled out and she wanted to weep with the loss of him.

He turned her to face him. "Say my name."

"Rafael."

Fingers squeezed along her lower back. "Again."

"Raf-y."

"Yes." His mouth claimed hers. It branded her with the kind of kiss that would leave her red and swollen later.

Hands lifted her and she wrapped her legs around his waist. They stood in the room, nothing supporting them, and fucked. His cock stroked in and out, making little noises of joy as it came out.

He kissed her. Frantic laps of tongue and teeth.

Kissed and fucked, until it was unclear how many times she climaxed.

When he finally released her mouth and drew out of her cunt, she was shaking on legs too rubbery to stand. He picked her up and laid her on the table again.

She was covered in sweat and without his warmth, started to shiver.

He watched her for a minute, then went to his luggage. Rummaging inside, he finally drew out a T-shirt, clean white cotton. The smell of detergent and bleach welcomed her.

He rubbed it over her body, drying her, cleaning her.

She was silent, agreeable. Rolling, lifting, opening as he bid. When he completed the task, he moved it over himself and tossed it toward the luggage.

Her head lolled toward him and she stared at his navel. Her tongue snaked out to lick a line over his belly. Before she knew it she was on her hands and knees eating over his flesh like a starved woman. *Caramel.*

He lay down on the table, and she moved over him. "A feast. My own banquet." With hands, teeth and tongue, she tantalized and teased his flesh. It was so much better than she imagined. Sugar warmed by butter and poured over muscle. She bit him and he cried out.

She could taste blood and felt his hand in her hair. "Don't worry, Raf-y, I shall not bite anything too precious."

A chuckle, deep and throaty, came from him and she had to

venture to his neck to lick around it. His Adam's apple bobbed up and down as he swallowed to keep up with her strokes.

"Enough."

She conceded his command, but grabbed the discarded silk scarf instead. She secured his wrists together and stretched his arms over his head. Then she climbed back on top and licked a line down to his nipples. Scoring them with her teeth, she did not stop until they shone red.

He hissed when she kissed them. Oh, so tenderly, she tortured him with her lips. Until with a satisfied grin, she nibbled her way down to his cock. His movement beneath her gave her great direction.

"So close, so far," she whispered over his tumescent cock. It lifted toward her words, her caress, and she caught it, drawing it into her mouth. Her lips wrapped around the head. "Mmmmm."

Closing her eyes, she let herself enjoy the taste of him. The faint hints of condom had been cleaned away earlier by the T-shirt and what was left was him: skin and cock.

She sucked hard like it was a chunk of caramel. In her mind it was the best candy, ever.

He groaned.

She repositioned herself so he could watch her. Breathing in, she eased him further in, an inch at a time. His cock overfilled her mouth, but she kept drawing. Her tongue flat against his cock stroked a welcome as he eased down her throat, until she could swallow him whole. She held him there for a second, then withdrew from the place of honor.

His breathing was shallow. She could feel his pulse race as it thudded against her.

"Now." The demand was solemn and strong. His voice rough.

Her mouth descended. She drew him completely down her throat. Giving him no mercy as she set a fast and furious pace.

Silk-tied hands came down and sank into her hair, changing the rhythm to one that wouldn't drive him over so fast, but she had other plans, other things she wanted. Her fingers drifted down, finding the sweet spot between scrotum and anus. Pressure combined with the delicate manicured fingers played steadily, in cooperation with the beat and balance of tongue and mouth, until the rhythms spoke and he could do nothing other than answer.

"Isa!"

She lifted her head and he came in giant streaking streams of come. She started to lower her head, but he yanked her up even with him.

"I wanted to take you again."

"I know, Raf-y, but there are other things we could do."

He pulled her head down to his and kissed her. Long devouring strokes of tongue.

She pushed his hands above her hand. "These were supposed to stay up there. If only I had brought my cuffs."

"Brought mine, they are in there."

"Do we have time before the flight leaves?"

"Always."

"What else did you bring?"

"Leather strap, a few more toys."

"They must have gone nuts in security."

"Told them the truth. I'm in Special Operations."

She laughed.

"What?"

"I should have given the porter a twenty. This is the best page I've ever had."

He nipped at her nose. "Better be the only page you've ever had."

Red eyebrows raised and green eyes twinkled at him. "Really, Raf-y. I missed you terribly."

"Missed you too, darling Isa. Next time, we cannot go this long or I won't be able to make it as far as a table in an airline club's conference room."

She licked his chin. Her teeth grazed the skin and she licked it again.

"Yes?"

"Like sugar and butter, warmed by heat, and poured over muscle, the best caramel ever. Raf-y, you are eatable. I need more of you. Let's skip the plane, the getaway, the whole thing and stay here. You are addictive. I cannot have you only once."

Laughter filled the room as he drew her onto his lap. His hand rubbed her tush.

She wiggled into the caress. The ache pleasurable.

"Oh, I have much more planned for you this weekend, Isa, than you can imagine." He leaned down, his breath teased her lips. His tongue laved the line of her mouth and she opened to him. When he lifted from her, his breath played over her. "None of it can be done here." He rocked her against him and her breath shuddered. "I'm going to make you come so hard, your shouts will make the neighbors wonder."

"Promise?"

"I am Latino, darling Isa. A Latino man, especially a Navy man, is always true to his word."

Tie Rack

ESTANTE DE CORBATAS

⤙⤚

SékouWrites

"How long is your dick?" Ms. Ramos asked in Spanish, her smirk teetering somewhere between devious and delighted, the index finger of her right hand pointed directly at her manager's crotch.

∞

The new Macy's store manager considered himself an expert in many things, including the seduction of women. After work, when his tie was loosened and he gathered his new coworkers around him at Dekk, a trendy SoHo bar where dim lights and strong drinks made everyone look gorgeous, he would brag that all it took was a compliment (the right compliment) to add yet another notch to his belt.

This was partly true. By use of compliments—but also by use of hungry smiles, cheap champagne, a voracious appetite for administering skillful oral sex and an uncanny knack for exploiting the biggest fear of pretty women (ending up alone)—he had found himself slipping and sliding within the moistened walls of many pairs of lips.

"That's sick, man." This comment was from one of the younger brothers in his newly created circle of men during their latest Dekk gathering. The young man wore his hair in a tightly tamped Afro and always found a way to keep his elaborate belt buckles visible, no matter how many layers of clothes he had piled on top of them.

"Sick how?" the manager asked in response. Sick, he knew from a younger cousin, was one of the latest euphemisms for "cool" but there was something in his young coworker's voice that made him think that there might be a more negative connotation at play. He was about to press the issue when one of the other men whispered Ms. Ramos's name and all of them made the sharp sound of sucking air at the same time.

Over time, the manager had developed sexual preferences. When available, older Latinas were his poison of choice, for he had come to find them passionate, nurturing, deferential and sexually uninhibited. All of which made Ms. Ramos, who worked the men's tie section of Macy's, his most obvious quarry.

He'd called her into his office for an impromptu "performance evaluation" because he'd noticed that she was wearing widely spaced fishnets and black ankle-strap pumps; he wanted a much closer look at both. He felt certain that he was only a compliment or two away from getting his tongue wet with the warm juices just inside her panties but that was before he looked at her personnel profile. He had no idea, until she was seated across from him, her prodigious cleavage and sculpted calves tempting him mercilessly, that the Panamanian beauty had been to medical school, had been a practicing doctor before coming to work at Macy's.

"Now, how is it that we have a medical doctor working in our tie section, Ms. Ramos?" he'd asked, striving to sound loose and conversational, hoping his tone didn't betray his anxiety. He specialized in pretty but dumb or desperate women. Women of superior intellect or solid self-esteem never fell for his hollow compliments and thinly veiled efforts to remove their clothes. He was already correcting his posture, sitting up straighter, determined to make this look like the professional evaluation that it was never intended to be.

"There are different ways to heal besides medicine," she'd said after a pause, her voice dreamy and distant, as if she wasn't fully present in the conversation.

"Like what?" He didn't care what she meant, but felt that this was the appropriate next question for a manager probing an employee. She shrugged and he fought to maintain eye contact as her chest shifted.

"It depends on the ailment," she said. "Men, they tend to have the same one. All the same one."

"Which is?"

"You should know. You have it."

"Do I?"

When she just stared at him without offering any further explanation, he switched to Spanish and threw out a compliment (just in case), telling her that she was far too pretty to be a doctor. Her eyes had narrowed and a few moments later she'd asked him how long his dick was. Despite his attraction to her, he was taken aback by the question.

Leaning back in his chair, he reached down to cup the thick folds of wool bunching between his thighs with one hand and let his libido guide his response.

"What? This?" he asked.

"Sí. That."

"Come find out."

She was out of her chair and coming around his desk so quickly that he felt a rush of apprehension. She seemed to sense his discomfort and revel in it. Her left Via Spiga pump came off the floor and perched on his right leg, giving him a perfect view of the landscape underneath her short skirt: an expanse of fishnet-clad thighs made grayish by the combination of smooth, copper skin and black netting. And, further up, at the intersection of her legs there was a dim sparkle of ornate but obscured lingerie.

The stiletto bit deeply into his thigh but he didn't want to reduce his masculine stock by acknowledging the pain. She shifted, her curvy hips gliding back to settle on his desk, and brought her right shoe up to dig into his left thigh. He tried to merely glance at the tantalizing tapestry in front of his face and then resume eye contact, but he failed and ended up staring between her legs intently, as if by sheer force of focused attention he could get her lips to moisten themselves, find their way to his lap, open wide for his entry and ease up and down on top of him for the rest of the day.

She leaned forward, bending at the waist between her upraised legs, and he licked his lips, parting them in anticipation. When she drew close enough that he swore he could feel her eyelashes on his forehead, he expected to be kissed but she only touched him enough to untie his tie and yank it suddenly from the folds of his shirt collar. His fear spiked with the sudden motion but, even so, he felt his body reacting to her proximity, her touch and the specter of danger. When she let her manicured fingers slide from his shirt collar down the front of his shirt, over his belt and below his waist, he was already stiff and throbbing. He couldn't remember getting hard so easily.

Her fingers encircled him and he expected a handjob or a blowjob—something direct, quick and explosive that hinted at pent-up passion, limited time and the possibility of discovery. He was completely unprepared for what she did instead: liberating him from the folds of his slacks and boxers only to wrap his tie around him in tight circles, starting from the base and cocooning him up to the tip.

When she was finished, he was happy to note that there was more of the tie wrapped around him than not. She seemed happy about it too.

"It's very long," she said, sounding aroused, still speaking in Spanish. "Thick too."

She smiled at him with her mouth, below eyes that seemed hungry in a predatory kind of way, then lowered her legs and backed away, pulling on the extra length of tie as she went.

She'd wound the tie so tight that he had to follow or risk having his circulation cut off, so he shuffled after her awkwardly as she led him around to the front of his desk. With his pants gathered at his ankles and his mummified member poking into the air like a makeshift flagpole, he felt more than a little silly but when she moved the guest chair she'd previously been sitting in out of the way, he got excited.

She told him not to move and then she backed all the way up to the door of his office like she was about to get a running start. He spread his arms out for leverage—her body was voluptuous and he didn't want to run the risk of dropping her. Watching her, he saw her eyes narrow again.

"Too pretty to be a doctor, huh?" she asked in English.

"What?" he replied, genuinely perplexed. He had no idea what she was talking about. Then it came back to him and he re-alized that she might have taken his compliment as an insult. This thought was just taking form in his mind when she abruptly opened his office door and walked out, leaving it all the way open.

Coño, he thought, as he scrambled to hide his disheveled nakedness from the view of the coworkers walking past his office door. He scampered behind his desk, knocking file folders and papers to the floor as he streaked by, and ducked down to straighten himself up, all the while fearful that the people he could hear passing his office would come in to check on him.

After he finally got himself together enough to walk over and close the door, it took him the rest of the day to calm down, feeling frustrated and angry but somehow extremely aroused by the encounter.

∽

Since he made most of his decisions based on the potential for sex, the idea of managing the Macy's at Thirty-fourth Street had appealed to him immensely. The place was so massive that he could conceivably "book and bang" for most of a year without getting caught, slapped or fired—probably in that order. He envisioned the Thirty-fourth Street Macy's as a player's paradise and, from his first day there, he had made the most of his new home-court advantage.

Early on, he'd made a few predictable choices. There was the short sister with an enticing tangle of natural hair that begged to be pulled and an athletic body that rippled and flexed under anything she wore. She had a penchant for wearing miniskirts that showed off thickly chiseled thighs powerful enough to crush his hips into submission. She worked in the beauty products section and, by virtue of sampling the wares, smelled enticingly different each time he sucked her clit into his mouth and licked it until she folded herself into a corner of his bed, panting and spent. He liked to enter her then, while she was still dripping wet from his saliva.

Then there was the tall receptionist from the corporate offices upstairs who wore colorful glasses but otherwise seemed subdued. He'd run into her in the elevator when he was on his way out to a music industry party. He invited her to come with him just to be polite and was annoyed when she agreed. Once there, though, he'd seen that there was a devilishly lusty side of her personality by the way she rolled her hips against his and the things she whispered in his ear. They'd rubbed and bumped against each other all night, until they were drenched in sweat and needful longing.

In the taxi to her place, he'd slowly coaxed his hand under her skirt. She resisted at first and then surrendered, spreading her legs wide enough to welcome any part of him inside her. Her moisture was so abundant that it felt like he was dipping his hand into a cup of water. The feel of her wetness flowing onto his fingers and dribbling into his palm made him want to keep his hand inside her for hours. He slipped his middle finger past her sodden panties and let it get lost in her flood. She came three times before they got to her house.

He liked to imagine that it was the power of his job position and his natural good looks that ensured an evening would end with his hands cupping cheeks and his fingers pinching nipples. Inwardly, though, he knew it was his ability to find the dumb or desperate ones and apply the right amount of "man shortage" pressure that worked to his advantage.

Not that it mattered. He was addicted to the chase and conquest of women the way some people couldn't function without a morning cup of Starbucks. For each new woman conquered, he felt a little better about himself. He'd sex them for two or three weeks and then stop returning their phone calls as he searched for the next woman he could make insecure enough to let him into her bed.

❧

He'd first seen Ms. Ramos as he was walking through the men's clothing section on his way to lunch. He slowed when he saw a long line of men in the tie section and was about to come over, apologize for the delay and get another sales representative to help when he caught a glimpse of her. Suddenly he understood why the men were waiting.

She filled out the golden dress she was wearing with curves so forceful they looked capable of cutting through metal. The crystals rimming her shoes would have kept him ogling what he could see of the firm calves just beneath her hem, if he hadn't been distracted by the beauty of her face and the fact that her sautéed butter complexion melted into her blond tresses so seamlessly that her face seemed to be shrouded in a halo of light.

He certainly wouldn't be doing the men any favors by getting another salesperson to ring them up, so he left well enough alone—but found himself wondering if she was the type of woman that would let him come all over her chest.

When he came back from lunch an hour and half later, he was surprised to see that there was still a large number of men waiting on line for her help. When he got closer though, he saw none of the same faces from earlier. This was a brand-new crop of men vying for her sartorial attention.

He asked around and found out that she had been consistently outselling everyone else in the store since the day she started. Even the folks who worked expensive counters like jewelry couldn't understand how she was leaving them in the dust with tie sales. But she was.

He observed her closely for a few days and decided that the compliment that might work on her was that if she was his woman, all those other men would have to buy their ties elsewhere. He got distracted by easy conquests for a while, but the day he saw her wearing those fishnets and ankle-strap stilettos was the day he decided to make his move.

A lot of good it had done him, though. If anyone had seen him running around half-naked with his dick wrapped up like a goddamn Christmas present, he'd have been fired for sure. He decided to let things calm down for a while before he tried again.

∞

"So, all you're selling is ties, right?" He didn't mean to sound wounded and insecure. He intended for his words to come off as a stern warning that any unseemly sexual behavior would not be tolerated. Not that he should be the one to cast stones, but still. He knew he had miscalculated as soon as his words hit the air. Ms. Ramos' look was frigid and at least two of the men in her omnipresent line of customers snickered.

"I'm just saying. I don't want to have to fire anyone today." He tried to infuse this with some bravado but it only partially worked.

"Are you here to buy a tie?" she asked, her voice distant and sharp. He noticed that she spoke English without the slightest trace of an accent. He shook his head.

"Are you going to fire me for selling ties?" she pressed. Again, he shook his head. She was making plenty of money for Macy's so she was a commodity. If he let her go he'd have to answer for it.

"Then I better get back to it," she said, turning away. He looked around just enough to see that the faces of the men in her line were alight with smiles, which only intensified the sting of being dismissed.

"Just make sure that's all you're selling," he mumbled as he walked away, more for the men's ears than for hers. He could already see how it would play out if he angered her. She'd be smart enough to claim sexual harassment and his pleasure playground era at Thirty-fourth Street would be over.

For days, he tried to stop thinking about her, but he couldn't. Even revisiting the conquests he'd already made was not enough to sate him. Frightened to confront her on the floor in front of her endless posse of men and equally fearful of what might happen if he called her to his office again, he settled for the only option available to him. He swallowed what was left of his pride and got in line to buy a tie with his employee discount.

"Only one, dawg?" the guy in front of him said with a derisive laugh. "Must be your first time."

He tried to shake off the feeling of inadequacy instilled by the man's comment, but when he looked around he noticed that everyone else in the line had multiple ties in their hand. He knew the tie prices by heart and saw that all the men had a single sale tie in their hands, in addition to a range of higher caliber ties, from Kenneth Cole to Joseph Abboud.

He noticed other things too, like the fact that many of the men in line did not seem to be the tie-wearing type. Not at all. As he noticed the other men in line, they noticed him too. Invariably their eyes would fall to his single clearance-sale tie and smiles and whispers would follow.

He thought about getting a few more ties, just to be on par with everyone else, but he didn't want to lose his place in line and, even more, he didn't want to feel like the other men had forced him into it. So, he stood there and waited his turn.

Ms. Ramos acted like she didn't know him any more than she knew the other men. Actually, even less so, since she seemed to have regular customers she'd been bantering with before she got to him. She held his tie up with her thumb and forefinger, examining it the way a woman might look at an expended condom after a disappointing sexual encounter. He heard chuckles behind him. There were outright laughs when she told him to take the tie back and find another. His pride flared and he insisted that she ring up the tie in her hand.

"It's not the right tie for you," she countered, holding it up under his chin and letting it drape over the tie he already had on.

"It's the one I'm buying," he said, trying not to snarl. She acquiesced with a glare and tapped on the cash register. With his managerial discount the tie came to $5.47. He reached for his wallet but she stopped him.

"This, you don't deserve to pay for," she said in Spanish before making a show of pulling a twenty from just underneath the pink lace fringe framing her breasts and putting it into the till.

"I'll let the house keep the change," she said, speaking in English again, and then she reached past him for the next customer. "Next time, get a better tie," she said to his back as he walked away. Male laughter followed him all the way to the escalator.

Over a greasy lunch procured in the food court of the Manhattan Mall, he mulled it over. He couldn't fire her. He couldn't write her up because she didn't seem to be doing anything wrong. He couldn't very well complain about the fact that she'd paid more than double the price of a tie and given it to him.

What bothered him more than anything was that he couldn't get her out of his head. In the days since she'd mummified him, his mind had become hardwired for Ms. Ramos and the mystery of her ties. It was an itch that needed to be scratched.

He waited a whole agonizing week before he tried again. This time, he followed suit: one semi-cheap sale tie, and three expensive ties ranging from $75 to $90. He spent some time trying to choose ties that were complimentary too. When he got to the front of the line, she gave his ties an appraising look.

"Much better," she rumbled, more purr than voice. "What's your home address?" He rattled it off without thinking before wondering aloud why she'd asked.

"I'll deliver these at eight o'clock. Be home."

"Ms. Ramos," he said, feeling a rare opportunity to reassert control. "We don't do home delivery here."

"I believe in personal service. Are you going to fire me for that?" She smiled the predatory smile again and reminded him she'd be over at eight o'clock, sharp.

He pretended to be annoyed while he was still facing her in the store, but by the time the digital readout on his microwave's clock read 8:00, he was waiting with chilled champagne, fresh strawberries and an assortment of chocolates. The intercom buzzer barked at him before the clock's time shifted to 8:01 and he was impressed by her punctuality.

She barged past him as soon as he opened the door, hardly giving him time to notice the fact that her trench coat wasn't nearly cinched tight enough to hide the undulating ripples of her oiled skin as she stalked inside, the sound of her heels clicking firmly across his hardwood floors sending tickles of anticipation across his skin.

"You're not naked under there, are you?" he asked, trailing behind her slowly. He'd dressed nicely, as if they were going out even though he was certain they wouldn't be. He was seasoned

enough to know that an unkempt man and house were the easiest ways to botch a night of expected passion. She stopped
walking when she got to the middle of his living room, gave the
place a brief, assessing glance, then finally turned toward him.

"You might want to take that off," she said, putting a crisp
Macy's shopping bag down on his metal coffee table.

"Take what off?" he asked, already feeling the power of control snatched away from him. He didn't like the feeling, it made
him uncomfortable, but he was intrigued nonetheless.

"Everything," she said, untying the belt of her coat and letting gravity pull it open only to be stopped and held in place by
her ample breasts while the ornate jewelry dangling from her
belly button sparkled in the light of the candles he'd lit for the
occasion. He felt like he'd be a chump for giving in to her demand easily, so he fought back.

"You first," he said, making sure he didn't sound annoyed.

"We don't have a lot of time." It was not the response he
wanted but he immediately understood that his opportunity for
sexual gratification would dissipate if he didn't act fast. Reluctantly, he took his clothes off, keeping a fake smirk in place the
whole time and hoping she was impressed by his gym-toned
physique. He stopped at his silk boxers, expecting her to take
over from there, but she just jerked her chin toward him and said,
"Those too."

When he was completely naked, and felt completely idiotic
and vulnerable, she pointed to the middle of his blue leather love
seat and followed him over to it, picking up the Macy's bag as she
did. When she straddled him on the sofa her coat fell away to reveal that she was wearing nothing but black lace boy-shorts, her
belly button ornament, and two black pasties over her nipples.
And the heels, of course. Green reptile-skin stilettos.

She leaned close and he licked his lips, eager, excited, expecting her to dip some part of herself into his mouth. With his face nestled into her cleavage, the thick, spicy aroma of sandalwood and lust wafting into his nose, he closed his eyes, waiting.

Instead of the delicate wetness of a tongue, he felt . . . silk. On his chest, up to his neck, past his chin, over his open mouth, his nose and finally coming to rest over his eyes. She was blindfolding him, he realized, and she was using one of his brand-new ties to do it. He smiled to himself. No wonder brothers were lined up for blocks to buy ties from her. He could get used to this.

When he was securely blindfolded, all he could see were brief glimpses of black lace when he tilted his head backward and peeked out from beneath the tie. Every time he did, she would gently push his head back down, blinding him again, but he liked the game and sensed that she did too.

There were two floor lamps behind his love seat, one at either end, and he felt her using two more ties to bind his left wrist to one and his right wrist to the other. Even though she hadn't tied them very tightly, he felt simultaneously thrilled and dismayed by the fact that if he moved either arm, he would topple his lamps and probably break them, so he found a comfortable resting position and settled in to enjoy whatever came next. He was very aware of the fact that she had only one tie left.

She trailed the nails of one hand across his face, down the side of his neck and over his chest and she must have felt his body responding because she scooted back on his lap, allowing him room to harden. When he was ready, rock hard and throbbing, slowly, delicately she tie-cocooned him again. Taking her time, squeezing occasionally, until he felt pampered by the feeling of being completely swaddled in silk. He could feel that she was holding on to the tip of the tie again and he was both excited and disappointed in himself that he felt like doing whatever her bidding might be.

She wrapped one arm around the back of his neck, leaned close enough that he could feel the heat of her body washing over his chest and put her lips to his ear.

"You like to have control over women, don't you? To feel superior."

He tensed, resisting the idea, fearful of reprisal. "Look, Ms. Ramos," he began, the well-practiced lies, apologies and deceptions ready to pour off his tongue before she cut him off.

"It's *Doctor* Ramos right now. And it's okay, I already know. Right?"

He nodded and hoped that was the end of it.

"You know, it wasn't nice what you said about me being too pretty to be a doctor." Again, he hesitated but a swift jerk on the tightly cinched tie was all he needed to remind him that she was very much in control and that she could hurt him if she wanted to. He nodded slowly.

"I can be pretty and still be smart, you know?" He nodded again.

"Bueno," she said, switching to Spanish, "I'm glad we got that taken care of. Now, to matters of healing."

After that there was only silence and the feeling of her nails all over him. For a while he moaned and rocked his hips in anticipation of release, but soon, he found himself becoming calmer, as if she was putting him into a trance. Before long he became sleepy, and even though he tried hard to fight it, he found himself drifting off only to be awakened by her nails discovering another part of his body before he drifted off to sleep again. The pattern continued until he woke up and didn't feel anything at all. He waited for a bit, called out for her and waited some more.

It took him quite a bit of physical maneuvering to free himself and remove the tie-blindfold without wrecking his living room. Once free, he noticed that there was a handwritten note on his coffee table.

> Hold the tip of the tie with one hand. Pull it tight. Masturbate. Think of me. I promise you'll have the biggest orgasm of your life. Next time, buy more ties. I always deliver.

She was right. In his own hands, all over his brand-new tie, he came hard enough to introduce Dr. Ramos's name to the neighbors across the street. He was no stranger to masturbation, but with the memory of Dr. Ramos's touch still playing over his skin, the phantom feeling of her full hips warming his lap, the thrill of being bound with his own new ties all fresh in his mind, his self-pleasuring experience was more profound than any previous one. He let himself drift toward sleep right there on the couch with the candles he'd lit still glowing, feeling more satisfied than any of his conquests had ever left him.

It was a blessing and a curse because he knew he'd never achieve the same heightened climax again without her. Maybe he would eventually, but for a while he'd need her to help him along. So, in the interim, he'd be buying a lot more ties—right along with all the other "patients" waiting in her line at Macy's. A long queue of men, he realized, that she was slowly retraining to appreciate the beauty of an emotional sexual connection rather than endless empty moments of physical release. Dr. Ramos had all of them tied up helplessly, her ties both binding them to her by desire and trussing them up with the previously dormant need to be sexually responsible.

"Never been whipped without having sex before," he mumbled to his empty apartment with a laugh. "She got me all wrapped up." Then he rolled over and went to sleep, dreaming of Dr. Ramos and her next home delivery.

On the Temptation Tip
AL BORDE DE LA TENTACIÓN

∼⤜∽

Michelle De Leon

So what do you think?" Irys asked as she drummed her fingers on the desk. "I mean, you're moving back here anyway in a few months. You can make a special trip to celebrate my engagement, can't you?"

"Irys, you know I'll be there. It's your time and I'm happy for you. But this other thing concerns me." Ileana confessed.

"I know it sounds a little far-out, but it would ease my mind."

"What I don't understand is if you feel you have to resort to this shit, why are you even marrying him?"

Irys considered her friend's question. Quentin claimed he was a reformed player and she believed him. At least she hadn't ever caught him cheating on her and was reasonably sure he hadn't. However, almost certain wasn't good enough if she was going to marry the man. "Ileana, you know no man alive has been able to resist you. If you come on to him and he passes, then I know he is indeed the man for me. If he responds, then I know to send his ass packing."

"You're crazy, you know that, don't you? I knew I shouldn't have left you behind in New York City; you're corrupted now." Ileana laughed. "All right, I'll put homeboy to the test for you. I just hope you know what you're doing."

"I know exactly what I'm doing. Thanks, girl. So you're sick of Sin City, huh?"

"Hey, Vegas is cool, but I've been offered a better position with the company if I move back to the Rotten Apple. Besides, a lot of the men out here have gambling problems." Ileana laughed again.

Irys looked across her desk to the full-length mirror on the other side of her bed. She knew she was attractive in an unconventional sort of way. She'd turned plenty heads. Ileana on the other hand was the ninth wonder of the world. Her girl was Dominican with dark exotic features. She had a small waist with curves to die for, but Ileana's ass made men do her bidding and wonder what happened later. Irys was not jealous of her girlfriend. They'd grown up in the same Washington Heights neighborhood and knew each other since elementary school. Even then, Ileana drew a lot of attention. She was a beautiful child and seemed to skip over that awkward stage most teens went through. Irys' own father had made a pass for her after his divorce from her mother was final.

"How is your job going?" Ileana asked.

"I got a promotion myself last month. Work is where I met Quentin, as a matter of fact. He's in a different department, but we're still the talk of the office. There are quite a few women there who wish they had my man."

"At least he has sense enough not to shit where he eats," Ileana told her.

Irys took the phone from her ear so she could read the caller

ID screen on the hand set. "That's him calling now. Hold on, Ileana."

As she waited, Ileana still couldn't help thinking that her friend was borrowing trouble. She wasn't conceited about her looks at all, but Ileana knew that she had a strange effect on the opposite sex. Was it even fair to set this guy up? Then she thought that Irys was probably right. If he didn't take the bait, then he had to be the real thing. Irys clicked back over to her. "Go and talk to your fiancé. I'll go online and purchase a plane ticket. I'll get back to you with my flight information."

"Thank you, amiga. I can't wait to see you."

"I can't wait to see you either. Behave yourself."

Irys laughed herself then. "What kind of fun would that be?"

Quentin was waiting for Irys to come back on the line. He was thinking how fortunate he was to be marrying her. She was a great woman; all that he could ever want in a wife. She was pretty, intelligent and had a great sense of humor. He truly cared for her and felt ready to be married. He found being a player was getting tired. Quentin had sown more than his fair share of oats, wild and otherwise. It was just time to slow his roll.

"So is your friend going to make it to our party?"

"Yes, she's going to get a ticket online right now. I can't wait for you to meet her, Quent. She's like a sister to me."

"Then I can't wait to meet her either. But right now I have more immediate needs," he said to her, turning the charm way up.

"And what are these needs?" Irys purred.

"I think you know. If you're going to be *my* wife you have to anticipate each and every need," he joked with her.

"And what about my needs? Can you anticipate what *I* need right now?"

"Oh, most definitely. If you were here you'd see how ready I am to meet that need."

"Well, bring it to me, then," Irys teased.

"I'll be right there."

Irys said, "I love you," but Quentin had already hung up.

◎

The party was in full swing. Coworkers, friends and family from both sides were there to celebrate the engagement of Irys and Quentin. Irys' younger brother had jumped at the chance to go and pick Ileana up from the airport while Irys attended to her other guests.

She slipped into the powder room to freshen up. Quentin came in right behind her before Irys had a chance to lock the door. "Enjoying the party?" she asked.

"Yes, I am, but I had to steal a moment alone with you. I'll be glad when all this fanfare is over and done with. I just want to get down to the business of being married to you, Irys."

She smiled at him with sincere love. He was deliciously good-looking with his bald head and neatly trimmed goatee. She asked him to wear his favorite Sean John suit; without a shirt. "I know, baby. I appreciate you going along with all the planning. You know, I just want the fairy-tale wedding."

"And you deserve it," Quentin said as he brushed a lock of dark brown hair from her forehead. She had large round eyes with long, luxurious lashes. He even thought the freckles on her face were precious. "You are one fine black woman. I'll find a way to get you whatever you want."

He pressed himself against her firm bottom and stroked her cleavage from behind.

"I'll think we'll be missed if we stay in here much longer, baby."

"I don't give a fuck."

"Well, a fuck is what you want and you know I hate quickies. I promise it'll be worth the wait."

He reluctantly pulled himself away and followed Irys back out to the living room. A small crowd had gathered over by the bar. Irys' brother was waving them over. "I guess Ileana is here, huh?" Irys asked rhetorically.

Irys grabbed Quentin's hand and walked quickly over to the crowd. She then let his hand go so she could embrace her friend. "I'm so glad you made it here safely. It's so good to see you. It's been too long."

Ileana hugged her back. "I know it has."

Quentin stepped closer to get a look at the woman he'd heard so much about. Ileana was indeed stunning. The most beautiful woman he'd ever laid eyes on. He suddenly recalled thinking the same thing the first time he'd met her. Ileana was not a woman whose face you'd forget even if you didn't remember her name. It had been a long time ago, but he'd been with Ileana.

Quentin waited for recognition to cross her face. "You must be the lucky man. Hello, I'm Ileana." She extended her hand to him.

"I've heard so much about you, I'm glad you could make it to the party," he said as he took her soft hand in his. Ileana's touch brought back the memory of how her body felt with him buried deep inside. Quentin couldn't believe she didn't know who he was. Then he realized she would hardly admit it at his engagement party.

"Come, get something to eat," Irys instructed her as she led her to the buffet table. Once they were out of earshot, she turned to Ileana. "So what do you think?"

"He is definitely one fine-ass man. I can't believe you never sent me a picture or anything."

"You know how scatterbrained I can get sometimes when I'm wrapped up in my love thang. I just hope you two don't get along too well," Irys said with a grin.

Ileana thought about just how well they had gotten along that one weekend years ago. She couldn't believe this was the same man. Back then he called himself Jontarius. Was that a fake name or was *Quentin*? Either way, this meant trouble for the three of them.

Sitting beside Irys on the couch, Ileana caught Quentin staring at her several times. He was even more handsome than he had been when they met at an after party Sean Combs had thrown. It was a wild time that lasted for two days. Ileana hadn't seen Jontarius/Quentin since then. His lovemaking was definitely memorable. He was the best she had. Ever. Ileana was not an easy woman to please in the bedroom. Most men tried too hard to impress her. Quentin was a natural. His strokes deep and hard. His tongue adventurous. His curiosity insatiable.

Irys' brother turned down the lights and the deejay threw on a slow jam. Quentin led his fiancée to the center of the room. They held each other as they swayed to the music. Near the end of the song, Irys whispered into his ear. "Why don't you ask Ileana to dance?"

Quentin couldn't think of a good reason to say no. And honestly he didn't want to. He walked over to her as she sat perched on the arm of the couch. "May I have the pleasure of this dance?"

Floetry's "Say Yes" began to play as Ileana took his hand. She wondered what he was going to say. "Are you treating my girl right?"

"I've never done anything to hurt her. I respect and care for her."

"Good. You should have a happy life together then." Ileana laid her head on his shoulder as they danced. Her bloodred tube dress clung to all the right curves.

"Where are you staying?" Quentin couldn't help asking.

"My mother has a place near the Cloisters. She's vacationing, so I'll just crash there until I head back to Nevada."

"Yeah, I've been there with Irys. Your mother's nearly as beautiful as you are."

"Thank you." She could tell he was waiting for her to say something. She wouldn't be the one to rock the boat. He subtly pulled her closer. Ileana could feel his reaction.

"I love this song."

"Yes, I can see that," she said, trying not to smile.

"Would you excuse me?"

"Certainly." Quentin expertly dodged Irys as he made his way to the bathroom. Ileana was ready to be out of there.

A few hours later, Irys asked for everyone's attention. "I just want to thank you all for coming and celebrating our upcoming marriage."

"Yes, thank you. And please join me in a toast to my bride-to-be," Quentin added.

All the guests raised their glasses. Ileana was glad the festivities had come to an end. Quentin wasn't the only one to have a reaction to their dance. She'd felt herself get wet and her nipples harden as he rubbed himself against her. It had been a while since she'd had satisfying sex. It was going to be a long night.

Irys pulled Ileana to the side. "Did he flirt or say anything while you were dancing?"

Ileana sighed. Did she really think her fiancé was that classless? "No, amiga. He didn't say anything inappropriate at all."

"I know you think the whole thing is silly. Thanks for humoring me." Irys hugged and kissed her. They circled the room with their arms linked as Ileana said her good nights. Irys' brother walked them downstairs as they hailed a cab for Ileana.

"See you tomorrow?" Irys asked as she held the door open for her friend.

"Yes, I want to hit the stores. Nothing like shopping in Manhattan."

"Get home safe. Call me in the morning."

⌘

Ileana tossed and turned as she tried to get some sleep in her mother's huge bed. The evening had gone nothing like she'd expected. She didn't want to do her girl dirty, but she had to admit that part of her wished Quentin would show up on her doorstep. She craved a good man. Then she realized that if he did come to her that would not make him a good man at all.

Just as she was about to drift off to sleep the doorbell rang. Ileana forced her eyes open and saw that the digital clock read three-thirty. She groped around for her robe to cover her nakedness. When she got to the door, Ileana was surprised to see Irys through the peephole.

"Are you okay? What are you doing here in the middle of the night?"

"I have a mystery to solve."

"Come on in. Talk at me; what's up?"

"The funny thing about all of this is I didn't have to develop a scheme to see how Quentin really felt. All it took was one look at you," Irys said.

Ileana didn't like the sound of what her friend was saying. "What does that mean?"

"Don't worry; I don't blame you. You didn't even let on to him that you knew him. I'm sure you remember, though. Quentin would be very hard to forget. For a lot of reasons."

Ileana didn't see the point of denying it. "When I met him a few years ago his name was different."

"Yeah, Jontarius. That's his first name, actually. He didn't think corporate America would dig it so he goes by his middle name. He said that he couldn't cheat himself or me by pretending that you didn't have an effect. He swore you never came on to him or vice versa, but he felt so drawn to you he wondered how he could call himself in love with me."

Ileana was shocked. "The wedding is off?"

"Looks like."

"Irys, baby, I'm so sorry." Ileana was a little concerned that her girl wasn't showing much emotion about the situation. "Can I get you anything?"

Ileana moved toward the kitchen, but Irys blocked her path. Before she realized it, Irys had covered her mouth with her own. An awkward kiss that felt strange to Ileana's lips.

"My so-called my man is leaving me because of you, my brother acts like an idiot over you and even my own father wanted to get with you. I just have to see for myself what is driving these men to distraction." Irys inched closer.

"I know you're upset; you have a right to be. You must be . . ."

"No, Ileana. I know exactly what I'm saying. I'm not even that upset about Quentin. Sure I wanted more than anything to be married to him, but something about it just didn't feel right even before tonight. I didn't really want to admit it to myself, but I don't believe he was ever in love."

Ileana felt uncomfortable as her friend stroked her face. She gently grabbed her hand. "How about I fix us a drink? Then again maybe alcohol is the last thing you need."

"I'm serious. I want to see what the mystique is."

"There is no mystique, stop playing. You can sleep in the spare room or we can sit up all night talking, but this other thing is not happening, okay?"

Ileana didn't want to completely spurn her friend, but she knew Irys' behavior stemmed from hurt and anger. It was not possible that she truly wanted to get it on with her. People often raved about her looks, but she always felt Irys was the beautiful one. Even still, she couldn't make love to her. Could she?

Irys could see wonder creep across Ileana's face. "You're considering it, aren't you?"

"Of course not. We wouldn't be able to look each other in the eye afterward. Have you ever been with a woman?"

Irys thought about if for a moment. "I did kiss this girl once in college, but it was a dare. This would be different. This would be testing the legend."

"You're getting sillier by the moment," Ileana said, then kissed her teeth.

"Are you afraid I'll get hooked, too?"

"What would doing it prove?"

"I'm not out to prove anything. I love you for who you are inside, but obviously there's more to the package. Listen, I know it's unorthodox, but right now I could care less. I just want to lie with someone I know loves me."

As hard as Ileana stared, she could see only certainty looking back at her. Irys was for real. Ileana did feel a little responsible for her predicament. She hadn't propositioned Quentin, but she had lusted after him. She wasn't sure what to make of his admission to Irys. If Ileana could ease her friend's pain . . .

She hesitantly sat down on the couch. Her robe came open, exposing one delicious breast. Irys knelt down at the couch. She traced Ileana's nipple with her forefinger. She was delighted that it hardened at her touch. Ileana parted her robe so that Irys could play with its twin. She pinched and tugged; gently enough so as not to cause pain, yet forcefully enough to cause pleasure. Irys boldly placed Ileana's left nipple between her teeth. Ileana threw her head back against the couch as Irys greedily took turns sucking and kissing each breast. Ileana was not surprised to feel the moisture between her legs. She wondered if Irys was getting wet as well.

She slid her hand beneath Irys' dress. Her girl was drenched. Irys moaned as Ileana moved the crotch of her silky panties to the side. She tickled and stroked her slick lips. Irys felt as if her clitoris was electrically charged. She scooted back, causing Ileana's hand to fall away.

"I can come and come again, but I don't want the first climax to happen this quickly."

Ileana nodded. She let Irys make the next move. She came closer and gave Ileana the softest, deepest kiss she ever experienced. She could vaguely taste strawberries and champagne on Irys' breath. Ileana seductively sucked on her friend's tongue. Her finger crept back between Irys' legs. She teased her opening with a finger, careful not to scratch her with a crimson nail. Ileana could hardly believe what they were doing; or how easy it was. Perhaps she was as starved for love as Irys.

Ileana felt a sudden curiosity to see Irys in all her glory. Ileana pulled the tie that held Irys' dress up at the back of her neck. The front fell forward revealing a silky strapless bra. Irys' chest was splattered with freckles and her breasts swelled attractively from her bra. Ileana planted tiny kisses on each mound. She moved downward and used her tongue to tickle Irys' navel. Irys squirmed as Ileana held tightly on to her hips. After what seemed like a thousand kisses, Ileana slid down the black Donna Karan until it was a heap on the floor. She had Irys lie on her stomach across the plush rug. Ileana nibbled at the back of her neck. She massaged her new lover's shoulders until Irys sighed with pleasure.

"I suppose it's not too late to stop," Ileana said in a questioning tone.

"Do you really want to stop, amiga?" Irys turned over to face Ileana.

"No, I don't. But . . . "

"You're talking too much. There are better uses for those lips."

Irys grabbed Ileana by her dark luxurious hair and brought her face down to hers. She kissed her with greater intensity than before. Ileana had to admit she enjoyed the roughness of their mouths meeting; the depth of Irys' tongue in her mouth. They groped and kissed every spot of each other's bodies. They paused when Ileana's mouth brushed against the wetness between Irys' thighs. She had never tasted another woman's essence. The scent was different from her own, naturally, but intoxicating. She brazenly traced Irys' outer lips with her tongue. Irys nearly cried out, but managed to control herself. She was totally enjoying the wicked feeling of their union.

Ileana swung her leg around and was careful not to bring all her weight down on Irys' stomach. Before she lost her nerve, she buried her face between her friend's legs. Sixty-nine was an old favorite and she hoped that Irys was also up to the challenge. Ileana need not have worried. Irys skillfully parted the way to Ileana's inner lips. In the dim light, she could see how swollen Ileana was with excitement. Irys wanted to be patient and take her time, but she began to suck on Ileana's button intensely. Ileana did not have the control not to cry out and did so very loudly. Irys was pleased with her girl's reaction. Then Ileana covered her entire sex with her mouth. Irys nearly bit Ileana but restrained herself before she could do any harm. Irys was completely smooth down below, but Ileana's silky hairs delightfully tickled her.

Ileana began to tease Irys again; darting her finger in and out. Irys gasped as the sensation of Ileana's finger and mouth working simultaneously nearly brought her over the edge. She decided to return the favor; however, Irys chose Ileana's other opening to torture. She wet her index finger before attempting to delve between the cheeks of Ileana's gorgeous ass. She tensed up at first, but Irys never stopped sucking her and Ileana felt like a ball of excited confusion.

Irys arched her back. She couldn't take it any longer. She was so grateful Ileana knew not to speed up, but to continue the slow motion that was bringing her to ecstasy in the first place.

Ileana was like a waterfall. She rode the wave of Irys' climax. As she delighted in her accomplishment, Ileana was not prepared for Irys' thumb as it entered. Her walls began to vibrate and she knew her release was near as well. She caught Irys' rhythm and moved her hips along with it. Moments later, she snatched Irys' dress to stifle her screams.

As they both came down from their high, Ileana hoped the

moment wouldn't be spoiled by regret. She slowly lifted herself off Irys. She turned around so she could face her. Ileana was relieved that her partner in crime was grinning from ear to ear.

"You are indeed magnificent," Irys said. She sat up and kissed Ileana. The taste of their juices came together in sticky sweetness.

"Thank you for sharing yourself with me. It was like nothing I've ever experienced before. You completely turned me out, *chiquita!*"

"I aim to please." Irys paused. "Are you okay?"

Ileana thought about it for a moment. "Yes, better than okay. This may be a once-in-a-lifetime deal, but I'm glad it was you. You know I love you, girl."

"I love you, too. But as much as I enjoyed this, I still think dick can't be beat."

They laughed hysterically before collapsing back to the floor. Ileana reached up and pulled down the sheet her mother left behind on the couch. She covered them both as they stretched and yawned. They knew they probably would never share their bodies that way again. But as they spooned, each was content that they got what they needed and their love did not suffer for it.

Drawing Reality

DIBUJAR LA REALIDAD

❧

Jocelyn Bringas

From afar I stared at her. Beautiful, I thought as I drew the flow of her dark black hair cascading down her back. Hair that I desperately wished I could run my fingers through just once. Hair that I dreamed of every night to feel. After a little more shading, my drawing of her was complete. I smiled at the drawing that was smiling back at me. It was a smile I wished was reality and not just some drawing.

I had to shut my sketchbook and attempt to focus on Professor Larson's lecture on Picasso but I just wasn't interested in learning about him. I was more interested in the beautiful woman seated six rows and two seats over from my desk. Jacelia Fernandez was her name. She was a beautiful twenty-one-year-old exchange student from Argentina. When I first saw her a few months ago, I was immediately taken by her exotic beauty. Never before had I seen such beauty in a woman.

Most of my days were spent drawing her in my sketchbook. She was my muse. I probably have over 500 drawings of her. Unfortunately, she didn't even know I was alive. The thought of approaching her mortified me—I could never gather up enough courage to talk to her. To save myself from embarrassment I just admired her from a distance and drew her.

Finally it was 3 P.M. and the class was over. Just like the other times I waited until she left first and followed her. I would follow her to the library, where she would study and do some reading for other classes. I took pleasure in watching and observing her. I loved how she concentrated hard on her work.

After pulling out my sketchbook from my backpack, I flipped to a blank page and began drawing her once again. I never grew tired of drawing her. First, I concentrated on her body. She had a voluptuous body that I longed to hold in my arms. I was grateful for the low-cut sweater she was wearing that showed me a good enough amount of cleavage. I longed to run my tongue on her smooth skin, between her full breasts.

Licking my lips, I continued to draw madly for the next few minutes. Drawing always gave me a pleasurable high. It was a beautiful rush to feel the drawing flow through my veins, to my hand, to the pencil, and right to the paper. When I finished drawing, I smirked at the page before me.

The drawing was of Jacelia on her knees staring up at me with her almond-shaped eyes, my hard cock between her full lips. Oh how I wished it was reality, her giving me a blow job. Her hot pouty lips sliding up and down my cock. I was hard now just thinking about it and decided it was time to depart the library. I needed to venture off to my dorm so I could take care of the problem in my pants.

∽

It was another day of class and like always I stared at Jacelia while I drew her in my sketchbook. She was dressed down today in a navy pullover sweater and jeans, her black hair pulled back tightly into a ponytail. She was wearing her glasses instead of her usual contact lenses, which made her look extra intellectual. Her chin was perched upon her left hand as her eyes focused on the professor's slide show on the Picasso.

My drawing today focused on her profile. Her hair pulled back into a ponytail exposed her neck to me. I longed to rake my tongue along the slope of it, to taste her sweet skin. My mouth watered just thinking about it.

A warmth passed through my stomach when she asked Professor Larson a question about the slide show. I loved the way she spoke. Her English was perfect but it still held a hint of a Latin accent. I dreamt every night of her moaning and sighing my name in ecstasy as I thrust into her.

"Now that was an interesting observation, Jacelia, which inspires me to give an assignment," Professor Larson said. The whole class groaned in frustration at the announcement.

I stopped doing my drawing and looked up as Professor Larson started writing on the whiteboard. In blue ink he wrote "Research Assignment."

"I am going to assign you each a partner. With your partner, you are to research a modern artist from the years 1920 to 1960. I expect a ten-page essay along with a painting or drawing of one of the artists' works. I will be selecting your partners randomly so that no one will work with their friends," Professor Larson said.

There was a part of me hoping that I would be paired up with Jacelia. My odds weren't good, though, since there was a total of fifty students in the class. I watched as Professor Larson pulled out a fishbowl filled with slips of paper from beneath the podium. For a few minutes he called out names and then I heard him say Jacelia's. My heart was racing in my chest and my brain kept repeating "pick me" over and over again.

"Jacelia Fernandez, your partner will be Nickolas Carter. Nickolas and Jacelia, please raise your hands so I know that you are both here."

I felt my eyes bug out of their sockets when Professor Larson said my name. I raised my hand and watched as Jacelia looked around the room to see who her partner was. When she finally spotted my hand, she flashed a bright smile at me. My head was swirling in shock and my stomach was filled with nervousness and excitement. I could not believe I had just received the opportunity to spend time with her.

When class was over, I stood up from my chair and walked toward her. My legs were shaking and my palms were sweaty.

"Hello, I'm Jacelia," she said sweetly as she stuck out her hand for me to shake.

"You can call me Nick, short for Nickolas," I said shyly. I'd never been so close to her and my body temperature felt so much hotter being next to her.

"I shouldn't have said what I said about modern artists and our lack of knowledge on them. I absolutely hate doing projects but at least I have you as a partner to help me out."

"Yeah," was I all I could think of say. My brain wasn't functioning normally and all I wanted to do was crawl under a rock and die from embarrassment.

"You're a quiet one, aren't you, Nick? Don't worry, I think I can fix that. Are you free right now or do you have another class to go to?" she asked.

"This is my last class of the day," I said.

"Great, do you mind if we go back to my dorm to discuss what to do for this assignment?"

"No, not at all."

The walk to the dormitories was quiet. I was not very good at initiating conversation.

Every once in a while I would glance at her walking beside me. It gave me a fuzzy feeling in my stomach seeing her right beside me. It was like she belonged there. When we finally reached the dorm, we had to climb a flight of stairs to get to the second floor. I couldn't resist staring at her abundant behind as I followed her up the stairs. I really wanted to reach out and run my hands over the roundness of her ass.

Finally, we entered her dorm and I was struck with the color pink. Almost everything in her room was pink, from the curtains to the rug and bedsheets.

"You must really love pink," I commented.

"Yes, it's my favorite color. Go ahead and have a seat right there," she said, pointing to the chair in front of her computer.

My eyes wandered all over her desk. She had lots of pictures of herself and various people. There were lots of her and one particular man. I couldn't fight the jealousy that was creeping inside me looking at how happy she was standing next to him.

"You have a lot of friends," I commented.

"Back in my country I do. I'm afraid I don't have as many friends here in America as I do back in Argentina. I miss my family a lot, especially my brother, Alejandro," she said, pointing to him in one of the photographs.

I let out a sigh of relief when she said "brother" and that the man in the pictures wasn't her boyfriend. I watched as she walked into her closet and came out a few moments later wearing pink shorts and a pink tank top. I did my best to suppress the arousal I was experiencing just gazing at the amount of skin she was displaying.

"Okay, I was thinking of some artists we could research and the one artist I really admire is the Mexican Frida Kahlo. I think her paintings are very powerful and unique," she said.

"Sounds good to me," I said.

"Let's get started with the research, then. I think today we should conduct a study on the databases online and then tomorrow after class we could head over to the library to find some books," she said.

I nodded in agreement and reached for my backpack, I pulled out my binder so that I could have some paper to take notes on. We spent the next three hours researching online.

"I really hate to cut this short but I have to attend a sorority meeting at the student union in fifteen minutes. We can continue this tomorrow after class," she said after printing out the last page from an information database we were looking at.

"No problem, I'll see you tomorrow, then," I told her.

When I left her dorm, I quickly went to mine, which was two buildings over from hers.

Flopping onto my bed, I couldn't wipe the permanent smile that was fixed upon my lips. For most of the semester I dreamed of spending time with her and now that I finally did, I felt so much happier. I had a rush of inspiration to draw, so I reached for my backpack to retrieve my sketchbook. My heart fell when I couldn't find it inside. I dumped everything out and only my binder and two textbooks fell out.

I started to panic and hoped my worst fear wasn't true. I hoped I didn't accidentally leave my sketchbook in Jacelia's dorm room. I spent the next few minutes looking throughout my room hoping I hadn't misplaced it but I couldn't find it. I wanted to go back to her dorm but she said she'd be at a sorority meeting. I had no idea when she would come back.

All I could do was painfully wait until tomorrow and hopefully get an opportunity to search her room.

∽

The next day I walked into class feeling uneasy. In my mind I
pictured Jacelia finding my sketchbook and being angry with
me for drawing sexually explicit pictures of her. All my fantasies
were in that sketchbook and it scared me to think of her looking
at them.

I entered the classroom and went straight to my desk. My
eyes drifted to where Jacelia's desk was and I saw she was already
there reading a book.

In a hoarse voice, Professor Larson said, "All right, I'm really
not feeling well today and I don't feel like speaking. Being the
nice person I am, I will be giving you all a free period to spend
with your partner to discuss your research assignment. I expect
you all to utilize this time wisely. I will also allow you to leave
class early. I suggest you use this time to go to the library and do
more research."

Everyone in the class shuffled out of their desks happy to
have a free period. Jacelia started walking toward me.

"Hello, Nick."

"Hi," I said softly.

"I'm really glad Professor Larson isn't feeling well, it gives us
extra time to do our research," she said.

"Oh yeah, it does."

"Come on, let's go back to my dorm room. I went to the
library this morning and checked out a few books on Kahlo.
We can sort through them and see which has the best information."

When we arrived at her room, I kept an eye out for my

sketchbook. My eyes scanned the pink room but I could not see it anywhere.

"Nick? Are you okay?" Jacelia asked.

"Yeah, I'm okay," I replied.

"Are you sure? If you want we can continue researching tomorrow."

"I'm sure."

We spent the next hour perusing the various books she checked out from the library. Every once in a while, I would divert my eyes from the page I was reading and sneak a look around her room for any sight of my sketchbook.

"Find anything interesting so far?" she questioned.

"Not quite," I replied.

"Are you sure, Nick?"

"Yeah."

"You seem very distracted."

"I'm not."

"Excuse me for a moment."

I watched as she stood up and walked to her closet. Closing the book I was reading, I decided to take the time to look more thoroughly around her room. I began my search under her bed and then near her desk.

"Looking for something?" I heard her ask all of a sudden, causing me to jump up in surprise.

"Oh, uh, no, I was just stretching my arms," I said quickly as I faked an arm stretch.

"Stretching, huh? I actually think you were looking for this," she said. My jaw dropped when I saw her holding my precious sketchbook.

"Jacelia—"

"Nick, I must say that your drawings are excellent. Not only do they have great details, they are *muy caliente*."

"What?" I asked, confused.

"Is this what you want me to do to you?" Jacelia asked while opening up my sketchbook, her fingers thumbing through the pages.

She smiled when she arrived at the page she was looking for and showed me the drawing I did a few days ago in the library where she had my cock in her mouth. My cheeks burned in embarrassment. I never thought she would ever see my drawings.

"And is this what you want to do to me?" she questioned as she flipped through the pages again and stopped at the one I drew two weeks ago in class. It was of me driving my cock into her, doggie-style. I was inspired to draw it because I had caught her bending over in class, her ass sticking out, trying to pick up a pen.

"Jacelia, I can explain," I said nervously.

"What is there to explain? It's all right here," she said, waving the sketchbook in front of my face.

"I'm sorry if I offended you. I promise to never draw you again," I said, nearly in tears from being totally embarrassed. My mind was racing; she probably hated my guts now and thought I was the biggest pervert in the world.

"Damn, you are so cute. If you wanted me, you should have just asked," Jacelia said seductively as she moved closer toward me. My eyes bugged out of their sockets; did I hear her right?

"Wha-wha-what?"

Jacelia got on her knees, her face inches away from my crotch, and said, "If you wanted to live out what you drew in your drawings, you should have just asked. I mean, why draw fantasy, when you can have reality?"

I stood there speechless as I looked down at Jacelia's hands caressing my thighs. She had a mischievous smile playing on her glossy pink lips while she stared at my crotch. I gulped because it was then I realized I had an erection that made a tent in my pants. The touch of her fingers raking down my thighs was arousing me to no end. My cock ached to escape out of my pants.

"So Nick, do you want me to suck your cock like in your drawing?" she asked.

A moan escaped my lips when I felt Jacelia's hand squeeze my cock through my pants.

I started to grind my hardness against her hand, relishing in the pleasure I was feeling.

"Tell me you want me to suck your cock," she commanded.

I was breathing heavily and still in shock that we were both in this position right now.

Never had I imagined her willing enough to want to give me pleasure. I had dreamt about it and fantasized about it for the longest time, yet I never thought I would be desirable enough for her. I always felt I was too ugly and nerdy for her affection.

"I want you to suck my cock," I said breathlessly.

Not waiting another second, Jacelia undid my pants and shoved them to my ankles. My erection bounced into view, standing proudly at attention, and wanting to be touched. She wrapped her tiny tanned hand around my cock and began to stroke it slowly.

"You have such a beautiful cock, Nick. It's so nice and big. I bet it has brought lots of other girls pleasure."

"Actually, you're the first," I said shyly.

"Wow, I'm your first ever?" Jacelia asked.

"Yeah, I'm a virgin," I quietly confessed.

"Mmmm, that turns me on so much more knowing that my mouth and pussy will be the first to take your cock," Jacelia said as she licked her lips.

I watched as Jacelia's tongue traced along the tip, smearing the pre-cum that had appeared. Then she licked down the length right to my ball sack where she massaged her tongue over my hanging balls as she gently jerked me off. She then opened her mouth wide and slowly inserted my cock inside. I groaned and felt my knees grow weak as her lips slid up and down my hardness. Her mouth was wet and felt amazing, rubbing all over my pulsating cock. This was better than I ever imagined. She kept sucking and sucking until she slid my cock out of her mouth. I frowned, hoping she wasn't done.

"You like this, Nick? You like me sucking you off?" she asked, her hot breath brushing my saliva-covered cock.

"Yes, don't stop," I whispered.

Her mouth returned to sucking and I absolutely loved it when she would bring her lips up my cock 'cause she would create a delicious slurping sound. This was all too much for me and I couldn't hold my orgasm any longer. The pressure started to build up in my balls and I could feel the cum ready to burst out. My hands grabbed a handful of her black hair as my hips started to lunge forward, causing my cock to drive in and out of her mouth like a jackhammer.

All I could hear was her moaning loudly in ecstasy as I thrust into her mouth. Faster and faster, my cock went. I was so deep inside her mouth I could even feel the tip of my cock going down her throat. My balls started to slap against her chin and within seconds a wave of pleasure ran through my body. I exploded into her mouth, my cum shooting into her waiting mouth. Never missing a beat, she kept sucking and swallowing my cum. When I came down from my high, I looked down at her; her mouth was glistening and a few drops of cum had leaked onto her chin.

With her perfectly manicured fingers, she wiped her chin, and licked the remainder of the cum off.

"Mmmm, *que delicioso,*" she commented as she smacked her lips in delight.

I was so frozen with pleasure that I was speechless. I could not believe I just experienced my first blow job with Jacelia. She stood up and gazed deeply into my eyes. Her hand reached up and caressed my face for a moment before she pulled my head down toward hers, causing our lips to crush together. Her tongue then delved into my mouth, urgently massaging my tongue. It was weird yet arousing to know that just moments ago my cock had been touching her lips and tongue.

I felt her push me forward and before I knew it I landed back first onto her bed. She then climbed on top of me and straddled my stomach; her brown eyes looked into my eyes with lust.

"I wonder what we should do next? Oh! I have an idea," she said as she hopped off me and went to pick up my sketchbook.

"Here, pick anything here and we'll act it out," she said, handing me my sketchbook.

"Are you sure?" I asked.

"Yes, I looked through all your drawings last night. It got me so hot that I started to touch myself. Your drawings are so good I bet acting them out will be greater," she said seductively as she planted some lazy kisses along the side of my neck.

A nervous feeling floated around my stomach as I looked through the various drawings of her and me. When I reached a particular drawing I did a few months ago, my cock began to harden just gazing at it.

"This one," I said, shyly pointing to the drawing I did after first seeing her in class. It was of her on top of me riding my cock.

Without another word, she climbed out of bed and began to strip out of her clothes. First she pulled off her T-shirt and then her shorts. She had on a cotton candy pink bra with matching panties. Her hands went to her breasts, cupping them and pushing them together. Her fingers then reached for the button on the front of her bra and with one flick her bra came undone, her breasts and hard nipples falling into my view. She shrugged her bra off and tossed it away.

Then she turned around and bent over, her round ass in the air. Slowly, she pulled down her panties to her ankles, exposing her bare ass. She shook her ass from side to side before standing up and facing me.

My mouth watered as my eyes drank in her naked body for the first time. Her skin was a beautiful caramel color, her breasts were full, and I noticed her pussy was shaved clean. I took a deep breath when I saw her climb on top of me and hover over my hard cock. With her hand, she guided my cock inside her and I groaned, feeling her tight wetness slide down.

Jacelia held my gaze with her eyes, her dark brown eyes burning with desire. She began to gyrate her hips in a circular fashion; her wet pussy felt so good squeezing all around my cock.

She placed her hands onto my chest and slowly her pussy began to slide up and down.

My hands went up and fondled her breasts as she was riding my cock. Her breasts were so soft and perky. When I began twisting her nipples, her moans grew louder, which made my cock even harder.

I couldn't handle the slow pace anymore and my hips began to thrust upward, creating a more delicious friction. Our bodies soon began to collide faster. Throwing my head back in pleasure, I let my body absorb all the amazing feelings running through me. All I could hear was the sweet moans she was making and the creak of the bedsprings. Deeper and deeper my cock went into her tight wet pussy.

My orgasm was fast approaching and just when I about to cum, she stopped. I opened my eyes and saw her get off my cock. My cock felt so empty without her pussy on it. She moved to the space next to me and got on all fours.

"Come on and fuck me doggie-style like in your drawing," she commanded.

Immediately, I got off my back and went behind her to position myself. My heart was racing as I parted her ass cheeks and gazed at her glistening pussy. It fluffed my ego to know that she was wet because of me. Holding my throbbing cock in my hand, I inserted myself into her. Her tight pussy walls contracted all around me and I couldn't take it anymore. I began pounding into her like there was no tomorrow. My body just slammed into her, our skin slapping together.

Jacelia reached out with her hands to her headboard and used that as leverage to meet my thrusts. She started to let out a string of words in Spanish that I had no idea what they meant but it was arousing to hear.

In and out my cock went. With each thrust, I was close to the edge. Our fucking was so intense that I couldn't hold back anymore. My balls were churning, and I could feel the cum burning in my cock, desperately wanting to get out. I thrust and thrust until a tidal wave of pleasure crashed over me. I let out one last hard thrust and pulled her ass close as I began to shoot what felt like gallons of cum into her convulsing pussy.

"Mmmm . . . yes, cum inside me. Fill my pussy up," she moaned.

My body felt so drained as I collapsed on top of her. After a few moments of silence, she pushed herself off my body. I turned onto my back and saw her pick up my sketchbook and flip through the pages.

"This one is my favorite," she said, pointing to the drawing I did a few months ago of her completely naked with my fingers in her pussy.

"You want me to do that do you?" I asked.

Jacelia nodded and lay back down, spreading her legs wide for me. I got between her legs and the smell of sex filled my nostrils. I slipped two of my fingers inside her drenching wet pussy and began to finger-fuck her. As I did that, she brought her hand down and began furiously rubbing her clit.

My eyes were glued to her rubbing her clit and I had this craving to taste it. Licking my lips, I pushed her hand away, and placed my tongue over her throbbing clit. Her juices tasted so sweet and I started to suckle her clit hard. I could feel her hands weave through my hair as she pushed her clit onto my tongue.

"Oh, *si,*" she moaned loudly as her hips started to go crazy.

Her back arched high and I felt her pussy walls tighten over my fingers and her clit explode on my tongue. When she finished her climax, she pulled my hand out of her pussy and brought it to her lips. Her mouth sucked in my fingers as she hungrily licked her juices off.

Taking my fingers out of her mouth, I smiled at her and leaned in for a passionate kiss.

"That was fun," she said after pulling away from the kiss.

"Yeah, it was."

"How about you draw how I look after we've fucked?" she asked, immediately getting in a seductive pose.

I picked up my sketchbook and went to get my pencil from my backpack. For a moment I stared at her lying contentedly on her pink bed. I began to draw her naked body, starting first with her perky breasts and then her pussy, which she had spread wide with her fingers. I felt my cock stir again as I drew. I tried to ignore my now rewakened cock but I simply couldn't. I had to fuck her again. Dropping my sketchbook to the floor, I pounced on top of her and began to thrust inside her drenched pussy. She seemed surprised by my abruptness but that soon faded away as I heard her moan in pleasure.

As I thrust into her I thought about how lucky I was. Who knew my drawings would end up becoming reality? Maybe next time I should start drawing being a rich and famous artist with Jacelia by my side supporting me.

What Tomorrow Holds

LO QUE EL MAÑANA TRAE

❧ ❧

Zane

DAY ONE

Take Me to the Moon

Joan Osborne's rendition of the classic "I'll Be Around" was blasting through my noise-cancelling earphones during my flight to Cancún. Technology can be such a blessing and a curse. It is a blessing because we get to experience things in our life-time that our ancestors could not even fathom. It can be a curse when we get so caught up in machines and gadgets that we start talking to people exclusively through emails and instant mes-sages. That was what my life had become. A fast-paced life in a microwave society. I had been so looking forward to spending New Year's Eve in Cancún, with my lover. Yet there I was, on the plane alone; caught up in the massive collection of nearly three thousand songs on my iPod.

When "I'll Be Good to You" by The Brothers Johnson—the next in alphabetical order—came on, I was ready to start danc-ing in the aisle. That was my jam! I decided to simply wiggle in my seat. I didn't want anyone to think I was a lunatic. In today's age, with all the threats of terrorism, I could see some idiot try- ing to be a hero by slamming me to the ground in a WWF move. Then again, there was a sister sitting directly across from me in the first-class cabin taking her braids out. Artificial hair was fly- ing everywhere. Good thing some meek man was occupying the seat beside her. If she had been sitting next to me flicking hair into my drink, without question there would have been serious drama.

I did glare at her like she was crazy when she got up to go to the lavatory. Even with my headphones on, I was able to make out the words she stated flippantly in my direction: "I'm getting a head start so one of those Mexican women can hook a sister up with new braids!"

I started to be sarcastic and ask if she planned to wash her hair on the plane also but, in all honesty, I could not have cared less about her or her hairdo. As long as it was not landing in my gin and tonic, I was straight. Still, I chuckled as I imagined her trying to bend over that tiny-ass sink and rinse it out. Since childhood, I had this wild imagination. Often I would picture people in "sticky situations" who were simply going about their daily business. Once, when I was on the subway, I imagined the cou- ple sitting across from me running from a serial killer on a dark mountain pass. An entire movie played out in my head by the time I reached my stop.

Damn, why did "I'll Make Love to You" by Boyz II Men have to be next? That was "our song." Korey had played that very song the first time I crashed over at his place. He had gazed deeply into my eyes and serenaded me with major seduction. It was amazing what effect music can have on one's soul. By the time "I'll Miss You Most" by Gordon Chambers came on, I was prac- tically in tears.

I still found it difficult to accept that I would be at The Moon Palace in Cancún—highly celebrated as one of the most gorgeous resorts in the world—alone. It was an all-inclusive resort and Korey and I had split the cost of a package for two. The money was nonrefundable because it was New Year's. I was not about to lose my half—fifteen hundred dollars—because he had chosen to act a fool. Ironically, the next song was "I'll Never B Another Fool" by Chaka Khan. How apropos. I was determined to never be played again. Fuck men and the big dicks they rode in on!

By the time we landed forty minutes later, "I've Got Love on My Mind" by Natalie Cole was playing. I certainly did not have love on my mind but lust was something different altogether. I was hot, horny, commitment-free and ready to explore new territory. I had never dated—or fucked—outside of my race but according to all my friends, dick is dick. If I had a quarter for every time I heard a man say pussy is pussy, I could have bought that new BMW featured in the airplane magazine.

The Moon Palace was the closest resort to the Cancún airport so the ride was short. I was greeted with a warm towel to soothe me from the heat while I waited for the cab driver to get my bags out of the trunk. Once inside, they handed me a flute of chilled champagne when they checked me in.

I had to be driven to my villa on a golf cart because no vehicles could access the secluded area of the resort. There were two large hotels on the property but I had opted for a cream-colored beautifully decorated villa on the golf course. The main draw was the villa's massive Jacuzzi.

"Korey, you fuckin' idiot," I said aloud. "This could've been the perfect vacation."

I called my Aunt Maxie to let her know that I had safely ar-

rived. I planned to stay on the phone for only a couple of minutes. Aunt Maxie was a chronic worrywart. The tension in her
voice almost got me all worked up. I tried to explain that even
though I was in a private area, the entire resort had more than
two thousand rooms, eleven restaurants, and at least a dozen
swimming pools—there were plenty of people around. Aunt
Maxie finally let me get off the phone when I said it was costing
a grip. She made me promise to keep my door locked. Like duh?

Aunt Maxie had been both mother and father to me since
my real parents were killed in a freak accident before I entered
the eighth grade. Their killer was a seven-year-old boy who
thought the gun he had found under his father's pillow was a toy.
He took it to school with the idea of getting back at a classmate
he was angry with. He yanked the gun from his backpack and
went to blasting. My mother was his teacher and my father was
there to bring her the lunch she had left at home that morning.
He gunned them both down in a pool of blood. Talk about
karma. I had often wondered if they had any premonitions that
they would both die together; or even if they ever desired to.
They had a strong love for each other; and for me. I got de-
pressed for a few moments, thinking about yet another new year
on earth without them. Then I decided to make the best out of
the situation. Hell, I was in paradise!

Lucky for me the resort offered twenty-four-hour room service—all included. I was too exhausted to venture out to one of
the restaurants. Too exhausted and, without a doubt, too embarrassed. I was still wondering how I would play off the fact that a
sexy, professional, educated sister like me would be in paradise
alone for a week. And for New Year's, on top of that. Surely, I
would be the only one. People were traveling with their spouses,

lovers, families or, at the very least, close friends. I would have to dine alone, lie out by the pool or beach alone. Shit! Sleep alone!

I ordered a steak dinner, a club sandwich, soup and every single dessert on the menu. Once the waiter, who had to be old enough to be my great-grandfather, dropped off the four silver trays, it dawned on me that I was binging—something I hadn't done in ages.

Every man that I saw on the way here seemed fine as shit to me. Every damn one. The brother who carried my bags into the airport on his cart since you could not check bags curbside for international flights. The ticket agent. The male flight attendant working the first-class cabin on the plane. The man who assumed that I was gullible enough to agree to a time share presentation in exchange for reduced event tickets that were not reduced at all. He was an asshole but, hell, he was still fine. The guy who handed me the warm towel outside the cab. The cab driver was female and a female agent checked me in at the hotel, so they did not do anything for me. I have been and will always be all about outies and not innies. But the young man who drove me to the villa on the golf cart had these succulent ears that I wanted to suck on like corn on the cob. Now the damn hundred-ninety-year-old waiter made me want to jump his arthritic bones.

I watched television while I ate to the point of nausea. I used to be bulimic and refused to go back there over my break-up with Korey. I loved Korey and I was convinced he loved me but the fact that we were both Virgos caused serious issues. We once looked up our compatibility on an astrology website. It said that since we were both so critical and determined by nature that we would fight for control over everything in the relationship. Truer words have never been spoken, or written, in that case. Every detail, big or small, led to arguments over who was right and who was wrong. The sex was off the chain, though. Virgos are very passionate people and Korey and I had grown to appreciate our strong sexual urges. Then the shit hit the fan. He cheated on me and even though I forgave him, he still had the nerve to dump me last-minute. He would come back to me; I was confident about that. I was also damn sure that I would never allow him back into my space again. I was going to do the damn thing all by myself.

Victory always begins with me, so I broke out "the gadgets." Some women never leave home without their favorite foundation, tube of lipstick or support bra. I never leave home without my favorite dildo, vibrator and set of ben wa balls.

The Jacuzzi thing was going to work wonders. My "dildo of the month" was a pink nine-inch with a suction bottom. It was perfect for water play. I ran the water in the Jacuzzi and stripped off my clothes. There was nothing better than a long, hot bath after a long day. The plane ride had been top-notch but it was still tiring. I wanted to climb in, listen to some more jams on my iPod using my portable speaker set, cum a good two or three times and then hit the sack.

I decided to back it up to the "B" songs and put on "Baby Come to Me" by Regina Belle; a classic. I climbed into the tub, placing a bottle of wine from the mini-bar beside me with a wineglass, and sank into the succulent water. My dildo was waiting patiently for me. I had suctioned it onto the bottom of the tub while I was running the water and watched intently as the water and bubbles covered it up until it disappeared altogether. Like an old familiar friend, it was right there and I slid my pussy right on top of it. I sat still as my body got used to it inside of me. Umm, that felt great!

There is a lot to be said for dildos. With men, they are so determined to prove they can dig a woman's back out that sometimes—when you merely want them to lie still with their dicks inside you—they still want to go all out and pump you like a tire. Dildos are well behaved and you can always have it your way. I started moving back and forth, up and down, on my "friend" and it was time to add some pressure to the mix. I hit the button for the jets; there was a short spurt and then nothing.

"Don't fucking do this to me!" I yelled out to no one. "Fuck!"

Now I was mad. The one thing I had to look forward to had been taken away from me. That was totally unfair. Someone was going to pay for this.

I climbed out the Jacuzzi, threw on the plush bathrobe they provided and called the front desk, demanding that they send someone to fix the Jacuzzi. I was relieved when someone knocked on my door less than five minutes later. I had to give it to them; that was great customer service. When I flung the door open, I did not know whether to scream or drop the robe.

He had on a workman's uniform and all I could think about was him doing some maintenance on my pipes.

"Hola," he said in the sexiest voice I had ever heard escape a man's lips.

"*Hola* right back at you," I replied.

"Cómo está usted, mi señora encantadora?"

"Hmm, I understood the 'how are you, lady' but what does 'encantadora' mean?"

"*Encantadora* means lovely," he stated in perfect English.

"Well, my Spanish is minimal but your English seems to be damn near better than mine so why don't we stick with that?"

He laughed, and his teeth were contrasted whitely against his smooth caramel skin and light brown eyes. He had wavy black hair that was brushed back to expose his chiseled features. His body was out of this world. He obviously had been doing major weight lifting.

"English is cool with me." He glanced at the Jacuzzi. "Having problems?"

"Yes, I'm having *temas.* I mean, issues."

"We going back to Spanish?" he asked jokingly.

"No, I couldn't resist since I actually knew a word to fit in there."

This time we laughed together.

"Let me take a look."

You can look at whatever the hell you want, I thought to myself.

I sat down on the bed as I watched him analyze the situation.

"Baby I'm Your Fiend" by Teena Marie was playing and I was damn sure craving some of what was across the room.

"Nice song." He looked up at me as he commented. "Who is that singing?"

"Teena Marie, off her *La Dona* CD. She's the shit!"

"Aw, isn't she the one who sang 'Fire and Desire' with Rick James?"

"What you know about Rick?"

"I'm Rick James, bitch!" he exclaimed, utilizing the famous saying.

"Well, in that case, just call me Mary Jane."

"You get high?"

"High?"

"Yeah, *fumado.*"

"Hmm, I guess they would have a lot of weed down here in Mec-ci-co."

"What's your name?" he asked, realizing that I intended to ignore his drug question.

"Doesn't it say it on your work order?"

He smirked. "What work order? They radio me and tell me what room or villa to get my ass over to and I get there."

"So you take orders—*órdenes*—well?"

I licked my lips. My wicked imagination had gone into overdrive and I pictured him butt-naked on the bed with me.

"Depends on who's giving them." Maybe it was still my imagination but I could have sworn he had said that in a "I'm ready to fuck" way.

"My name is Taneisha, and yours?"

"Carmelo."

"Hmm, nice name. It matches your skin. Caramel. Carmelo."

"You have nice skin also."

He got up to get another tool out of his box.

"Carmelo, are you getting fresh with me?" I asked.

"Would it do me any good if I was?"

I started contemplating the situation. I was in Mexico. Did not know a damn person down there, or even in the entire country, for that matter. All of my friends had already had plans for New Year's and would not even take a free trip to Cancún on Korey's ticket; the heifers. I was horny, there was a fine man in my room and he seemed "approachable."

"Carmelo, have you ever fucked a guest at this resort?"

"*No, nunca,* never."

"Would you fuck a guest at this resort?"

"This is wild." He laughed. "I knew something strange was going to happen to me today. I just didn't know what it would be."

"So you're saying that I'm strange," I stated offensively as "Back to the Hotel" by N2DEEP came on.

"Actually, you're fine. It's like this." He sat down on the edge of the Jacuzzi and eyed me from across the room. "My girl, she's been treating me bad lately. She got this really great job and I'm proud as hell of her but now she acts like she's better than me." He held up the wrench in his hand. "She doesn't consider this honorable work."

"Is she still your girl?"

"I have no idea. I guess, but it doesn't feel right. Anyway, this morning when I woke up, I was happy for no reason; excited about coming to work. I'm *never* excited about coming to work. But, here you are, sitting over there on that bed, dripping wet under that robe, and my dick is so hard it could bend this wrench."

"Let me see it bend the wrench."

He chuckled.

"I'm serious."

"Serious. You know I'm kidding. That was only a figure of speech. A dick can't bend a wrench."

"But I bet the wrench can do interesting things to a dick."

He laughed again but this time uneasily.

I got up, untied the belt of the robe and let it glide to the floor. "You like my body."

"Shit, who wouldn't?"

"My man cheated on me. Can you believe that?"

"He's a *tonto*, a dummy."

"He thinks I'm too controlling."

"Are you?"

I sat back down on the bed and patted the space beside me.

"Why don't you come over here and find out. Bring that wrench with you."

Carmelo stared down at the wrench, hesitated for a minute, but brought it with him as instructed.

I grabbed the wrench, pushed him back on the bed, and ripped open his work shirt. Buttons popped everywhere.

"They're going to make me pay for another shirt."

"I'll pay for it." I ran my fingertips up and down his chest. "So your woman doesn't appreciate all of this. She's a *tonta,* too."

"You ever been with a Mexican?" he asked out of the blue.

"No, you ever been with a black woman?"

"No, but I've always wanted to be with one."

"Why?"

He shrugged. "Curiosity."

"Well, you won't be curious anymore because I'm about to lay it on you."

Carmelo grinned. "Lay it on me?"

"Yeah, lay it on you. *Quebrarte la espalda;* blow your back out,"

"Sounds interesting."

I unfastened his pants and was glad he was not wearing a belt. It gave me easier access. I pulled his pants and boxers down in one swoop and took it all in with my eyes. "Nice. *Agradable.* How do you say 'scrumptious' in Spanish?"

"*Riquísimo.*"

"*Riquísimo?* That's what your dick is. *Riquísimo.*"

"I bet your pussy is *riquísima.*"

"Have a taste and find out for yourself."

I quickly swung myself around and sat right on his awaiting tongue. Then I took the head of his dick in my mouth and went to work. There was this recent porno going around with much hype surrounding how the sister gave head. She did not have a damn thing on me. Spitting on dicks was skank but men thought that shit was actually sexy. She and I did have one thing in common; we were both passionate about sucking dick. However, I did it with class.

Carmelo was trying to yank away from me in less than a minute. Yes, I can make men run from blow jobs because I suck them in like a pit bull with lockjaw. I tasted a little pre-cum and was thinking, *Damn, not yet!*

He must have read my mind because he pushed my pussy up off his mouth for a second, just long enough to whisper, *"Puedo quedarme,"* meaning that he could hang.

"Before I Let You Go" by Blackstreet was playing; one of my all-time favorites. "That's good because before I let you go, I'm going to make sure that you remember me always."

He went back to sucking on my clit with a perfect intensity; confirming that his woman truly was a dummy. I had no idea what I planned to do with that wrench but after talking all that shit, I decided to experiment and see if he stopped me.

I picked it up and adjusted it until I could fit it around the base of Carmelo's dick; all the while still slobbering on him like an all-day sucker. When I tightened it, he flinched but did not yell out. I did not think it was possible but his dick got even harder than before. I gyrated the wrench back and forth on his dick while I went up and down on it with my mouth, deep-throating him like a pro. I would never prostitute myself but if I ever did, I would be the richest whore on the block.

Carmelo was about to explode but I was not having that. I needed him to stay hard so I could take a ride. My juices were trickling down the insides of my thighs as I turned back around and straddled him, immediately sliding my pussy onto his dick. I never let go of the wrench. I keep working his thing like I was the maintenance worker. His face was a mixture of pain and pleasure. All he could say was. *"Mierda!" Damn!*

I clamped onto the head and shaft of his dick with my pussy. I don't care what anyone says, ben wa balls are worth their weight in gold when it comes to learning pussy control. I had been using them for more than ten years, since I was in high school, and I could smoke a cigar with my pussy if I wanted to. I rode Carmelo for more than thirty minutes until I sensed he could not take any more. Every time he was on the brink of having an orgasm, I would pull off of him, rub my pussy lips on his dick to make it good and hard again, tighten up the wrench, and then reinsert him with my free hand.

Carmelo got a bit rough with me also by pinching my nipples and yanking on them. I bent down so he could suck my tits, one at a time, then both together. "Um, that's right, little *bebé*. Suck on them like you own them."

We fucked through several songs: "Between the Sheets" by the Isley Brothers, "Body" by Me' Shell NdegeOcello, "Boogie Oogie Oogie" by A Taste of Honey, "Bravebird" by Amel Larrieux, and "Brown Sugar" by D'Angelo. Korey crossed my mind for all of five seconds and then I remembered that he cheated on me. I saw the chick once in passing at a Starbucks. I recognized her from a photo he had taken with her at a cookout. She had been all on him by the pool and I should have known they were fucking from the way she had her arms around him, as if saying, "This man is mine!"

Carmelo had a woman but you would not have known it that night. I was cool with that because it was not like I was planning on moving to Mexico. I wanted to do a quick drive-by fucking and move on. In fact, even though I would be there a week, I decided that it would be that one night and nothing more for me and Carmelo. I could not risk catching feelings and since Korey had been my man for more than three years, anything was possible on the rebound. I was not used to being a whore, but I was good at it.

When we took a break, Carmelo asked me if he was a "revenge fuck."

My reply was, "Am I?"

He didn't comment.

I was lying there in his arms when I suggested, "How about you try to fix that Jacuzzi one last time? I would love to get busy in there with you."

He laughed.

"What's so funny?"

"I fixed it in less than thirty seconds. I didn't want to leave and was hoping it I dragged it out, things would develop."

I sat up and glared at him. "You planned to fuck me from the time you knocked on the door."

"I have a confession to make."

"What?" I asked apprehensively.

"I saw you when you checked in, found out which villa you would be staying in and while they were still getting your bags on a golf cart, I came out here and broke your Jacuzzi."

"*Increíble!* Do you do this shit all the time with guests? What number am I?" I was fighting mad. "You asshole!"

"I swear, I have never done this before. I have never been with a guest. I saw you and you were so beautiful and I really didn't think it would lead to this. I wanted the chance to talk to you; that's all. Why would I assume that I could have some of you by breaking your bathtub? Think about it!"

I did think about it. There was no way he could imagine that I would be a willing fuck partner. "So you wanted to meet me?"

"Yes, I only wanted to meet you."

"How did you know you would get the service call?"

"This is my section. Fate was on my side. How could I not take advantage of it?"

I laughed. "In that case, we should take advantage of the rest of the night."

"How do you suggest we do that?" Carmelo asked excitedly.

"By fucking in that Jacuzzi."

We jumped up from the bed and damn near ran to the Jacuzzi. The water was freezing. Carmelo ran some additional hot water in and turned on the jets while I decided that I had heard enough of the "B" songs and went to dial the iPod to the "G" songs. "Grown & Sexy" by Babyface came on as I climbed in the water with Carmelo right behind me. He jumped when his ass hit the dildo.

"What the fuck?"

"Oh, say hello to my little friend," I said with an accent, imitating Al Pacino from *Scarface*.

Carmelo chuckled. "So this was what you planned to use to get off?"

"Yes, but luckily for me, some real dick came along. Some real, juicy, *riquísimo* dick."

"I like you," he whispered in my ear as be pushed my hair back to gaze into my eyes.

"I like you, too, but you know this can go no further than tonight."

"I have no problem getting on a plane to come see you."

I sighed. "You have a woman and I sense that you love her;

regardless of her recent attitude. The two of you will work things out and I don't want to play second fiddle."

"What about your man?"

"Korey and I are history. I'm going to live *la vida loca*. I'm going to have the time of my life this week; starting with you. Now, let's have a little less talking and a lot more fucking."

We started tonguing each other down as "Grown Man Business" by Mos Def began to play. We fucked in the Jacuzzi for another hour before Carmelo's radio started going off. Someone had overflowed a toilet in the villa three doors down. Before he left I made him use the dildo on my pussy while he fucked me in the ass. Yes, it was going to be one hell of a week!

DAY TWO

You Can Ride a Bull but Can You Ride Me?

The day after my arrival was Wednesday; a bullfight was in town. I was hesitant to go because I hated the sight of blood but it was the equivalent of being on *Fear Factor* for me. Watching a bull get massacred was going to be right up there with licking maggots off a windshield in hopes of winning fifty thousand dollars.

I took a cab from The Moon Palace to Plaza de Toros in downtown Cancún, a small bullring, the kind where the poor bull does not stand a chance. He is half dead before he is even brought out. I was more amazed by the entertainment before the actual fight began. Dancers were dressed in vibrant colors and dancing around on the dirt like it was a celebration, instead of a murder in the making. Women came out giggling and smiling on horses and young men in ruffled shirts and tight black pants did tricks with ropes.

They picked some people from the audience to go down and participate. This drunken man—who had screamed at the top of his lungs when the announcer asked if anyone was from Canada—grabbed my wrist and pulled me down the bleachers with him.

"Come on, sweetness!" he said. "You look like you can ride a mean bull!"

"I'm not riding shit!" I exclaimed, trying to yank away from him. Then I got hyped when people starting applauding and prodding me to be the only woman down there. I'm a competitive person who thought the women needed to be represented.

"I can do this," I whispered to myself as they handed me some pads to put on. "I can get over my fears."

Silly me, but I thought we were going out there to run from bulls or ride some bulls or even be in the ring with some bulls. But they sent a scrawny-ass goat out there instead. We had to run around the ring chasing it and trying to pull it down to the ground. The alcoholic from Canada got knocked up in the sky when the goat ran into his slow ass. I almost died laughing.

They gave us all T-shirts and then sent us back to our seats. On the way, I spotted what could only be described as "the finest thing in Cancún." He was tall, at least six-three, and had a bald head. That's all I needed to see. I had a predilection for two clean heads on a man, one to lick and one to rub while he licked on me.

He was dressed in the same tight black pants all the other men were wearing but his fit him like a glove. I could see the massive bulge in between his legs and hoped it wasn't a jock cup. Those damn things can be so deceiving. Back in high school and college, I used to think the boys on the football team were seriously holding, only to discover a bunch of pencil dicks in the aftermath.

I tried to get his attention backstage before they forced me back upstairs. He eyed me and winked. That was enough to make my panties wet. When I got back to my seat, I whipped out my camcorder. I had no intention of taping the bullfight. But him, I had to immortalize on film to show my friends back home. Seeing him, alone, would make them regret not taking me up on my offer to take Korey's place on the trip.

The bullfight was awful. The matador was skinny but "my dick" was one of the men who helped him contain the bull and I almost lost it when the matador had to stick the bull twice in the heart before he died. He actually cried and whined like a baby. It was a tearjerker. In fact, I started crying and left the plaza wiping my eyes.

A little boy started pointing at me and laughed. He yanked on his mother's skirt. "Look, Mom, she's crying."

It's a shame that kids are so desensitized by video games and movies that they are immune to violence by the time they are ten. The woman looked at me apologetically and was about to say something when a younger child, a little girl of about four, came up to her, pouting.

"Mom, that man over there won't take my play money. He wants real money."

Watching her hold up three fake ones from a board game lightened my mood and I found myself giggling along with the mother. The older boy shook his head and seemed ashamed of his younger sibling when he should have been ashamed of himself.

I was suddenly starving and there was nothing of interest within walking distance of the bullring. A lot of Cancún was still being reconstructed after a recent hurricane. Many of the hotels along the water were still closed; pending refurbishment. I went upstairs to the bar adjacent to the plaza and ordered some wings and fries. I was washing it all down with a Corona with lime when "my dick" came in, wearing regular street clothes. Even in the jeans and faded T-shirt, his body was banging. He spotted me and winked again. One of the waitresses, clad in barely nothing, sashayed up to him and started flirting by rubbing his arms and telling him in Spanish what a great job he had done. Being a Virgo, I have a jealousy streak; even when the man is not mine. If I am even thinking about fucking a man, no other woman better look in his direction.

I sat there, trying to size up the situation and determine if they were "friends with benefits." I drew the conclusion that she was way more interested in him than vice versa. He kept glancing in my direction. I was sitting in a dim corner and there were no more than ten other patrons in the entire place, since the show was done for the day. I had on this pair of shorts that were so tight that they were causing my white lace thong to ride up in my pussy.

I thought back to the bold night of lovemaking I had shared with Carmelo the night before. I had made it clear to him not to come knocking on my door for the remainder of my stay. He was hinting around about going at it again but I was determined not to let that happen. Yet, there I was, as horny as a damn bull; even though I had witnessed one being slain less than an hour earlier.

Could I possibly be bolder than I was last night? I asked myself. *Why the fuck not?* I answered.

I took the lime out of the Corona and squeezed it on my breasts. I was wearing a halter top, showing much cleavage. I sucked the remaining juice from the lime, maintaining eye contact with "my dick." The waitress had taken the hint and the few other men in the place were staring at me as well, but I had my sights on only one.

I lifted my left foot and placed it on an empty share, spreading my legs for all the world to see. I ran the lime up my thigh and let it disappear between my legs, rubbing it on my clit through the lace fabric. Then I started rubbing it more vigorously and squeezing my breasts with my free hand. You could have heard a pin drop in the place if there had not been music playing. Even the waitresses were engulfed in my performance. I almost got scared but then I remembered that none of these people knew me. Two tears in a bucket; mother fuck it!

I spent the next ten to twelve minutes masturbating myself into an orgasm. I stood up halfway through the show and sat on the table, spreading my legs even further. I fingered myself, moaned, threw my head back and got lost in myself; imagining "my dick" was helping me out. I am not sure when life began to imitate art but his hands were suddenly upon me; his fingers taking the place of mine. I gazed up into his eyes as he looked down on me; removing his fingers barely long enough to lick them before putting them back.

Was this really happening?

A man yelled out, *"Ustedes no pueden hacer eso aquí!"* You can't do that here!

"My dick" replied, *"Usted no tiene que miranos. Cierre y vayase."* You don't have to watch. Lock up and leave.

Everyone cleared out of there like bats. Whoever the man was that I was about to fuck, someone either owed him something or respected the hell out of him. I suspected it was a little bit of both. Seeing him up close, he was definitely older than me; at least forty. Fine by me.

"Dámelo, Papi." Bring it on, Daddy.

He did not ask my name; nor did I ask his. What did it matter? We had one mutual goal; to fuck the shit out of each other. That was apparently clear. That is exactly what we did.

We helped each other strip down to nothing. He pulled my thong off with his teeth; taking it and sucking on the middle like it was licorice. Then he pushed my breasts together and devoured them for a good five minutes. I had never cum before from a man sucking on my breasts but I squirted like a water gun.

I fingered his bald head as he ate my pussy and I was yearning to suck some dick; "my dick" but he was not having it. He wanted to get inside me and he rammed into me and took me for the ride of my life. My shoulders were the only things remaining on the table as he lifted my hips and caught a rhythm that damn near scared me. I had never been fucked so royally. Yet, there I was, on a bar table in Mexico, on a vacation by myself, fucking a bullfighter who had a dick so big that I could not fathom a jock strap big enough to hold it.

I thought about Aunt Maxie and how ashamed she would have been of my behavior. But Aunt Maxie was not there, Korey was not there, and I was going to be free; if only for a little while.

"My dick" never said a word to me directly. After everyone else left and I called him Papi, he simply tried to break my back. We fucked for a good two hours before I had to almost crawl out of there with an aching pussy and ass. I had this thing about ass play. That day the Corona bottle had done double duty.

I took a cab back to the hotel, took a long shower and then fell asleep until later that night. About ten, I woke up thinking about sucking dick. Shame on it but that was the first thing on my mind between the time I opened my eyes and the first blink. "My dick" was history, for we had not spoken; let alone exchanged contact information. Too bad because I knew he would not try to catch any feelings for me. Carmelo was a touchy matter, on the other hand. There was something about the night we had spent together that bothered me; it was too *real*.

Everything within me tried to prevent me from calling the front desk to complain about a dripping sink that was keeping me awake. Of course there was not a drip; except for the one between my legs from my natural juices waiting to be licked off of me. Within ten minutes Carmelo was knocking on my door. Less than two minutes off of that, we had commenced to fucking.

DAY THREE

A New Year, a New Dick

Carmelo was off for New Year's Eve. Just as well. I was getting too accustomed to being with him after a whooping-ass two days. There was a big celebration in the grand ballroom at the resort open to all who had reserved a seat ahead of time. I snagged the last seat at one of the tables closest to the stage and entered, wearing a tight gold-sequined floor-length gown—the one originally meant to make Korey's eyes pop out. There was a man occupying the seat next to mine. He was gorgeous and, as it turned out, very, very nice.

His name was Enrique. He was from California. A long way from the motor city, Detroit. He was traveling alone because he needed a vacation. He said that he had been too busy lately chasing Benjamins to chase skirts. He was an IT guy—CEO of a privately held corporation—and thirty-three years old with no kids. For a second I thought he might be gay and able to afford the trip because he was in a DINK—double income no kids— situation. Sometimes they'll leave their lovers at home to put on a front. After a few flutes of champagne and two dances with his hard dick pressed against my aching pussy, I knew he was down with the puddy.

There was an awesome band, an awesome show and even some performers there from Cirque du Soleil. They began to count down to the New Year, but I was already toasted before the toast. Enrique and I bumped glasses and then bumped lips. His tongue was sweet from the champagne. He was a fantastic kisser. I had been ready to get busy less than an hour after we began dining together. Now I did not want to waste another minute.

"Your villa or mine?" I whispered in his ear.

"Doesn't matter, as long as wherever we go has a bed," he replied. "Are you sure you want to do this? You seem a little tipsy and I don't want to take advantage of you."

"Trust me, this week is all about me taking advantage of the situation." I eyed him seductively. "I want to go to your villa. I want to lie on your sheets and smell your cologne in my hair, all over my body, on my pussy. I want to lick every inch of you, from head to toe, as long as you return the favor."

He grinned. "I'm an extremely good licker."

Enrique was so fine in his tuxedo as I grabbed him by his bow tie and issued a weak threat. "You better be good. You better be damn good or else . . . "

"Or else what?"

"Or else I'm going to make you fuck me over and over again until you get it right."

Enrique laughed, grabbed the back of my hair and yanked my head back. "Then I might mess up on purpose so I can keep you in my bed longer."

Enrique and I did not leave his villa for the next three days. We ordered room service three or four times a day, licked food off each other's asses and fucked and sucked like the final days arrived.

We did briefly leave the room one night. We snuck over to the pool. It was deserted at that time of night, we eased down into the corner of it, and fucked each other slowly against the wall. I went underwater and sucked him back into a hardened state; breathing through my nose and using his dick as a snorkeling tube. He grabbed my head and for a second, I thought he might drown me; he was so into it and not wanting me to come up for air.

After he was hard again, I stood and palmed the side of the pool while he entered me from behind. He lifted my feet up off the ground and my toes were dangling as he drilled his thick dick into my pussy. I heard a noise and just knew we were busted. It turned out to be an armadillo, an iguana, or some shit.

Enrique chided me. "What were you going to do if had been a person?"

"Shit, I don't know. Ask them if they want to join, maybe?" We both laughed.

"You know, I have to leave first thing in the morning," he said solemnly. "Are you going to come to California to see me? We've spent some special time together. I would like to continue to see what develops."

I sighed; even though he was still digging my insides out. "I like you, Enrique. I like you and I love the sex but I'm confused right now. I didn't come here to find a new man."

"Then what did you come here for?" he asked.

"At first, I had no clue. I was disappointed that I had to come alone." I had revealed my Korey drama to Enrique at some point during our three-day fuckathon. "Now I am glad that I did. I am glad that all my girlfriends had other plans. If one of them had been here, I could never have been myself; not like this."

"Then I'm glad their asses didn't come either," he said jokingly.

For the next few minutes, Enrique shut up and handled his
business. We came together underneath the water. As we were
walking back to his villa so he could pack, he added, "Take your
time and think about it. I'll give you my number and I hope
you'll consider giving me yours. I won't pressure you but I
would really like to see you again."

I decided to spend the remainder of that night in my own
villa. Saying good-bye to Enrique as he left for the airport would
have been too much drama for me. He had caught feelings and I
was straight-up confused. My message light was blinking when I
got back to my unit. There were five messages from Carmelo,
wanting to know where I was because he wanted to see me before I left. There were two messages from Aunt Maxie, worried
about my safety since she had not heard from me in days. Then,
there was one from Korey; short, straight and to the point. "I
hope you're having a good time. That's cold that you would go
on a trip without me. Well, I guess you've made your point. Have
a nice life."

Maybe it was just me but I could have sworn that Negro had
cheated on me, disrespected me, tried to control me and then
dumped me. He was acting like I had victimized him. Yes, that
shit was definitely over!

DAY SIX

Reminisce Over Me

Carmelo was banging on my door bright and early the next
morning. You would have thought the sky had fallen; the way he

was panicking. I struggled out of bed, turning off my iPod. "He Is" by Heather Headley, one of my "sleep" selections, was caressing my brain until now as I staggered toward the door.

I knew it was him I did not even bother covering up the bra and panties I had fallen asleep in after an early morning shower less than four hours earlier.

"Carmelo, what the hell is wrong with you?"

"*¿Dónde has estado?*"

"What do you mean, where have I been?" I asked angrily. "I've been in my skin."

"I left you a ton of messages."

"Five barely constitutes a ton but I did get them last night."

Carmelo started sniffing the air and examining my sheets.

"Um, excuse me, what are you doing?"

He glared at me. "Searching for evidence."

All I could say was, "Wow!"

He stopped in his tracks as he rearranged the pillows on my bed. "Wow what?"

"I'm stunned. You're acting like my man and, last time I checked, we only met about five days ago."

Carmelo sat down on the bed and buried his face in his hands. I sat down beside him and rubbed his back.

"Carmelo, you're really sweet but I have to go back to the States tomorrow and we'll never lay eyes on each other again. You need to get a grasp on reality."

He did not utter a word for a few minutes. Then he stunned me again. "Okay, okay, since you're going back, spend today with me."

"Carmelo . . . I . . ."

"Please, Taneisha. What else do you have planned for today?"

"Actually, I was going to go to Playa del Carmen and catch the ferry to Cozumel."

"Then I'll go with you," he stated insistently.

"Don't you have to work?"

"I'll get the stomach flu. I never get sick or miss work. They won't give me a hard time."

Everything within me told me to put Carmelo off and insist that he leave and get back to work. Everything but the part of me that wanted to spend my last day in Mexico with the man who had clearly stolen my heart; despite all the whoring around I had been doing. Even with three days of fucking with fine-ass Enrique, Carmelo was the one who made me feel most special. I could not be honest with him and tell him that I had gone to the bullfight, fucked a man on a table at a bar and then spent seventy-two-plus hours with a Californian.

I got dressed while Carmelo went to go tell his supervisor that he was sick. We could not be seen leaving the resort together so I took a cab and picked him up outside the main gate at a bus stop where employees arrived between shifts. It took nearly an hour to get to Playa del Carmen. So, Carmelo and I jacked and jilled each other off in the backseat. The driver was visibly aggravated but did not say anything. He rather demanded his payment upon arrival and rushed us out of his cab.

Waiting for the ferry to arrive, watching the locals with their beach bags and swimsuits getting ready to go spend the day on the white sandy beaches of Cozumel, was so romantic. It reminded me of how cruel Korey was for trying to punish me by sending me there alone. The last laugh was on me. I felt like a contestant on that show *Temptation Island*. My relationship with Korey had not survived the test. It was never meant to be.

Carmelo and I located a secluded spot on the top level of the ferry for the thirty-minute ride to Cozumel. We kissed each other passionately the entire time. I had never kissed someone so long and hard before in my lifetime. One woman walked by with a younger child and I tried to pull away from Carmelo's tongue but he refused to let the fire die down. The woman shook her head and walked off with her child in tow to find somewhere else to sit.

We arrived at Cozumel and had frozen drinks at Fat Tuesday, then walked around the town so I could pick up a few trinkets and souvenirs from the shopping areas. Most of the items—particularly the silver—was overpriced, but I was able to find some reasonable things. I bought a marbleized gray dick to add to my collection. Okay, so I am a freak. I love my toys. Heaven knows, I would not and could not ever deny that one.

I was surprised to see how readily available amoxicillin, penicillin and other drugs that require prescriptions in the States were and purchased a few bottles right over the counter to prepare for the winter months. We grabbed some lunch at La Parilla Grill and then headed down to a secluded area on the beach. It was breathtaking. The water, the sand, the clear sky, the man beside me. All breathtaking.

Carmelo surprised me by taking off his shirt and shorts right there, in broad daylight. "There's no one around. Get naked," he demanded.

I giggled. "And what do you propose to do to me if I do get naked?"

"Ever made love on the beach?"

"No, but would we be making love, Carmelo? I thought we were simply fuck partners."

He sighed in disgust and collapsed beside me in the sand. "Why do you try so hard to be hard, Taneisha?"

I brushed his question off. "I'm keeping things in perspective. I live in Detroit; you live in Cancún. You have a woman, to boot."

"No, I don't have a woman. I told her three days ago that I was in love with you."

"What did you just say to me?"

"*Te amo.* I love you."

I stared at Carmelo, sitting there naked next to me, proclaiming his love for me. I reached out and took his hand. "Carmelo, you don't even know me. If you only knew . . . "

"Knew what?"

That I've been the biggest whore in Mec-ci-co this week, I thought to myself.

I could not get the words out. Instead, I started getting undressed. I wanted him; right there on the sand. After I was nude, I lay back and watched him climb on top of me. We kissed, even deeper than on the ferry. He caressed my breasts and I felt renewed; reborn by his touch. No one had ever brought out those emotions in me before; no one.

He licked a trail down the middle of my chest and then dipped the tip of his tongue in my belly button. I grabbed his shoulders and stared up at the blue sky. There was not a cloud in sight. It was truly paradise. Carmelo went down on me and I spread my legs to welcome his face between my legs; right where it belonged. He spread my pussy lips with his fingers and lapped at my clit until my moans became uncontrollable. I tried to back my hips up away from him but he sucked me right back into his ecstasy.

Once I came, I pulled him all the way up so that his knees straddled my shoulders. I commanded him, *"Aliméntame con tu dick."* Feed me your dick.

"Damn, Taneisha! You sound so sexy when you say that."

He positioned his dick right at my lips and I ate my dessert. It was good, too. I took the head of it in and suckled on it like an orange. He was excited and wanted me to deep-throat him but I worked the shaft with my hands for a while; working magic with my fingers and my mouth. Then I relaxed my throat, took it all in and held it there. He shuddered and stared down at me. I gazed into his eyes and wondered what had carried me to this place; lying on the white sands of Mexico with a dick in my mouth that was not attached to the man who had been my world for more than three years.

The waves started crashing against the shore as the tide was about to come in. I did not want to stop, though, and it was a sensual feeling to have the water cascading through my hair and over my skin, mixed with sand, as I continued to devour Carmelo's dick. This had gone beyond lust. I realized it at that moment. I realized it even more when he entered me and slowly worked my G-spot with all the right moves. I let out a yelp when I came.

By the time we caught the last ferry back to Playa del Carmen, I was exhausted. Still, Carmelo insisted that I go into town with him to meet his family. I was totally embarrassed when I shook his mother's hand; thinking about all the nasty and freaky things I had done with her son whom I had met mere days earlier. I sat and ate dinner at her table. Her English was minimal but I had gotten better with my Spanish so we somehow managed. She was a sweet woman who had been dealt a tough hand in life but like sisters united in all races, she had lived up to her responsibilities and done the best that she could do. She had managed.

Carmelo saw me to a cab. I did not want him to get in trouble by going back to the resort with me in a cab and the buses had stopped running. Besides, our good-byes had to take place there that night. I could not see him the day I was leaving. I was not dick-whipped; I was love-whipped and I knew it.

Korey did as I suspected and attempted to get back with me the day after I returned. I told him to forget about it and go crawl back up in the bed with that cave witch he had cheated on me with. I returned to work as an investment banker. I had never mentioned my profession or how much money I made to any of the men in Cancún. I wanted them to assume that I was struggling financially and had merely saved up for the trip of a lifetime. I was actually very well off and lived on a two-million-dollar estate that was nearly paid off already. Within another year, I would own it lock, stock and barrel.

For months I tried to forget about Carmelo. I had to admit that while I did not think he was beneath me like the woman he had been dating in Mexico, I was not sure that he could fit into my world. It was a hectic world, my microwave society, and things were much slower in Cancún. Life was more carefree. I tried to stay even busier than normal and fucked a new man every now and then; simply to satisfy basic needs. None of them could give me what I needed.

By June I had phoned Carmelo and told him that I needed him. I had already purchased him a plane ticket and he had less than four hours to get to the airport. I prayed he had what he needed to travel to the States; he did. He had never left Mexico but had always dreamed of it.

He was only supposed to stay for a few days but that turned into a few months. Now it has been a few years. Carmelo not only fit into my world, he is my entire world. My husband, the

father of my twin sons and my business partner in CT Contract-
ing, which I lend my financial know-how to while he runs the
day-to-day operations. It is funny how things turn out. But, you
know what? *La vida tiene valor cuando no se sabe lo que trae el
mañana.* Not knowing what tomorrow holds is what makes life
worth living.

ABOUT THE CONTRIBUTORS

CURTIS L. ALCUTT was born and bred in Oakland, California. He walked many career paths before deciding to give writing a try. He now resides in Northern California with his family and is a writer masquerading as a small trucking company owner and computer geek. Please visit his website at www.mralcutt.com.

JOCELYN BRINGAS is a young Filipina who resides in Northern California. She is currently a student at San Jose State University. In her free time she enjoys writing stories, watching television, shopping, traveling, eating, listening to music, and going to concerts. Her website address is http://bboys-style.com/delicious/.

NIOBIA SIMONE BRYANT's a nationally bestselling and award-winning writer of both steamy romance—as Niobia Bryant for both Harlequin/Arabesque and Dafina Romance—and mainstream fiction, as Niobia Simone, for Kensington/Dafina Trade. For more on her romance novels—eight to date—and her upcoming drama-filled mainstream release, *Live & Learn,* go to her website www.geocities.com/niobia_bryant.

PETULA CAESAR, from Baltimore, Maryland, has authored an erotica anthology called *Lipstick and Other Stories,* published by Phaze (www.phaze.com). Excerpts are available on her website, www .tulabooks.com. She also writes for *Mic Life* magazine, (www .miclifemagazine.com), a publication covering all aspects of microphone culture, including music and spoken word poetry.

WILLIAM FREDRICK COOPER is affectionately known as "Mr. Romance," and his first novel, *Six Days in January,* was published in February 2004 by Strebor Books. A trailblazing piece of literature that explores the heart of an African-American man damaged by love, the novel received rave reviews in major periodicals in the United States, Canada, and the United Kingdom.

Mr. Cooper is a contributing author to several erotica anthologies. "Legal Days, Lonely Nights" appeared in Zane's *Sistergirls.com;* "Watering Cherry's Garden" was a story for *Twilight Moods: African American Erotica;* "Snowy Moonlit Evenings" was composed for *Journey to Timbooktu,* a collection of poetry and prose, as compiled by Memphis Vaughnes; and "More and More" as well as "Sweet Dreams" were included in *Morning, Noon and Night: Can't Get Enough*—a collection of erotic fiction. His second novel, *There's Always a Reason,* which explores topics ranging from the psychological effects of hysterectomies to restoration of faith in love, will be published in Spring 2007 by Strebor Books.

MICHELLE DE LEON, author of *Missed Conceptions, Love to the Third, Once Upon a Family* Tree and *Evangie's Fortune,* has been creating chaos with her pen since the sixth grade. Born in the Bronx, she graduated from City College of New York with a degree in English. She lives in the Atlanta area with her husband and daughters and is currently writing her first Christian fiction piece, *We Never Danced to a Love Psalm.*

Susan DiPlacido is the author of three novels: *24/7, Trattoria, and Mutual Holdings.* Her short story, "I, Candy" won the Spirit award at the 2005 Moondance International Film Festival, and *Trattoria* has been nominated for the Romantic Times Reviewers' Choice Award. She can be found online at susandiplacido.com.

Anne Elizabeth enjoys stories that catch the mind. Body and spirit work in synchronization, so must the path of sharing a story. If you enjoyed this diehard romantic's tantalizing tale, check out her website for additional creations at www.anneelizabeth.net.

Tracee A. Hanna (Bell), author of *A Little Bit of Sinning,* was born and raised in St. Louis, Missouri, and currently resides in Arizona. She is the mother of two lovely daughters and is currently working on her second book. Visit http://alittlebitofsinning .tripod.com. She thanks Lisa and Travis for their endless support.

Naleighna Kai, a Chicago native, is the author of *She Touched My Soul* and coauthor of *Speak It into Existence* and *How to Win the Publishing Game.* She is a motivational speaker and developmental editor who is currently working on her next projects: *Open Door Marriage* and *Right Place, Right Time.* Visit her on the web at www .naleighnakai.com.

Geneva King (www.genevaking.com) has been published in *Erotic Fantasy: Tales of the Paranormal, Who's Your Daddy, Ultimate Lesbian Erotica 2006,* and *Best Women's Erotica 2006.* She intends to publish a collection of her stories, if her professors ever give her enough time to do so.

Keeb Knight was born in London, England, and resides in Philadelphia. He enjoys writing multicultural short stories, erotic fiction, and romantic suspense. He started writing six years ago and plans to make a career of it. He's currently working on his first erotica novel. Visit his website at www.keebknight.com.

TERESA LAMAI's stories have appeared in several collections, including *Best Women's Erotica, Mammoth Book of Best New Erotica, Lips Like Sugar: Women's Erotic Fantasies,* and *Dying for It: Stories of Sex and Death*. She has recently completed a collection of dance-inspired erotica, entitled *Swayed to Music*.

JAMES W. LEWIS is an up-and-coming author living in Southern California. He has several publication credits, including stories in *Chicken Soup for the Mother's and Son's Soul, Help! I've Turned into My Mother,* and *Truth Be Told: Tales of Life, Love, and Drama*. His website is www.jameswlewis.com.

SYDNEY MOLARE, a Mississippi native, is the author of five novels including *Grandmama's Mojo Still Working* and *Devil's Orchestra*. A veterinarian by profession, writing has become her latest passion. Please visit her website at www.sydneymolare.com.

MICHELLE J. ROBINSON is the mother of ten-year-old identical twin boys. She resides in New York City and studied journalism at New York University. She has written several short stories and is currently working on two novels, *You Created a Monster* and *Fraternal*. She can be reached at Robinson_201@hotmail.com.

SÉKOU WRITES is the New York–based editor of the serial novel *When Butterflies Kiss*. His fiction has been published in *UPTOWN* magazine and the anthologies *Wanderlust: 14 Erotic Travel Tales* and *Intimacy: Erotic Stories of Love, Lust and Marriage by Black Men*. Sékou Writes also authors two online relationship columns. More at www.sekouwrites.com.

Nikki Sinclair publishes fiction in a variety of venues both in print and online. She lives and writes in Minneapolis, Minnesota, the Rome of the North. Or the St. Petersburg of the South. Or . . . you get the picture.

Pat Tucker is an award-winning broadcast journalist. She currently works in news at a Houston radio station. She is also a freelance writer for the *Houston Defender,* Houston's oldest black newspaper. Pat has worked for TV and radio stations in San Jose, California, and Texas. Her career in front of the camera began in Victoria, Texas, where she served as a TV and radio news reporter. She also held positions at the ABC and NBC affiliates in Waco, Texas, and at News 24 Houston in Houston. She is a member of the Houston and National Associations of Black Journalists. Pat is the author of the urban soul novels *The Hook Up* and *Infidelity.*

Zane is *the New York Times* bestselling author of nine books and the contributor and/or editor to nearly a dozen more. She is the publisher of Strebor Books/Simon & Schuster and a partner of de Passe/Zane Entertainment. To join Zane's mailing list, please send a blank email to Eroticanoir-subscribe@topica.com.